D1020164

FALLING SIDEWAYS

BY THE SAME AUTHOR

Fiction
In the Company of Angels
Crossing Borders
Unreal City
A Weather of the Eye
Drive, Dive, Dance & Fight
The Book of Angels
Cast Upon the Day
A Passion in the Desert

Nonfiction
Last Night My Bed a Boat of Whiskey Going Down
Riding the Dog: A Look Back at America
Writers on the Job: Tales of the Non-Writing Life
(as editor, with Walter Cummins)
The Book of Worst Meals (as editor, with Walter Cummins)
The Literary Traveler (with Walter Cummins)
Realism & Other Illusions: Essays on the Craft of Fiction

FALLING SIDEWAYS
A Novel

THOMAS E. KENNEDY

BLOOMSBURY

NEW YORK · BERLIN · LONDON · SYDNEY

Copyright © 2011 by Thomas E. Kennedy

All rights reserved. No part of this book may be used or reproduced in any manner whatsoever without written permission from the publisher except in the case of brief quotations embodied in critical articles or reviews. For information address Bloomsbury USA, 175 Fifth Avenue, New York, NY 10010.

Published by Bloomsbury USA, New York

This is a work of fiction. Any resemblance of characters depicted in this novel to real persons living or dead is purely coincidental.

All papers used by Bloomsbury USA are natural, recyclable products made from wood grown in well-managed forests. The manufacturing processes conform to the environmental regulations of the country of origin.

The Rumi quotes are from *The Essential Rumi*, translated by Coleman Barks with John Moyne (HarperCollins, 1996). The quotes from the Koran are taken from *The Essential Koran*, translated and presented by Thomas Cleary (Castle Books, 1993).

Chapter six of the novel appeared originally in altered form in *Arts & Letters: Journal of Contemporary Culture* (Georgia College & State University, Milledgeville, Georgia); another portion appeared under the title "Let Everyone Forget Everyone" in *South Carolina Review*; and portions of chapter three were read aloud on the Harper College documentary film *Copenhagen Quartet*—at a time when the novel in progress was entitled *Breathwaite's Fall*.

LIBRARY OF CONGRESS CATALOGING-IN-PUBLICATION DATA

Kennedy, Thomas E., 1944–
Falling sideways : a novel / Thomas E. Kennedy.—1st U.S. ed.
p. cm.
ISBN: 978-1-60819-081-2 (hardcover : alk. paper)
1. Business enterprises—Employees—Fiction. 2. Corporate culture—Fiction. 3. Middle-aged men—Family relationships—Fiction. 4. Midlife crisis—Fiction. 5. Domestic fiction. I. Title.
PS3561.E4277F36 2011
813'.54—dc22
201002370

First U.S. edition 2011

1 3 5 7 9 10 8 6 4 2

Typeset by Westchester Book Group
Printed in the United States of America by Quad/Graphics, Fairfield, Pennsylvania

To Copenhagen with love,
its seasons, its light, its dark, its people,
home of homes.

There are so many people I would like to thank for their friendship, support, and encouragement throughout my life, over the years and in recent times. It is not possible to name them all. But I would be remiss not to name the following:

Daniel and Isabel Kennedy
Leo Kennedy-Rye and his father, Søren Rye
My beloved sister, Joan

Anton Mueller and Helen Garnons-Williams
Nat Sobel and Judith Weber
Roger and Brenda Derham
Duff Brenna, Walter Cummins, Greg Herriges, Michael Lee, Robert Stewart, and Gladys Swan

> . . . we should be careful
> Of each other, we should be kind
> While there is still time.

> —Philip Larkin

CONTENTS

CHARACTERS (IN ORDER OF APPEARANCE)

EMPLOYEES OF THE TANK

Frederick Breathwaite, married to **Kis (Kirsten) Breathwaite**
   Parents of twenty-two-year-old **Jes Breathwaite**

Harald Jaeger, divorced from **Vita Jaeger**
   Parents of six- and four-year-old **Amalie** and **Elisabeth**

Birgitte Sommer, married to **Lars**

Claus Clausen, unmarried, friend of Harald Jaeger

Martin Kampman (CEO of the Tank), married to **Karen Kampman**
   Parents of seventeen-year-old **Adam Kampman** and five-year-old
   twins, **Helle** and **Hanne**

OTHERS

Jytte Andersen, the Kampmans' seventeen-year-old au pair

Jalâl al-Din (owner of Dome of the Rock Key & Heel Bar), married to
   Khadiya
   Parents of **Zaid** (teenage son, estranged from father)

Tatyana, Polish mistress of Harald Jaeger

WEDNESDAY

The Mumble Club

1 . Frederick Breathwaite

Breathwaite woke to a screaming from the courtyard. He knew who it was. Still groggy, he amused himself in the dark behind his eyelids, assembling the Winchester underlever locked away at the bottom of the antique chest in the hall, screwed on the telescopic sight, braced his elbow on the ledge of the back terrace, and targeted the screamer, a bawling red-faced four-year-old. Pick her off and her coddling self-loving yuppie parents, too. Bing bing bing. One, two, three. Thank you, Charlton Heston.

Assassinations complete, he slipped back down for another half hour of blessed nothing.

He had fallen asleep reading the night before and woke this time in a beam of rare October sunlight through the bedroom window of his Østerbro, East Bridge, apartment, book splayed open on his chest. Beside him in the antique four-poster bed, slight and blond as a Renaissance angel, Kirsten lay curled against his shoulder, delicate fists tucked up beneath her chin. Conscious of his own bulk, he studied the calm repose of her face, still mysterious to him after half a lifetime together. Who knows the mind of a woman? He imagined the silken feel of her skin to his fingertips. But he did not touch her.

Kirsten was a morning lover, even now, in her sixties, but despite the fact that he was younger, he had alas nothing left to offer in that department, morning, noon, or night. When he was a boy, hostage to desire, he used to pray to be free of it; now, it seemed, he was, and he would never have guessed how utterly it changed everything, how quintessential was appetite. Kis was five years older, but her appetite still flamed briskly on.

He slid from beneath the eiderdown and slippered softly across the broad-planked bedroom floor to the bath. Sitting to pee, he looked into the novel he'd been reading, at two lines he had underscored: *Choose carefully who you pretend to be, for that is who you will become.*

Shoving the paperback into the wall rack beside the bowl, he spied an advertisement on the back of a magazine there—men in suits seated around a table—and remembered the meeting today. He had a premonition something might be coming.

He rose and washed his hands, crossed twenty meters of gleaming hardwood floor, an archipelago of antique carpets—from Iran, Afghanistan, Tibet—through the library with its ceiling-high shelves and gliding ladder, to the long, dark kitchen. He thrived in large rooms. These rooms. Broad floors, high ceilings, tall windows. Space. Without them he would smother. He brewed coffee and took it on the chilly, sunny fifth-floor balcony in his dark blue robe, a CD playing softly from the player inside: Cannonball Adderley, Miles Davis, "Autumn Leaves." Moody variations of dead men celebrating death's prelude.

He tugged the lapels of his robe closer to his throat. He was proud of the robe, an elegant one from Magasin du Nord, a gift from his colleagues at the Tank two years before, on the occasion of his twenty-fifth anniversary on the job. His secretary told him it had cost two thousand crowns, money contributed voluntarily, out of pocket, from the headquarters staff. They had lined the long hallway when he'd come in that day, unsuspecting, and when he'd stepped off the elevator he had proceeded through a gauntlet of them, waving paper Danish flags and cheering him. At the end of the gauntlet stood the new CEO, Martin Kampman, holding aloft between thumb and finger a minuscule paper flag on a toothpick, which he'd flicked back and forth at a twitch of his wrist, smiling—a small, horizontal smile bracketed between tiny verticals.

Coffee cheer lifted his brain. The day was immaculate. Vast, flawless, blue autumn sky above his head, yellow and red sunlit leaves on the tree-tops below, and golden sunlight warming the green-copper towers of Copenhagen, the adopted city that had become his home, where his sons were born, his grandchildren. This sunlight he recognized as the gift it was, the most beautiful autumn he had seen in his decades here, where sunlight and warmth could never be relied on. The days were already being chewed short to feed the lengthening nights as winter prepared to pipe in the darkness. Even *that* he had grown to love about the country that was now his home, the yearly share of death, later repaid to those who survived by the white nights of summer.

The moody, cozy notes of Miles Davis's trumpet lulled him into an agreeable melancholy.

Curious, he thought, that there is no religious festival to celebrate autumn, no sacred autumnal ceremony. Harvest, of course, but that was end of summer, that was the feast of plenty, not the first smell of death. Not that the Danes had so very much religion to start with, though they *were* a Christian nation, their whole society built on its secular equivalent. And they had their ritual seasonal touchstones—Easter, Christmas, even Pentecost, Whitsunday, which they celebrated by drinking all night until the sun danced at dawn and them with it. But nothing for autumn. St. Morten's Eve was a ritual-less feast of roast duck or goose. No. There were only the falling leaves to mark the secret reverence of accepted sorrow, reverent natural metaphor of inevitable death. Rake the leaves and strike a match, witness beauty consumed in flame, rising to the sky in smoke.

From the breast pocket of his robe he lifted a Don Tomás, smelled and wet it before striking a match to roast its nose in a cedar flame and filling his mouth with the fine Honduras smoke. His cheeks hollowed deeply as he drew on the cigar, then puffed out as he released the white smoke through pursed lips. He smiled at the Chinese archer on one knee in the corner of the stone balcony. He had purchased the sculpture for a song at a Bruun Rasmussen auction on the other side of Langelinie Bridge. Why an archer? he wondered. Why an antique kneeling Chinese archer on their balcony? He could find no other reason than that the bid had been so low and easy, the only piece of art they owned that he'd bought because it was cheap. All the other pieces—paintings, masks, sculptures—he had acquired because they would not give him peace until he did. Didn't matter what they were worth in money. Fortunately, he and Kirsten—Kis—shared the same taste. They liked pieces that unsettled them or made them smile or, in the best case, both: an ironically ferocious Inuit mask; an enormous Gunleif oil of an angel sitting like a hen on a woman's head; a cast-iron blue-and-red amphibian that looked like a cross between a snail and a pterodactyl, by the Finnish sculptor Heikki Virolainen; a three-foot ebony Senafu bird with a meter-long bill in profile; a ram's head, tongue jutting downward while a rainbow bird pecked into its brain . . .

And an antique kneeling Chinese archer for a song? He chuckled at his own evident corruption, even of his taste for art.

"Why didn't you wake me?" Kis asked softly from behind him, standing between the white-lacquered frames of the double glass doors.

He turned his smile to her. "Because I wanted you to miss me, *skat*."
Treasure. The word was not ironic.

"Don't you come back to bed?" A tender question, tentative. She knew
he had a problem but would not let him think she was not willing to help
and reminded him discreetly from time to time that such problems passed,
but also that problems should be addressed. Difference between men
and women: Women wanted to talk about everything, even if doing so
caused pain and confusion.

"Wouldn't blame you if you took a lover," he said.

"Such rubbish!" she growled, the way Danish women growl to indicate
no-nonsense honesty. "Have you one of those meetings today? They always put you in a sour mood."

"What a blessing this sun is," he said, and warmed his eyes on her
sweet aging blond face.

2. Harald Jaeger

Forty-seven, forty-eight, forty-nine . . . Due north from Breathwaite's east-side windows, Harald Jaeger did push-ups on the dusty wall-to-wall of his Nørrebro, North Bridge, two-room. He entertained the fact that he was halfway to Friday to avoid thinking about the Wednesday morning management meeting he would soon have to suffer at the Tank. The Mumble Club.

Pleasure burned through his blood with the tensing and flexing of his biceps and triceps as he pressed up from and dipped down again to the dirty beige carpet, enjoying the gathering sweat on his brow, beneath his arms and T-shirt.

Demons lurked around the dim little room. He held them at bay with the steamy images assembling in his brain as he worked his blood and muscle, sculpting his arms, his abs, his pecs, feeling the radiation down to the cherished clockwork at the center of his universe.

Ninety-six, ninety-seven, ninety-eight . . . Finally, midway on the hundred and first, his arms gave out and he dropped to his belly, panting. He sneezed, nostrils tickled by the dust particles dancing in a beam of smeary light. Then he leapt to his feet, shoved a CD into the stereo, and threw himself into the rhythm of Manu Chao, dancing himself into a lather, stepping, dipping, leaping, twisting, until he collapsed into his armchair, gasping, halfway through "Welcome to Tijuana."

Calm then, he wiped the corners of his eyes, demon free, guzzled half a liter of cold grapefruit juice, belched with openmouthed pleasure, scratched his butt, and stepped under a steaming shower. Beneath the scalding water, behind his pink-black eyelids, images of Amalie and Elisabeth drifted across his consciousness.

No. Not today. Please.

No use. He remembered when last he had phoned, and six-year-old Amalie told him she thought about him every single night when she lay down in bed, kept seeing his face in the dark. The demons moved closer again. Wrapped in a black plush bath towel, he dialed, only too aware what the voice of his ex could do to him if he caught her in the wrong mood—and when was Vita *ever* in the right mood? The phone burred half a dozen times before he dropped it back into the cradle and sat there, palms on knees, staring at the grimy sun-smudged window, thinking what a fucked-up mess he'd made of his life, of their poor sweet innocent lives.

No.

He rose again to the all-important oblations at the glass altar of his little bathroom sink. With a snazzy black plastic razor, he shaved the hairless portions of his lower face—cheeks, neck, up to the sculpted slant of his midear burns, tiny arrowheads pointing to the corners of his 'stache, sculpting his motherfucker beard, as it was called. He wondered why: Because bad guys sported the style? Or guys who fucked mothers? Mystery there. All mothers would have had to be fucked, making every father a mother-fucker. Or was it the sexy motherfucker that Prince sang about? What exactly did the Americans mean by this term?

He selected the tiny folding scissors given him as a gift thirteen years before by a woman whose sexual beauty he remembered in detail to this day. Mystery there. Why had he chosen the irascible dark Vita over the light loveliness of Janne? Complicated by the fact that Janne was, in fact, the dark-eyed brunette, Vita the blue-eyed blonde. Ice blue.

Thumb and finger in the handle holes of the little scissors, reverently recollecting the vision of Janne's perfect, pear-stemmed breasts and shy, bright smile, he inserted the pointy tips of the blades into his nostrils and snipped short the bristling red nose hairs, trimmed his blond mustache and its architectural extensions to the neat, square beard that framed his square, dimpled chin under the clear expanse beneath his full lower lip.

He viewed the beard with satisfaction, trimmed a stray darker blond hair from his eyebrow, spotted a boary bristle from the chamber of his left ear, and clipped that, saw as it fell to the edge of the black porcelain sink that it was not blond but gray. He picked it up between thumb and finger and held it close before his eyes. No doubt. Gray. He leaned closer to the mirror for a minute inspection of his beard, but it was blond, all blond, no gray at all. Not yet.

Relaxing again, he reverently refolded the scissors, laid the minuscule folded instrument in the palm of his hand, and gazed at it tenderly, thinking again of Janne and how she had been, how she had looked last time he'd seen her, only a few weeks ago, in the supermarket, wheeling an unpleasant-looking child in her grocery cart, her own face bloated almost beyond recognition. It had become a face that Jaeger could not love, a face that precluded desire, a fact he acknowledged with disagreeable self-awareness but acknowledged nonetheless. *No more games*, he thought. *I am what I am. For better or worse.* He smirked. *Till death do I part.*

His eyes were still on the blond beard reflected in the frame-lit mirror above the sink, one of the few beautiful things in this dingy little apartment to which the divorce had relegated him. He was ashamed to take most women home to it, had to prepare them for the shock, fearing the surprised disappointment that might flash across their faces. *A man of your position! A man of your background!* Or just, *You live* here?

The neighborhood was okay, no problem there, fashionable even, or on its way to becoming so, though he was half a generation too old for it. But the building was terrible—right from the battered and graffiti-spattered outside door and on up. There was not even a lobby and the shabby, dumpy stairwell no self-respecting academic would, as the saying went, subject his mother-in-law to. No elevator, either, so you were forced to mount by foot every dingy landing, through the lingering stench of gone generations of brown-cabbage eaters, to the fourth floor, only to find at the end of the ascent a shabby two-roomer that matched the stairwell.

Thank God his mother and father had not lived to see this downward turn, this further downward turn. By half. He had married up economically—Vita was the daughter of a plumbing contractor—down socially. He was a third-generation academic, Vita a never-employed dental assistant and cultural autodidact. He did it all to himself, he knew, and had no one else to thank.

Harald Jaeger, this is your life.

But his face, illuminated in the frame-lit mirror, was still blond and young and, he had to admit, though one wished not to be self-loving, handsome. Handsome enough, anyway. His dark blue eyes were almost violet and his lashes and brows so much darker than his beard and head hair that a woman had once asked him, with evident fascination, if he used eye makeup.

"Women sense my power," he said aloud to his reflected face, quoting one of his favorite films. "I do not avoid women, but I do deny them my essence."

But that was the trouble. It was theirs for the taking. Women were his everything. Women. Plural. He knew it, no need trying to deny it. He was a ladies' man, and that was it. Not a skirt chaser, but a woman adorer.

From the elegant bottle of Armani Acqua di Giò, he dashed a generous puddle into his palm and anointed his shining cheeks with the agreeable scented sting. Dashed a bit beneath his arms, inside of his thighs, on the butt cheeks. Never knew when you might be glad you did.

But he had been alone now for nearly a month since the infatuation with Caecilie had petered out. *Losing your touch.* One day perhaps they would all be gone and he would be alone then forever, and what then?

That time, that sorrow.

After a last lingering glance at his illuminated face, he switched off the mirror lamp and withdrew to the inner dump to dress: crisp black Boss jeans, mint green shirt, charcoal gray cashmere necktie, his good handwoven Irish tweed jacket. And jogged down four flights, averting his eyes from the shabby institutional green woodwork to the courtyard, averting his eyes from the overfull Dumpsters, unlocked his bicycle, and mounted it at a run, coasted through the arched portal to the grime of North Bridge Street, and started pumping through the morning traffic toward the Centrum.

3. Birgitte Sommer

Still farther north, in the coveted north Copenhagen inner suburb of Hellerup, in a yellow-brick bungalow a few streets down from Vita Jaeger's classic Gentofte minimanor, Birgitte Sommer woke from a dream in which she and Lars had been painting the walls of their Gilleleje summer house the sunniest shade of sun yellow. They had been naked in the dream, their lean, long bodies glistening with daubs of the beautiful paint; Lars's dark hair somehow was yellow in the dream, golden, even the thick hair matting his chest and his groin, and he turned to her with a dazzling smile and exclaimed, *Birgitte, you're fan*tas*tic! This is the* perfect *color! It will last all winter so we can sun ourselves naked out back!*

And the children? she asked.

Suddenly his face looked like someone else's. It swooped toward her, grinning, whispering, *Yes! Like this!* as he cupped his hand between her legs.

She woke smiling beatifically up at the molded stucco fringe of the high white ceiling, only to find her own hand between her legs and the bed beside her empty. She sighed and ran her palm over the rumpled sheet where Lars had slept, lowered her face to it, and breathed the sweet-sour scent left by his body. In a sun-yellow mood, she donned a crème silk robe (sixty-nine crowns from an unassorted bin at ALDI) and paused for a moment, running her long fingers through her curly black hair, gazing across the pleasantly muted light of the bedroom to the luminous gauze curtains that faced the garden she had expended nearly every weekend of the summer tending.

Now, as the season ended, she had it nearly where she wanted it. Next year, she would turn it over to the local retiree who had offered his services for a monthly cash payment they could afford—*if* they shopped, *without exception*, in the Netto and ALDI and Fakta supermarkets instead of the upscale Irma or ISO or Brugsen—while she turned her attentions to the garden of the summer house they had closed on two weeks ago in Gilleleje. Like the garden here, it was completely sequestered by tall, ligustrum privet hedges. They could go naked there all weekend if they wished. And the necessary economies would keep them trim even as the value of their properties grew.

Still damp from her lovely dream, she stepped into the espadrille home shoes that displayed the cleavage of her toes and padded out to the nook at the front of the house where they took their breakfast.

Lars sat alone by the shady window over a single mug of coffee, reading the newspaper and picking his nose.

"Good morning!" she sang out, and felt the smile of her voice emanating from the surface of her skin.

He took his finger from his nose, brushing it on his thumb, and said, "Morn," without looking up. And, "You forgot to buy milk again."

"*I* forgot?" She was still smiling.

He smiled now, too, a tilted smile, and laughed a single quiet note of irony.

"You could run up to the dairy on the corner," she said.

Another note of scornful laughter. "*Dairy?* It's a goddamn Pakistani kiosk. Forty percent markup to fund the cousins in Jakarta."

Birgitte was not to be daunted. "Well, good morning to you, too, sunbeam," she said with a smile he did not see but no doubt heard, and she went to the kitchen and switched on the radio, sawed off a couple of slices of yesterday's French bread, and laid them on the toaster.

On the radio, Gustav Winckler was singing "Little Summer Bird," a song her father used to sing to her. How she missed him, the whiskers around his thick lips and the spaces between his smiling teeth as he sang; "summer bird" meant "butterfly" in Danish—*Lit-tle but-terfly, lit-tle but-ter-fly*—but it was also a play on their family name so that *she* was the little butterfly he sang to.

Her father had frequently emphasized to her the importance of owning property. Land never devalues, he'd told her. She had grown up in a small rented apartment and had not thought so much about it, but then she'd met Lars, who shared her dead father's dreams of property, even if he didn't possess her father's sentimental side.

She was still smiling as she glanced into the oval mirror tacked above the kitchen sink and saw the best of her face, the frame of dark curls, the burgundy eyes, disregarding their narrowness and the knob at the end of her nose. But as the aroma of toasting bread lifted to her nostrils, her narrow gaze shifted from her smile to the round white face of the wall clock, and she realized it was Wednesday.

"Shit!"

"I *can't* hear you," Lars grumbled from the other room.

She hurried out to him on swift light feet. "I've got a meeting at the Tank, nine sharp. Watch the toast won't burn!" And she ran for the bathroom, calling back, "I'll have to take the car!"

"Like hell you will!" he called back, following her. "I'll drop you off."

"I can't be late!"

"It's just a damn meeting."

"It's the principle. We're doing the annual resource report. I have to be there if there're questions!"

"You'll be there, for hell's sake," he said, tall and narrow-shouldered in his baggy, crap brown jogging suit (49.90 crowns at Netto, available in pee yellow, crap brown, and mucous green), his protruding Adam's apple bowing over her at the bathroom door. *"Relax!"*

Beneath the shower, she forgot the sunny yellow dream and her father's song, disregarded her husband's morning sourness and the increasing incidence of his nose picking and the lengthening time since they had last made love, and ran through the Tank accounts in her mind as she lathered herself with an egg-shaped cake of lemon soap. The fragrance lifted on the steam, and the feel of the soap in her palm coincided with a tweak of hunger in her stomach. She would eat toast in the car. But she wanted an egg, boiled, soft. *What am I thinking?*

She opened her eyes in the steaming glass shower cabin, saw her steamy reflection in the full-length mirror on the back of the bathroom door, straight up and down from narrow hips over flat belly to the flare of her C-cup breasts. She focused on the breasts.

There was still time.

She was only thirty-seven. Lars was ten years older. He had a better position than she, but he worked for the county; in the private sector, she made more. He was always insinuating the extra she made was somehow dishonest. County salary scales were reasonable. The private sector shoveled it in at the expense of the public. The world according to Lars.

She remembered his face in her dream, when it changed to someone else's. Whose? It had been bearded, a little yellow beard. She realized with a start that it had been Harald Jaeger's face, from the Tank. Why would she dream of Harald? Then she recalled that she had seen him the weekend before when she was out jogging in the deer park. He was walking with the cutest little girls. One on each hand, a tiny one and a taller one. Birgitte had stopped to chat, stooped down, and the littlest one asked her, "Who are you? You're *nice!*" So sweet. So very sweet.

She shut off the water and stood shivering, wet, in the steam, and a thought she had not quite considered floated across her consciousness: *Where was the time?* With the summer house closing, she would have to work *at least* two or three or more years before they were above the water-mark again. She would be forty, forty-one. So where was the time that was supposed to be?

The door rattled. "If you're in such a devil-me rush for your devil-me meeting, you'd better shake your little devil-me backside in there!"

4. Claus Clausen

South and west again in Vesterbro, West Bridge, Claus Clausen sat at his little kitchen table spooning cornflakes and milk into his mouth, watching construction workers down in the street doling out bottles from their box of morning beer. He nearly gagged at the sight. He reached across the width of the narrow kitchen and took the jar of aspirin from the cupboard shelf, opened the refrigerator, still without rising, and lifted out a liter of orange juice, popped two pills into his mouth, and washed them down with juice straight from the carton.

He had been out with Harald Jaeger the night before—their first time out together since Harald's promotion. His lips twitched back from his teeth as he considered again the fact that Harald was now his boss. The head of his department. How in the fuck had that happened? Okay, Harald had been there longer, but Claus was faster, more focused, and there was nothing Harald knew that he didn't know just as well. In truth, all Harald was interested in was chasing pussy. How the hell had it happened? Claus suspected it was that fucking Fred Breathwaite. For some reason, he always held a hand over Harald. Why? What did he have against Claus? And how had he convinced the CEO that Harald should have the promotion over him? No warning, nothing. Just one day a memo goes around inviting everybody in for coffee and cake to celebrate Harald's promotion.

And Claus had to go in and eat fucking dry cake and find out from a friend in accounting that Harald was now making 30 percent more than he was. Claus hated looking down into the little man's face and being told what to do. The little peacock.

The little *fuck*! And he hated sitting at his metal desk in his crummy little windowless office—an alcove, really!—and watching Jaeger and the other department heads wander past his doorless door arch on their way to the department head meeting every Wednesday, knowing they sat there behind the CEO's closed door discussing matters over which he himself had no control, decisions in which he had not a word to say, decisions that might deploy him in their projects. Then Harald would reappear and suddenly there would be a new plan, and Claus would have to take instructions from the little fucker and report back to him.

The little motherfucker bearded fuck.

With thumb and forefinger he blotted a tear from the corner of each eye. The only thing he wanted to do today was *not* be there as they walked past him on their way to the meeting. And that was exactly the thing that he *had* to do. Because if he wasn't there, his absence would be noticed.

No, the thing to do was to be there long before they got there. To be there where the CEO could see he was the first one into the office, bent over his computer. Even the CEO must notice that Harald was *never* in by nine on any other day than the day of the department head meetings, while Claus was *always* in well before nine.

The little cunt-chasing fucker with his pseudoponderings, looking as though he thought he'd swallowed the stone of cleverness. "Tell me something, Claus," he'd said last night in the northside dive where they'd ended up, the only available woman hanging close to Jaeger at the bar. "Tell me, what do we actually *do* in the Tank? Do you have any idea? Do we actually *do* anything?" Clausen had given him the bland puss, thinking to himself, *What we do, you asshole, is to keep the money moving from hand to hand. Know-how. Consumption. What do you expect, you jerk? We're a little piece of a big picture.* But he'd said nothing, given nothing that might later be marshaled against him.

Now, remembering with embarrassment the rebuffed pass he'd made at that woman, Clausen chugalugged the rest of the juice and, gasping, dragged his butt into the shower.

5. Vita Jaeger

The au pair was sick again, and Vita's mother could not be there for an hour. So if the day was going to hang together, Vita had to get the girls ready for kindergarten herself. Already dressed in her golfing tweeds, she smoked a cigarette at the bathroom window, gazing down to the tight-cropped grass of the back garden while the girls splashed and giggled in the tub. The grass was impeccable. It made her think of the green where she was due for a lesson in less than two hours. The day was perfect for it. Crisp and sunny. Vita would never have believed what pleasure it gave her to be out on the course.

All her life she had despised golf as the snobby, snooty activity of people spoiled by privilege. She still referred to the game as *galf* in a mocking echo of the snobby, overclass pronunciation of the word, just as she referred to Gentofte as *Shantofta*—in parody of the accent of those who were born to it, born to money in their big villas, the type that went skiing in winter and to the sunny south islands for spring break and who got a brand-new Volvo or Mercedes sports car for their high school graduation, never having to earn anything for themselves.

To them, she was an *upcomling*. But her father's success had come from his sweat and was new enough that she remembered life in the poorest streets of North Bridge, growing up in a two-room flat with no shower and a shared toilet—the very street that Harald lived on now. Her lips tightened at the thought of him. A cheat and a liar and a lech. They could have had a good life together. He'd had promise, and he earned enough and had a good background. When they moved into this house, she thought they would be happy together forever. With two beautiful little girls and so much that life could promise within their reach. Her father had seen it right from the start. "You sure he's not a skirt chaser, honey?" She couldn't see anything, but . . . But what? She could no longer remember whatever in the world she had ever seen in him. It was painful for her now to have to turn the girls over to him every other weekend. The mere *thought* of him got her piss cooking. She drew on her cigarette, inhaled deeply, and closed her eyes, chasing his image with a picture of herself on the green, driving from that fine third hole, the joy of her muscles in full flex, grace of swing, shock of impact—*thwack!*—follow-through, slice of the ball arcing into the sky as she exhaled the smoke.

"Pee-yew!" said Amalie from the tub, and Elisabeth giggled, picking up on it as she did on everything her older sister did. Amalie was six, Elisabeth four.

"Yeah, pee-yew, Mommy! That cigarette *stinks*!" The two of them were giggling now, egging each other on.

Vita ran the cigarette under the cold-water tap and flushed the butt down the toilet. "Okay, okay," she said. "That's more than enough. Are you all clean now, girls? We have got to hurry if Mommy is going to be on time."

"You got to wash me unner here like Dad does," Elisabeth said, pointing beneath her arm. "It tiggles."

"Did your father give you a bath?"

"We were all mud," said Amalie. "From the deer park. The big daddy deers were ready to make the little girl deers into mommies."

"Yeah!" Elisabeth chipped in. "And Birgitte was there. She's *nice*!"

Vita's eyes narrowed. "Oh? Who is Birgitte? Did Dad bring a friend along?"

"Yeah, she's *nice*. And she's pretty."

"But not as pretty as you, Mom."

"Where did Dad wash you?"

"In his shower."

"Where on your body?"

"Unner here," Elisabeth said again. "And back here!"

She burst out giggling as she pointed behind her, but Amalie snapped, "He did not!"

"Did too!"

"He *never* did! He said *you* should!"

"Why are you objecting so strongly, Amalie? Did your father say you shouldn't tell?"

The girl blinked, gazing at her mother, her mouth open as she shook her head no. "It was because we were all mud. From the deer park."

Vita pointed at Elisabeth's vagina. "Did he wash you there?"

"No, he told *me* to," she said, and started giggling again. "He said, 'You got to wash everything you own when you take a bath!'"

While the girls toweled themselves, Vita stepped into the hall with her cell phone: "Mom, it's Vita. Would you ask Daddy if he could come by with you, too? Just for a few minutes. It's rather important."

6. The Mumble Club

Nine A.M. sharp: another Wednesday morning in the Mumble Club.

Jaeger sat sober-faced, occasionally caressing his trim blond beard, his shirt still damp with sweat beneath the arms and on the back from cycling full pump through rush-hour central Copenhagen traffic. He listened as the CEO's quiet voice said important things. October light slanted golden through the big window at the CEO's back so his face was invisible, his shadow cast like a Giacometti sculpture down the center of the steel-legged, crème-lacquered Piet Hein meeting table. Around the table sat the assembled department heads of the Tank, each in a crème-lacquered, steel-legged Arne Jacobsen "ant" chair with arms, while above hung an unlit Poul Henningsen pinecone lamp that looked to Jaeger like an unpleasant creature a diver might encounter hanging in the depths of the sea.

Out the window, the vast blue sky canopied the October trees of the botanical garden below. Jaeger pondered the CEO, Martin Kampman. He was two years younger than Jaeger. Which was strange, to have a guy born two years after you as your boss. Only thirty-nine years old. Made Jaeger feel kind of retarded. Maybe he was. Neither tall nor physically imposing in any way nor, for that matter, brutal or harsh of manner, Kampman had a way of keeping Jaeger unsure, even fearful to an extent. Jaeger's own father had been something like that, and he found himself responding to Kampman sometimes as though he *were* his father, a guy two years younger! Somehow, almost passively, Kampman made it clear that he was not to be fucked with, that a wrong word would put you in a bad place. Jaeger would so like to understand how this was so, but he did not have the patience to concentrate on it for very long. The whole idea bored him. It was so unsexy.

Kampman had been CEO for not quite two years now, and their initial unrest, after the departure of Jørgen Fastholm, who had been tough but fair, had settled. Kampman's reputation as a hard-nose had preceded him. But now it began to appear that Kampman would make no changes after all. People had begun to feel safe again.

The CEO had been speaking for some time now, addressing the assembled department heads—"chiefs," they were called. "How," said one of Jaeger's colleagues to him the day he was promoted, raising his palm like an American Indian in greeting. "How, Chief." And, "Ugh." That was Claus Clausen, passed over for the job that had gone to Jaeger, who was a little bit older, maybe a little bit more productive, and, well, let's face it, less physically imposing and thus maybe less threatening to Martin Kampman. So Claus Clausen was passed over, barred from these Wednesday morning department head meetings. The lucky devil! Jaeger hated having to be here, even as he recognized the importance that he was.

Before he was admitted to the circle, Jaeger used to worry about what was said behind the CEO's closed door. He still wondered. The room was still but for the occasional grumble of an overcoffeed gut and the CEO's murmuring voice.

Here, thought Jaeger, *we speak quietly about important things, though unfortunately not distinctly enough to be understood.* At first he thought he was going deaf and consulted an ENT specialist, who clapped earphones on his head and had him respond to a series of electronic chimes in annoyingly decreasing amplitudes.

"Your hearing's fine," he said. "Perfect as a forty-year-old's could be expected."

"Then why do I have trouble hearing what people say?"

"We Danes do tend to mumble," the doctor's gravelly voice mumbled. "Especially when we're afraid of being quoted."

There were six of them around the table. Six chiefs and the CEO, Martin Kampman, who chaired. Four men, two women. Fingers caressed the handles of cups of steaming coffee, occasionally lifted to their lips, and their eyes were sleepy in enjoyment of the CEO's shadow down the middle of the crème-lacquered table, the CEO's face and torso dark with the golden light behind him, and the crème surface around the long thin shadow. His voice—soft, low in his throat—might have been an articulated Buddhist chant. Every second or third word rose clearly above the rumbling flow.

The subject, Jaeger knew from the agenda, was the annual time and resource consumption review, the report that would display in graphic fictional form a breakdown of precisely how much it cost for each department to produce its dubious results in the unclear (to Jaeger) overall interdisciplinary policy mission the Tank served. Jaeger knew only too well how much fiction went into the review—a born bullshitter, he had no problem fabricating the results of his own department—how much time was wasted on the review, how intangible the results of their work in fact were. Whether or not the results were meaningful was another matter—one he had not yet succeeded in coming clearly to terms with. But he assumed they were doing *something* since substantial state subsidies and profit revenues of a not inconsiderable amount continued to finance their efforts to keep doing it.

After fourteen years here, Jaeger was the third senior manager under the CEO, who had been here a little under two years, recruited for his impressive political network and his reputation as "the clean knife" that had sliced away 30 percent of the 750 staff members of his previous firm.

Jaeger was not worried. Not about his position. Not about losing it. He had already lost everything but his position—a position he had engineered for himself by making use of his strengths and avoiding his weaknesses—and the bulk of his respectable, though not dangerously enviable, salary went to pay alimony and child support and would continue to do so for the next twelve years unless his ex-wife remarried or found a job, neither of which was likely since her well-heeled father would never allow her to suffer want, given her gift of stoking guilt in him.

Jaeger wondered if he was unfair in his judgment of her. They say there are always two sides to a story. But as far as he could see, there was a good deal more to blame on her side than on his. He had thought they could tough it out together, for the sake of the children, for the sake of their beautiful villa and their promising future; but when the violence started and began to escalate, he knew it was time to get out. It started with a heavy glass ashtray on his head and the two of them on their knees cleaning blood out of the expensive white-shag carpeting. She seemed at first to go always for the head, drew blood three times from his scalp, but then once when she came at him, he covered his head, and she lowered her sights, caught him full in the testicles. He swung wild and clipped her on the ear, damaging her eardrum. Thank God it healed. He could never have lived with himself if he had done permanent damage to her, and the prospect of that made it clear to him that it was time to end it.

He did not know why these things had happened. All right, he had cheated on her. More than once. But she had cheated on him, too. With the next-door neighbor, a man named Felix who worked as a poultry expert for the European Union offices in Copenhagen. Another northsider. Jaeger did not mind. In fact, he was pleased. He felt liberated to pursue his own interests, but she seemed to feel that his cheating was less forgivable than hers. There was nothing to do but end it as the mistake it had been from the start. If only they had done so before the girls were born— but how could he ever regret the existence of his two little angels?

Jaeger had eagerly agreed to the unfairly weighted terms of his divorce, had proposed the terms himself. Even the judge presiding in her chambers had requested the clerk to enter in the record that the terms were unfairly weighted against him and required him to affirm that he was aware of that fact before approving the agreement.

The judge, the clerk, both lawyers, and, of course, his ex-wife had all been women. Jaeger had been the only man in the room. Sometimes, in the dark kingdom behind his eyelids, as he made love to some woman or his hand, he reentered Judge Dorrit Kierkesen's chambers and reorganized the proceedings as the true Dionysian ceremony for which they were a metaphor. Judge Dorrit had not been bad-looking for a woman in her late fifties, nor had his own lawyer been, or his ex-wife's, who he later learned had herself been divorced from a history professor who kept locks on the refrigerator, telephone, and television set at home, for these, he asserted, all belonged to him and not to his wife or children.

On either side of him now at the Piet Hein table, in their regular places, sat Signe Cress, head of the legal department, slender and sharp as a knife with a tuft of curly blond locks atop her narrow head; and Holger Hansen, chief of public relations, recently recruited from a regional news service, an owl-faced man whose voice when he spoke rattled out of his sinuses. Across the table were Frederick Breathwaite, chief of international affairs, the Tank's token foreigner, a large, bulky man who walked slowly through the headquarter hallways, speaking Danish like a broken arm; and the newly acquired spin doctor, Ib Andersen, a slender, sprightly man with glistening clean-shaven jowls and manic blue eyes. Andersen was their press spokesman—chosen for the position, Jaeger was convinced, because no one could understand much of what he said, although he spoke with intimidating emphasis and achieved successful results. Jaeger wondered if perhaps that was the secret of success: to emphatically pronounce things no one could quite understand. The CEO was good at that, too. They studied these things in their management courses. Team building and such. Went out to climb mountains together, ford rivers, paddle canoes, eat wild birds cooked over fires built without matches, and learn to mumble double-talk.

Even sitting silently at a meeting, Andersen was his usual hectic self, guzzling coffee, chewing and clicking his trademark red ballpoint pen, shifting in his chair, folding and unfolding his arms, then suddenly sitting bolt upright and flinging the pen down onto his pad and slouching back again, refolding his arms, immediately unfolding them to pick at the corners of his eyes and inspect whatever came away on his fingertips, then, as if suddenly inspired, lunging for the thermos can to refill his coffee cup. He had a restless smart mouth, too, and Jaeger avoided him and his eyes, not to be subjected to one of his sudden epithets or rhetorical questions: *Nobody likes a clever dick*, he might spurt. Or, *What would* you *say if you had something to say?*

It grieved Jaeger that he never had a response ready. His mind was usually elsewhere, often immersed to the waist in the wisps of sexual fantasy, and if he replied off the top of his head, he risked voicing inappropriate scorn and resentment. The right response always occurred to him only later, when it was too late. To *Nobody likes a clever dick*, he might have said, *Are you saying you have no friends, Ib?* To *What would you say if you had something to say?* he almost shot back, *I'd say you have a big mouth!* But that had too much surface feeling. Subtle sarcasm was called for. Like: *Say to* you? *Not a pin.*

Jaeger shifted his gaze to Frederick Breathwaite, doodling on his pad. Breathwaite had been there longer than any of them. He had chaired the committee that hired Jaeger and had been instrumental in his recent promotion to department head, too, beefing up his work with portfolios from his own department.

Between Fred and Ib, directly across from Jaeger, sat Birgitte Sommer, chief of finance, an angular woman with dark curly hair and burgundy-colored close-set eyes, small and very slender, though with wonderfully round breasts. Even as he considered this, the burgundy eyes turned toward

Jaeger for a moment. He looked away and wished he hadn't, remembered meeting her the Sunday before in the deer park when he'd had his little girls out to see the rutting deer. Birgitte had been out jogging and stopped to chat and had been so sweet with the girls, hunkering down to chat with them, her smile so light, before she'd jogged away again.

Someone's stomach rumbled. Ib Andersen straightened his posture and touched his middle. *Guilty!* But then he tilted his head and gazed quizzically at Jaeger, as if to cast the ball of guilt over to him. Stomach can't take all that coffee, eh, Ib? he considered saying but decided it was better not to tempt the spin doctor to start spinning him.

The sun had moved. The CEO's shadow on the tabletop now slanted to his right, blurring at the far edge. Half his craggy face was now visible, the other half in shadow.

Rather, Jaeger thought, the world had moved, not the sun. The sun was stationary in relation to the earth. That had been proven hundreds of years ago by someone. Who? Galileo? Who went to prison for daring to assert that the sun, not the earth, was at the center of the planetary system. Yet we still talk about the sun rising. The sun, Jaeger remembered having read somewhere or other, suffers unendingly and owes us nothing. Jaeger owed things. He owed money to his ex-wife and daughters that had to be paid every month for at least twelve years, perhaps more if the girls went on to university, as he fervently hoped they would, debts he was grateful for and eager to pay. The girls were six and four years old, blond like their mother. But blond Vita's shadow was dark as the pit.

His eyes turned to the great oil painting on the wall at the opposite end of the conference table from where the CEO sat. The subject was hard to identify. It looked like some kind of deep canyon viewed from the rim above, red and blue at the same time, like cold flames, like those blue flames on a gas-run fireplace, like a chilly hell. He could not recall how long it had been there or who had selected it. Perhaps the immediate past administrative chief, a toad-faced blond-headed Clever Dick who lasted only two years in the organization and whose dislike of Jaeger was evidenced by his habitually forgetting to include Jaeger's name on meeting invitations. He had even once invited the assembled staff to a reception at his own home without inviting Jaeger. But Jaeger was still here and Clever Dick was gone, a matter of grim satisfaction. Jaeger's feelings had been hurt by the man, but he'd never disliked him, had wanted the man to like him, or at least not to dislike him. It had been clear Clever Dick had wanted Jaeger gone, and he suspected that Breathwaite had saved his backside for him. Not the only time, either. Why? Goodness of his heart? Or to stockpile favor vouchers?

He glanced over at Breathwaite again, still doodling elaborately on the pad before him. Jaeger tried to get a glimpse of the doodles, but Breathwaite's free hand was cupped around the pad. His gaze lifted toward Breathwaite's face, took in his necktie, a broad, sporty slant stripe of silver and blue knotted neatly at his throat, and the sporty robin's-egg jacket he wore. The lapels, Jaeger noticed, were hand-stitched. Elegant. The lapels of Ib Andersen's gray jacket were hand-stitched, too, though a bit frayed. He wore the same jacket every day. Jaeger wondered when it had last been cleaned. Then he tried to remember when he himself had last cleaned the jacket he had on, one of two he owned, handwoven Irish tweeds he'd bought on sale at Cleary's in Dublin some years before, on holiday when the punt was low. Pre-euro money. Before the green tiger. Before divorce. He couldn't recall if the lapels were hand-stitched and didn't care to bend his face down now to see, but he was quite certain they weren't, even if the jacket *was* handwoven.

The CEO was tieless, wearing a black turtleneck shirt with the word *Boss* emblazoned black on black at the collar, his beige, glove-leather jacket on the chair back behind him. With a glove-leather jacket, you hardly needed hand-stitched lapels. But did a CEO really need a turtleneck shirt that said "Boss" at the collar, even if discreetly black on black? A mounting sense of insufficiency rose in him. He didn't have money for a new jacket. He wondered if the other two men on his side of the table also had hand-stitched lapels, wondered if this was noticed about him. Cheap-ass clothing. He remembered . . . Lost the thought.

The woman beside him, Signe Cress, head of the legal department, also one year younger than Jaeger and one step higher on the hierarchical totem, was taking notes with a silver Cross pen in a fine script he could not quite decipher. It worried him vaguely that she seemed to understand enough of what the CEO was saying to take notes. Maybe there really was something wrong with his ears. Or perhaps she was only writing a grocery list or some private ruminations. Perhaps she was planning the menu for a party she would host. Or writing a poem. Fat chance. Now Breathwaite might be writing a poem, although he was not writing at all at the moment or even doodling. He was only staring down into his glass of water—he never drank coffee at the meetings as the others did—as though he saw in its depths some foreign epic of great tragedy. Breathwaite was a great reader of books, which reminded Jaeger of the days when he himself used to read books. Jaeger was once placed at the international table of the annual banquet with Breathwaite and an American couple, the male half of whom had been trained as an astronaut and whose wife said that her husband read to her at night in bed. "What does he read?" Breathwaite asked.

"At the moment he is reading me *Lassie*," she replied. There was a silence, and then she asked Breathwaite, "Read anything good lately yourself?"

"Yes," he said. "As a matter of fact, Neruda's memoir."

"Who's that?" she asked.

"A Chilean poet. He won the Nobel Prize in 1971."

"Oh, how cool!" she exclaimed. "A *poet*!"

Even if his English was not all it ought to be, Jaeger had enjoyed the exchange, although it made him slightly uneasy that while he did know, vaguely, who Neruda was, he had never read a word the man wrote—in Spanish, English, or Danish.

The CEO cracked a joke, and everyone laughed. Jaeger heard only half the joke and did not get it.

Birgitte Sommer, across the table from him with her exciting, curly black hair and narrow burgundy eyes, laughed by opening her mouth wide so he could see all her teeth and her tongue. The end of her tongue, a small red bulb, wobbled in the dark vault beneath her palate, and her round breasts jiggled alluringly.

Jaeger tried to figure out the joke even as he laughed. He wondered if all the others understood the joke, whether he was the only one who did not get it, though in his own defense he reminded himself he had only been half listening. Idly he wondered what would happen if he said now, *I don't get it.*

He glanced at Breathwaite and noticed that there was no merriment on the man's bulky, jowly face. Jaeger liked Breathwaite, a loner, a somewhat shadowy figure, though always approachable, always helpful and quick with sage advice. Nearly twenty years Jaeger's senior, Breathwaite alone was not placed in the hierarchy of the department heads, for his sphere of responsibility was not linked with the others. Breathwaite was the Tank's eyes in the greater world outside of Denmark. What Danes usually termed "the big world," meaning the "real" world that did not really matter, for it seldom enough rippled the water of this little kingdom of islands. Such had it been since 1864, when the last great battle was lost, in Jutland, to the Germans, and the nation's spiritual adviser, N. F. S. Grundtvig, advised the country, "What we have lost to the world we must regain from within." Or something like that. Jaeger could not remember all the details.

Breathwaite would surely know precisely what Grundtvig had said and meant even if Breathwaite was a foreigner. He had once heard Breathwaite remark that if Denmark had not lost to Germany in 1864, Bismarck would never have been able to unite Germany and neither the First nor the Second World War would have happened. Of course, he'd added, something else, maybe even worse, surely would have filled the vacuum.

Jaeger was intrigued by Breathwaite's book reading. He always had a book with him, on his messy desk, in his bulky satchel, novels and poetry and other things. It worried Jaeger that he himself had stopped reading years ago. Periodically he tried to begin again and would start some book or other, but invariably he got so excited by the first sentence or paragraph or page that he would close the book and start thinking about it, pour a drink, turn on the TV, and never get back to it.

What good were books really, anyway? Words. Escape. A pose. Illusion.

Birgitte Sommer with her burgundy eyes was peering merrily across the glossy Piet Hein table at Jaeger, as though inviting him to share a moment of mutual personal understanding of the humor being experienced at the management group, behind the CEO's closed door. He nodded and grinned as if to say, *The CEO is some card, hey?* He understood suddenly the pleasure of release being experienced in the group's laughter. It did not matter what they were laughing at. Those in the corridor outside this sequestered room would hear this laughter and worry. *What are the chiefs laughing about? What merriment are the chiefs pursuing in there? Is their laughter perchance inspired by some crack about* me? *About my performance? Appearance? Manner?*

Jaeger had forgotten why he wanted so badly to be part of this inner circle. Claus Clausen, now in his tiny windowless alcove-office across the corridor, was no doubt staring at the CEO's closed door, hearing these notes of shared laughter, and lifting an index finger to flick a pearl of sweat from his brow.

It intrigued Jaeger to consider that Clausen, although physically larger and more imposing than he, was now a little bit afraid of him. Jaeger had a definite edge there and could back Clausen down when they disagreed on something. He had tried it just to see. All he had to do was level his gaze and say something curt like *That's not how things work here, Claus.* Or *That's not how we play the piano here.* Clausen was probably his closest friend in the Tank, maybe his closest friend period, maybe his only friend, and Jaeger never hesitated to protect his comrade, as best he could, if he sensed any threat to him, or to put in a good word when he could do so without being too obvious. He enjoyed Clausen's respect and camaraderie. Clausen was divorced, too, after a very brief marriage to a schoolteacher, though childless, and he and Jaeger spent time together occasionally, especially in the summer at the beach, where they sat on the sand behind dark glasses, watching the topless, even sometimes totally naked, women sunbathers, or at serving houses—as they had done last night. Clausen had clearly consumed more draft beer than he could handle, in fact, and had come on too strong to a woman at the bar, who had turned her back and ignored him.

Jaeger was also more successful with women and enjoyed Clausen's little-brother admiration of that success. Clausen was a reader, too, though he seemed mostly to read thrillers, and they both liked films and jazz. Clausen didn't drink as well or fuck as much as Jaeger did, which amused Jaeger, made him feel that he had mastered access to some of the prime skills of manhood that Clausen could only sniff around the edges of. He sometimes suspected that Clausen was deeper than he, that his intellectual range was greater, but that was all right, it was okay that his friend had some strengths greater than his own, especially—well, admit it—less significant ones.

Jaeger's eyes lingered on Birgitte Sommer's narrow burgundy ones, took in those sexy black curls, then dropped to her smooth, slender, eminently kissable neck and lower still to her breasts, so wonderfully large for such a slim body. He remembered the backless dress she had worn to the office Christmas dinner last year. Her back was completely naked so you could see clear down to where the split of her rump began, and the dress somehow held tight up just over the nipple line of her wonderful breasts. How did she keep it up? Some kind of tape, maybe, two-sided tape in the bra cups. No visible straps. Her husband was tall and gawky and wore a stupid-looking pearl gray bow tie, and Jaeger caught him shoving a finger way up his nostril between courses. Jaeger could not help but wonder why Birgitte wanted to look so sexy while her husband looked so drab. Wanted to be admired? Was she lonely? Neglected? Jaeger danced with her a couple of times, and she smiled so nicely into his eyes as they moved around the floor, but when he tried to get close enough to show her how she made him feel, she shifted expertly, blocking him discreetly. Funny how some women let you, even if nothing is to come of it, and some women don't. Maybe she was afraid it might get her excited? God, he would love to bury his fingers in those black curls! Why else would she dress so sexy unless she wanted to be desired? But her husband was there, too. Maybe she did it for him. Maybe he got his jollies watching other men ogle the goods?

For nearly ten years now, he had felt sexual desire for Birgitte. What excited him about her was the thought of how her face might unfold in an intimate situation, how the surface of those sharp small burgundy eyes might crack, emit a dazzling light. He imagined looking down into those eyes as they mounted to orgasm, saying something to her that would make her inhale sharply through an open mouth, issue a pleading moan. He felt that he could please her sexually, could surrender to a profound desire if she was open to it. If she was not open to it, however, the whole experience might be regrettable.

Imagine failed love with a fellow manager. Imagine sitting here in the Mumble Club next day knowing suddenly so much about each other, knowing a failed touch.

Could be the opposite, of course. Eyes meeting as their pulses mounted unbearably. *You! Yes!* What, then, next day across the table? Shared secret of a glance? Plots? Assignations? Meetings in a hotel—perhaps over in the Palace Hotel, looking out onto the Town Hall Square? Lengthy lunches. Cocktails, cigarettes afterward, nakedness, the raw language that excites, his face between her gorgeous breasts, her slender thighs, and her joyous groans as he buried his face in the essence of her?

That heady feeling at the annual banquet seeing her with her husband, Lars. Jaeger shaking Lars's hand in greeting, a tall, thin man with a scrawny throat who wouldn't have a clue. Or would he? What then? Narrowed eyes? Hostile words in the cloakroom?

The head of the legal department, Signe Cress, was now interjecting a word, and this no doubt was what she had been jotting with her silver Cross pen. A prepared statement. Annoying, for now she had spoken, others would feel required to speak as well, to assert their presence, and this meeting could drag on for another hour, for God's sake! Jaeger too began plumbing his mind for some worthy comment.

I could thrash you, he thought, hearing Signe Cress's words, her grainy voice, *seize your pad and tear off that sheet of notes and crumple it into a ball and pitch it into your face.* He was immediately ashamed of his excessive, inappropriate, and uncharitable thought.

A stomach rumbled in the silence between words. Stomachs already thinking of lunch. He tried to concentrate on the words being conveyed in the grainy voice of Signe Cress, whose mumble was as unclear as the CEO's, but he could not stop thinking about how he hated these meetings even as he knew he must guard his place here. People were always saying, "It is important that we talk, that we communicate."

The CEO had invited in a communications expert to address them all once, and after a lengthy presentation about the importance of open, honest, direct communication, Jaeger had chanced a question. An honest, if ill-considered question, the intention behind which seemed to have been misinterpreted.

"I've always wondered," said Jaeger, "why and how it is that when we close a letter by writing 'With friendly greetings,' it is actually *less* friendly than if we write just 'Greetings'? Just as in English I understand that writing 'Yours truly' is sort of less *true,* so to speak, or 'Sincerely yours' less *sincere,* than if you just write 'Yours'?"

Jaeger thought it an interesting question, even a perceptive, clever one, but everyone cracked up laughing, and the presenter shot him a sarcastic smile, then said to the audience in general, "Are there any sincere questions?" and didn't bother to answer. Jaeger noticed then the CEO smiling at him in the way the CEO always smiled—ungaugably. Did that smile say, *You and I, Jaeger, know just how much pig trash this all is. You and I, Jaeger, know the depth of distrust that exists among all of us. You and I know, Jaeger, how we keep this pecking order in function, with tiny withholdings and tiny alleviations.* Or even—could it be?—*Jaeger, I see right through you, you piddling lower middle manager, which is all you'll ever be. You skirt-chasing waste of a human being who is useful to me and therefore tolerated but by no means nonexpendable, by no fucking means, Jaeger. So watch your back.*

It seemed to Jaeger that people here were always talking, always meeting, always *communicating* over a cup of coffee and a piece of cake or a bottle of sparkling water. Every day, at least once, sometimes twice, even three times. And in between the meetings, people dropped by one another's offices to chat. He noticed that when people came in to chat, most of them said the same thing three times: once when they came into the office, once again after they sat down, and then once more to signal that they were about to leave.

Jaeger had many such visitors. He was considered a good listener because he didn't speak much. He didn't speak much because he had found that if you also spoke instead of only listening, the chats were twice as long. If you remained silent and only listened, it was finished in half the time, and then he had peace to try to do some work and get it over with so he could have some time to himself.

But when he was finally alone after all that chatting and listening, all he usually wanted to do was gaze out his window or contemplate the quality of the light on his crème-colored walls or think about some of the women in the office whose smiles or bodies or way of moving down the hall or glancing at him filled him with hope and pleasure or who asked how his daughters were doing and really seemed to care, really seemed to want him to tell them about the cute things they said or the things they were interested in. And why shouldn't they be interested? He wanted to hear about their children, wanted to see their little darlings if they popped in for a visit, wanted to crouch down and smile at them and ask their names and enjoy their shy little faces and big wide eyes, offer them a mint if he had one or colored pencils and paper to draw pictures on or say preposterous things to them that made them smile skeptically at him, suddenly trusting him because he was so clearly teasing to win their trust with outlandish statements.

Sometimes he wondered if anybody actually did anything at all in the Tank. They must have, though, because some things did get done. Even his own work got done despite all the meetings and talking and communication and "chats." The quality of his work was even complimented occasionally by a higher-level manager or member of the board of trustees, although he could never quite remember having actually done the work or what it might mean in the long run or in the overall scheme of things.

All the talk and the words and the chatting and the shuffling of paper and the composing of reports, and half the time, most of the time, perhaps, he felt like a fake hiding in the bush, wondering if he would ever make sense of it at all.

Actually, it suddenly occurred to him, he loved it here. He loved this place. He loved these people. Nothing was perfect. No one had the right to expect perfection. He was one lucky asshole to have this job, and he was eternally grateful for having it. Only a fool would be an ingrate! What was wrong with him?! He looked up, beaming, in the grip of his sudden epiphany and gazed around the Piet Hein table from face to face, loving them each and all.

But something was happening now.

He could sense a tension rising along the table. Eyes were going tight. The CEO picked up on something or other that Signe Cress had said, and it seemed at once to Jaeger that her words were a setup, agreed upon before the meeting between her and the CEO to start a scene no one had expected.

The CEO's face was now almost fully visible as the light behind him slanted over the faces across from Jaeger. Only one eye of the CEO was in shadow and a fragment of his forehead, one ear. His lip moved firmly over words that now fell clearly onto the tabletop between them.

"It hasn't hit us yet, but there will be a substantial deficit in the last quarter of this year. It might be as high as one hundred and fifty million. So I have to ask every one of you to draft a plan for cutting costs, to absorb the loss."

The narrow burgundy eyes of Birgitte Sommer were rigid. Jaeger wondered how the chief of finance could have failed to know this.

Holger Hansen, chief of the public relations department, asked through his sinuses, "How could this happen, Martin?"

The CEO's eyes fixed on him. "You all know—or should know—what has been happening these past many months with foreign investments as well as that both the state and the county have decided to cut our subsidies."

"We discussed that nearly two years ago," Breathwaite said. "And again last year. It was not seen as a threat."

The CEO's gaze was almost casual on Breathwaite's jowly face. The corners of his mouth drew out into a little smile. "The possibility was clear."

"Then we *knew* it was coming and—"

"The possibility was clear."

"But then . . ." Breathwaite didn't finish the question Jaeger would himself have liked to ask: *Why did we just let it happen, then?*

7. Harald Jaeger

Claus Clausen watched from behind his desk across the corridor as the department heads straggled out of the CEO's office. Jaeger avoided Clausen's eyes, hurried through the anteroom where his secretary sat outside his own office.

"Anything of interest . . . ," she began to ask, peering at him with tense blue eyes from behind the big frames of her blue plastic spectacles.

"Nothing special," Jaeger said curtly, and closed his door behind him. He could see from her eyes she already knew something, was trying to get more out of him, information, especially gossip, but anything would do, to feed those around her in the lunchroom. Gossip was the currency of importance. Unfair. She had a right to know.

But not from me. Not just yet. No doubt she already knew some of it, maybe all of it, maybe more than he himself had. *Maybe go see what she has? No, find your own footing first.* A voice from within offered instruction: *You can survive this. Just turn the spotlight on someone else. Be the guy focusing the beam. And be seen to be. Show you want to help cut away the deadwood.* Then he heard his own thoughts and shuddered. He would not be that person. Kill or be killed. No. Live and let live. Live to fuck another day. The image of Birgitte's black curls rose to the screen of his mind. *Oh, Birgitte, Birgitte!* Her slender chest and lovely round breasts! It occurred to him that after a while the splendor of a woman's body was kind of used up. The glow dimmed from use. The aura of each of its parts wore out. But with Birgitte it might be different. It *would* be different. The real thing. This was a woman he could truly love forever.

He sat over his opened laptop, elbows on the desk, mouth pressed against his fists. He was sweating. *Am I going to get fired?* He thought of his little girls, his little angels. What would happen to them? What would happen to him? *No, no. Work. Prove your value. Work.*

He hit the mail receive on his laptop and watched the new messages fall into place. Spam, mostly. Few that needed action. Favors, mostly. Easy stuff. After all these years, he knew most of the answers without having to think. He directed a query from the secretary of a member of the board to a fellow whose name he knew in a parliamentary tourism committee. Good one. Answered three more in a row. Greetings. Friendly greetings. Best greetings. Loving greetings in response to one who had signed off with "MKH"—with loving greetings. Modern type. The subject line of the next mail was, Check out my wife's butt and tell me it's not hot! Click here. With regret, Jaeger deleted. Can't risk a virus on a ruse like that. He continued scrolling down.

Spam.

Spam.

Sex spam.

Political spam.

Political spam.

Sex spam.

Jaeger had once been surfing porn sites and got into a series of pretty hot S&M pages that he checked out at some length. Later that day, in the canteen, he glanced across the room and saw a young woman from IT, big lovely butt and blond braids piled atop her head, smiling at him. Then, eyeing him, she casually clapped her open palm against her bottom and winked at him. This was a woman he had never said boo to. She didn't know him well enough to seek his eyes with a smile like that. What was she thinking? Of him checking out the butt of some spam man's wife? Did this mean the IT people could amuse themselves watching what he was watching online?

He didn't like it.

No more surfing on the job.

8. Frederick Breathwaite

Across the hall and two doors down, Breathwaite's telephone rang. He was tipped back comfortably in his five-footed hydraulic safety chair and did not feel like making the effort to reach for the telephone. The view out the window of the yellow wisps of a weeping willow on the other side of the street was soothing to his eyes. He did not want to think, he wanted only to gaze upon the shadows and light on that tree and the grass around it. But the phone did not stop. Normally on the fourth ring it would channel automatically over to his secretary if he didn't take it, but now it was ringing five times, six times. He jerked forward and reached for it.

Quiet voice: "Don't you read your e-mail?" Kampman.

"Uh, no, I have to admit, not yet today, I haven't."

"Why not?"

"Sorry," he said. "I'm not the biggest gadget guy in the world. Was there one from you, Martin?" Using Kampman's first name reminded Breathwaite of the fact that his boss very rarely addressed him by his name, either first or last. Occasionally he spoke to others about him in his presence as "Fred Breathwaite." Sign of respect, or distance?

"Never mind. Why don't you come on in here. And would you bring the Irish file with you?"

"That's not really a file so much, just a couple e-mails."

"Well, then, why don't you bring the e-mails? That is, if you've looked at them, being that you don't always do. Look, I mean. At the e-mail." Followed by a "heh heh heh" that Breathwaite recognized would be accompanied by a rhythmic lift and fall of shoulders, simulating laughter.

Before Kampman's desk, Breathwaite remained standing and handed the e-mails across to his CEO.

"That's it?" Kampman asked. "Two sheets of paper? No file?"

"It's . . . so far it's been pretty informal. These are people I've known for some time. I can tell they want to open a cooperation, and they have a fat

European Union grant. Green tiger and all. We're talking many millions of euros."

Kampman was nodding, his face bland. "Good," he said with a flat intonation that conveyed neither praise, encouragement, nor enthusiasm. "Would you brief Harald Jaeger on that. I'd like him to take this over."

The sunlight that had previously illuminated Kampman's conference table was at the far edge of the room now and glinting through the slats of the blinds into Breathwaite's eyes. He shifted his position and tilted his head to be free of the glare. "Uh . . . ?" *How to address this? These Irish guys are* my *contacts.*

"I'm hoping you're willing to follow it through with Harald to the end." *Am I hearing this?* Breathwaite only watched the younger man.

"Yah!" Kampman said then, and slapped his palms onto his thighs before moving them to the arms of his chair and raising himself to his feet. "Let's go sit at the table, Fred." He picked up his chrome thermos can. "Coffee? Water?"

An old Danish song kept running through Breathwaite's consciousness. Gnags. Late 1980s or early 1990s, perhaps. Århus rock. A song about a man whose plan for his old age was just to sit on a bench. It was all Breathwaite wished to do just now. A slow stroll out into the late October afternoon sunlight to sit on a bench and watch the city walk by in its curious shoes. Warm enough still to be out without a topcoat. Unseasonably mild for Copenhagen.

He had been about to look in to his secretary to say he would be gone for the rest of the afternoon when he heard her quiet sobbing from the office next door, and he held back, listening behind the opened slit of his door. She wasn't getting the ax. Was she sobbing for him? He wasn't even sobbing for himself. Had she heard already? Or maybe she'd known in advance. Secretaries know everything that is essential—the human side, at least. He did not feel prepared to offer comfort just now. Then he heard footsteps in the corridor and Jaeger's voice: "Marianne! What is it?"

Breathwaite pictured her at the desk, behind her keyboard, a large, capable, diligent, pretty, sweet-natured woman, a hankie balled at her nose. And himself too small to go in and tell her. But Jaeger could never resist a woman in distress. He'd do fine. *Just hold your panties up, Marianne.*

He returned to his laptop, open on the wing of his desk, and sent her an e-mail:

Dear Marianne,
I'll be gone the rest of the afternoon. See you tomorrow. Chin up.
Greetings, Fred.

It was Marianne who had nurtured their e-mail culture here, insisting on formal salutations and complimentary closings. No staccato telegrams here.
Breathwaite: You're fired. Kampman
He hit send and hurried out quietly, down the back stairwell, his mental litany shifting to Auden's poem about the one-eyed veteran who did nothing with his single eye but look at the sky.

A plan already forming in his head, he lifted the cell phone from his breast pocket and keyed in Jaeger's number to leave a message: "Harald, listen, I'm sure you heard. Could you stop by my place for coffee this evening? Say, eight? Got a splendid malt to crack. Not a word to Kis, okay? No need to call back if you can make it."

Something good could be salvaged out of this. Jaeger owed him a couple of favors—although, of course, that did not mean he would necessarily deliver. Still, he could try. As the Danes said, If it works, it works, and if it doesn't work, well, maybe it will work anyway.

Headquarters were on East Farimags Street, beside the old Commune Hospital, across from the botanical garden. Breathwaite slipped past Ole Suhrs Street and paused on the corner, uncertain where he wanted to go, as a short, craggy-faced, black-haired man walked past with a German shepherd on a leash, tugging him forward. "Easy, Samson," the man grumbled. October air slid gently through Breathwaite's hair. Hard to believe such gentle air this time of year. The galleries and northside lakes to his left, Silver Square cafés ahead, East Park to the right. Any number of amusements available here: He could drink a sugared absinthe at Krut's Karport just ahead and bask in the light of that sweet waitress's smile. Or wine and a delicate selection of excellent cheeses at the Café Kaava farther down. Café Under the Clock, diagonally across, still had tables out. Rare for October. Could enjoy a thirty-crown beer there from big, quiet Hans. Try to carry it up from the basement bar yourself, and he always says,

"I'll bring it up to you." Down in the cozy basement with the bookcase of glasses imprinted with names of the regulars. Breathwaite had never made the bookcase.

There were two museums to choose from—the Hirschsprung Collection there on Stockholms Street, sculpture outside of a small equestrian barbarian, three heads hung from his saddle. *Put mine there, too.* Or the National Museum, across from Brandes Place. He hadn't been there in an age. Strange sculpture in the doorway—what was it? He'd noticed it one day last summer. Couldn't remember, but it was strange.

But he had it in his head to go sit on a bench, so he turned toward East Park and strolled among the tree sculptures, dead of elm's disease and transformed into art. Ought to do that with human beings. Bleach and carve the mighty bones of the dead. *There stands my father's white thigh like a narwhal tusk, pointing to the sky. And there my mother's pelvis through the port of which you can view the reverse story of my life.*

Might as well admit it now, Breathwaite: We have fucked up this world, and you did not a pin to stop it. *Guilty as charged. So do I burn in hell? Does, say, Hitler burn in hell? Or not? Because if Hitler's not burning, I must deserve a peaceful sleep.*

He came at last to just the bench he sought. He sat in a dapple of sunlight through the wizening leaves and watched a pack of young men on a small field, grass still green enough, run furiously at soccer. He himself was that rare American who had managed his way through grammar and high school without ever having engaged in any manner of team sport apart from a few mandatory hours on the basketball court, a tiny bit of lacrosse, softball, soccer even. He had been agile enough and large, sought after for football, but it didn't interest him. The spectacle of bulk smashing bulk to capture a ball. The whole idea of competing, of fighting to win a symbolic battle, had always seemed so . . . unnecessary. If you work hard, you will prosper; no need to try to bring the other man down.

It made him sad now to see these young men fighting together, testing themselves against and for one another, hooting, groaning, laughing, cheering. Red sweaty faces full of grin and grunt. Clapping of hands and triumphant pump of the arm: *Yes!* How unlike Molly's "Yes." The Y of YHWH.

Sport, he thought, *serious sport has nothing to do with fair play.* Orwell said that. It's bound up with hatred, jealousy, boastfulness, disregard of all rules, and sadistic pleasure in witnessing violence. In other words, it is war minus the shooting.

Or what?

Maybe I was wrong.

Then he remembered, some forty years before, knocking out Hugh Powers's teeth. That sick, pointless feeling of ugliness.

He rose, his solid black Lloyd 46s strolling him on dirt, north, toward where his youngest son lived, the only one of the three who still interested him, the only one who was making a fuck-up of his life. The others were all so . . . *set.* IT consultants, the two of them, with their villas, respectively, in Brønshøj and Albertslund, three kids between them so they jointly matched the national average. They didn't drink, didn't smoke, went out running every day, mountain biking on the weekends (in the flats of Zealand). They watched television in the evenings, had voted central right, both of them, flat and happy as clams with kids to match. No doubt in ten years or so they would divorce to match the statistics in that sector of this disintegrating society, too. A terrible confession he would never make, secret observations locked inside the vault of his skull.

Only Adam (what a handle to give a kid!)—named for his mother's brother, middle named for Breathwaite's beloved dead brother, Jes, the name he went by—only Jes gave him cause for concern and hope. But the kid didn't have a chance. Too many dreams. He'd dabbled in post-modernism, and he'd dabbled in post-traditionalism and in post-colonialism, and he'd dabbled in post-ethnicity and in behavioristic post-ethicism and no doubt in post-postism, too, leading up to pre-ism, retro-ism, which could end only in now-ism, and then on to neo-nowism ad infinitum, until time stops its survey of all the world. As far as Breathwaite could determine, he was a very bright kid with an understanding of everything and a grasp of nothing. The boy had all the right ideas and not a chance of realizing them. He worked in a bloody key-and-heel bar run by a Pakistani, and every year that passed, the limb he was out on grew farther from the trunk. At least he had an apartment. He'd invested in a three-room on Blågårds Place at a time when such a place was an idiotic investment for a quarter million. Breathwaite had tried to talk him out of it, but the boy would not be swayed. Twenty-one-year-old Marxist capitalist. Breathwaite only wished he himself had had the good sense to follow the boy's lead and buy three such condominiums, for he would have quadrupled his money already. At least the boy had that to fall back on, but you needed someplace to live and you couldn't eat bricks.

Breathwaite crossed the lakes, chiding himself for his hard and pessimistic frame of mind. *What the hell? Just been fired. Got a right to be sour.* He followed Nørrebrogade past the grimy streets where he'd had his own first apartment in Copenhagen, he and Kis when they'd started out, a two-room on Peder Fabers Street that they'd bought for nothing, sold for triple what they paid, but which now would have been worth a cool million. Mistake to sell that, too. Now, apart from their summer house, they had nothing, a rented luxury flat. Money out the window every month.

Mistake.

He paused on the avenue to gaze across through passing traffic. In the gaps between the cars whizzing past, he could make out the broad face of a burial association. Danish terminology always made him smile, straight from the shoulder as it was. No portentous purple metaphors here. No funeral parlors—which was to being dead, he thought, as a cocktail lounge was to being crocked. This particular shopfront advertised, ARBEJDERNES LIGKISTER—literally, "Workers Corpse Boxes."

At Blågårds Place, he stopped at Café Flora and ordered a pint, sat in hopes his son might happen by, and found himself thinking about his conversation with the CEO. Shit-canned at fifty-nine.

"Unfortunately we have to cut from the top as well as the bottom," Kampman said. "I'm sorry."

Breathwaite had entertained this possibility but considered it a long shot. The international work at the Tank had grown increasingly important with the growth over the past decades of the European Union from six member states to nine to twelve to fifteen to twenty-five, soon to twenty-seven. How in the world could they do without his experience? Well, clearly, they could. His salary was second only to the CEO's and equal to the administrative chief's. He had counted on staying until he was sixty-five to build up his pension in the last five years. By stopping him now, they saved at least six million plus benefits. The arithmetic was simple and clear. But even though Kampman was only thirty-nine, he had finesse enough to let that say itself.

Breathwaite knew he had to say what he had said next, though he profoundly regretted it. "And if I took a cut?"

Kampman only shrugged slowly, smiled ruefully, more a firming of the lips than a smile. An answer that was not an answer. Unquotable. They learned these things in their management courses. He would get not a golden, but a silver (rather a silver-plated) handshake. A half year's severance. Half a million crowns. He converted to dollars—something he still had to do to get a real sense of the value of the figure. Not quite eighty thousand bucks gross.

Nothing, really. Nothing. Considering the Danish tax structure.

And conditional, it went without saying, on his delivering his Irish contacts.

Breathwaite considered what else he might say. He found himself thinking how old guys know how nasty young men are because that's how they once were themselves, covetous and impatient, overrating themselves as they lunged out after what they wanted and did not have, what some older man was occupying, blocking them from. *I was never like that. I wasn't. I fought with hard work. Or am I kidding myself?* If the soul is ever to know itself, it must gaze into the soul. *That is, if you even have a soul. Anymore.*

Then he remembered what he'd wanted to say to Kampman: "We knew this was coming. We saw it coming two years ago. Longer."

"It was a possibility," said Kampman with firm lips.

"Why didn't we prepare for it?"

That shrug again. That rueful smile that was not a smile. Conveying what? An answer that was not an answer.

You saw the advantage in this, Breathwaite did not say.

Now, in the café, a black fly landed on the back of his hand resting on the tabletop. He flicked it away. It rose and landed again on his wrist. Another flick and it buzzed his nose. He backhanded at it, but it landed again a few inches from his beer, lifting and falling on its spindly legs that sawed against each other. Hideous little bat the size of snot. Breathwaite wondered if he would be fast enough to flatten it with the tip of his index finger, but at his first movement, the fly was up and buzzed his ear. This was unfair. It buzzed him again, and then he thought, *What is that fly trying to tell me? As if it had an urgent message. As if I am a glorious planet, it lands here and there on me, touching down again and again despite my every effort to discourage it, to indicate that it is not welcome. Does it want me to kill it? Is life as a fly so miserable?*

He finished his beer and strolled back toward the lakes, stood on the bank of Peblinge watching the swans float around like question marks. A duck crawled up onto the concrete lip of the bank and waddled over to him, perhaps thinking he had bread to share. The duck looked up at him and honked twice.

Which, Breathwaite thought, translated from duck as, *No bread*.

9. Kirsten Breathwaite

It was love at first sight. Leaving him behind about broke Kis's heart. An eight-week-old golden retriever pup she had been offered by her boss for practically nothing. He looked like a little furry clump of golden sunlight, and the minute she set eyes on him, a name popped into her head. Amon-Ra. Who was that again? Then she remembered it was the name of the Egyptian sun god. Or, no, it was just plain Ra, wasn't it? Better yet, and that was what she would call the pup. *Ra*. If she could call it anything.

Fred would never go along with it.

She stepped away from the building front on Østergade where she worked and felt the ache of emptiness in her arms where the little thing had been. So sweet. *So* sweet. She felt like a child whose father had refused her a pet. Helpless. Hopeless. She would do *anything*. I'll *take care of it, Fred, you won't have to do a thing*.

Turning up Strøget, the Walking Street, she decided that if Magasin's outdoor café was still open, she would stop for a cappuccino—*no*, for a glass of wine—and do some thinking. But it was not open. So—to hell with it!—she pushed through the side doors of Magasin and rode the escalator down to the basement café and ordered a glass of merlot.

She lit a cigarette and found herself thinking about the pope. It was *his* fault that she couldn't have a puppy. Fred was all locked up in guilt. Martin Luther was right. The Catholics had it all wrong. Guilt and shame. Kneeling and bowing the head—bowing for what? the butcher's knife?—and beating the breast. *Mea culpa, mea culpa, mea maxima culpa!* Ow my tit, ow my tit, ow my most battered tit!

And that story about the guilt wheel in the heart that some damn priest had told Freddy when he was a boy. *If you do a bad thing, the guilt wheel starts to turn and its sharp edges cut into the tender skin of your heart and the blood of shame and pain spills from the cut. But the more bad you do, the duller the edges get, so finally you can't even feel the pain anymore. You just sin and sin and sin and you don't feel a thing.*

Sounds like a plan to me, Freddy.

He had liked that. He didn't want the guilt, and he'd come a long way from it, she thought, but still it was the guilt that made him fold into himself and cut him off and fear being engaged with others. If you were engaged with someone, you might do something wrong, something to hurt them. When you were alone, there was no one to hurt but yourself. Not even a puppy!

It's not that he doesn't care, it's that he doesn't dare. She was certain of that. It *had* to be that. If it wasn't that, she didn't know him at all, and if she didn't know him after all these years, why then . . .

He had done so much better when the children were little, when they needed him. Such a loving father. But his expectations were so great and his disappointments, too. When the children didn't do what he saw as best for them, then the guilt got cooking, and it was *his* fault, and there it was again.

Sometimes she wanted to shake him, shock him. *Freddy, you're your mother's son! You've got an Italian heart, not an Irish one. You're not Catholic, you're an amorist! A hedonist! No wonder your mother cheated on your father! Who could stand to live with all that guilt and piety? It's enough to make a sinner of anybody!*

But of course, she wouldn't say that. Such words were not spoken or even insinuated.

She lit another cigarette and signaled for another glass of wine, which the waiter brought with a dazzling smile, a tall, slim boy with tight black pants pinching his delightful ass. Tight at the front, too. Nice thick wad to wrap your palm around. Oh, to have Fred's prick in me again! But all he thought about these days was his disappointment with Jes.

"That boy has greatness in him, Kis," he had told her once.

"Who needs greatness? Let him live and be happy. All a person really needs is a little love in his life, Fred." (*Or her life,* she didn't add, but he heard it anyway.)

"Want me to try Viagra, Kis?"

"No! What if you get a heart attack? Anyway, it only works if you have the desire—I read all about it—and if you have the desire, why in the world would you need Viagra? This is all mental, Freddy."

"Since when are you such an expert on everything?"

"I know a few things, Freddy. It's the Sermon on the Mount that matters about the church, about any church that calls itself Christian. In the Sermon on the Mount, Jesus says that we should love our neighbors. That's what matters. Not all that guilt and sin, but love. That's what Jesus said."

"In fact, Jesus did not say that in the Sermon on the Mount. In fact, it is from the Old Testament. God to Moses as reported in Leviticus. And in the same chapter, God instructs Moses that certain women, if they are not free women, that it's appropriate to scourge them for adultery. That's something of a conflict, wouldn't you think?"

"You know so much, Freddy. But how much do you really understand? Who cares where it's written, it's true."

"It's your truth."

"The only truth."

He was smiling at her. He reached to touch her face. "Sometimes I think you're the only real Christian I've ever known."

10. Harald Jaeger

"My God!" Jaeger yelped, following Breathwaite through the entryway of his apartment into the triple en suite living room. "What an apartment!"

Breathwaite spoke over his shoulder. "As a wise man once said, If you have to be bored, it might as well be in comfortable surroundings."

"You don't strike me as particularly bored," Jaeger said, running his fingertips over the multicolored spines of books in the library shelves, floor to ceiling. He calculated quickly—four meters by four meters. Sixteen square meters of books. He felt his knees might buckle under the weight of the diminishment he felt. It occurred to him he could never invite Breathwaite and Kis home to his own measly apartment. He felt ashamed. He felt like nothing.

Kis floated lightly in from the next room with a bright smile of greeting. She kissed Jaeger lightly on the lips. "Hello, Harald. Welcome."

"Jesus," said Jaeger. "This man has *everything*. A beautiful home, a sweet beautiful wife, three grown successful kids . . ."

"How're your little girls?" Kis asked.

"I just love 'em to death," he said in stilted English, a line from some American movie. "They are so sweet."

"Enjoy them," said Breathwaite. "Those are the best years."

The thought of his girls cheered him. At least he had that.

"Do the girls have a puppy?" Kis asked. "You should give them a puppy. Every little girl should have a puppy." She glanced at Breathwaite, who rolled his eyes. "How about Vita?" Kis asked then. "How is she holding up?"

"I'm sure she's fine as she can be," Jaeger grumbled. Then, "I envy this apartment," he said, trying to get control of the envy by confessing it. "What a place!"

"It's okay," she said, "but you know what? I never asked for this. I could be happy in a construction shed."

"Says you," said Breathwaite, and Jaeger laughed sarcastically.

"I mean it," Kis said, then added, "As long as I could have a puppy."

Breathwaite grunted.

"Really," Kis insisted. "I was up and down once in my childhood. My father lost everything, and my mother became a bitter woman. It killed her and it killed their marriage. She thought she was a displaced princess deprived of all the things she had a right to, so she couldn't enjoy what she did have."

Jaeger glanced at Breathwaite, who shook his head almost imperceptibly.

"What did she have?" Jaeger asked. "Other than a puppy?"

"Don't ask," said Breathwaite. "Excuse me while I fetch the drinks."

"We had a nice little apartment in Rødovre."

Jaeger guffawed. He could hear the strain in the laughter and in his own voice. "Jesus Christ, you know what? When I got divorced I started seeing a psychologist to help me deal with how it might affect the kids . . ." The words slipped out too fast. They were part of a funny story, but he hadn't realized what the story would reveal about him.

"That was a good thing to do, Harald," Kis said softly.

"Yeah, and he was good. He was really good." No graceful way out of it now. "He was really helping me sort through it all. We really hit it off. So much that he wanted to be friends with me. Then he invited me home to meet his family . . ."

"Do psychologists do that sort of thing?"

"What sort of thing?" Breathwaite asked, returning with a tray of glasses and bottles.

Kis clammed up. "Oh, we're just jabbering," she said.

Jaeger was impressed by her discretion. *She respected my confidence.* He realized that she had recognized his own surprise at stumbling into his story. But he wondered if she wouldn't tell Fred about it later anyway, so he thought he might as well plunge right on. "I was just telling Kirsten about how I went to a psychologist to help me deal with my divorce, with how it might affect my little girls."

"Anyone sees a psychologist should have his head examined."

"Fred!"

"That was ironic, dear."

"Well, don't *be* ironic about such things."

"Anyway," said Jaeger, and wondered if he had any chance in hell of salvaging the humorous twist that had been his point in the first place.

"This guy invited me home to meet his family. We really hit it off, and he was helping me, but he invited me home and it turned out he lived in one of those god-awful rows of ten-story shoebox apartment complexes in Rødovre. I had to take the train out to Glostrup, and he met me at the station and led me across Rødovrevej. Jesus, their main street was a bloody highway with a metal fence in the middle of it. He brought me up to his apartment, and honest to God . . . He was always reminding me to be frank with myself about what I felt about things, and when I saw the, the *joint* he lived in, I was like, frankly, how can you take psychological advice from a guy who lives like this?"

Kis made a face at him. "Snob!" To Breathwaite, she said, "That was Harald's response to my tale of a happy childhood in Rødovre!"

"You *told* him that!"

"What a couple of snobs!"

"Time for some elegant whiskey," said Breathwaite.

"Not for me, thanks," Kis said. "Harald, will you stay for dinner?"

"Thanks, no, Kirsten, it's nice of you to ask, but I have an appointment."

"And we all know about Harald's appointments," Breathwaite said.

Jaeger laughed and let him believe it. At least he had that to envy.

It was too chilly for the terrace, so they sat in the library and Breathwaite shut the sliding panel door. There were two bottles of malt on an expensive-looking table of dark wood between two red earflap chairs. "Did you want coffee, too?" Breathwaite asked. Jaeger smiled at the whiskey bottles and shook his head.

"This one is a prize," Breathwaite said, and measured out a dram for each of them into crystal rock glasses.

Jaeger looked around for an ice bucket. "Got any ice?"

Breathwaite smirked. "If you want ice, I'll give you a blended. This whiskey is thirty years old. You want it neat. With just a drop of distilled aqua." He applied water from a glass beaker. "Listen, you know how to taste whiskey?"

"Yeah, with my tongue."

"Do yourself a favor, try it my way just this once. First, nose it pretty good, let your nostrils sort through the strands of aroma. With this one you can expect a mix of nuts and sweaty socks . . ."

"That's good?"

"That's very good. Then take a little bite of it onto your tongue, right in the center of the tongue, hold it on the tongue by curling the sides up. Then let it roll over the sides, and when all your taste buds are getting a jolt, breathe in, just a bit. Whoa, whoa, don't inhale it! Just sip a little air into the chamber of your mouth and feel how it—"

"Whoa!" said Jaeger. "Combustion!"

"Right. Now let the whiskey roll slowly down your throat."

Jaeger sat back in his chair. "Jesus! I'm converted."

"Right? Good?"

"Incredible."

They tasted again, and Jaeger closed his eyes with pleasure. "I always thought all that stuff was pure snobbery. It really matters."

"You bet it matters, buddy," Breathwaite said, and reached across to a humidor and flipped up the lid. "Help yourself, Harald."

"Jesus, are you going to offer me a job, or ask me for a loan, or what?"

"Suspicious little fucker, aren't you, Harry?"

They prepared their cigars in silence. It occurred to Jaeger as he inhaled the aroma of the Cuban tobacco that for what this would have cost him he could have bought a liter, maybe two liters, of his usual Netto-blended whiskey, guaranteed not fewer than three years old, and have enough left over for three Flora Danica stogies if he absolutely felt like a smoke. But on the other hand, this wasn't costing him anything. Yet.

Breathwaite torched him with a burning strip of cedar, and Jaeger filled his mouth with smoke and watched it drift up along the shelves of books, settle in a wispy blue ceiling halfway up. "How're the kids and grand-kids?" he asked.

Breathwaite shrugged. "The older kids are all set in their right-centrist rut. Young Jes is having trouble getting started."

"He's at Roskilde University Center, right?"

"In principle."

"What does that mean?"

"It means in fact he is working at a Pakistani key-and-heel bar while he decides whether or not he wants to go further than a bachelor's."

Jaeger tasted the whiskey again. The inhalation process made him feel as though the whole top of his body were tasting it. As much as he was enjoying the drink and the smoke, he could smell depression hanging in the air of the elegant room and began trying to think of a graceful exit before he got depressed himself. He wondered if Breathwaite knew that he knew what had happened to him this morning.

"You get called in to Kampman after the meeting this morning?" Breathwaite asked him.

"No." A little bubble of fear popped in Jaeger's belly. Who knew what negotiations might have been made since the last news he heard? What tables might have been turned? "Called in for what?" he asked, his throat fumbling a note.

"To get the sack."

Instantly Jaeger saw Amalie's and Elisabeth's sweet young faces in his mind, thought what might happen if he was going to get fired after all. Vita would have help from her father, but that was not the same. The thought of not being the one to provide for his little girls, of Vita being able to treat him as a father who did not provide for his daughters, opened a window onto the worst dread he could imagine, and he realized suddenly that truly he was nothing. All he had left in the world was his position at the Tank, and suddenly he understood that he had been allowing himself not to consider how vulnerable that might be, *was*. Had Breathwaite traded him off, somehow got his own back by selling him out? What the fuck could he do? He needed a smoke screen to hide his terror but didn't dare raise the cigar to his teeth for fear his hand might tremble and give him away. He went for the whiskey instead, lowering his face to it so he didn't have to lift the glass so high, and drained it, forgetting all the tasting techniques. It helped anyway, but not much. He thought of asking whether Breathwaite was on a mission for Kampman, but some instinct told him to keep his mouth shut.

"That's what I got," Breathwaite said.

"No!" Jaeger hoped to hell the grin in his heart did not shine through the mask of shock and sympathy. Breathwaite nodded, smiling wryly. Did he see?

"That's right. Kampman is a fox." Breathwaite sucked at his cigar, but it was cold. "He's setting up a whole machine. Everyone's going to take a course in how to lower the ax. All department heads. They're going to offer psychological counseling, reemployment counseling, and a bag of money."

The fear was crawling down into Jaeger's testicles now. There was only one question in his mind, and he didn't dare ask it, so instead he asked with appropriate shock, "You're getting fired?!" Hoping to Christ Breathwaite did not already know that he knew.

Breathwaite put a finger to his lips, got up to check that the sliding door was shut tight. "I don't want to upset Kis unnecessarily. No, I'm quitting."

Was this bullshit? "I don't understand."

"As soon as we agree on what I get, I quit."

"A golden handshake."

"Golden shower is more like it. Kampman is a fox. Everyone knew this was coming, but when he didn't do anything about it, he created the illusion that everything was fine, that there was some kind of alternate plan. Well, everything *was* fine. From Kampman's viewpoint. Now he has an excuse to hack away all the deadwood before he rebuilds . . ."

"But *you* . . . ?"

"*I* am an idiot. He's got my whole network. It never occurred to me to wonder why he's taken such a keen interest in my work for the past couple of years. He gave me everything I asked him for, so I gave him everything he asked me for. Now he's got it all, and I'm superfluous. Seven years before my time."

"But your contract . . ."

"Verbal. I made a verbal contract five years ago with Jørgen Fastholm. We had such a good relationship that I got lazy. Jørgen was not an easy guy—a CEO can't be—but he always kept his word, and he didn't pull this kind of crap on you."

"But the Academic Union would—"

"Not a member. Like I said, I'm an idiot." Breathwaite turned his eyes on Jaeger, who could see he wanted something, but Jaeger's own need was stronger. "Who, who else, is—"

"You're safe."

"I'm safe?"

Breathwaite nodded. "You're just going to have to work a little harder. You'll be taking over a good piece of what I do. The rest will be farmed out." He relit his robusto, puffing vigorously, cheeks hollowing with the effort. "Kampman asked me whether you were strong enough to do the job."

"He did?" Despite himself, Jaeger whispered again, "He did?"

Breathwaite nodded. "I vouched for you from the start, and I'll do it to the bitter end."

Sweat was oozing down Jaeger's back. Why was Breathwaite telling him this? Could he believe it? He had to. He did. Was it a trick? A strategy? Jaeger knew that he was not a strategic thinker, he knew that about himself. He ran on instinct and was meticulous about not being a threat to those who could hurt him. But why would Breathwaite tell him all this?

"You're empty," Breathwaite said. Jaeger heard it as an accusation and raised his eyes, startled, but Breathwaite reached for the thirty-year-old, refurbished Jaeger's glass, then his own. "So what do you think?"

"I don't know what to think."

"You must be thinking something."

Jaeger shook his head. "Why are you telling me this?"

"I've got a favor to ask."

"Anything," Jaeger blurted. "Anything I can. You always stood up for me. Without you, I wouldn't be here." Breathwaite had chaired the hiring committee fourteen years before that selected Jaeger out of a slush pile of over one hundred applications for his job. And had saved his arse more than once since. He would do whatever he could for Breathwaite. Within reason.

"You're going to need some part-time help. Someone with English. To help with some of the international portfolios. Someone who can write perfect English and who can translate and who knows Denmark and Danish, too."

"You don't mean . . . You mean *you* want to work for me?"

Breathwaite's gaze went chill. Jaeger saw a brief flash of disdain—or did he imagine it?—before the man's mouth opened in laughter. "No! No no no. I'm done. I would appreciate your telling Kampman you need some part-time help and suggesting, very strongly suggesting, my son for the job. My youngest. Jes. Which I will already have suggested."

THURSDAY

DOME OF THE ROCK KEY & HEEL BAR

11. Martin Kampman

With true discipline, the routine and its rhythm are internalized. Into the body. At 4:59 A.M., Kampman opened his eyes. He lay neatly on his back on his side of the bed. His right hand reached swiftly to the night table and lifted the clock down before his eyes: 4:59. He smiled at the green luminous ciphers, which confirmed what he already knew and stopped the alarm an instant before it sounded.

His aim was one day to so perfectly incorporate time into his bloodstream and nervous system that he could live without a clock. Simply know the time and trust that knowledge. Like the primitives. Only this would be the other end of the evolutionary cycle. Primitive understanding refined in modern managerial consciousness.

After folding back his side of the eiderdown, he rose smoothly in the dark room, glanced at Karen asleep in a heap across the mattress, tangle of tight yellow curls showing against the pillow, lit by a shaft of pale light from the driveway lamppost. The swell of the bedclothes over her hip stirred him; quickly he stepped into his slippers and crossed the room quietly, down to the foyer toilet, where he wouldn't wake anyone, and watched the rod deflate as he leaked quietly against the porcelain. Piss hard-on. The urges sank away with it.

In the kitchen he did jumping jacks before the open back-garden door, watching morning mist lift off the grass, cool October air sweet in his nostrils. He touched his toes, touched the floor, flat-handed the linoleum, did side bends, back bends, squats on toes, and squats on flat feet until a light sweat filmed his flesh. Then he poured and drank seven centiliters of prune juice and climbed down the stairs to the basement bathroom.

Watching the calm of his blue eyes in the mirror, he brushed his teeth, shaved his lean jowls. Just before the prune juice kicked in, he stepped on the electronic scale. It was his custom to weigh himself, naked, before *and* after shitting each morning. Sometimes as much as a half-kilo difference. He looked before he flushed to read the day's augury in what he had dropped. Two large brown nuggets. Neat. Internal harmony. Promised a good day. He

cleaned himself meticulously with wet serviettes and relegated his produce to the plumbing system.

At five fifty A.M., in luminescent Helly Hansen running suit and self-
illuminating Nikes, a purple-and-gold terry-cloth sweatband around his
head (colors of the Tank logo), without knocking first, he briskly opened
the door to his son's room and entered swiftly, clicking on the overhead
light.

"Adam. Y'wake?"

Silence. Scan the covers for telltale bulges. "Adam?"

"Yeah, Dad, thanks."

Forced politeness. Self-control. It annoyed Kampman a little that the
boy's sleepy smile seemed exaggerated, effusive. And it annoyed him a
little more that he didn't rise with alacrity, that he was still in bed.

Hands beneath the covers. *Drop it, son!*

It annoyed him that he had learned it was necessary to budget five minutes of a tight morning schedule for this reveille process. And it also annoyed him that these things annoyed him, for he wanted very much to
respect his son, his firstborn by a dozen years, who had a lot of potential.
If he would just get his butt in gear. He told the boy that from time to
time. Not too often, but at certain moments when he judged it might have
an effect.

You've got potential, Adam.

Thanks, Dad.

Use it.

That smile. *Thanks, Dad.*

Now his voice was crisp, though not without affection. "Carpe diem,
sonny!"

"Right, Dad."

"Come on."

The boy sighed—true colors there—threw back his covers, and slid his
legs out so his feet were flat on the antique plank floor. But sitting, not
standing. Kampman could see he'd slept in his underwear. Sloppy habit.
We provide pajamas. Use them. Maintain form at all times. Demonstratively,
he shot his cuff and looked at his wristwatch.

"You *are* up, are you not?"

"Yo, Dad."

"Good. I'm counting on you now. Up early and work hard. You'll never regret it."

"Right, Dad."

"Good. Have a good workday, sonny. Love ya."

"Love you, too, Dad." Rubbing his eyes.

Kampman leaned forward and gave the back of the boy's head an affectionate smack.

Down the hall, he looked in on the twins, still sleeping in their little twin beds. He wanted to kiss their golden brows but feared it might wake them, complicate the morning before Karen was up or the au pair here to deal with it.

Across to Karen. He could see the blue shadows of her open eyes in the pale darkness. He bent to kiss her, could smell she'd had a cigarette yesterday, decided not to mention it. Sometimes the secret of a successful marriage, he thought, was simply keeping your mouth shut. Pity, though. Weakness there, for all the world to see. Aside from the health problem, the stink, and the economic waste of it.

"Have a good day, honey," he said.

"You too, honey." Her sleepy smile of admiration. "How do you do it?"

"Easy. Just do it."

"But where do you get the energy?"

"From just doing it."

At the bedroom door he turned to wave, and she twinkled her fingers at him. Both of these actions, they knew, were necessary parts of the turnkey operation that started their day, kept each part balanced in the flow of the harmonious whole that was the life of their family, *his* family.

As his cushioned Nikes hit the pavement outside their villa on Tonysvej, he glanced at his watch and was rewarded to see the time was precisely what he'd felt it to be, 6:02, and he was jogging west to Bernstorffs Way, south toward the city. He jogged on the bike path that ran parallel to the road, past Gentofte Town Hall and the fire station, heading out of Charlottenlund into Hellerup, heights to middle heights, through the fine-misted damp air. The rain hung in the air rather than fell, haloing the objects that furnished the semidarkness along the road, early bikers in their slicks humped over handlebars, cozy blur of their headlamps, houses, a red mailbox. The streetlamps were not yet extinguished, light smearing pale in the mist, as did the headlights of the slowing, thickening motor traffic. The stretch and contraction of his muscles was agreeable, elbows pumping steadily with his heart, lungs, all in smooth high function. He felt light and agile as he slowly built speed through the boring streets past Helleruplund Church and Rygaards School—little to engage the eye. A good leader is never bored, can always find engagement. The stretch of his legs was long and easy as his jog built to a quick trot, to a sprint, past St. Lukas Hospital and Fragaria Way. Odd name for a street—Fragaria. Strawberry? Strawberry Way? Kilometer and a half behind him already, but he reminded himself to keep the measure simple and objective. The journey, not the distance. Stay in the moment of the run. Seven kilometers total. A sixty-minute run normally, fifty on a better day. Started out at 6:02 today, should be there by 7:02 the latest. First one in. Annoyed him if someone came in before him, but no one ever did. God forbid they should give a little extra. Difference between the leader and the led. Clausen sometimes—8:30, 8:40. Clausen the only one. Keep him in mind.

This was his prep for the day. Two and a half kilometers straight down Bernstorffs Way to Tuborg Way, veer right along Fragaria Way and across Lyngby Motor Road for the next one and a half kilometers, past Emdrup Pond, across Emdrup Way, past the little shopping center there toward Hans Knudsens Place. Time it so you reach Hans Knudsens on the green and jog toward the big polar bear sign on the Polar Bodega. Dismal place. Gave him a shudder. Kind of joint his father used to frequent. *Damn loser.*

He broke into a sprint for the next one and a half kilometers past Vibenshus Center, the Magister House (Medister House, one of the twins called it once, Sausage House, Meatball House), Vibens Motor Circle, and open to a full run down Nørre Allé, past the Commons, west wall of the Rigshospitalet, the State Hospital, and hook right on Tagens Way. Not thinking, letting thought find him. He knew there would be many thoughts preparing themselves today, and he would not rush them. Let the pick get the meat out of the nut for him, just let it happen, no rush, let thought come to him.

A million details were grouping themselves into bunches, preparing themselves for his attention now that things were falling into place. Breathwaite on the catapult. But what had already appeared first thing, way back alongside the misty face of the fire station, was Adam's effusive smile. He rejected the image at once. This was not a thought he wished to spend time with right now. It threw him off his stride. He had to skip a beat, two beats, to catch his pace again. The soles of his Nikes popped an easy half-dozen steps against the tarmac in proper sync, and the unwanted thought was gone.

But now here it was again, nearly five kilometers afterward. That smile. Effusive. Why? *Deal with it later.*

Yet it threw him off into thought streams that were subterranean. Couldn't be dealt with. Then the big glowing white polar bear reminding him of the old man, wasting himself at a smoky bar. Cigarettes. Schnapps. Beer. No doubt women, too. The kind who sat at the tables of serving houses. Slurred voices and greasy hair. So easy. Easiest thing in the world was to lose. Lose a chance, a negotiation, lose a window of opportunity, a whole season, lose your whole damn life and end up like him, eating weiner-brød pastry with beer in the morning. Goddamned loser. Adam looked like him. Same traits. Days abed and morns of slumber were not meant for man alive. Adam would not lose. *Keep at him.* Slow and sure. Karen was too easy with him. *He's a sensitive fellow, Martin.* Who isn't, Karen? *The boy needs love.* Yes, indeed, he does; now tell me your definition of love, please. We live in a culture of dependency, my friend, and dependency neither yields nor breeds love. Contrariwise. That is *not* love. That is *not* nurturing strength. That is encouraging weakness. Adam will be a leader of men, not a follower of his own desire for comfort. A leader of men and women. He will not repeat his grandfather's sorry life. That is a model we scrap right from the start. Break the mold and throw it away.

The south wall of the State Hospital loomed up above him on his left, Panum Institute to his right, high red brick studded with small black windows. Like running through a valley. Through the valley of sweat ran Martin Kampman. He liked that. Sweat of triumph clinging to his back, his flanks, the muscles of his ass and thighs and calves working with his blood, his pump, tight swing of elbows.

As he aimed for the green traffic light at the corner, a dream fragment fleeted across the screen of his consciousness: He had been in the airport, and he saw a Swedish colleague, Anders Sachost, and was about to say hello, but the face looked wrong. Kampman watched it, transfixed, as it began to mutate into one face after another; it became the face of a fly, of a wasp, but green as a grasshopper. Frightened, Kampman asked brusquely, *What are you, celebrating carnival early?* And Sachost's face grew purple mandibles between which his teeth spelled out, "Early Carnival," and all the people around them began to laugh at Kampman. Ugly dream.

He missed the light on Blegdamsvej and had to stop while buses and cars and trucks rumbled past. He leaned forward, palms on knees, catching the breath the interruption cost him. Sweat dripped from his forehead, headband soaked through. He crouched there in the pale shadow of the ridiculous huge sculpture of Finsen, hands raised melodramatically to the heavens to receive radium. Like that crazy Swede in the von Trier film on TV: "With plutonium we will force the Danes to their knees!" Funny joke. Had to hand it to those damn Swedes, though. Built their nuclear power plants at the farthest outpost of their waters—a stone's throw off the waters of Copenhagen. They get the energy and we take the risk. Had to hand it to them. They never flinch. Make a joke about it to try to give them a dig in the rib and they laugh right along with you. Make like nothing. Okay, so they promised to close it, but only after toughing it out for how many years? If it works, it works, and if it doesn't work, well, maybe it works anyway. Tough decisions to tough out in this life. Like Breathwaite: "We knew this was coming, so why didn't we do something to prepare for it?" Give him a shrug, firm smile, say, *"We knew it was a possibility, but . . ."* Shrug again. Meet his eyes and he gets the message. *I know that you know that I know, so what are you going to do about it? Not a thing you can do. Try. See what happens.*

Then he sensed some connection between the dream about Anders Sachost and the Finsen statue and the Swede in the von Trier film. *Keep that in mind. Something to keep an eye on. Anyway, even if the Swedes were closing down their reactors here, I'll believe it when I see it. They closed one once before, then opened it up again.*

The light went green, and he jogged across, along the long green oblong of Peace Park, where they had raked away those slummy buildings years before. Public outcry to save some rat-infested firetraps. Tough decisions. He waited for the next thought, running past that odd sculpture to his left. Big tilted stone monolith with a keyhole in its center. *Now what in the hell is that supposed to mean? They call that art? Waste.*

He crossed here past another crummy bodega of the sort his father hid away in half his life or more. Over the Peace Bridge. Black Dam Lake beginning to sparkle black silver in the slowly lifting dark. Magnificent. This was his city. *His.* On to Silver Square and a sharp right past the Chinese clinic, the Thai restaurant, along East Farimags Street, and he was at the great carved-walnut double doors of the Tank, handsome purple-and-gold logo in brass at the center of each door.

He estimated it to be 7:04 before checking his watch: 7:03. Pleased, he spent a few minutes stretching and destressing his legs against the door, up on the edge of the wrought-iron fence. Then he removed the master key from the pocket of his sweats and let himself in.

On the top floor, he stepped out of the little elevator and briskly followed the darkened hallway to the opposite end of the building front, passed through the anteroom that housed his secretary's desk into his own office. He plopped down in his swivel chair, sidewise to his desk, picked fruit from the bowl on the Finnish shelving beside him, lifted a bottle of grapefruit juice from the little paneled refrigerator beneath, and wet his dry tongue, swallowing carefully.

Sunlight cut a sharp white crease between the dark sky and snaggled horizon of building tops off behind the botanical garden and glinted off the glass roof of the central hothouse in the garden below, looking like a Russian summer palace. The garden was still morning dark. Eyelids at half-mast, his gaze played with pleasant endorphin-induced languor across the shadowy October trees, the dim yellow glow of pathways, sculptures looming like pale spirits in the agreeable gloom. The drug of his run stilled the pressure of his blood, suffused his body with a glowing calm.

This was his. The best hour of his day. Before any of the others were here. He peeled a banana and ate it slowly, quartered a grapefruit with the Swiss Army knife in his desk drawer, sucked out the juice, and chewed the fruit to the white underside of the peel. He ate two tangerines, orange skin loose and easy to tear with his fingers from the fruit inside, popping the agreeably dryish segments into his mouth.

On the pad beside his B&O telephone, he jotted, "Sweden. Anders Sachost. Finsen. Plutonium. Barsebäck. Early carnival."

Then, from the cabinet beneath the shelves, he took a clean folded shirt—a charcoal Boss turtleneck—from the pile there, clean folded CK shorts and sleeveless T-shirt, Boss socks, black. Clean slacks hung neatly in a clear plastic sheath from the dry cleaner's on his walnut butler, along with a selection of cleaned and pressed jackets of beige, gray, and black suede. He stripped off his sweated joggers and jockeys and dumped them in the wicker hamper in his bathroom, flicked on the light, and paused. Something was off.

Someone had used his bathroom.

His gaze scanned the room to identify what had signaled him, and sure enough, he could see that one of the two plush white towels on the rack between the shower cabin and toilet had been used. He could see it at once by the drape. Someone had tried to be discreet about it, drying fingers in the fold without lifting the towel from the rack, but he could see it.

Sneaky. He didn't like sneaks. Who?

He lifted the lid of the toilet seat. A pale streak of red along the inside of the porcelain. He toed the pedal of the chromium wastebasket so the lid popped up, saw something wrapped in paper inside the plastic sack, bent closer. It was a bloody tampon. Must have been Bente, his secretary. Maybe that explained her curtness two days before. PMS. He let the lid of the pail drop back into place. (Another thought: maintenance crew getting careless.) Bente was a smoker, too. He had seen her on the sidewalk outside at lunchtime with Fred Breathwaite, who also smoked—cigars—and drank, too. Smelled it on him sometimes. Once had the effrontery to ask if he could light up in this office when they had been going over a budget together. Long session. Took out a little green box of Nobel Petits.

"Do you mind?" he'd said.

"Do you really need it?" Asked mildly. With a smile.

"No, I guess not."

Told him with my eyes how pathetic he made himself appear. Like my father. Sentimental drunk. Sad, really. Victims of themselves. Naked to the world. Mystery to themselves. The old man always nattering about the sadness of time, sitting alone in church and trying to get me to join him to pray to his dead mother. My poor mother, her life was so sad, son. *The only thing sad around here, Dad, is you. Sad sack.*

He ran his palm over the close-clipped brown stubble on his skull, waiting for thought to find him. It was as though his faculties had abandoned him today. All he got was his father and Adam's effusive smile, and he didn't have any use for either of them just now.

Then his bowel called him down to the perch, where he deposited a large bean. He wondered what that might weigh.

After adjusting the shower to the right temperature, he stepped into the glass cabin and surrendered to the pleasure of the steaming water, discovered himself then thinking about Bente's husband. Some kind of tradesman, plumber. Black-haired, constant five o'clock shadow. Virile type. *Why am I thinking of him?*

As he soaped his chest, beneath his arms, his groin, the image of the bloody tampon came into his mind. Fertile. *She must be off the pill. Trying to get pregnant?* And that's what the girl had told him, using his toilet, leaving the bloody tampon. Sneaks always left clues. Did it on purpose or unconsciously. Wanted to be caught.

So. Bente wants to get pregnant.

He smiled in the steamy air, hot water beating against his skull, rolling off his shoulders, down his back. And then before long they wanted another. One maternity leave after another. Smart. And everyone's hands tied. State regulations covering it all. They knew their rights. This would cost the Tank a lot of money. Lot of money. Not to mention all the accompanying difficulties—advertising for a temp to replace her, screening hundreds of applications, getting agreement of key people in the participatory democracy scheme, interviewing. We live in a dependency culture, my friend.

Put her on the list. *Speak to you for a moment, please, Bente? I'm sorry to have to . . .*

And he bowed his head beneath the shower, water streaming toward his bare feet, and watched the effusive smile gather and twirl amid the soapy water sucking down the drain.

12. Adam Kampman

Adam was still seated on the edge of his bed, feet on the cool plank floor, when he heard the front door click shut. The house was silent. He got up and switched off the overhead light, let his butt sink back onto the bed. Slowly, he toppled sideways, drawing his legs back beneath the eiderdown, shivering as his chilled arms and hands and feet warmed beneath the soft folds of the feather-stuffed blanket, then arcing his body sensuously in the cozy warmth. He had at least an hour, hour and a half, before his mother rose, possibly another half hour after that before the new au pair arrived and got the house into motion and people started nagging him to get up.

Ninety minutes of respite. His eyes were heavy, the sweet hole of sleep drawing down at him, but he mustn't allow himself. If he slept, the time would evaporate. He would cease to exist and it would be as if a single moment, a few moments later the tapping at his door would start, the grainy, sugary voice of his mother, the disturbing footfalls of the twins pounding down the hallway as they shrieked and argued, and his ninety minutes would be gone as if they had never existed.

He would stay awake. He would savor this little cave of time, this hideaway. It could as well have been eternity from this end of it. A ninety-minute eternity of ease. But only if he stayed awake.

Then his hand was moving downward, and he thought about the new au pair, Jytte. Her smile. The dimple in her right cheek. So pretty. But he didn't want to think about her that way. Then he remembered the magazines he had found the Sunday before. His parents had been at the dining table over a late Sunday breakfast, sunlight slanting in the leaded windows from the garden to mix with the light of the PH lamp over the maroon Piet Hein table, laden with fruit and cereal and bread and cheese, the teapot, pitchers of juice of every color, the heap of newspapers they went through for hours, every one of them except the tabloids, leaning back in their maroon Arne Jacobsen chairs. Twins on the floor on their stomachs, chins propped on palms, leafing through their Barbie comics, studying the pictures, making up stories to fit them.

"Adam, Adam, will you read to us!"

"No."

"Is that a way to talk to your sisters, son?" his father said without looking up from *Berlingske*.

"Sorry, no, I can't, I'm going out."

His mother looked up with a smile. He could see into the split of her robe, the swell of her breasts, and turned his eyes away. He zipped his jacket.

"Where are you off to, honey?" she asked.

"Going to church."

Only then did his father look up. He said nothing, but the expression on his face was clearly skeptical for anyone who knew his father's face. *Doesn't believe me. What* right *do you have to doubt me?* It worried them. He could see that. Well, it worried her. His father was only annoyed by it. They went to church once a year. Christmas Eve. Apart from the occasional requisite baptism, confirmation, marriage, funeral. Adam could see the question in her smile, her searching blue eyes: *What have we done wrong?* But what she said was, "That's really nice, honey."

"Sunday's family day," his father said. "You know that."

"Yeah, yeah."

The cocking of his father's head said he didn't like the tone, so Adam repeated the words more gently. "Yeah, yeah, Dad, I'll be back later this afternoon."

"Long service?"

Adam was at the door now, not a meter from freedom. "Take a walk afterwards. Maybe see a film."

"Sit in the dark on a day like this?"

"Oh, let him, Martin."

His father was smiling, but his eyes were steady on his son. "What film?"

"I dunno." Doorknob in his palm. "See what's on at the Palace, maybe." The door open to the cool sunny air. "See you later."

"Bye-bye, Adam!" the girls chimed, and he was out the door.

He walked. Hands in the slash pockets of his jacket, shoulders hunched, head down, scuffing through the yellow leaves drifted across the pavement, heaped in the gutters. Down through Hellerup, and he cut across the intersecting pavement of the old age home, sheltered housing. Ancient faces of people bundled in wheelchairs on tiny balconies outside their tiny apartments, staring out wordlessly at him, joyless, blank as he felt. Thinking what? Seeing what? As a seventeen-year-old kid shuffled past in the chilly sunlight? *Did you have a good life, you sad old coots?*

I hate this, he thought.

He caught the city train from Hellerup and got off on the platform at Østerport, East Port, climbed the stairway up into the station house, and went into the DSB railway station kiosk. He slipped a copy of the morning tabloid *Ekstra Bladet*, bare-breasted woman in one corner of the front page, from the newspaper rack and folded it face in, plopped it on the cash desk. A dark-eyed young woman, pretty, ran the bar code across the scanner—it took several swipes before it registered, and she smirked at him. "Seventeen crowns."

Blushing, he paid and hurried out the swing door, double-folding the tabloid beneath his arm, and waited outside the locked post office for the Oslo Plads light to change, crossed, and turned right down the street that ran parallel with the train tracks, then left into a little green square with a large sculpture of a naked woman on horseback, leaning back sensuously, sunlight glittering on her bronze breasts, head flung back and one arm raised. He paused to study the line of her body, the fork of her thighs on the horse's back, then turned away, followed streets of apartment buildings occupied by people he did not know. He thought of the Dan Turèll poem they had read in school: "Behind every single window people live." Who? Families. Singles. Couples. People arguing, talking, watching TV, reading newspapers, and eating morning bread with pots of coffee. People fucking in a bed. Jesus, God, he wished he could be in a bed with a woman naked, kissing her breasts, her cunt, fucking her. The bronze woman's cunt right on the horse's back, riding, riding . . . He wished he lived in one of these apartments. He wished he could live alone. Be himself, alone, in an apartment where no one was always *watching* him. Asking questions. Expecting something from him. Disappointed.

He shuffled past the Russian embassy, turned in through Garnisons Churchyard, and threaded along the paths between gravestones marking where people whose lives were finished lay rotting in boxes in the earth. He envied them. Free forever. Forever.

Past the rear wall of the American embassy and past the backs of some other old buildings he hardly bothered to look at or think about, dark stone, old dusty places, and he was out on the street again, passing in front of an apron of café tables where a few people in jackets, some with blankets on their knees, huddled in the chill sunlight over steaming cups of cappuccino, gleaming glasses of draft beer. Up along the end of the street were lakes where people strolled with children, baby carriages, fed the swans and ducks, couples with arms around each other. Ahead of him on the boulevard, a couple walked lazily, arms slung across each other's shoulders. The woman's palm drifted down to the man's ass and squeezed it. Adam slowed his pace to watch, felt himself get stiff, thought, *Oh no!* and hunched, speeding up to get past them, away.

Beyond the three-cornered square of Trianglen, he turned right, down a street shabbier than any in his own neighborhood in Charlottenlund. Big deal. He would rather live here. In an apartment over a shop, over a bar. Alone. With a girl who would let him fuck her and put his face between her hot, cool thighs.

Oh no!

He hunched, sped up again, crossed, turned a corner at random. Three dark, foreign kids were coming toward him, talking loud. One of them stared hard at Adam. He crossed the street and turned again, passed a shabby church, turned again, saw a sign that said, HOLSTEINSGADE, along a narrow street lined on either side with shabby apartment buildings, a short stout sloppy man in a doorway, smoking a cigarette. He saw a bench between two young trees and thought he might sit down and look at his newspaper, glanced to see if the man in the doorway was watching him, but then something on the bench caught his eye, a glossy smear of light, a magazine.

He had a feeling. He knew what it was. He wanted it. But he kept walking, turned the slanted corner, and stopped, breathing heavily, back to a brick wall. He hesitated. Why was it there? What was it? He knew what it was.

Doubling back, he scanned the street from the corner of his eye. The man in the doorway flipped away his cigarette and went inside. Adam came to the bench and grabbed the magazines—there were two of them—folded them into his newspaper, and kept walking. He turned at the next street onto an empty sidewalk, hastily unzipped his jacket, stuffed the magazines down the front of his pants, and zipped his jacket again. On the corner, he pitched the unread tabloid into a refuse basket and headed toward the city train.

At Østerport Station, in the men's room, in a locked toilet cubicle, he sat with his pants around his ankles and studied the magazines hastily. The one was *Rapport*, filled with glossy color pictures of naked women. You could see everything, their cunts and everything. There were also stories, articles he did not have time to read but scanned quickly, a lump in his throat, blood beating in his ears. The other was something called *The Devil's Scrapbook* and contained nothing but pictures, no text. Pictures of things that seemed to see into the corners and shadows of his own mind. He stopped turning pages and stared at one picture, a woman with a teasing, mocking smile and eyes that seemed to stare directly from the page into his own eyes and to know him. *I know who you are*, her eyes said. *I know what you want. I know you and all your secrets.*

The men's room door opened. Through the space beneath the cubicle he saw sloppy black shoes pass to the urinals. He held his breath, heard the sound of a zipper. With trembling hands, he flushed the toilet to cover the sound as he stuffed the magazines behind the bowl, stood and raised his pants, and flushed again, let himself out. The sinks were parallel to the urinals, and from the corner of his eye, he saw a man standing there. Was it that same man from the doorway? The man stood back from the urinal, and Adam could see his penis. He was shaking it. He sighed loudly. Then he looked at Adam and asked, "What's your name?"

Adam hurried out the door, jogged down the stairway to the platform, and hurried to the far end. Were there footsteps behind him? He didn't dare look. The train was just sliding into the station. Adam opened the door and stepped in, sat quickly in a corner seat with his back to the car, hunched low, staring at the dirt and paper scraps on the floor.

Now, in his bed, savoring his ninety minutes, he cursed himself for having discarded those magazines. All of these things had been discussed in school, in sex ed, but nothing of what he felt, nothing of these images, their power, could surface there. There, it was jeering and jokes and feigned disinterest and vague, embarrassed teachers. What he wanted was secret, had to be secret. That magazine had been a treasure. He would never have another like it. He didn't dare to buy one, to risk revealing his most private thoughts and dreams to the person at the cash register.

He took hold of himself now beneath the blanket, and in the current of pleasure that coursed through his skin, his blood, an intense joy enveloped him. In the dark behind his eyelids, he saw that woman's smile, those knowing eyes, and felt the smile opening across his face, in the pit of his chest, his belly, *up!*

And then he slumped, wiped his hand on the sheet, disgusted with himself.

That's all it was. Those few moments. Then the gloom. Disgust. Here in his bed. In this room. This cage. As his time alone, his little eternity, evaporated. He checked his watch on the night table. Seven. Half an hour left. At best.

He threw back the covers and rose, went to his computer to check his e-mail. There they were again: *Virgin pussies first-time sex. Tiny girls huge cocks. Hot young pussy girls. Horny ebony teens waiting for you. Dirty sluts on film. Add inches to your cock now. Girls giving head to strangers. I need to feel a huge cock. Hi, watch me suck cum out of his cock. Produce stronger rock hard erection. Cum-covered girls. Nasty cum sluts. We like it up the butt. Doctor-approved instrument enlarges your penis. Need a stool softener? Adam K: Want a big penis?*

They even had his name! One by one he deleted them, then deleted his delete box. He was convinced that the reason he received this porn spam was that one day he had discovered there were sites on the Web that contained all manner of interesting things and he spent several hours with them. Then, by a fluke, he accidentally hit some combination of keys whose function he did not understand, and a list of the sites he had visited appeared on the screen. They were recorded there. He had left fingerprints. Anyone—his father, his mother—could log on and see where he had been. They shared the same server. They could even log on to his e-mail by switching IT identities. So he had the Sisyphus task each morning before school and evening before bed of deleting and then deleting the deletes. He didn't dare open any of the mails for fear of what kind of trail *that* might leave.

All deletes completed, he sat slump-shouldered before the glowing screen in the still dark room. He felt weary again. The crumpled bedclothes drew him. He crawled back in beneath them, found himself thinking about

those magazines again, about the tabloid he had discarded without even reading the pages he had bought it for. The classifieds. All those women offering to sell what he wanted. Some of them even showed addresses. He had seen one with a Holsteingade address: *I got whatever you want, baby, and I know what you want.*

He started thinking about Holstein Street then, about the bench, about the man smoking in the doorway and the man in the train station men's room. Was it the same person? Did he see him take the magazines, watch from behind the windows of that door, follow him? Did he leave those magazines there? Was it a trap? Did he follow him afterward? Could he have followed him all the way home? Was he watching the house?

He turned onto his belly, buried his face in the pillow. Was he going crazy? He remembered then last night in the dark as he lay waiting for sleep he had suddenly felt there was someone in the room with him. Someone standing with his face just in front of him. He thought that all he had to do to dispel the fear was to open his eyes and see that no one was there, but he couldn't. He didn't dare. If he opened his eyes and a face was there, peering into his, he feared his heart would explode. He would die. Of fear. Shock. Who could it be? Who did he fear could be there, staring at him? That man? *What's your name?* Standing back from the urinal. Shaking his penis. Fat.

Then he got it into his head that there were snakes under his bed and that one had coiled and risen over the edge and was staring at him with a red glowing eye but would hurt him only if he opened his eyes to look. He knew it was nonsense, but he was too frightened to open his eyes and end it. What if it didn't end? What if someone really was there, staring at him? That man. Forcing his penis. Into his mouth. Adam moaned. He was stiff and ashamed of his stiffness. What did it mean? *Am I gay?*

There was a tap at the door. His mother. He recognized the way she tapped. With the tips of all her fingers, drumming lightly at the wood.

"Adam!" she called gently. "Honey? Time to get up."

"I'm sick."

"What's wrong, honey? Can I come in?"

"No! Don't. I've got a stomachache. I couldn't sleep all night."

"Shall I call the doctor?"

"No. I just have to sleep a little more. I'll get up later."

"You'll miss a class."

"The first two classes are canceled."

Silence. Then: "Are you sure?"

"Yeah, of course I'm sure!"

"Well . . . Okay, then, I'll ask Jytte to wake you at nine, okay?"

"Yeah, yeah."

"Oh, Adam, honey, would you do me a big favor today and make copies of the house keys for Jytte?"

He groaned.

"It's important, honey, she needs to have them, and I don't have time. I'll lend her mine for today, but she'll need her own. I'll leave a note so you remember. And a hundred crowns. You can keep the change, okay? Buy yourself a hamburger and a Coke."

"Yeah, yeah."

"Don't forget now, honey, okay?"

"I *said* yeah!"

Then peace at last. Another ninety minutes! He closed his eyes and felt the ease again, a little hideaway of time, eternity, drawing him down toward the place of peace. There were dreams this time, good dreams, though he didn't really experience them, only as some sense of well-being, warmth, so when the knock on the door came, it seemed part of that distant warmth and goodness, and he woke smiling. Until he opened his eyes and saw his room, daylight blurred around the edges of his curtains and the gloomy air pressing down all around him. Missed classes. He'd already missed so many. His average had already fallen to a B. And that man in the men's room. Shaking it at the urinal. Then he remembered the dream. It was about Jytte. She looked into his face and said, *You're an old pair in a soft stool.* She was naked, smiling—that dimple—and she was holding a condom that was full of come, which she raised up above her mouth as though she were going to swallow the whole thing, smiling. *Don't you eat the condoms over here?* she said, and he woke, feeling good. Why would that make him feel good? Was he gay?

Another knock. "Adam?" Again. "Good morning, Adam! You awake?" Was he gay?

The door opened slowly and Jytte's pretty face peered in. That smile. Dimple. The room filled with her light. Adam blinked.

"So sleepy," she said, smiling. She wore a long-sleeved turquoise T-shirt that clung to her breasts and followed the trim line of her shoulders and chest and waist. Her nipples were clearly outlined against the green blue cotton. His penis stiffened.

"Are you awake now, sleepy-John?"

"Yeah, yeah."

She crouched threateningly, fingers curled into claws, smiling. "You want me to tickle you awake?"

"*No!*"

His response was angrier than he'd meant it to be, and he was disappointed to see her drop the game at once. She moved closer, and he saw her eyes look at the place in the blanket that had lifted. Could she see? He turned on his side and feared that had only given him away all the more. Her smile was owlish. She seemed about to speak when there was a crash down the hall and one of the twins hollered, "You stole my phone!"

"Did *not!*"

"Did *so!*"

There was the sound of thumping footsteps followed by thumping footsteps in pursuit and a scream of terror, and Jytte was out the door with a flash of her butt and long legs in tight beige jeans.

Adam could hear her out in the hall reasoning gently with the twins while he squeezed his stiff prick in agony and began to pump it rapidly. *Come back come back come back and see see see see* see*!*

She looked in briefly—"There's coffee downstairs"—and was gone again, and it seemed to him her blue Jutlandic eyes had taken it all in at a glance, surveyed and registered his hopeless emptiness. How he wished he could tell her how he felt. But he didn't really know how he felt. *I love her. God, I love her.* But he didn't trust her, certain things. He loved her dimple. What could you do with a dimple? He could just look at her dimpled face for hours, just look. She was almost a year younger than him, but she seemed older, more sure of herself, her blue gaze so steady and direct when they spoke, and her energetic politeness, her warm eyes and smile, her readiness to laugh and joke. Did she know what she did to him? What would she think if she knew? Once in a while, when she laughed, she opened her mouth wide, and the look on her face, the clumsily rhythmic rise and fall of the laughter, seemed to reveal a profound stupidity concealed behind the lovely country-girl mask of her face. Her *body*!

She was from Tønder. Adam's mother always hired au pairs from Jutland: "Wanted: Jutland girl with a bone in her nose to care for energetic twins in CEO home in Charlottenlund." How he hated those expressions: "bone in the nose." It sounded like one of those porn spams—*Hot Jutland girls with bones in the nose.* And "CEO home in Charlottenlund." What the fuck is a CEO home supposed to be? Big shot, CEO. Big deal. And who the hell wanted to live in Charlottenlund? Rather live in fucking Albertslund or someplace where the real people lived.

He wiped himself off with the bedclothes and got his robe from the back of the chair, crossed the hall to the bathroom, stood staring at the tub. He pictured sitting there with his knees up to his chest while Jytte sponged his back the way she sponged the twins, pictured her kissing him, him kissing her dimple, the bone in her nose poking into his face. Her nose *was* big, but it was sexy. What did it mean, really? Bone in the nose? Opposite of cotton prick. That's what *he* was. A cotton prick. That guy in school, in gym class, Sandemark, with his ugly teeth, calling across the basketball court, "Hey, Kampman, you cotton prick!" And the others laughed. Girls, too.

Fuck you, Sandemark, you snaggletoothed fuck! he should have shot right back at him. But he said nothing. Slunk away. *I'll punch your ugly snaggled teeth out, Sandemark, you ugly fuck! Come on. You want some of this?* He held his fist up threateningly in front of the bathroom mirror.

But what if he couldn't follow through? Or worse. What if he went too far? Really hurt the guy? *Why did you do that, Kampman?*

Because he called me a dirty name.

That doesn't give you the right to hit him. And certainly not to hurt him so badly. We'll have to report this to the police. You might go to jail. And you know what the older men do to the young boys in jail. Maybe that's what you like.

Fuck you! I don't! It wasn't fair.

Once, at the end of gym class, in the showers, Sandemark and some of the others grabbed that tall skinny awkward kid Hansen, and they hung him naked over the walls of a toilet cubicle and dunked his head into the toilet bowl. And everybody laughed. No one stuck up for him. Afterward, the story got out around the school and people snickered every time Hansen came down the hall, so gawkish, even girls laughed, whispering with their pretty mouths to one another what had been done to Hansen. And one of them called out, "What is that shampoo you're using, Hansen?" and they giggled, the bitches. Put his head in the fucking toilet, those bastards!

Adam pictured himself barging in on the scene, kicking Sandemark right in the balls so he doubled over, groaning, while Adam elbowed the others away and caught hold of Hansen, lowered him gently to the floor, helped him up, and gave him a towel to cover himself with. *Want me to kick their asses for them, Hansen?*

Dogs. Pack of dogs. Boys will be boys. Just a prank. Innocent prank. Don't be so sensitive, Adam. *Sensitive! They stuck his fucking head in the fucking toilet bowl! How'd you like them to do that to you! Would that be so fucking funny!*

Boys will be dogs. Pack of fucking dogs. Like those American soldiers in Iraq. Women, too! Stripping prisoners and making them touch themselves, humiliating them. Stacking them up naked in a pile and that woman soldier there smiling and pointing at them! And she was pregnant, too!

He became aware of himself then, leaned over the sink, gripping the edges and staring at his own face in the mirror, gritting his teeth.

"Adam?" Jytte outside the bathroom door. "Are you okay? Your mom said you were feeling sick."

"I'm okay."

"Want me to come in and help you?"

Teasing voice. Was she mocking him? "No!"

"Well, you want some breakfast before you go to school?"

"No!"

"Well, excuse me! And don't forget your mother left a note for you to get some keys!"

"Yeah, yeah." He was too tired to shower, too tired to brush his teeth. He cupped his hand under the cold tap and rinsed his mouth, splashed his face and the back of his neck, rolled a stick of Odorono beneath his arms. Two black hairs clung to the ball of the roll-on, and he stood there staring at them, disgust and futility rising like a tide within him.

13. Jytte Andersen

Along Bernstorffs Way, Jytte walked the twins to their Montessori kindergarten, one on either side of her, holding their hands. They were much easier to manage that way. Hanne, on her left, was a little prettier and a little smarter and a little sweeter than Helle, on her right, who was quick to anger if she thought Hanne was getting more attention. As if Helle already knew she had been shortchanged somehow. Their mother had explained this to Jytte, who felt an immediate sympathy for the unhappy twin.

Not that she was *so* unhappy. Mostly the girls enjoyed each other. But there was that wound of nature, and Jytte understood. She herself, when she was a child, had always been favored over her older sister, Sara, who was very plain, and it had always seemed unfair to Jytte. Sara had never taken it out on her. They had been fiercely devoted to each other. But the older girl developed a dark, sarcastic relationship with the world, and the other kids didn't like her. They called her "Sara Sarcastic" behind her back or "Sarca" or sometimes "Castic," which developed to "Casti," and then they started saying it to her face, too.

Sara started smoking hash when Jytte was only eleven and moved away just a couple of years later, and she rarely came back to visit anymore. She lived in a collective in Århus, had shaved her head bald, and worked in a tattoo-and-piercing studio. Jytte was afraid she was taking harder drugs now, too.

Little Helle reminded her a bit of Sara, and Jytte was determined to try to redress the balance in any way she could by lavishing her affection on the girl. She stroked the back of Helle's hand with one finger as they walked, and Hanne chattered away, oblivious to the inequity that her sister was victim to—just as Jytte had been oblivious to Sara's unhappiness for many years. Helle responded to Jytte's caress on her hand by reaching up with her own free hand to lightly nip with her fingers at the tiny golden hairs at Jytte's wrist. It was sweet. Cozy.

The Montessori kindergarten was a part-time institution. Jytte would have to return at two to pick up the girls again and then get back home before Karen did, because Karen had let her borrow her own house keys until Adam got the new ones for her. She wondered why Karen didn't just let *her* have the new keys made. Didn't she trust her?

There was plenty to do between now and then, but Jytte took her time at the kindergarten, helping the girls off with their jackets and getting them settled. They were placed in separate rooms, which Jytte thought was a good thing, especially since she noticed that one of the pedagogues, Gunilla—a tall, dark-haired girl with very big hips—tended heavily to favor Hanne when the girls were together, constantly shushing Helle and telling her to let her sister speak. Jytte had disliked Gunilla on sight. Gunilla was only a couple of years older, but she acted so high-assed. She literally *was* high-assed; her legs were too long for her body. Jytte had noticed that homely girls were sometimes unkind to other homely girls. It seemed so unfair, so ridiculous, to be less kind to people because of the way they looked. She was very glad that Helle was not in Gunilla's room. The pedagogue in Helle's room seemed much more sympathetic. She was also prettier. Jytte wondered if she found her more sympathetic because she was prettier, but she didn't think so.

From the Montessori, Jytte walked briskly up toward Gentofte Street so she could shop at the ISO supermarket there for the things on the list Karen had given her. In her backpack she had two folded plastic bags that she had retrieved from being used for garbage; it offended her to have to pay good money for new plastic bags that would later be used for garbage. Even if Karen herself didn't seem to care, it offended Jytte's sense of thrift to spend six crowns on two trash bags. It was also bad for the environment. Even if Mr. Kampman was a big director and made a lot of money—probably more than a million a year, maybe two million—there was no reason to waste.

She didn't like Mr. Kampman. He seemed to her terribly happy with himself, even if he also seemed to think he hid that away pretty neatly. You could see in his smile how full of himself he was. Jytte's chemistry fit perfectly with Karen's right from the start; Karen was cozy and friendly, always had time for a chat or a cup of tea at the end of the day, and was interested in hearing what Jytte had to say about the cute things the twins had done that day or her appraisal of possible problems developing.

Once, when Mr. Kampman was not there, Jytte had seen Karen leaning out the kitchen window smoking a cigarette. She'd jumped when Jytte had come up behind her. Palm on her chest, she'd said, "This is our secret, right? I *am* quitting."

Poor woman, was she afraid of her husband? "I smoke myself," Jytte had said. "But not in front of the twins, of course."

She wondered if Mr. Kampman bullied Karen. Also, she was pretty certain that it had been he who got his wife to change her mind about letting Jytte live in. Even if it was nice having her own room away from them, it would have been nicer if she had been allowed to decline the room herself, which she probably would have done anyway, maybe.

She had an idea what was behind it. Mr. Kampman was probably afraid she'd snatch their precious Adam from the cradle. That wouldn't be difficult. The way he looked at her. And the bulge under his blanket there today. She smiled at the thought. He was cute, too. In a way, he seemed like the little brother she'd never had, even if he was almost a year older than her. But when she saw that bulge under the blanket, the feeling that came over her was not exactly sisterly.

Jytte knew about boys. She had two older brothers, and she knew what they did with themselves and just about any girl who would let them, too. Last summer, her brother Bertil had been in bed with two girls at once right down in the basement room when their parents were away for the weekend. Bertil hadn't known that Jytte was home. She'd sneaked down and watched through the stairway railing and seen them there, three of them under the blankets together, giggling at first and then getting quieter and then making other noises that were exciting, and they didn't have their clothes on, either. Shirts and pants and socks had been thrown all around. Underpants, too.

When she'd seen Bertil later, she'd said to him, "Bet you had fun today, huh?" and looked him right in the eyes.

His face had turned red. "We were just messing around."

"That was obvious."

"Don't you start getting any ideas, Jytte. We were just playing around. Don't you start thinking about trying anything like that, you'll ruin your name."

"Oh, I won't," she'd said. "I'd be afraid of being tickled to death, the way you three carried on."

And his face had turned red again, beet red.

She had already been with two boys, scored them both, but one at a time. They had been older, too, but she was braver. Johan, a great big baby-faced farm boy. And Peder Ehler, who worked as a bellboy in the Hotel Romantic in Tønder. She liked it, too, even if it wasn't as much fun as she had expected. But she kept thinking it might be more fun with someone else. And she could tell by the way a lot of boys looked at her that she would have plenty of chances to try.

14. Adam Kampman

Adam locked his bike and shoved it into a slot in the bike rack, circled around the side alley of the schoolyard. Old Hellerup High School. God, he hated it.

A lot of kids were in the yard, standing in groups, sitting on the backs of benches. Three boys from his homeroom kicked a soccer ball back and forth, and a bunch of girls were lighting up cigarettes over by the shed. He recognized one of them as a girl who had laughed about Hansen, the one who had asked about his shampoo. She had two rings in her nostril and a chrome stud in her chin. Sandemark was there, too, leaning up against a wrought-iron fence, back to it, long-faced, his arms draped out to either side as though he thought he were Jesus Christ on the cross. *Like to crucify you, you cocksucker.* Three or four of his friends were ranged around him, talking loudly, laughing, sucking up to him, while he never showed any expression at all on that long face. *Ugly snaggletoothed cocksucker.*

Adam wanted to charge him. Just get it over with. Charge in swinging his fists, punch the ugly face bloody. What if he wasn't fast enough, though? He pictured Sandemark blocking easily, punching back, faster, harder, everyone saying, *Fucking Kampman's gone nuts!* Or just laughing at him.

"Hi, Adam!"

He turned to see a smiling girl from his history class coming toward him. She was short and a little plump, with a squared, slightly underslung jaw that looked cute, and her smile was so bright that it lit up her eyes and her smooth round cheeks, and her short blond hair glittered in the sun. He knew her name, Nina, but didn't feel like saying it, so he just said, "Hi."

"I just can't stop smiling," she said.

He couldn't figure out what she meant, and he couldn't figure out if you were supposed to keep looking in someone's eyes when you talk to them, and if so for how long, so he looked from her eyes to her nose to her mouth and worried that he might look sneaky, shifty-eyed. She seemed suddenly so much prettier than he had ever noticed, smiling at him. He was confused. He smiled back.

"It is hard to stop smiling once you start," she said. Then: "I have met someone."

When he didn't reply, she added, "A boy. He is so kind and nice. I cannot stop smiling."

"Great."

"He is not from here," she explained, as though he'd asked. "He is from Øregaard. He plays the trombone."

"Great." It occurred to him then that she must have felt very lonely to be so very happy now about meeting some guy who played trombone. He wondered if he would have had a chance with her, if only he had guessed that.

The bell rang for next session and the students started straggling toward the building entrances, taking last hasty drags of cigarettes, gathering the soccer ball. Sandemark glanced at Adam with a smirking nod, and Adam realized suddenly that he was finished here. Done with it. He watched the other students drifting toward the door as the second bell rang, and they started moving more quickly. He stepped backward away from them, gripped by a certainty that suddenly seemed so obvious, irrefutable. He gripped it tight to him.

To seal the pact, he stopped at the refuse can near the side alley, slung his backpack from his shoulders, and zipped it open. He turned it upside down and watched his school books drop into the heaped paper and bottles and McDonald's wrappers there, sinking, settling, one with covers bent back like the wings of a bird.

15. Karen Kampman

Karen parked the Toyota down the street from the clinic, where she would not be seen. Martin knew her boss, Flemming Vesterberg, and she didn't know how much they talked together. Martin had arranged the receptionist job here for her. It was good to get away from the house, from the twins, from Adam and Martin and all of it for a few hours every day. Flemming's wife had a job that Martin had arranged for her in the Tank.

Flemming was nice enough—maybe too nice—but she worried sometimes that he might "report" back to Martin about her, or to his wife, who might pass it on. Not that she did anything to report on, but, well, there was the smoking. She didn't want him to see her smoking. Martin was always harping on that, too. *Aside from the damage to your health, it's a sign of weak character. It's like saying to the whole world, I am a weak person; I have no control over myself.*

Anyway, she *was* quitting. She didn't smoke nearly as much as she used to. And when this pack was finished, she planned on not buying another. Maybe.

She snapped open her bag, dug into the bottom for the squashed, near empty ten-pack of Prince Silvers. They called them "Silver" now because of some law that didn't allow them to be called "Extra Ultra Lite" anymore. Plastered across the front of the pack in a black frame—like an obituary—was the warning "Smoking is extremely harmful to you and your surroundings." And on the back: "Smoking reduces life expectancy." She had seen others, too: "Smoking can kill" and "Smoking leads to hardening of the arteries and causes heart conditions and stroke" and "Smoking can cause fertility problems." It seemed smoking was responsible for just about all the evils of the world now. It had gotten to be embarrassing even to buy cigarettes. Maybe they would pass a law that would require you to say to the shop clerk: *I am an idiot. May I have a pack of Prince Silvers, please?* And if you didn't: *Sorry, madam, but you didn't say you were an idiot. The law requires . . .*

She poked her finger into the packet—only three left—and fished one out. It was slightly bent. Delicately she straightened it, then rolled down the driver's-side window and lit up with the flame of a blue plastic lighter. Just as she inhaled, a big yellow bus rolled past, fuming exhaust into her face, and a spasm of coughing gripped her lungs, causing her to whoop and gasp for air, almost ruining the pleasure of the cigarette. She leaned her head out the window, breathing deeply and slowly until her lungs settled.

Then she smirked, thinking, *Bus Yellow, Extra Ultra Heavy.* She had read somewhere that inhaling the carbon monoxide from the traffic in any medium-large city was equivalent to smoking fifteen cigarettes a day. But of course, you couldn't say that. That would be like supporting terrorism or something. *So why smoke even more, voluntarily?* would be Martin's response.

Anyway, she knew he was right. It was a stupid, harmful habit.

She drew on the cigarette, filling her mouth, then inhaled it deep into her lungs. God, she loved smoking. She would never be able to quit. But she had cut way down. She had read in the Sunday papers that the sign of real addiction was when the first thing you did when you woke was go for a cigarette. Karen's first cigarette was more than an hour after she got up, longer if Martin was home. Of course, she had to admit that one of the first things she *thought* about when she woke was a cigarette. Her first of the day were the two she had here in the morning before work, then two at lunchtime (she came back out to the car for them), and two or three in the evening before Martin got home from the office. Compensation for his working so late every night.

If only she had his willpower. He'd be able to quit just like *that*. Except he was too clever to have ever started in the first place. How could a person have such self-control?

Even in bed he had control, the way he built her up. She liked it that way. His hands were so strong and just a little hard with her, touching all her soft places just a bit hard, like letting her know he knew where she was soft, had access, could, almost did, then didn't, so he got her all built up for it before he got on top of her, and he was in such good shape that he could balance there, dancing in and out, so fast, with his eyes locked on hers always. Fierce, he looked; she liked that, another side of him—no, the same side, only revealed now, all the polite control and smiles stripped away with his clothes.

She drew on the cigarette again, pulled the smoke down to the bottom of her lungs, excited by her thoughts. Not as often anymore as it used to be, though. Once a month. Twice at most. Couldn't really expect more.

Up the street she saw Flemming's silver Mercedes roll to a stop in the parking space beside the clinic. She watched him climb out of the car and zap the locks with the thingamajig in his hand and jog up the steps into the clinic. Jaunty. Danced practically when he moved, even if he was heavy. And older. In his fifties.

"Slip out of your pants and climb up on the table, let me take a look at you," he'd said that time when she'd asked something about a discharge, and she almost had . . . but no, no, she couldn't.

"Thanks, Flemming. I have my own gynecologist." A woman. What would Flemming have thought if she had done as he'd said? Looking at her like that.

"Are you shy?"

"Flemming, a woman who's had three babies can hardly have an ounce of shyness left. Just the same, though, I'll stick with Amanda. She knows me. But thanks. Really."

Picture him looking. Fingers up in me. Would he have called in the nurse? Would he have said something to Martin? She had heard him comment on a couple of the other patients. Not very kindly, though he had made her laugh. Or did she laugh just to accommodate him? One of the nurses had told her, "Flemming has to protect himself from all the patients who fall in love with him." She had leaned closer. "You know his reputation? They say he's the only gynecologist in Denmark who never has to lubricate his finger prior to an internal."

"Are you shy?"

"Not a gram of it left." After all the prodding, poking fingers and God knew what else up inside and the cutting and the stitching with half a dozen people surrounding your lower half. That was with Adam. *Easier with the twins. Put me to sleep.* Cesarean. Adam's had been a long birth. Twenty-three hours. She thought she never would again. He was enough for her, sweet Adam, so troubled now, but he'd come through. He was softer than Martin. They had to understand that about him. A shy boy.

"Are you shy?"

If you could only read my thoughts, Flemming, she didn't say.

Smiling tartly, she flipped the cigarette out the window and lit her second. It occurred to her perhaps she should have waited a few moments, but she was already drawing on it, filling her lungs. If only Martin smoked. Even just a little. That was a terrible wish to have. Better wish for some of his self-control. She thought again of his strong fingers finding her soft spots, that fierce look in his eyes, fixed on hers. Thinking what behind that stare, those eyes?

Even after eighteen years she didn't know, only little bits here and there, tiny breaches in the facade, or was it a facade at all? Maybe he really was just Martin all the way through and down and in, Martin and Martin and Martin.

One more drag of the second cigarette, and she flipped it away into the road, leaned back against the car seat to enjoy the last inhale, down to the base of her lungs, while her eyes lingered on the withered linden leaves along the street, slender branches and twigs twitching in the gray, autumn air. Slowly she exhaled the pale gray smoke.

Time to go in.

She slid the plastic lighter into the crumpled pack alongside the last remaining cigarette and buried it in her purse. The realization that she had only the one cigarette for her lunch pause tickled a tiny edge of panic in her. Perhaps she would skip lunch, walk up to the kiosk by the train station, buy another pack of ten. Or maybe she wouldn't. Maybe.

Maybe just one last pack, and that would be it, then.

16. Harald Jaeger

Behind the cloakroom on the top floor of the Tank was a door to a small elbow of space that gave access to a WC that for some reason was rarely used by any of the staff. Jaeger thought perhaps no one knew about it other than the few old-timers. Because of the sense of privacy it gave and that little anteroom to isolate the noise, whenever he had to shit at work—which was usually at least once a day—here was where he did it.

And this was one of the days. Besieged by a spastic colon as he'd sat, "chatting" with the CEO. Bonding, maybe. Kampman had "invited" him to come in ("Would you like to come in for a moment, Harald?" *Do I really have a choice?*) but had yet to explain the reason. Jaeger had seldom seen Kampman so forthcoming and personal.

"You're looking fit, Harald."

"I try to keep in shape, Martin." The first name was stiff on his tongue. He usually didn't call the CEO anything at all. It felt too servile to call him by his last name when he called Jaeger by his first, but somehow the first name popped out today and alerted Jaeger to watch himself, which triggered his colon. He tightened the sphincter.

"Good," said Kampman. "Reflects."

Reflects? Reflects what? That was the kind of thing that worried him. *What am I to understand of that? Guess? Deduce?* Jaeger had always hated crossword puzzles and riddles because he was so bad at them. *What should I say now? Thanks?* "Thanks," he said.

And Kampman lifted his glance alertly, as if to examine on his face what Jaeger might have meant. But Jaeger had not meant a thing. He retightened his hold on his sphincter and smiled. Kampman tilted his face. A question. But what question? *Why am I sitting here? Why did you call me in? Why did you invite me to join you at the conference table instead of keeping the desk between us?* Jaeger wanted to ask questions, but he was afraid anything he asked might be contaminated by the information Fred Breathwaite had given him the night before—right or wrong, honest or deceitful. *I'm not cut out for this.*

"Well," Kampman said then. "Have you given some thought to it all?"

It all? "You mean, economies?"

Kampman nodded slightly, watching him. Or *had* he nodded? Jaeger could not stand it; he plunged on. "Actually I was thinking a lot of small economies could easily be . . ."

Kampman's mouth wrinkled, as at a bad taste. "Afraid this isn't small," he said.

"No, of course, but a lot of small economies add up, don't they? I was thinking about the plastic folders we use. Hundreds of them. And the open supply cabinet. I mean, it's a luxury. All those nice fiber-tip pens and Scotch Tape and yellow sticky pads. Rulers! I mean . . ."

Kampman smiled. "I admire your loyalty."

Jaeger smiled and did not go on.

"The biggest item on our budget, the obvious item, is personnel. We have to be looking at that now."

Jaeger retightened his sphincter and held the agonizing question he yearned to blurt out: *Me? Was Breathwaite shitting me? Do I go?*

"I'd like you to work with Fred Breathwaite, keep cultivating the international connections. There's income there. Not inconsiderable grants and grant sharing. How is the Japanese contact coming?"

"I've been e-mailing Ito regularly." Kazumuri Ito was Jaeger's counterpart in the Japanese Tank. He had never met him, only e-mailed to invite him to visit the Tank in Copenhagen. "He seems definitely interested." "Seems definitely" sounded lame in his own ear, so he repeated, "Definitely interested." And remembered a dream. He'd dreamed he met Kazumuri Ito as twins, one male, one female. The twins were also man and wife. The male Ito said to him about the female Ito, *She got her pocket picked empty.* Now what the hell could that mean? Ito? I too? I too what? But *I to* in Danish also meant "you two." You two what? Or just You too?

"I want you to take the lead on the Irish cooperation."

Jaeger blinked. "Those are Fred Breathwaite's close friends, aren't they?"

"They're *our* friends, I hope," Kampman said vigorously, with an indignation that seemed more for effect than from emotion. "Let's make sure of that. When they come in next week, we'll be holding a dinner for them. I want you there. And I'd like you to speak."

"Speak?"

"At the dinner. Set the keynote. Say the welcome. You're not afraid to speak, are you?"

"Not at all," said Jaeger, constricting his sphincter more tightly.

"Let's get you out from behind the desk, then. Would that interest you?"

"I . . . certainly."

"Good. Let's talk again later this week." He rose. Jaeger rose. Time's up. He moved for the door and Kampman said, "Tell Fred."

"Right, Martin, thanks," said Jaeger, and was halfway down the hall toward the secret WC, taking quick short cautious steps, before he asked himself, *Tell Fred what, for Christ's sake!?*

He preferred not to be seen entering his sanctum, so it seemed a lucky break that no one was in the hall or the cloakroom. He was inside and seated not a moment too soon, face in his hands, trousers around his feet, sighing.

Tell Fred what?

It occurred to him sitting there that he had half a hard-on, which seemed very odd to him. Hard-on of irritation, perhaps. He recalled hearing or reading somewhere that in times of crisis and threat, people tended to copulate more. Explained the post–World War II baby boom.

Finished with his business, he sat there and watched himself stiffen further.

Why is this happening to me?

He needed to collect himself. No time for this. He considered relieving the tension with his hand, remembered then the terrible moment that Vita had caught him at it. Beginning of the end right there. He didn't know what got into him. Yes, he did, but that had been his defense. Non-defense. *I don't know what got into me, honey.* What had gotten into him was the desire to sit naked in one of their new beige leather armchairs in the living room, holding over his face a pair of Vita's used panties, retrieved from the bathroom hamper, inhaling and kissing them as he jerked off there, knowing full well that Vita might walk in at any moment. That was part of it. A large part. That agony of tension at the possibility of being discovered. But it was only the tension he wanted, the possibility, not the fact, and the fact was that she did walk in. When he heard her keys in the front door, he tried to make a break for it, but she caught him halfway across the living room carpet, in flagrante, chasing his hopping pole to safety, panties in his fist.

She smiled at first. For just a fragment of an instant. Like a gas pain. Then the storm broke: "You fucking *pig!*" She circled him, hurling epithets and insults. There were questions, too, demands. What exactly was that in his hand? What exactly was he doing with it? What exactly was he thinking? What else did he do when he was alone? Where else did he do it? What if the girls had walked in? And then, the light of unswervable enlightenment and conclusion in her eye, she summed up the case against him: "You *wanted* me to catch you." She watched him, a fascinated glint of horror in her eye. Then she whispered, "You are *sick.*"

Now, in his sanctum in the Tank, the memory helped deflate him enough to facilitate the zipping of his trousers. He washed his hands and let himself out, and in the little elbow alcove, he heard a loud whirring sound just outside the window. Eager for distraction, he flipped the latch and shoved open the casement in time to see a helicopter in the air immediately above, lifting over the roof of the Tank building. A brown helicopter, flying low, headed north toward the State Hospital just a couple of blocks away. It was a medical chopper, he knew, flying in a frozen heart from a patient who had just died in Århus or Ålborg to a patient here who would die without it. Or maybe a liver, a kidney. Could be from Sweden, too. Land on the roof of the State Hospital and people come rushing out for the icy box. Packed in dry ice, maybe. Or would that damage the tissue?

A sense of awe rose within him at the accomplishments of human civilization. *Just think: a fucking machine that flies in the air delivering a heart that surgeons equipped with the most refined technology have salvaged from a dead man in order to prolong the life of another man or woman who would otherwise die. Just think of all the factors, all the things, that have to go right to complete this successfully, and it is being done every day, everywhere.* The thought overwhelmed him with an immense gratitude for all those who had built and kept his civilization functioning, followed immediately by a sense of his own futility, his uselessness. *What do I contribute? What if it was me who needed a new heart?*

Imagine someone else's heart in your chest. Seat of emotions. *You are in my heart. My heart is in you*, says the dead man, now heartless. Hole in the chest where his heart should be. *Will you be my valentine?* asks the heartless man of the transplant. Paper hearts on the Christmas tree, strung on a thread. *My heart is in your hands. Your heart is in the surgeon's hands, about to be stuffed into me.*

No thanks. Wouldn't want it, wouldn't want another heart. They cut with a saw right down your sternum, crack the bone like a lobster shell, and pry open your rib cage. Snip out the old, sew in the new. There's a reason we have no hinge in the sternum; protect the soft heart in a hard cage of bone. Heard about a man who got a woman's heart once. Would it make a difference? Couldn't, really. It's the endocrines that matter there. Ductless glands pouring hormones directly into the blood. Can't really picture it.

I'd just as soon die as go through all that. Wouldn't take it. Don't think I would. Rather commend my spirit to the great whatever. Now, a prick, *maybe*. Give me a new prick if this one wears out. Helicopter flying prick and balls from Sweden. Here comes the cavalry. Whole new set. Learn to do it like a Swede. Swedes are supposed to be good in the sack. This one I have comes too fast. Give me a slower one that only stands on command. Maybe a bit bigger. Definitely not smaller. Make that a condition. Eight inches minimum. Everybody adds an inch or two. Preferably nine or ten. And every bit as stiffable as mine now, please. Stands at attention to watch me shave in the morning, not hanging down to watch me tie my shoes. Remember Clausen's dick that time in the showers after we swam? He tried to hide it in the towel, but I saw what a little dinkle it was, on such a big body. Thank God mine is okay. Still, a man could always use an extra inch or so. Imagine if they flew in a horse prick, grafted it on. Whale prick. Me with a whaling three-footer like the petrified one I saw at the Erotic Museum on Købmager Street. Looked like an elephant tusk, only a bit straighter. There goes Jaeger with the meter-long sausage. Sell tickets to the girls.

As the sound of the chopper faded in the distance, another sound caught his ear. From the cloakroom behind him. It sounded like someone sniffling. He opened the door and saw Birgitte Sommer there, big-breasted and slender in a midthigh mini, hand in the pocket of an elegant gray herringbone coat that hung from a wall hook. Her hand was just emerging with a bunch of Kleenex that she put to her nose, but she started when she saw Jaeger there. Her left hand flew to her breast. "You frightened me!" Her eyes were red. She looked sweet.

Jaeger peered into her face with concern. "Are you crying, Birgitte?"

"Of course not, I have a cold." She blew her nose.

"Oh, sorry! I thought for a minute . . ." Then: "You don't have a cold," he said, and she hunched around the crumple of Kleenex and the water-works started for real. Tentatively he laid his palm on her slender shoulder, warm to his touch, and made the move with his body that moved her into his embrace, where she let go and sobbed, twitching in his arms. He was in heaven.

"Here," he said softly. "In here." He led her behind the door of the little alcove.

She drew away, wiping her eyes with that same wad of Kleenex, which grew smaller and more ragged with each application to nose and eyes. Her nostrils glowed pink against the creamy pale skin of her face, and as luck would have it, he was able to deliver a clean white linen handkerchief to her, albeit slightly wrinkled, which came away from her eyes with streaks of black mascara on it. *Mysterious paint they use on their eyes.*

"Excuse me," she said. "I don't know what's come over me."

Which carried associations he wished to hold away from his consciousness just now. "Nothing wrong with a good cry," he said. "You're lucky you can. Wish I could."

Her red, puffy eyes took him in. Smiling lips and charming black smudge beneath her damp eyelids. *Like to kiss her mouth. Careful. Wrong move could be dangerous. Chief of finance here.*

"You haven't had an easy time of it, either, have you, Harald? How are your babies?"

"I just love 'em to death."

She touched his arm. Sympathetic smile. And he stepped closer. "You're not in trouble with the job? The economies?"

Comprehension took a moment. "Oh, no," she said. "No. It's . . . personal. It's, oh, it's Lars, he is so . . . cold."

Lips nearing hers, he whispered, "How could he be? I just, oh, Birgitte . . ." And their mouths fused, his heart hammering crazily. Soft skin of her neck on his palm, her hands bracketing his face in position for her mouth. *She wants me. To kiss.* "Oh, Birgitte, I—"

"Sh . . ."

"I—"

"Sh . . ."

Their eyes met and held. Hers always narrow, little spots of burgundy, but now glistening, soft, and their gazes explored each other's faces while he moved so she could feel what the nearness of her did to his body.

"God, Birgitte," he whispered, "I *want* you so—"

"Sh . . ."

He wanted to do it right there, but she took a step back, leaned away from him, shaking her smiling mouth, saying, "Sh . . . Sh . . . No. We'll talk. Later."

And left him there.

Later? Talk? *Talk?*

But one sweet fact was irrefutable. She had put her tongue in his mouth. Of her own volition.

17. Jes Breathwaite, Jalâl al-Din

The Dome of the Rock Key & Heel Bar was tucked in between the Trafik Cafeen and a 7-Eleven kiosk on the southern edge of St. Hans Square in North Bridge. Outside the little shop, a small leather-harnessed carousel pony of battered, painted wood was mounted on a banged-up red metal stand, an electrical motor plugged into an external wall outlet. A note, printed in black marker on the red stand, alongside a coin slot, read: "2 x 2 kr."

Inside, Jalâl al-Din sat behind his shoeless last, sipping tea. He wore a gray dishdasha robe and black kufi cap. The wall behind and beside him, spreading toward the front of the shop, was stippled with little hooks from which hung blister packs of shoelaces, innersoles, key rings with an array of first names and signs of the zodiac, key chains, nail clippers, bicycle locks. There were shelves of spray cans, tins, jars of polish, silicon, waterproofing, shoehorns, shoe brushes, and buffer cloths, and a pegwood board from which hung many kinds and colors of uncut keys.

Farther toward the street in the deep, narrow shopfront, Jes Breathwaite leaned against the wrought-iron key grinder, elbow propped on the little work platform, chin propped in his palm, contemplating the little carousel pony. He had never seen a child ride on it.

Jalâl's wife, Khadiya, came swishing out of the back in her blue-and-silver jilbab robes, a silver hijab around her long black hair. "Ay," she said, and placed a glass of tea before Jes. She dragged over a stool and patted the seat. "Sit," she said to Jes. "Time for relax now." And she reached deep into a hidden pocket in her jilbab to produce a large bar of dark chocolate studded with bits of fruit and nut, which she placed beside the tea. The shy pleasure of her smile flashed gold.

"Thank you!" Jes said, bowing a little. "*Thank* you." A bar like that cost about twenty crowns, no small amount for him.

"You are a boy," she said. "Boys like something sweet on the tongue."

"He is a man," Jalâl said quietly.

"Yes, he is a man, and all men are boys," Khadiya said, laughing. "And he needs more fat on his long body. Look at him behind, he is haunchless, it is a wonder he can sit at all, there is nothing there."

Caught by surprise, Jes blushed, smiled, and she laughed merrily. She disappeared again through the blue curtains into the back of the shop while Jalâl barked, "Respect! Show this young man respect!" To Jes he said, "Thee women have no more respect for thee men." But Jes could see the pleasure in the man's eyes at his wife's spirit.

Jes remained standing, opening the wrapping of the chocolate bar self-consciously. He extended the opened packet to Jalâl, who raised the back of one finger with a pleasantly stern set to his lips. "Is good for you, not for me. I must to honor the Ramadan."

"But you're drinking tea."

"In my interpretation there is way that this is permitted, for tea is of the innocence. It give necessary strength of the body in order to support the requirements for the spirit. Why you don't sit? Relieve the veins of your legs. No mind what Khadiya say. Sit."

Jes felt funny about sitting during work hours, even if there was nothing to do at the moment. He felt funny about that, too, that Jalâl didn't just send him home when it was so slow. His unaccustomed delicacy here was agreeable to him. He found himself admiring the firmness of Jalâl's personality, his character, the seeming lack of necessity for conscious consideration of his speech or actions. He was who he was, said what he said, did what he did. At the same time, however, he felt a near irresistible urge to mimic and parody the man. A customer had come in once, and Jes began to serve him without greeting him first, and afterward Jalâl had said to him, "My friend: Always remember to greet and to treat with good words. Even the customer who does not impress you with his own good manner. Especially him. If you treat your neighbor as good neighbor, you help him to become the good neighbor he might become."

Jes was dazzled. Could this man be for real?

"Sit!" Jalâl exclaimed now, and Jes finally acquiesced. He sat there with one foot on the chrome rung of the stool and munched the chocolate, gazing across the square. A single linden tree rose from a patch of earth on a little concrete knoll directly across from the window, behind a sculpture that looked to Jes like a huge black iron tarantula in attack mode—or maybe like a solid iron house of cards. Not to be toppled. Beyond that, a

Tulip sausage wagon stood with its back flush against the spigots of the fountain, which sprayed three low streams of water into the cool, sunny air. The heavyset sausage man munched a medister inside the windowed cabin of the wagon. The square was empty but for a little girl in a yellow dress and yellow jacket who methodically chased the pigeons pecking for crumbs around the sausage van and beneath the linden.

"So slow today," said Jalâl, and sipped loudly at his tea.

"God is merciful," said Jes. "He gives us leisure."

Out of the corner of his eye, he saw the back of Jalâl's index finger shoot up. "My friend: Do not sorrow your own soul with poor wit."

Spoken with a mild smile, but Jes was embarrassed that his private condescension had leaked through unwittingly. "Forgive me," he said. "I meant no harm or disrespect." Increasingly when he was here working, he found himself imitating the phrasings and rhythms of Jalâl's speech.

"You are forgiven."

The little girl wheeled around the side of the sausage wagon for a fresh attack on the newly settled pigeons, scattering them one after another. If they only flapped their wings without taking flight, she stamped her shiny buckled shoes harder behind them to make them fly. Her mother and father sat over drinks at one of the few remaining outdoor autumn tables around the beer kiosk attached to the Pussy Galore serving house. They were tall and blond and sat with open jackets, seemingly oblivious to the chill. Jes could see the woman was drinking a cappuccino and the man a large draft. He wondered if Jalâl understood the name of the bar, and if so, what he thought about it and what he might say. Jes kept a little notebook that he had titled *The Sayings of Jalâl* with which he entertained his drinking friends, repeating the man's pronouncements with an ironic portentousness that belied the affection and admiration developing in him for Jalâl. He imagined Jalâl's judgment of Pussy Galore, *The Perverter is a wretched companion*, and covered his mouth with the side of his fist to hide his smile.

At just that moment, the little girl made the mistake of coming too close to a full-throated bull pigeon that had been near success in mounting a sleek gray little dove. The girl stamped her foot behind the pair, and the male flapped up into her face as though to attack. The little girl screamed and began to weep, running for her parents. Both Jalâl and Jes burst out laughing.

"What is so funny?" asked Khadiya, thrusting her face out from behind the curtains.

"Even the dove knows wrath," Jalâl said with mock portent.

Khadiya surveyed the square. "Do you laugh at a weeping child?" she demanded mildly. Jes was impressed with how quickly she had assessed the situation.

"There was no harm," said Jalâl. "Our laughter is to ourself as well as the girl. She has learn to respect for the birds. We learn this, too, with her."

"I think idleness is curdling your wit," Khadiya said, gathering their empty glasses. "Tea time is over. Make some work now."

Jes looked away, not to embarrass Jalâl with his witness; but to his surprise, his boss only smiled owlishly at him. "Thee women are always good to us. They save us from idleness and self-importance."

Jes itched to write it down in his notebook but feared that might appear odd. Maybe it was odd. Why was he collecting all these quotes? Just to play the clown for his drinking buddies? He thought with relish of their laughter, their delight, as he did his imitation of the shoemaker in the North Bodega each evening. Not only what Jalâl said, but the way he pronounced words. For example, when he dyed leather he wore rubber gloves and asked Jes to fetch them for him from the shelf over the door—Jes stood half a meter higher than the older man.

"Jes, please, to take down woba golves to me."

Jes could barely wait for him to request them again. This was now a saying among his friends; for no reason at all, one might suddenly look at the other, perhaps in displeasure, perhaps in response to a reminder that it was his turn to buy a round, and say simply, "Woba golves!" and everybody present would crack up.

Yet Jes's feeling for the Afghani was not simple, he knew that. The more he came to know of him, the more he recognized that he had made an assumption at the start—that he was inherently superior to this man. But each day in his presence was a challenge to that assumption. There seemed no end to it.

Jes had been working for Jalâl for not quite two months now, since his leave of absence from *RUC* started and his student salary stopped. He'd seen a hand-lettered sign in the shop window in some kind of Arabic,

English, and Danish. How perfect it seemed! Practically just around the corner from his apartment on Blågårds Place, and it was not an office job. He was willing to do practically anything that would keep him out of an office. It seemed to him that almost nobody in Denmark actually did anything anymore; they all just sat in offices sending e-mails to one another or went to meetings where they sat around a table and talked about the e-mails. His father had got him a student job at the Tank two years before, and Jes had been amazed at how little anyone seemed to do. They wrote e-mails or sometimes letters, photocopied and filed them, sent them, and received responses, which needed new letters, new photocopies, new files. They went to meetings. Sometimes some of the big shots went to meetings in other cities or other countries where they apparently had their e-mails translated into other languages so they could talk about them with foreigners. Meanwhile, there were a million truly important things that needed doing in the world, things that were a matter of life and death for people who lived in poverty and misery. Jes wanted a foot into that door. And meanwhile, he wanted to do something concrete.

When Jes went into the shop and introduced himself to the smiling little pop-eyed man behind the shoe desk, Jalâl said in English, "Your name is Yes?"

"Yes: Jes. With a 'J.'"

"Please to write this for me. . . . Ah, 'Jes'! But spoken as 'Yes.' This is good name. Much better than 'No.'"

Jes laughed.

"So you want to come to work for a foreign man in your own country? You know, when I was only the little more than age of you, I had to select if I must to spend my life repairing and polishing the boots of the Russians. I am Kabuli. Was born in Kabul, the city of my father, and I thought it was also my city. But Kabul has many master in the three thousand year. I was only tenant in rented house that pass from the hand of one foreign to another. Arab, Persian, British, Russian. Now American. But I did not know about the American was coming like this. I only knew the Russian came and killed my father, and they wanted me to take their boots in my hands. To repair the boots of other man is humble, there is honor. But not the boots of man who kill your father. My father was good man. He teach me to read, he teach me many thing. He teach many people, the young people. I think they kill him because he teach. It says in Koran that whoever flee in cause of God will find on the earth many a spacious refuge. This I have found here where I have now lived since twenty-five years. That is one year more than I live in Kabul, which has have many master and destructions and pain in the years since I leave her. Now is Copenhagen my home, and you, a young Dane with father who came from other land, come to *me* for an occupation. This honors me. I consider. Return here to me tomorrow and we shall decide together if you are to take this little job of work for me."

That night in the North Bodega, Jes was quickly the star of the evening. Even the old-time regulars were amused. But now it occurred to Jes that they would refer to Jalâl as a perker, a spic, and anger stirred in him—at them, at himself. He despised that word.

Next day, Jalâl said, "Do you wish to work for me still? The pay is not great."

"Thank you, Mr. al-Din."

"Please, no 'Mr.' Is not necessary. I am Jalâl, like the great poet, you know him? No? You read him sometime. I have name from him. But they have sometimes call me Al-Jariz because my eyes, you know, they stick out. Al-Jariz it mean, how you say, 'the Goggle-Eyed.'" He made a comical show of displaying his pop eyes. "They have said it indicates force to have the eyes protrude, but I know it indicates only a slight disturbing of a gland behind my throat. For this I swallow the heart of a garlic morning and night. This way there is no odor. For me to smell of the garlic is to invite the Danes to call me perker. Not wise to tempt. To swallow the garlic also regulate elimination system very well. So, how you say? The situation win-win."

Now a woman came into the shop with two pair of men's oxfords in a plastic bag. Jes marked them with the thick stub of yellow crayon Jalâl kept beside the cash register and passed them over the work desk to his boss. He watched Jalâl fit the shoes over his last and with a wide-jawed pliers peel away the remains of the old heels in one sweep. With another dark iron tool he clipped off the nail stumps and hammered flat the leather beneath. Then he painted the heel space of each shoe with glue and laid on a square of nylon that protruded all around the heel. Holding each shoe, in turn, to his chest, he carved away the excess nylon with a sharp knife. Jes's fingers itched to try it himself.

"It must be nice," he said. "To have a trade like that. To do something, you know, real."

"My father was teacher," said Jalâl. "It was no meant for me to repair boot. But it feed my family."

"I would really like to have a trade like that."

The back of the index finger rose and twitched before him. "No for you. You father would be sad."

"My father is a big shot, but he's not happy. He spends all day in an office doing nothing as far as I can see."

Jalâl tilted his head, and his eyes glistened as he peered into Jes's face. "You say this to me of your father?"

"Don't get me wrong, I love my father, but his work . . ."

"Do you know your father recommend you to me?"

Jes was confused. "You know my father?"

"When you apply I see your name and I look in telephone book and I call to your father. We speak on telephone. I tell him I like you for this job for me, and I ask if he approve that. He tell me about his work, what he do. He is important fellow. Educated. You must become educated, too."

Jes felt his confusion faltering on the border of anger. He felt like a child, being discussed by two men. He didn't need his father's approval, goddammit! Yet the mild, good-natured certainty of Jalâl was too much for him, and he stilled his own sharp, quick tongue. He couldn't be angry. "The problem here, Jalâl, is that there is nothing worth being educated for."

Jalâl laughed. "Nothing? My son Daoud will be doctor in three year time. My daughter studies the IT. My young son Zaid, he is confusing. He listens only to the music techno. All day, all time, the music techno. Boom boom boom. It drive a nail of tympanics in the soul. He is no happy." Jalâl's eyes glistened, and he looked at Jes. "You know, seven weeks now I no see Zaid. His mother he see, but not his father. He is no happy. The young are confusing. You are of much intelligence, I see this in your face, but your intelligence is like the morning sun when there are many clouds before it. The clouds will pass in time, and you will see light."

Jes watched the man's thick hands place each shoe on the last of the nailer before he toed the pedal, turning the shoe as nails slammed neatly into the nylon, affixing it to the glued surface, and he felt as though he had wandered into the great cliché factory. He got an idea for a little skit he would play out at the North Bodega, then: *Another Day at Jalâl's Great Northern Cliché Fabrik*. Yet he was tempted by Jalâl's words; if only such simplisms could be believed! Maybe they could. Or maybe he was being tempted by candy floss.

When the heels were in place, Jes took the shoes over to the finishing machine, hit the drive baton, and ran the edges of the heels against the waxing wheel, watching the raw pale nylon take on a deep black luster before he painted on polish and buffed them on the spinning brush. As he worked, Jalâl began speaking again.

"It is said that God has sealed the hearts and covered the eyes and ears of the ungrateful and placed them in the torment where they cannot hear or see or feel what is true. But I believe it is the ungrateful who refuse to open their eyes and ears because they have fallen in love with their own lies and no longer can to see the falseness of them. They have become obsessed and made themselves so sick they will not know the good."

If only it were so simple, Jes thought. "Do you know the good, Jalâl?" he asked, thinking the question a subtle form of rebuttal. Surely the man could see reality was more complex than that.

"Yes," Jalâl said.

"Yes?"

"Yes. Is simple. Worship nothing but God, be good to your parents and relatifs and to those who are without parents and to the poor and to the animal. Speak nicely to people, very important. Treat your neighbor as good neighbor so he can become good neighbor. Remember to pray and to give charity."

Jes's instinct was to scoff, but he tempered his challenge into the form of a question. "Can it really be that simple?"

"Yes."

"I respect you, Jalâl, but I don't know."

"My friend: Do not wrong or sorrow your own soul."

"Jalâl, my father's country is destroying the world. My own country is helping. I think more than simple homilies are needed."

"I understand these words and their source, my friend. Someday those who oppress will wish there were a great distance between them and their evil. My friend: Ways of life have passed away before us. If you travel the earth, you will see how scorners have ended up. Do not wrong your own soul."

Jes decided to say nothing more then as he took the last shoe in his hands and leaned into the turning wheel, welcoming the high, shrill whine of it into his ears.

18. Frederick Breathwaite

Breathwaite closed Kampman's door behind him and moved slowly along the hall, hand in his pocket, stirring the coins there. He remembered then how his own father used to do that and how that sound of dimes and nickels and quarters and fifty-cent pieces clicking against one another had seemed wondrous to him when he was a boy. The wonder of money in the possession of adults. Pockets full of jingling coins. Wallets fat with green folding currency. The very word *cash*. The silver money clip his father carried in the buttoned back pocket of his suit pants, bills folded in ascending denominations from ones to twenties, the occasional fifty. His mother's black purse with the snap clasp, inside of it a smaller purse with its own snap clasp and separate compartments for coins and bills.

Many years had passed before the unconsidered assumption that adult pockets came filled with cash revealed itself as false, before he recognized the relationship between labor and monetary recompense. It embarrassed him now to think how old he was. Not that he'd been lazy. Breathwaite had worked all his life. Newspaper routes, delivery boy for a grocery store, runner for a druggist. Unlike most of his friends, he was allowed to keep and use what he earned as he pleased. Candy, comic books, movie money, popcorn and, later, cigarettes, clothes, pizza, even restaurants, six-packs of beer. It was not until after high school when, for reasons still murky to him—was it his father's drinking, his mother's infidelity, a tight economy (but this was the 1960s!), or just bad karma?—his parents had sold their house and moved into a three-room apartment that Breathwaite recognized the ride here on out would not be free. That he awoke to the fact he would have to work for the rest of his life to earn his keep.

Late waker. Until then he had a little ironic motto he used to employ on people he considered unnecessarily and ostentatiously industrious: "You have got to get up early and work hard; otherwise other people will look at you and say, 'He doesn't get up early and work hard.'"

With his mother and father living in a small apartment, Breathwaite slept on a pull-out sofa bed for a while, then got a room of his own and began to turn the fruit of his labor to essentials—food, rent, college tuition. If he got a toothache, he had to pay the dentist to make it go away. A shot of penicillin for the flu cost money. Razor blades and shaving cream, toothpaste, toilet paper, the use of a washer and dryer, shoe leather, the dry cleaner's, meat and bread and cheese and condiments, ketchup, mustard, subway tokens, bus fare—everything cost money. And that was not even to mention luxuries, which cost a lot of money. A lot more than he was earning as he, with painful slowness, inched his way toward the American dream of having everything you wanted and your parents never quite had, until it began to appear that everything you wanted was at the cost of everything you had to give. You could have it, everything, but you couldn't have the time to enjoy it.

The Danish dream, on the other hand, was more modest and manageable. All you needed here was a house or apartment in the city, a house in the country, a car or two, maybe even a time-share in the south of France, TV, stereo, delicious furniture, a cozy, well-equipped kitchen and bath, a garden, and a six-week holiday to enjoy it all in, as well as a society that takes care of everything else for everybody so you could enjoy what you had without guilt and without too much worry about being envied, robbed, or murdered for it. Breathwaite pretty much had the furnishings of his Danish dream in place. Or had had, before this pulling of the plug. He could already hear the water of comfort gurgling down the drain.

Marianne, he was pleased to note, was not at her desk, so he didn't have to muster energy to raise a mask with which to reassure and comfort her that he would be okay. He closed the door of his office behind him and sat with his feet up on the desk, gazing out his window toward the autumn-withered botanical garden.

His work for an NGO in his twenties had brought him to a conference in Copenhagen, where he got a glimpse of the Danish dream, with which you didn't get everything, just a nice piece of it all (town house, summer house, a car or two if you wanted), and you still got to keep something of yourself. What really sold him was the six-week annual holiday leave, not to mention the numerous three-, four-, and five-day weekends and a society that seemed not quite so predicated on the shaft. Taxes were high, but you got something back for them—education, health care, and a security net if you fell on your butt.

Well, now he was on his butt, or about to be, and that net did not look quite so attractive from this position. And it was beginning to look worse.

He'd just had that one piece to get into place—Jes's future—and he realized now his mistake: He had assumed that Kampman might feel he owed him something for agreeing to leave quietly after twenty-seven years of service, but a man like Kampman did not think that way. He had also tried to flank him with surprise, and that was always a mistake with someone like Kampman.

"I've been thinking about the new international structure, Martin, and it would work, but you'll still be missing one vital thing."

Kampman lifted his brow. The question that was not a question. *I didn't ask, so whatever you offer might well be gratuitous. Answer at your own peril.*

Breathwaite answered nonetheless. "Someone who is perfect in English."

"Not a problem."

"Believe me, it's a problem. When you represent the Tank—I don't mean you, but one—with pidgin applications, the Brits will shoot you down as sure as Nelson and Wellington did. If for no other reason, they'll do it because they see a way of doing so."

Kampman lifted one brow. Danger. He didn't understand. *Don't embarrass the man.*

"We can buy the language expertise we need in town," he said. "Ad hoc. Which is a lot cheaper than the little butter-hole we have been maintaining in the international department." He laughed then, as if his frankness excused his insult.

Breathwaite ignored it. "Fee for service," he said. "Will cost you a fortune. And you'll have no means of quality control because no one here has the English."

Smiling broadly, the CEO lifted his hand expansively. "*Everyone* here has the English."

"Everyone here has school English. There's a difference."

"I take it you have a suggestion."

"I do. Would you like to hear it?"

Kampman only stared at him, smiling inscrutably.

As though there had been an affirmative reply, Breathwaited plunged on. "Take someone on. Part-time. Trial basis. Assistant to the chief. A right hand for Jaeger."

The smile was sweetly incredulous with pity. "You?"

Sit on the outrage. Even if it sticks up the butt. Breathwaite shook his head mildly. "When I'm gone, I'm gone. My son."

"That might be a thought, but . . . Don't have a budget."

"Take it from the translation budget."

"Already used most of that on your, uh, handshake."

More like a kick in the ass—as a prelude to this one. All lies, but it was imperative that Breathwaite maintain the mask. "The first two years wouldn't cost more than two hundred K. Quarter million tops. I know what the boy can do. You'll get more than the value of the cost. You'll be glad."

"And you'd be glad?"

"Of course, but I wouldn't suggest it if I didn't know that he can do the job you need done."

Kampman's lips soured as if on a bad taste. Breathwaite saw the inevitable. He had to give something here. "Give him a two-year contract and you can skim the half of it from my, uh, handshake."

"The half of it won't pay the half of it."

"How so?"

"Overhead, for example," Kampman said. "Contingencies." Then he smiled.

It cost Breathwaite not quite 30 percent of his settlement. His little bag of good-bye moneys was now little more than a pouch. Like the little pouch of useless jewels between his thighs.

But the boy was in the door. And that, anyhow, was something.

19. Adam Kampman

The sense of conclusion, of release, buoyed Adam's step up Callisens Way, past the drear rows of villas and ligustrum privet hedges. House after house of the sort he knew his father expected him to throw away his life for, day after day, just for the hope of locking the remainder of his days in one of these yellow-brick boxes. For what? To be able to say he lived in Hellerup or Gentofte or Charlottenlund or Rungsted Kyst? Why? Who wanted to?

But now, with each step along the chilly street to Ryvangs Way, he felt he was leaving them behind forever. Now it was all changed. Now his future was uncertain, and he was released from the certainty that had always been assumed for him. How could he have failed to see this option before? Every time he had ever voiced anything even remotely like a question about the necessity of an academic education, his father's response had always been quietly relentless: *Do you want to destroy your future?*

A question that had always seemed unanswerable. It answered itself irrefutably. There was only one future for him, and it must not be destroyed, for then all that remained was the yawning pit of futurelessness that awaited all boys who failed to attain an academic high school diploma with a high average followed by six years of university education in law, political science, or government with a high average. There were also medicine and dentistry. *But are you sure you're hard-nosed enough for that, son?* There it was again. The nose. And, of course, theology. *But really, Adam, is that a viable option? You might as well take humanities and ensure yourself a spot on the unemployment line.*

The questions always answered themselves. *If you think you might like to try an M.B.A., well, let's discuss that when the time comes. But IT is a one-way ride to oblivion. Journalism? Oh, come on!*

Oblivion. The pit again.

The only option that had never been discussed. If you destroy your future, then some other future could be waiting. All the other futures. It might be anything. Maybe even happiness. To destroy one thing was to create another.

Outside Hellerup Station, the smell of frying sausage coiled out the open window of a grill bar into his nostrils, and the water began to run in his mouth. He took a step toward it, but the sight of a man standing in the doorway deflected his course. The man was fat and sloppy, smoking a cigarette.

Without understanding why, Adam went instead for the stairway down to the Hellerup Station platforms and lost his balance. He glimpsed a poster plastered to the wall advertising a film called *Graceland*, and his knee went loose. He stumbled, clawed for the railing, and fell, banging his hip and the small of his back as he slid over the sharp edges of the steps and rolled to the dirty concrete floor below, biting his tongue so that he tasted blood.

Blushing furiously, he rose at once. Someone, a man with a cigarette, was descending toward him, speaking. He spun away and hurried for the Copenhagen track, ran for a train whose doors were sliding shut, jammed them open, and leapt in. The doors remained open as the train signal sounded, and he glimpsed someone, a man, boarding the car farther down. Then the doors slid shut, and Adam started hurrying, limping, toward the opposite end of the car. He still tasted blood in his mouth and spit into his handkerchief, wiped his lips.

At Svanemøllen Station, he got off the train and ran, hobbling, for the next car. He saw dirt smudged along his hand and the side of his gray jacket. He took a seat but saw he was in the smoking section, rose again, and moved farther up as the train pulled into Østerport. A small heavy man boarded—had he come from farther down in the train?—and stood in the aisle outside the smoker, lighting a cigarette.

At Nørreport, Adam waited until the train signal warbled over the PA system and leapt through the doors just before they closed. The man with the cigarette stared at him from behind the glass windows of the doors. Without looking behind, Adam limped rapidly up the steps to Frederiksborg Street and headed north, toward North Bridge.

The pain in his hip was getting worse. He shoved his hand in under his shirt and his fingers stung against the skin of his back. He was cut. He leaned over the curb to spit into the gutter and saw the pink gob fall from his mouth. He limped quickly up Frederiksborg, looped through the vegetable market on Israels Place. He slowed, pretending to study the wares, glancing at the sexy women in tight slacks, who were hawking fruit.

"Hey, ten bananas for a tenner! Ten good bananas for a tenner!"

"Oranges! Juicy! Oranges! Seven for a tenner! Can I help you, honey?"

Honey! In her tight, tight jeans. He stumbled on, shaking his head, trying to see if the man from the grill bar was behind him. Had he been the man on the train? Was it . . . ? But he couldn't tell, couldn't remember. *Am I going nuts!*

Continuing north, across the lakes, he hooked over to North Bridge Street. The shopfronts and the dirty sidewalks here seemed embedded in the mystery of his new future. Details caught his eye. Signs written in Arabic script. The old signs of now defunct businesses still imprinted like pale shadows on dirty brick, old and new jostling together. Odd names in shops whose purpose he could not imagine. One with a sign that said, "Function 2." An old chiseled brick sign spanning several windows: "L. V. Erichsen A/S. Al Rafiden gold and silver watches." Across the lintel between a GUF record shop and a sportswear store, a flat gray canopy advertised, HOTEL CONTINENT.

Adam gazed up at the four floors of grimy windows above the sign: one with a lit yellow lamp behind checkered curtains. Who was in there? Doing what? Across the street from him a shop sign said simply, "Food Store" and "Dhadra Indian Specialities." A pub called Munkestuen, the Monk's Room, with a price list propped outside the door: "House Spirit 12 crowns a unit. Beer schnapps bitters 15 crowns. Billiards and Pool One Flight Up." Who was in there? Behind the dark windows? People who would have been excluded from the life of his old future.

He crossed Stengade and glimpsed a tall fence dripping with withered wisteria. Women with scarf-covered heads walked past, and a dark man said to another, "*Salaam aleikem.*" Then there was a cemetery, Assistens Churchyard, where he knew Søren Kierkegaard was buried, Hans Christian Andersen, too. Tall trees rose from behind the yellow wall—firs and poplars, leafless elms and lindens. He doubled back, past a street called Solitude Way, a dead end closing on a bunch of chestnut trees and a grimy-fronted bar named the North Bodega. He heard the chant of an Arabic voice drifting through the air. The call to morning prayer? How strange it seemed suddenly, how foreign, to call to prayer, to pray. When had he ever really prayed?

Crossing over along Fælled Way, he passed a burial shop, the Restaurant

Opium, the Restaurant Barcelona, Rita's Danish Open-Sandwich Shop. He looked into the window of a halal butcher, and a thin man with a stubble of gray hair looked out with a dark smile.

At the corner, he came into a square with a single linden tree, saw a sign over a café that said, "Pussy Galore." He felt a little dizzy, and the aroma from a sausage wagon drew him. In his pocket he found a hundred-crown note and an envelope on which his mother had written, "Adam, honey, please don't forget to copy the keys for Jytte. Keep the change. Love, Mom."

He was famished. He ordered a fried medister with raw onion and stood at the counter of the wagon munching it as he gazed around the square. The raw onion dice stung the cut inside his mouth, but he kept chewing, dipping the meat into the blobs of ketchup and strong dark mustard the sausage man had dolloped onto a square of butcher paper.

As he swallowed the last bite, the elation of the fatty meat lifted, and he felt sleepy. He sat on the edge of a strange sculpture there and felt desolation descend upon him. Idly, he watched the sausage man behind the window of his van. He wondered what you had to do to get a job like that. The man was reading a newspaper, one of those they give out free on trains and buses. It seemed it might be a simple life, a good life. You could live off the sausage, read free newspapers, just sit in there all day by yourself and watch the world go by, no one breathing down your neck all the time. By comparison, his own life seemed impossibly complex and frustrated.

Then he noticed a key-and-heel bar across the street. He could give the keys to Jytte himself. It would give him an excuse to talk to her.

When he entered the shop, a short foreign man wearing a black cap and gray robe seated at the shoemaker's bench called out, "*Salaam aleikem!*" And, "Good day, my friend, welcome." He rose from the bench. "My colleague will help you," he said, and pushed through a dark curtain to the back.

The young man behind the counter looked familiar to Adam. He put the keys down on the Formica.

"One of each?"

"Yeah."

Adam watched the young man's hands move deftly to place the shank of the key into the jaws of a kind of vise, flip a switch, and begin to file the key pattern into a red metal blank. The young man looked back at him.

"Don't I know you? You look familiar." Then, "Are you Martin Kampman's son?"

"Yeah." Uneasiness began to crawl inside Adam's stomach, turning the sausage there.

"What's your name?"

"Adam."

"No shit? My name's Adam, too. But I use my middle name, Jes. No offense, but like, you know, *hello? Adam?*"

Adam laughed. "Actually, Adam is *my* middle name. My real name is Isaak—for my mother's father—but my father didn't like it."

They looked at each other and cracked up over the coincidence.

Jes removed the key from the vise, blew away the filings, and started on the next. "My old man works with yours at the Tank. Works *for* him, I should say." He glanced up, as if assessing, then plunged on. "The downsizer, huh?"

"Huh?"

"Your old man. Professional downsizer. They bring him in to fire people. Read about what he did at Western Gulf. It was in *Information*."

"I think he worked at Western Gulf a couple years ago." Adam thought the young man was maybe a Communist.

"Damn right he worked there. He shit-canned thousands of people. Hundreds, anyway. You want a bag for these?"

"Huh? Nah."

"So what do you know about that?"

"Huh? Nothing. I don't know anything about it."

"No, I mean about our meeting like this." With an exaggerated sing-song Danish accent, he said in English, "Danmark iss a lit-tle land."

Adam paid and tried to think of something more to say to prolong the conversation. "So you work here?"

"Yeah, it's fat. Best boss I ever had."

"Who, that guy there in back? He's your boss?"

"Owns the place. Got out of Aghanistan before the Taliban. 'Course the Americans put the Taliban in. Then they took them out again. Except, of course, they're still there. Some world. Listen, I get off in like five minutes. You want to have a beer?"

"Uh, I'm only seventeen."

"So?"

"Well, you have to be eighteen, right?"

"Right," Jes drawled. "You mean you never even been in a bar? Come on, it's time, boy."

20. Breathwaite's Whiskey

For the second day running, Breathwaite left the Tank early. Down the back stairs. *Getting to be a habit.* But not for long. Outside the botanical garden, he decided to cross through and take the city train home from North Port. Crisp air livened his cheeks and leavened his spirit as his big feet walked him slowly along the paths of brittle leaves, their dusty smell lifting to his nostrils with an agreeable edge of death. He had always loved that about autumn, the chill sense of dark ahead of him.

He was in no hurry, scuffling his shiny black Lloyds through the crinkly foliage. Dust on the shine. He crossed paths with a woman leading a golden retriever on a leash. The dog smiled at him. Such a kind animal. Sad for Kirsten that she had been so yearning for a dog ever since Jes moved out. He remembered her hinting about her boss's golden having puppies. But Breathwaite saw no reason for taking on avoidable unnecessary baggage. Now they had their castle to themselves, why complicate things? Sad for her. And how much longer did they have their castle, anyway?

Past the palm house and observatory, the pond and botanic museum, past the statue of Echo leaning forward, calling out her own name in the woods, and out on the corner of Gothers Street, down into the subway at North Port, and right into a waiting train. Good timing. Lucky. The warbly, high-pitched sound of the door signal, it occurred to him, sounded exactly like the opening notes to the *Mission Impossible* TV series theme. Then the train wheels clicked into a long fast starting riff of *naynaynaynaynaynaynay*, faster and faster, before quieting to a smooth slide, rolling out the tunnel into the light as he gazed dreamily through the dirty window, seeing nothing, thinking nothing that he was aware of.

And he missed his stop at East Port. No matter. He got off at North Harbor and stood on the platform, gazing over the water. To the left, black warehouses with blue trim, the brown concrete towers of the agricultural firm DLG. An orange yacht cutting the harbor water before it in a white V and, to the right, red cranes reaching up into the sky. Farther out, the tall spinning steel propellers of windmills against the chill blue sky—windmills no Don Quixote would get worked up over—and just fifteen miles across from Copenhagen, the evil humps of Barsebäck. Swedish nuclear reactors. After all the years of Swedish promises, now finally closed. But for how long? Let's see them dismantled first. And where will they dump the waste? Why have so few people ever been particularly worked up over them? More concerned with closing Christiania. Picture a meltdown. Sound the alarm! Run for your life. Run, don't walk, to the nearest exit. See them boil up a tidal wave laced with strontium 90. Here comes everybody's worst nightmare! Another flood is coming, but not the kind you think, there is still time to shrink, and think. Incredible shrinking man. All worldly goods swept away. These small problems of today dwarfed by it all.

Or not?

He lifted a slender tin box of Henri Wintermans Royales from the side pocket of his jacket, and his eye caught the warning plastered there: "Cigar Smoking Can Cause Cancers of the Mouth and Throat, Even If You Do Not Inhale." Tell it to Bill Clinton. Funny, how they capitalize the words. Old-fashioned types. He lit one. The secret to enjoying cigars was variety. The rough dry smoke in his mouth was bracing. He wondered if he would get cancers of the throat and mouth. Why plural? More than one kind?

A smiling woman approached him. Unpleasantly plump, she put her false smile in his face and said in twangy American, "You are stinking up a perfectly good day!"

"Madame," Breathwaite said, "turn and observe those humps of evil out in the bay. *They* are stinking up a perfectly good city. Turn your attention where it is needed."

Clearly she hadn't expected that. With outrage tight in her lungs, she pronounced, "You are *very* selfish, sir!"

Breathwaite stepped away from her and chucked his cigar to the tracks in the path of an incoming red city train, considered chucking himself after it, and cocked his head with interest at the impulse.

You can't die yet. Think of all the great whiskey in your cabinet.

The train jiggled him back to East Port, the American woman glaring at him all the way. Breathwaite was surprised at himself. Normally he would have simply trampled the cigar underfoot without a word. *Growing confrontational in my time of crisis?*

Kirsten was not home, so he installed himself on the balcony with an honor guard of bottles on the little wrought-iron table before him, admiring their different shapes, the quality of the afternoon sunlight filtering through their different hues. From the pale yellow amber of the Glen Grant, to the deep dog-eye glowing brown of the Wild Turkey 101-proof eight-year-old straight bourbon whiskey, to the similar but slightly lighter red brown of the Balvenie DoubleWood and the mellower, yellower Bushmills Black Bush triple-distilled in sherry casks, to the elegant reddish yellow thirty-two-year-old Bunnahabhain Family Silver Vintage 1973 Limited Edition, which he had been nursing for the past five years and was now slightly less than half-full. Or to put it another way, slightly more than half-empty.

It occurred to him that it was highly unlikely he would ever have another bottle of that. He could not even recall what he had paid for it, other than that it was pricey. One hundred dollars? Two hundred? When these bottles were empty, he would have to develop a taste for cut-rate supermarket whiskey.

Hello, my name is Fred, and I am not an alcoholic, I just love whiskey. I am a connoisseur. Who will take whatever he can get however he can get it.

With these bottles he could entertain himself an entire evening, taking a dram every half hour or so. Correctly tasted, a single dram warmed your mouth and your chest, your heart and your consciousness, keeping the reason from stifling for at least half an hour.

How optimistic seemed the bottles that were full or near full, how sad the single remaining finger in his Glen Grant. The Family Silver still had five fingers—five skimpy drams—five more tastes. Properly stewarded, a week's worth of evenings.

He considered starting with the Glen Grant but was reluctant to kill the bottle. One less soldier in his guard, even if a short-timer. So he went for the Wild Turkey and cracked the seal. Bonded bourbon. Legs to stand on. He nosed it well. Sweaty socks, chocolate, nut. Poured a third of the dram into the furrow of his tongue and let it roll, ignited it with air, and swallowed, smiling, happy as any southern gent, chest full of the home fires.

Like a cigar, Fred?

Why, yes, Fred, thank you.

Not at all, Fred, my pleasure.

Know what, Fred? I don't mean to be sentimental or anything, but you are a true friend.

Right back at you, buddy! Now fire up at will! Take a good one!

Fresh robusto, all Cuban, rolled to the lyrics of Neruda. Smell of fertile earth and sun and skilled peasant fingers. With his hole cutter, he pressed a neat dime-sized opening in the head of the cigar, studied its even contour, ran the tube beneath his nostrils again, then struck a long cedar matchstick and roasted one end before putting the other between his teeth and drawing the flame up to it.

Thank you, God, for the fruits of this good earth. And thank you, Fred.

Right back at you, buddy.

As his mouth filled with smoke, stimulating the benevolent phlegm at the top of his throat, he regarded the lines of Langelinie Bridge spanning the train tracks below. Jerry-built footbridge that replaced the graceful structure that had been there for a century before, since 1896. A new bridge was coming, but not for another few years. Would he live to see it? Beyond that, the domed roof of Bruun Rasmussen's auction house, where he had passed many a pleasant evening battling for the objets d'art and furniture with which he had decorated and appointed his roomy shelter here. Figuratively speaking "his." Rented. *Dear landlord, please don't put a price on my soul.* He remembered battling for the Dan Turèll barber chair two years before. He gave up at nine thousand. It went for ten thousand. Breathwaite would have placed it on this very balcony so he could sit in Uncle Danny's elevatable stool and contemplate the view over the city, hoping that the chair would exude some old infused Dan T poetic sentiments.

Breathwaite could sense that Kirsten was home now. Connected by the invisible tendrils of their years together, he knew her movements. He needn't look. From where he sat on the balcony, his back to the apartment, he knew. The aroma of her thoughts, her dreams, her concerns, wafted through the labyrinth of rooms between them. Sour and sweet, her breath, never foul unless she was ill, the heady fragrance of her body, sea salt, seaweed tang below, her soul the floor of an ocean. Sweet angelfish. All sweetness and light while the sun shone.

Then abruptly he recalled the turd of hers he saw floating in the bowl the other month, black and ragged as a cheap Italian cigar, ginny stinker. A sweet-ocean angel's secret. Odd to have lived together so long and that the first time in thirty years he ever saw her shit. That was not a turd to be proud of, but certainly an interesting one. Inconsequential, of course. *My mistress's shit is nothing like a rose.* No need to tell her he saw that twisted little marvel, yet he was uneasy with secret knowledge of her. If he kept something from her, what might she keep from him? Surely it was mad to extrapolate at such length over a little ginny stinker of a turd.

What would she say if he said suddenly, burst forth with confession: *I saw a piece of your shit the other day. It looked like a ginny stinker.*

She would say, *Your mother again?*

And then he heard what he was thinking. *Ginny stinker.* His mother was the ginny stinker. Her angelic face, angelic name (Raffaella Belmare), her sweet nature, kind touches, her sensuous Italian lips, and she was the ginny stinker. Story of his life. Incomplete puzzle. Little piles of broken images. Explanations built from grains of dust.

His mother, Raffaella Belmare, had been born out of wedlock in Naples, in Caserta. As was the custom for those born out of wedlock in Caserta, her last name was conferred upon her by the mayor, who gave her the name Belmare because her eyes were the green of a beautiful sea. Did the sin of her own mother haunt and follow her?

Whatever the reason, perhaps simple lechery, perhaps neglect, perhaps just a moment's weak hunger grown from discontent at her husband's virility or lack of it, Mom cheated on Dad. With Jimmy Powers, handsome wiry mick who drove the van that collected our laundry once a week. Dad and I went to the one o'clock show instead of the four, to see Gregory Peck in *Moby Dick*, cultural experience, and when we got back, the laundry van was in the driveway, but Mom was not in the kitchen. Mom was not in the dining room. Mom was not in the basement or the living room or on the porch. Dad said loudly, "Okay, let's see if she's out in the backyard," and when we were out back we heard the ignition of the laundry van kick in and then Mom came out and said, "You're early!"

The flush of her face and edgy smile told the story. Dad said nothing, but his eyes were sad. He was a pacifist. Or was he afraid? I was not afraid. Jimmy Powers was the father of Hughie Powers, with whom I went to St. Gabe's. Hughie with his chiseled face and dazzling smile of teeth, so admired by the girls. I found him in the schoolyard next day. His eyes were frightened as a baby's when he saw me, and that only fueled my intention—for his fear announced the fact that he knew all about what had happened, that everybody knew all about what had happened.

I approached him, not certain what I meant to say or do. And then my right hand decided for me. It swelled up like a cement hammer and blasted him full in his fake-smiling teeth. One of them flew out, and another one lodged in my knuckle. He bowed forward at the waist, whimpering, hands cupped in front of his mouth to catch the blood as if he could use it for anything once it was out.

No satisfaction at all. Solved nothing. Helped nothing. Did not ease my pain. Made it worse. I had felt so certain that action was the only viable path and learned from that, that certainty was not necessarily a good foundation for action. Best to make decisions and to act when you are not feeling so certain and self-sufficient. Certainty is a drug whose effect is fleeting and fickle.

That evening, I was reprimanded in the kitchen by my father. Gently but firmly. While my mother sat with her hand over her sensuous, angelic lips. The reprimand was unnecessary. I was already disgusted with myself for the way my knuckles had felt smashing into his teeth, for the sight of his broken tooth that I had to pick out of the skin of my knuckle.

Dad said, "You know, or ought to know, and should have thought about, the fact that Hughie Powers's mother is in the hospital having a baby. These things have to be taken into consideration."

Oh, Dad. Did you take into consideration that Hughie's dad was so horny because his wife had a bun in the oven, is that it? Well, why was *Mom* so horny, Dad?

Those mean Sunnyside streets Breathwaite had left so far behind, where the currency of negotiation was a punch in the mouth or a kick in the balls. Might is right. Walk it like you talk it. Are you good with your dukes? Solved *nothing*. So much more civil here in the shelter of beauty and art with my dear Kirsten. She thinks all this is not important to her, but I know better. What she fails to realize is the importance of its importance to me. If we lose all this and have to move into our little summer house or into some dismal northwest-side two-room—as my own parents had to do for unclear reasons forty years ago—her brave smile each morning will be a mirror of my failure, and she will see that in my face as surely as my mother saw it in my father's doubt, whether he was a pacifist or a coward, and it will make her sad.

Being sad is the most damaging weapon Kis has against me. She doesn't complain or nag or bitch or argue; she just deflates, loses her sweet happy vigor, and when I ask, *Sweetheart, what's wrong?* she only says, *I'm sad.* Or, *I get sad.*

I sometimes wonder if she is fully conscious of this and the debilitating effect it has on me. The total capitulation. Calls for a reshuffle of all priorities. Only thing that matters is to undo Kis's sadness. How tyrannical is your sweet love, how powerful in its gentleness your tyranny.

It makes me sad. Oh, the tyranny of a sweet angel's sadness. Sweet angels have the power to swangle you. That's what it was, a swangling—a force that drained all color, sweetness, joy, hope, from the day. Copyright that word. Coin it and copyright it. Patent it. *Swangle*, verb, transitive: the action of a sweet angel to crush with sadness a man's fragile sac of gems.

Such methods of withholding: no morning kiss, no smile, no good-bye when you leave for the office, unless you go in to her and say, *No good-bye? No kiss?* And you have to lean down for it, and it is not much of a kiss or a smile, and she doesn't see you to the door as she otherwise always made a point of doing, waving as you got onto the elevator down to your day.

Swangled.

Now she stepped out onto the balcony with a smile. "You're early," she said. And bent to kiss his mouth. Then straightened to take in his honor guard. "Bad day?"

"It just occurred to me to claim this rare afternoon of October light for myself."

"Good idea!" she said. "You should do that more often. Worry them a little. Make them appreciate you more."

She will know, he thought. *If I am not careful, she will tune in and suck the information from the secret recesses of my mind. Or read it subliminally in the language that my body transmits without consulting me.*

But she left him with a smile to tend to her own affairs, and he went on to the Black Bush and the recollection of a conversation he had with his youngest son, Jes, some three years ago, when the boy had still seemed to consider his father worthy of listening to. It was the boy's eighteenth birthday, and Breathwaite had introduced him to the secrets of whiskey with a dram of Black Bush. Breathwaite liked a whiskey that was corked rather than capped. He loved the sound of the cork popping from the neck of the Black Bush, the fine bouquet it dispersed. He explained this to Jes, who tasted in accordance with the ritual suggested.

"Wow, Dad! That is fantastic!"

On the second dram, Breathwaite grew expansive: "Son, the secret to a happy life is good whiskey, good sex, an appreciation of poetry, a large living room, a trustworthy accountant, and a reasonably hefty net surplus in the bank."

Jes's smile was all admiration. "You forgot family."

"I did not forget family," said Breathwaite, instantly reframing. "Family is a sine qua non which I take as a given. Without your mom and you, I . . . and your brothers, of course . . . I might as well cash it all in."

Yet now he saw he had left out another vital element: the job he thought he didn't give a fiddler's fart for. How ironic to be undone by that. Blindsided.

And in those three years since, something had changed. Instead of going on through to his master's degree, Jes took three potentially fatal leaves of absence.

"Aren't you afraid you're making a mistake, son?"

"I'm not afraid of making a mistake, Dad. Even if it's for the rest of my life."

Touché. Breathwaite caught the reference: *"Portrait of the Artist as a Young Man."*

"You're very well-read, it's well-known," said Jes.

Touché again. Dylan. They had all the same references. Only the slant was different.

"Dad, listen." The boy sat forward, elbows on his knees. "I'm sorry to say it, but your life is not the life I want for myself. I know you make good money, and you have this great pad and all, but that's not what's important for me. I want to do something that matters. Sorry."

"That's admirable, Jes," Breathwaite said. What he did not say but only thought was, *I hear the sound of violins, I see Barbra Streisand and Robert Redford, I hear the smarmy sound track of* The Way We Never Really Were.

Breathwaite had been startled by the force of his own cynicism, which he had never before confronted head-on.

Now he fished his wallet from his back pocket and flipped through the credit card section to gaze at the platinum AmEx and Diners and the gold MC there, his gold pass to the airport lounges, his supply of company taxi vouchers. Could as well clip them into pieces right now.

At least I don't have to travel so much anymore, he thought, and felt an immediate nostalgia for the comfort of being on the move, that period of suspension, being nowhere, no longer where you were and not yet where you would be, an intense present during which you were tended to by smiling, business-class stewardesses proffering unlimited free drinks from cozy, rattling trolleys, free cigars in the airport smoking lounge for gold card holders only. Pour-your-own triple vods on rocks, XO Hennessy, Bloody Marys ad libitum, chips and peanuts and Japanese snacks, free newspapers in many languages, taxi to and from the airport at company expense.

Now into Bowmore Islay Single Malt twelve-year-old, Hebridean isle of Islay (color: warm amber; nose: lemon, pears, honey; palate: peat smoke, dark chocolate; aftertaste: long and complex), and, contrary to his custom, a second robusto, he recalled a quote from Seneca: "No one can win without the other losing." Which he had years before set out to disprove, thinking he could have it both ways. Win-win. Build a life of cooperation, sharing information, helping himself by helping others. It hadn't always been possible, but it had seemed to work better than he might have hoped. Accumulating win-wins for the Tank.

Doesn't really work that way, I guess. You were piping smoke.

Memo to file: Autobiography. My name is Fred. Means "peace" in Danish, engraved on every churchyard stone. Rhymes with dead. Better to call me Lance. Not peace, but a sword. Buddha's sword of wisdom slashes through incorrect thinking. My daddy was a cuckold, descended from a Lambeg informer. My mom was a ginny tart, like her Neopolitan whore of a mother before her. The B of my initial separates into a one and a three. Thirteen. Bad luck been waiting all these years like a catch clause on a pact with the devil. Entered into when? Negotiating with my first CEO, who hired me three decades ago, when I was just a few years older than Jes now.

He asked, "So, Fred, what are your thoughts on the job?"

I said, "This is a cause I would be pleased to serve. I believe in Europe."

He named a figure. I raised by a half. He laughed and cut the half in half. I smiled and cut the severed half in half, and we shook hands and I thought, *You will now direct me. I will be your subaltern. But I will live well and not betray my mind. I am not selling you my soul, only a piece of it.*

That's not really me. That wasn't me. The way I was. The way I am.

Just as it is not really me who had to write that speech for Jaeger to make at the Irish dinner, signaling all his old contacts that Fred is now out, Harald is in. I wrote it out in longhand on lined paper. Page and a half: "Here's what you say, Harald. Tickle their Celtics. You say, 'It is a pleasure to welcome to the Danish capital our Irish friends from the other old Danish city of Dublin, Dubh Lin, the Dark Lake, beside which our Viking emissaries founded the first Danish-Celtic cooperation some 1,200 years ago.'

"That will get you a chuckle. You leave implied the fact of the rape and pillage the Vikings perpetrated there. Then you touch your red blond beard and you say, 'But Brian Boru gave better than he got and sent us all home again smartly with a few Celtic genes in our kit.'

"That'll get you a chortle, and then you say, 'What better way to seal this important educational cooperation between us, the modern Irish and the modern Danes, than with a few words and a toast from the great Danish bard Mr. Yeats.'

"That'll get you a laugh. And then you say, 'To our guests and their beautiful ladies.' And you recite:

> *Wine comes in at the mouth*
> *And love comes in at the eye;*
> *That's all we shall know for truth*
> *Before we grow old and die.*
> *I lift the glass to my mouth,*
> *I look at you, and I sigh.*

"And then you raise your wineglass and you say, '*Sláinte. Skål.*'"

Breathwaite did not add, *And then my Irish friends and colleagues become your Irish friends and colleagues. And my Jes becomes your right hand and gets his arse the hell out of that Paki key-and-heel bar.*

Now it was time for that last finger of Glen Grant pure malt highland, no age statement, 40 percent (color: gold; nose: fruity, flowery, nutty, faintly spirity; body: light but firm; *palate*: dry, slightly astringent at first, becoming soft and nutty; aftertaste: herbal).

Thank you, God, for the grains that you provide. And God, if You do exist, Your intelligence is so far beyond mine that I would be akin to a flea on Your divine butt. Pig without arsehole, amen. He placed the empty Glen Grant on the floor of the terrace beside the kneeling Chinese archer, diminishing his honor guard by one.

They would all be better off without me, he thought.

"What're you up to out there?"

Kis with a mischievous smile at the balcony doors. *Dreaming of a magic poker I cannot provide.*

Breathwaite smiled and said nothing.

21. Harald Jaeger

The breeze on the Coal Square was from the north, chill. It was too cold to sit outdoors and too warm to sit in. Jaeger took one of the few remaining outdoor tables, close to the wall of the White Lamb, and sat watching the quitting-time pedestrian traffic hustle toward North Port Station. The flower and green stalls had packed up their wares and departed, and the sausage wagon puttered off behind the sausage man. The trees were growing balder by the day, and it occurred to Jaeger that he still had not secured a new love. At one of the other tables, half a dozen young men and women gabbed loudly, laughter hanging above them like a cloud of hysteria, unnerving him.

A large draft on the table before him, he hit the repeat button on his cell phone. He nursed the beer. Would not do to be high if he got hold of Birgitte. Might give the wrong impression. Without beer, Jaeger would never have made it through the year since his divorce. He drank every day, sometimes just a little, sometimes more. He was a happy drinker. If he felt bad, drink made him feel good; if he felt good, it made him feel better. Sometimes he took schnapps with the beer, too, and sometimes—not often, maybe once every other month—he got so drunk that when he woke the next day he couldn't remember what had happened. Sometimes after such an experience he would quit for a week or more, drink only Diet Coke or juice or Danish water, and during that time, he would think he had been redeemed from the person he had become, back to the path of the person he had always been meant to be; but slowly, he would realize that that person lacked passion and imagination, tended to be ignored and overlooked in company, and was of little interest to women. In fact, that person hardly knew what to say to a woman or what to do if he happened to get one talking. So it seemed to him a choice between sobriety and passion.

He wondered if this meant he was an alcoholic. He looked at the AA site on the Web, but it seemed much too extreme and religious to him. Perhaps he could solve the problem with some antidepressants. He went to his GP, who administered a multiple-choice test to which Jaeger did not answer yes to enough questions to qualify him for an antidepressant prescription.

"Everything in measure," his GP told him—a man ten years his senior with a port-wine nose. "Don't quit drinking altogether, just quit drinking alone. Quit drinking at home. And make sure there are at least two days a week, in a row, where you don't drink at all. That's important."

So Jaeger mostly stopped drinking at home. He went out to drink. The two alcohol-free days per week were difficult, but sometimes he did hold one. Still, those blacked-out nights appeared with a certain regularity every other month or so, but he never knew when. Every time he ordered the first beer of an evening, it occurred to him that in the blink of an eye, morning might be upon him with a smudged-out memory peppered here and there with a blurry glimpse of something that may or may not have happened, something he may or may not have said, a woman he may or may not have groped for or tried to kiss or succeeded in kissing or feeling up. Nobody had ever come after him. When he returned to the scene of the excess—say, to the office after the annual Christmas party or after the summer outing—no one made any cracks, not any that he could put his finger on, at least, and he never knew for certain whether those little broken fragments of warbly memory were founded in fact or dream.

The most useful advice he ever received about it was from Breathwaite, to whom he had confided his problem once, in a moment of lonely worry. Breathwaite had said simply, in English, "Many a good man's weakness."

That was the mantra that helped him through now: *Many a good man's weakness.* But not tonight. He had nursed the first half of his beer for nearly an hour. It hung like dishwater in the pint glass, sticky streaks of foam clinging to the walls of the glass as he tried Birgitte's cell phone number yet again. Her cheery voice kept coming on, and every time, at the first sound of it, he was duped into thinking it was really her voice; but then the canned electronic qualities crackled through and he killed the call without leaving a message.

The day had been torment for him ever since the excitement of this morning, the magnificent surprise of suddenly having her in his arms, her tongue in his mouth. *She* had initiated that part. How sweet and fresh and smooth and moist it felt slipping between his lips. His hand trembled now lifting his beer glass with the memory of it; he poured the rest of the lager down his throat in one long draft and signaled down into the bar for a refill, which was carried out promptly to him by a waiter with one arm. The waiter adeptly balanced the tray on the edge of the table, placed Jaeger's beer in front of him, made change for the fifty-crown note. Jaeger watched him return down into the bar and felt somehow the man was more complete, more balanced, more sturdy, than he himself was.

He had waited in his office as the long hours of morning dragged by, met with Breathwaite to plan the Irish speech. Kampman had told him to "tell Fred," but Fred already knew everything about it. So why had Kampman told him to tell Fred? To confuse him? To confuse Fred? Implement friction?

Back in his office, he phoned Birgitte's extension, but there was no reply, so he strolled down the corridor to where it crooked around the opposite end to her office. Her room was dark. Birgitte's secretary, Lise, a cute plump girl, tight jeans riding the big curves of hip and rump, smiled out at him from her door across the way. Above her smile, her brown eyes seemed knowing. "She had to take half a personal day, Harald."

"Oh? We had an appointment." Those knowing brown eyes; routine babble from the mouth while the eyes X-ray your soul. And that butt, which never worried about humility.

"She must've forgot, Harald. Anything I can do for you?"

You teasing bitch! You see my need and mock it! Or . . . ? "No, thanks, Lise. You think she's home?"

"Is it that urgent?" Lise asked.

He saw the calculations being shuffled around behind her keen brown gaze, so he shrugged it off. "No, no, it'll wait."

But it wouldn't wait. He had to know. He had to have her. As if on cue, he noticed that the music seeping out the door of the cellar bar behind him was Bob Marley asking himself over and over again if it was love that he was feeling.

Life's startling synchronicities. Or, he wondered, had he subconsciously heard the song and then thought that?

Against his better judgment, he swallowed a fourth of the new cold pint in one pull just as a woman with a plain appealing dark face and beautiful, perfect breasts walked past. Pear-fect. Pair-fect. The cups of them like two bonbonnieres filled with sweets. Her rump was gorgeous, too, and turned him speculative: *How can this form so move me?* But then he began to feel as though he were being unfaithful to Birgitte, so he pressed the redial button again, got the electronic voice.

Across the square, outside the window of a bookshop, a man and woman leaned the fronts of their bodies together and kissed passionately while waning sunlight glinted off the brown cobblestones. Jaeger felt simultaneous happiness and loneliness at the sight of them. He thought of Birgitte's tongue in his mouth. The young woman was pressing up against the young man's chest, and Jaeger was fascinated by the urgency of her movement. She was so hungry for his body. Her sweater pulled up over her backside so he could see how her blue black jeans conformed precisely to each of her buttocks and to the cleft between them as well. The material was all the way up her crack. He wondered how she did that. Ask a tailor, Please take these in so the denim goes right up my crack? Lucky tailor, to touch her there. How did it feel for her?

His phone rang, and he took it quickly, his heart lifting as he heard Birgitte's voice.

"You've been calling, Harald?"

"Why did you leave without telling me? We were supposed to meet."

A long silence ensued, and he was about to speak again, but she said, "I was confused."

"Birgitte, I need to see you."

"I can't."

"Birgitte, I need to see you. I *need* to see you."

Silence. Then: "Why?"

He rose from the table, walked away into the doorway of a clothing shop alongside the bar, whispering, "Birgitte, please, we've just got to talk this through. Please, meet me. Just half an hour. For a cup of coffee. I'm so worried about you."

Silence. Then: "Just half an hour."

"Just half an hour."

The only decent piece of furniture he had was the coffee table, a curved trapezoid slab of raw beech hardwood, low to the floor above an antique red brown Turkoman carpet he'd inherited from his mother. He had arranged half a dozen pillows around it and lit half a dozen candles in a silver-plated candelabra, set the table with antique mocha porcelain and hundred-year-old cognac glasses, also inherited, and a sterling silver bowl in which he'd placed the little olive tree his last girlfriend had given him at the end of the fortnight they'd lived together. It looked like a bonsai tree in the candlelight. He hoped this little island of elegance might distract her from the seediness of the rest of his tiny apartment.

What she said to him at the door after climbing four flights up, slightly winded, was, "I never thought you would be such a Bohemian," and suddenly he saw his apartment in another light, through her eyes—or her diplomacy. She slipped off her shoes at the door, and he heated water for Nescafé espresso. His heart leapt as she sat back on the pillows, her skirt crawling up her slender thighs so he could see the shadow between them. And one of her opulent breasts tipped downward beneath her furry sweater, a nippled nod. She smiled at the candles. "So romantic."

He cracked the seal of the split of VS Courvoisier he'd invested in. The scent of the cognac chuckling into the crystal snifters lifted to his nostrils as Al Green sang softly from the stereo. "Let's Stay Together."

He could see in the sheen of her burgundy eyes that there would be no pretense, no contest. She knew why she was here. Optimism sang in his blood as he reached across gingerly to touch her toes, took her foot in his palm, and began to massage it. She watched him curiously for a moment, then hummed the pleasure of her acceptance, and he bowed forward to tenderly kiss her toes.

"No!" She pulled her foot away. "I haven't showered."

"Birgitte," he whispered, "Birgitte, goddammit, *je t'adore*," and pressing his lips to the salty arch of her foot, he murmured, "God, God, I have wanted you so long." And they tumbled together on the carpet, his heart pounding at the wall of his chest, and nothing in the world existed beyond the glow of this candlelit oval in the dark of night.

Afterward, she lay with her cheek on his naked chest, and he stared up at the dim, crackled ceiling, thinking about the fact that when you're married, all the uncertainty of being single, of wondering whether you will have sex tonight, is gone; because when you're married you pretty well know for sure you're *not* going to have sex tonight. The thought tickled him, and he considered sharing it with her but feared she might misunderstand and think him cynical. He was not cynical. He was in recuperation from a loveless marriage. At this moment, hearing Al Green's baritone on repeat, he was as happy as he could ever be.

Birgitte excused herself to use the toilet, and he watched her naked, graceful body as she crossed through the candlelight to the little water closet. He considered how slightly disappointing it always was to see a woman naked, how their faces always sort of decomposed as masks fell away, barriers removed themselves. It was the barriers that excited, the masks. Or something deeper at the heart of what they were, of what the beautiful allure of their bodies seemed to be, to stand for, that which drove them to paint themselves, their faces, their fingernails, toenails, to adorn their bodies with jewels. He felt a desire to devour then that he knew could never really be fulfilled. And so there was nothing to do but try again in order to experience the ecstasy of hope that this time, this time, it might succeed, might happen, a moment of ecstasy that became permanent.

She emerged from the WC, looking around for her panties, but he reached up to her thigh. "Wait, wait, no." He caught her hand and drew her down, turned over, and put his face between her thighs, kissing the silken skin along the glowing flat plane that led to the dark plant of her delta. "So beautiful," he whispered, and again, whimpered, "So beautiful! *Angel!*"

She groaned, murmured his name. "Harald! Oh, Harald!"

"Birgitte! Birgitte!"

Yes!

Midnight, and he pleaded with her to stay the night.

"I can't, darling," she said.

"Darling? That's me?"

She nodded, smiling, and he wrapped his arms around her and buried his face into the flesh of her neck and moaned, "Jesus Christ, I cannot let you go."

She laughed, happy, looked into his eyes a long moment, then kissed him deeply on the mouth.

And then she was gone. He stood at the door, listening to her footsteps on the stair—pretty little feet!—descending, retreating from him, and finally the click of the door below, closing.

He sat up alone by his window, gazing out over the rooftops of North Bridge, sipping cognac, thinking, *I will marry her. I will. She will be mine forever. This time it will last. This is the woman of my life. To whom I will be faithful until I die. This time I will.*

"What happened with your marriage to Vita, Harald?" she had asked him as he lay on his back and she traced a fingertip through the hard creases of his abdomen.

"Yeah," he said, hands behind his head. "What happened?" And he tried to explain to her as the words he discovered in his mouth now explained it for himself: how he had married a woman he did not really love because she loved him. Or at least she wanted him. At the time he did not know what to do with his life, so he decided—not necessarily with full consciousness—it was better to be loved than to be lonely. Or at least better to be wanted than to be lonely.

It took very few years for him to realize that this was not the case, and it took even fewer years for her to perceive that he didn't love her. When she came to that realization, they already had two beautiful daughters, and her love turned cruel. To his surprise, battling to maintain his identity against her cruelty strengthened him, but at some point, he realized it was a battle to the death. She grew violent; finally he responded with violence; then there was nothing to do but file for divorce, which was the last cut to her pride.

The pain he had caused her hurt him far more than her violence or her cruelty ever could. To compensate, he gave her everything he had won in the dozen years they were together, everything that his newfound strength had gained for him. Which made her hate him even more. So she took not only the two houses, selling one and keeping the other, and all his money, but their two little girls as well, his little angels, and now he was at her mercy when she would allow him to see them beyond the alternate weekends the court had granted.

Well, he still had his strength, his passion. He knew he would never love again. "Women like that," he said. Birgitte smiled quizzically at the statement. "Most women," he modified. "For a while." As a result, he had

had several women passionately involved in trying to make him love them. When they realized it was a hopeless cause, they left him, right about the time he was ready for them to do so.

"A regular Don Juan," Birgitte said, not without admiration in her tone. Then, caressing his flat hard navel, she added more gently, "It sounds so terribly lonely."

He sipped his cognac. "Yes and no."

"What is yes, then, and what is no?"

"Well, the yes is that now . . ." He looked into her eyes. "Goddammit, Birgitte, I . . ." He shook his head, shed a tear into his fingers while her fingers played in the hair at his neck.

"How long can a man run from love?" he said. He touched her face. "You," he said, and peered deeply into her eyes. "Are you the woman of my life?"

22. Martin Kampman

Kampman ordered his limousine at six forty-five P.M., early for him, but it was Thursday, and he had a standing appointment every third Thursday evening. He shoved his dinner plate to the corner of his desk, knife and fork assembled at five o'clock on the bone china, swallowed the last of the wine (one glass a day), and clicked off his desk lamp. The entire headquarters floor of the Tank was quiet. And that's how it was to be on top. First in, last out. He stood there in the dark of his office, in the silence, and felt a sense of contentment, of power, rise within him and with it an agreeable tingle of anticipation. *Slowly and evenly does it.* Breathwaite and Jaeger were now in place. Marianne he would speak to in the morning. The others would follow.

I am in charge. I make the decisions. I steer the ship. I take care of things.

And with that, in the shadows around him, the pleasurable fear of what lay before him this evening.

The black company Mercedes waited at the curb on East Farimags Street outside the Tank. Karl, the chauffeur, stood beside the rear fender, his jacket buttoned, tie knot flush to his throat. He touched his cap. "Evening, Mr. Director."

Kampman nodded. "Evening, Karl. Everything well? Family?"

"Excellent, sir."

Then he was settled back in the black leather upholstery, glass partition between them. Silence. Karl would survive the cut. Breathwaite was in place—that was the biggest single savings, five and a half mil. More, actually, with the new agreement to let his son come in for two years. Family charity. Saved him a good quarter mil more. Jaeger would take over what they still needed of Breathwaite's function—without a raise for now, later with a cut. Kampman was pleased with the day's work. He was even more pleased to be free of the oversize, pompous oaf. Much too long in the tooth. No one should be allowed to stay more than ten years, a dozen at best. Jaeger would soon be up for review. If young Breathwaite was quick enough and less oafish than his father and didn't smoke, he might be good to take over Jaeger's functions at half the price. But the key now would be the secretaries. There were forty of them in the Tank, earning between a quarter mil and 350,000. And big envelopes of time during which they did nothing but hold meetings that in fact were sessions of the coffee club. Gossip sharing, but also sessions of strategy planning, on how to milk the Tank for more—on Tank time. *Paid* Tank time.

Each of thirty of those secretaries was attached to one case handler, consultant, or department head, a completely unnecessary luxury in the age of the personal computer. With the implementation of role-efficient procedures, each of those thirty could serve three or four, and the other twenty, who were serving two or three, could be serving four or five. A minimum savings right there of thirty million or more. In the next round. And the next round after that to slice away unnecessary case handlers, consultants, and department heads. Then unnecessary departments. In five years' time, the Tank would be sailing at racing trim, and Kampman would have earned his negotiated bonus before moving on.

As Karl signaled left on Bernstorffs Way and turned onto Tonysvej, Kampman felt the glitter in his own eyes as he contemplated the remainder of the evening.

"Have a good night, Mr. Director," Karl said, holding the limo door for him.

Kampman nodded. "Remember me to your family, Karl."

One side of the double garage door was up, and the space where he normally parked his silver BMW stood empty. He stepped into the space. Only Karen's orange Toyota was there. He let himself in through the garage entry, which opened onto a vestibule that gave access to the kitchen. He stood there amid the row of family Wellingtons, rain capes, hats, and garden workclothes. There were voices from the kitchen. Annoying.

Adam and the new au pair girl, Jytte, were seated at the kitchen table, a cozy-draped teapot between them.

Kampman smiled at Jytte. "Overtime?"

"Karen asked me to stay on and watch the twins. There was a meeting she forgot."

"Well, no need to keep you up so late. Adam can watch the twins, can't you, son?"

Adam's mouth jerked into a smile. "Uh, sure, Dad, I could do that."

Jyttle looked skeptical. "I don't know. Karen asked *me*. . . ."

Kampman chuckled. "It's okay. Believe me." He turned the heat of his smile on her. "I can drop you off on the way to my meeting."

23. Adam Kampman

Adam poured another cup of tea, spooned in sugar, and watched his father touch Jytte's elbow to guide her out the kitchen door. It pissed him off, that touch. *Fuck you, Dad*, he thought. *Keep your hands off of her.*

His father glanced back with a smile. His nose twitched. "Beer," he said. Adam saw that Jytte was watching. Her eyes seemed to question him, to challenge him to defend himself.

"I had a beer with a friend."

"Fine. Who?"

"A fellow I met."

His father did not pursue the matter, but Adam could see he was not done with it. He didn't want to tell him who it was. He didn't want to tell him anything. Not until he had his thoughts better organized.

"Tell your mom not to wait up. I'll be beat when I get back. I'll probably sleep in the basement room so I don't disturb her."

Adam listened to the rustle of their movements through the boot room, heard Jytte say something, but could not make out the words. Sound of his father's voice and the smacking of the door. Then the whir of the garage door on its automatic switch, the Toyota ignition, and the growl of its engine backing out the drive.

Have a good day, son?

Yeah, Dad. I killed my future.

Good for you, sonny! What else did you do?

Went to a bar in North Port.

Great! Was it fun?

It was fucking terrific! I drank beers with my new friend, Jes. And he introduced me to his friends there. And you know what he said when he introduced me? He said, "This is my friend Adam." There was this tall skinny funny guy named Bjørn and a guy they call Zack who owns a big farm in Jutland, and he invited me to come stay there anytime for as long as I want. They really liked me, and I told them I quit school today and they cheered and bought me a Gammel Dansk, and we toasted my freedom. They invited me to come back again tomorrow, and you know what else? I felt so good when I got home that I had this great con-versation with Jytte, and I told her all about everything, and she listened to all of it, and I could see in her eyes and in her smile that she liked me and that she thought it all sounded exciting, and you know what else? She's going to meet me in North Port tomorrow, and she's coming with me to the North Bodega.

She's coming with me.

So you see, Dad: My new future is starting already. I was right. You were wrong. And Jes told me about what you do for a living. You fire people. How come I never knew that before, Dad? You keep it a secret? Ashamed, maybe? 'Cause I sure am.

The tea was lukewarm, but it quenched the arid thirst of his mouth left there by the beers and schnapps. He wondered if there was any beer in the house. Sometimes when his mother and father had dinner guests, after the coffee, cold drinks would be served and cold bottles of beer. Maybe there were some down in the basement refrigerator, but there was a pad-lock on that. Where did he hide the key? If Adam could find it, he could get Jes to make a copy for him.

The thought of Jes made him smile, remembering how at the bar Zack had said, "Speak to us of the sayings of Jalâl, O wise Jes."

And Jes got them all laughing. He got this expression on his face that made him look foreign and raised one hand like some kind of Arab priest or something and said, "Those of whom God has made apes and swine and slaves of seduction, theirs is indeed an evil state." And, "The life of this world is nothing but play and sport."

"Heard," little muscular Zack shouted in Danish. "Heard!" And he lifted his beer and all of them were cracking up with a high giggling laughter that made Adam feel a certainty he had not known since he was a child, perhaps had never known before.

"Adam?"

The twins stood at the kitchen door in their white nightdresses, bare-foot, with big shy hopeful eyes. "Will you read to us?"

The sight of them filled him with a sadness he did not understand. *Poor kids*, he thought. *Poor sweet little kids.* "Sure," he said. "Sure I will." And he followed them up the stairs to their room.

24. Martin Kampman

Kampman looked from the wheel to the girl as he pulled out onto Tonys-vej. "You ought to get yourself a bicycle," he said.

"I have one. My parents are sending it from Tønder." She sat far from him, pressed up against the door.

He glanced at her with a smile. "Are you afraid of me?"

"No."

He chuckled, lifting and dropping his shoulders rhythmically. "Good." He could feel himself relaxing already in the thought of where he was headed. "What do you think of me?" he asked.

"Nothing," she said.

Kampman laughed again. "See? You *are* afraid of me. You're afraid to tell me what you think of me."

"Being polite is not the same as being afraid."

Another laugh barked from his throat, and suddenly he was interested in what might be concealed behind her huffy face. She was warm to everyone in the house except him. To him she was only polite, and he could sense she disliked him. Or perhaps she was just afraid of men in general. Maybe her father had given her a hard time. He glanced at the long slim line of her leg, crossed over the other, then up at her breasts, which looked like half oranges pressing against her aquamarine T-shirt. She pulled the lapels of her jacket together and zipped it up, and he turned to her face with a smile on his lips aimed to tell her he could see her thoughts and acknowledging that she had interpreted his correctly.

"Are you a slave to good manners, then?"

"It's the way we are. But if someone is impolite or naughty to me, he'll get to know it pretty fast."

"*Naughty?* I like that." He stopped for a light at Trianglen, then turned up East Bridge Street, hooked right on Århus. "Just for fun, try just once to take off the mask of your good manners. Just like that. Like removing a hat. And tell me what you think of me. Open and free. I won't hold it against you. On the contrary."

"Okay," she said. "I think you're not very nice."

This was good. "And why should I be nice?"

"It's nice to be nice."

He turned left at the foot of Århus Street. "Not for me it's not. If I went around being nice all day, the company I'm responsible for would go right down the slippery slope. I'm not paid to be nice. I'm paid to run an organization. Everyone else is free to go around being nice. My job is to take care of things."

They were on Strandboulevarden now.

"It's just up there," she said, "where the red mailbox is on the wall by the tall windows. That's my room right there."

He pulled in along the curb. "Nice place," he said. "One of those high-ceilinged places with fancy plaster moldings. Rent-controlled."

"I just have a room."

"What do you give for it?"

"Isn't that a personal question?"

"Is your room furnished?"

"Yes," she said with annoyance. "Why?"

"Because I bet you're paying two thirds of the rent on that whole apartment. If your room is furnished, the law allows that. So you get to live in one fifth of the place and pay two thirds of the rent. That's not very nice, either, is it?" He grinned and leaned across to open the door for her, being careful not to touch her.

"Thanks for the ride," she snapped.

"You should thank me for the lesson. Think about it."

He watched her let herself into the front door of the building, saw the lobby light come on, then a few moments later the light in the first window to the right of the front door on the ground floor—just as she had said, right alongside the mailbox. Funny she would have told him that. Volunteer information. To someone who was not nice. He could see the outline of her body behind the long-curtained window. One of the vent windows up top was open. *Typical Jutland girl. Sleeps in a cold room. Fresh.*

Clutching, he threw the Toyota into gear and pulled out.

He parked up near the Teachers College, around from the Radiometer offices, and sat behind the wheel, thinking. He was excited. The girl had excited him. He would have to talk to Karen about her, about letting her go. *Are you certain she's suitable? She seems to be getting a little too friendly with Adam.* He chuckled mirthlessly, lifting and dropping his shoulders.

The dashboard clock said eight. He would be late. The thought brought a bemused smile to his lips. He raised his haunch to get his billfold from the hip pocket of his runners, removed two thousand-crown notes and three hundred-crown notes, which he folded and buttoned into the inner pocket of his jacket. Then he chucked the billfold and his omega wristwatch into the glove compartment and locked it. He zipped his key ring into the hidden collar pocket inside his jacket, pulled his halfpenny running cap low on his forehead, and got out of the car.

Through the dark chill autumn evening, alongside Emdrup Pond he jogged, inhaling the crisp, mulchy air as anticipation built in his blood, in his lungs. He was trembling as he came out into the light of the streetlamps on Emdrup Way, past a row of old yellow-brick apartment houses to a newer building, red brick, clean, well lighted.

He rang, spoke into the two-way, was buzzed in, crossed the bright lobby, and rode the elevator to the third floor, where he pressed the bell on an unmarked door. He was admitted by a smiling middle-aged woman, dressed more like a receptionist than the receptionist at the Tank—primly middle-class, though with a touch of silk-and-wool British elegance. He liked that. It excited him. He already had two of the five notes folded in his palm, two of the hundreds, and he passed them to her.

She thanked him, counting them quickly, discreetly, then gave him a large plush black towel and showed him to a door in the hall. "You can change there, honey," she said, and returned to her place in an armchair by the door, took a magazine from the tabletop beside it. *See and Hear.* Kampman could see, on the cover, a picture of the crown prince and princess. "Honey," she had called him. Again. Vulgar. It blemished his entry. When he left, later, he would slip her the last hundred and tell her, for next time, not to call him honey. He wanted this to be perfect, and that one detail was bothering.

Now he entered the dressing room and locked the one door behind him. *The undressing room,* he thought. His hands trembled as he took off his clothes and folded them on a chair, and his knees felt loose as he tapped on the other door.

A woman's voice said, "Come."

He watched his hand shake as it rose to turn the knob. The room was tastefully furnished, a little old-fashioned, a parlor. A long, slender woman sat in an armchair in the center of a red Persian carpet, her long, bare legs crossed. She was naked but for a narrow, black-leather mask. Blue eyes watched him from the slits in the mask.

He looked at her body.

"Lower your gaze," she said.

He did as he was told.

"You're late."

"I—"

"Be still."

He shut his mouth.

She motioned him forward with her forehead. "You will regret that," she said.

FRIDAY

Vita Nuova

25. Martin Kampman

Every third Friday was Kampman's day to sleep in. He woke in the basement guest room, opened his eyes to the white ceiling, and reached for the alarm watch he had set for seven.

Six fifty-eight.

He smiled, deactivated it before it could ring. Then, gazing at the blank screen of the ceiling, he gingerly stretched his limbs beneath the covers. Each detail of his body's discomfort contained a minuscule fragment of mystery he knew he must push from his consciousness lest he become morbidly fascinated by it. If he dawdled here, savoring it, reconstructing what was now behind him, he would surrender force to the experience, rather than winning from it. Abruptly he threw off the bedclothes and limped naked into the bathroom, turned the cold tap on full, and willed himself beneath it, counting slowly. Only at sixty did he allow himself to begin to add warm water to the stream, soaping himself gingerly, refusing to wince when it hurt. *Of course it hurts; I am stronger than pain.*

Dressed and shaven, he went straight up to Adam's bedroom, meticulously stifling the annoyance that was already asserting itself at his anticipation of having to wake the boy even though he had also been allowed to sleep an extra two hours today. Lazy.

Adam's bed was empty, unmade. Adam was not in the room. Adam was not in the bathroom. The twins were still asleep, and Adam was not in there, either.

Back down the stairs to the kitchen, where he could hear Karen fussing about. He smelled coffee.

"Are you limping?" she asked when she saw him.

"Strained a muscle. It's nothing. Where's Adam?"

"He was off early today."

Kampman blinked, annoyed. Something fishy here. "Off to where?"

"Why, to classes, I presume."

Fishy.

He took the BMW and was in his office at the Tank by eight twenty. Even that late, he was still the first one in. No, Clausen was at his desk.

"Morning, Mr. Director," he said as Kampman passed his doorless office.

Kampman drew the corners of his mouth into a little smile. "Early bird."

"Yes, sir."

26. Harald Jaeger

At last there was hope, at last the chance for love, for Birgitte, a woman he could love. And his little girls liked her, too. "You're nice," Hanne had said to her in the deer park. Spontaneously. And today he could tell them, hint to them that they might be seeing more of Birgitte—maybe even this evening. Jaeger had taken a half personal day to get a head start on his weekend with his little angels. He opened the white wrought-iron gate and stepped into the little front garden of the house he had owned for ten years and to which he no longer even possessed a key. The grass, front and back, was still green and tight as a golf course. Vita's pride. She practiced her putting here. *Galf*, she called it, a parody of Gentoftian High Danish that to Jaeger was beginning to sound less like a parody than an assimilation. Let her. She had taken up golf after their split. He pictured himself telling her, *Well, some people work and some play*, but quickly dismissed the thought. Nothing but trouble in that direction.

Beneath his arm he had a little gift for her, a book of golf cartoons wrapped in silver paper and tied with a dark green ribbon. Last time he came, he'd got the idea of bringing a little present as a surprise and saw that the gesture had startled and moved her, and he was eager to repeat that success.

He gazed from the grass to the agreeably uneven assortment of trees—larch, lilac, pine, the brittle rose vines that in spring and summer blossomed with fat blooms of red, yellow, white. The forsythia hedge was nearly bald now in the gray early afternoon, but in the eye of memory he saw it as an explosion of bright yellow late April leaves, his two yellow-haired baby girls standing before it with their big, sweet smiles. Returning here was always like a dream fragment for him, the unreal real. A return to the life he had always assumed temporary until it took root, grew clinging vines he had to hack away, and somehow he had managed not to realize the result would be pain, blood. Yet had he not decided—*now! quick!*—he was certain they all would have died slowly and with a greater, all-consuming pain.

"I feel so fucking guilty," he had told his psychologist.

"So feel guilty for a moment, then move on. The guilt helps no one. Learn from it."

"But I did a terrible thing. To marry a woman I didn't love was—"

"The mistake of a confused man. Move on."

"But the babies . . ."

"As a very wise man once said, Harald: Shit happens. Move on."

Now he moved on down the garden path to the neat white front door with its neat rectangle of little square white-curtained windows. He pressed the bell and listened to its pleasant chime.

Vita opened the door wide and looked at him. Then she closed it halfway and kept staring. She wore tailored jeans and a tailored tweed jacket. She looked terrific. He held out the gift. "Hi," he said. "How are you? How are the girls? Here's a little present for you."

She did not take the package and she did not speak, only stared at him, and she did not step aside to let him enter.

"You look great," he said. "Have you lost weight?"

Vita was slim as an eel, with close-cropped yellow hair that glittered silver. She was eight years older than Jaeger. She let the question hang in the air. Then she said, "What have you been up to? Who is she? I can see you've met someone. Again."

It did not occur to Jaeger that he did not have to answer. "Do you remember Birgitte Sommer?"

"From your office? She's married."

"We . . . well, it just kind of happened. I—"

"Oh, I know all about you and things that just happen. You really take the bloody biscuit. You desert one wife, then steal one from another man. Do they have children, too?"

"No, I—"

"Because I ought to warn her not to let you be alone with them."

"What do—"

"I have to ask you straight out now, and I want an honest answer."

"What? I—"

"Did you bathe the girls last time you had them?"

It took a moment for the question to make sense to him. Was she complaining that they were dirty when he returned them to her? Then he remembered he had taken them to the deer park and it was muddy, so he'd washed them under the telephone shower back at his place. "Well, yes, I . . ."

She stared at him, lips slightly parted with distaste, eyes narrowed, and she whispered, "How could you do that? To your own daughters."

"What are you . . . They're my daughters . . . they needed a bath . . ."

"They do *not* need to have you undressing them and . . . You disgust me."

"Where are they? It's my weekend to—"

"You will not see them. I have to consider what to do about this now."

"You can't do this. I'll complain to the—"

"Go ahead. And I will tell them what you did."

"What I did? I didn't do anything. I gave them a bath because they were muddy. I sprayed them with the telephone shower. There was nothing."

"I knew you were sick, but I really never expected *this*. Now get out of here." And she closed the door.

Jaeger was trembling. He rang the bell, knocked. "Vita, you can't do—"

The door opened again, and Jaeger started. It was not Vita but her father, Frank, a short muscular man with kinky yellow hair and a broad, porcine face. He stepped close, and Jaeger could smell coffee on his breath.

"What do *you* want?" he demanded.

Jaeger was less afraid of the man than of what he himself might do to him. He felt his right fist ball up. His breath was ragged, and he saw the bulky little man as a door behind a door blocking him from his daughters. He wanted to bury his fist right dead in the middle of the piggy face. Words rasped from his throat in a grating whisper.

"I want to see my daughters!"

"You can get the hell out of here," Frank snapped. "We know what went on. It's not going to happen again."

"That's a fucking lie, Frank. Repeat it, and I'll smash your fucking face for you!"

Frank spoke over his shoulder as he shoved the door between them. "Call the police, Vita! He's violent!"

Jaeger put his shoulder to the door, and they struggled from each side of it. Moving his foot for traction, he lost his balance and the door slammed on his little finger. He yelled out with pain. The door opened a crack, and

Frank muttered, "Sorry," then slammed it again and the finger was caught once more. Jaeger bellowed, and the door opened a crack so he could pull his finger free. "Sorry," Frank muttered again, and shut the door.

Jaeger heard the dead bolt mesh shut, and he stood there on the little brick stoop, cradling his injured finger, muttering, "Fuck fuck fuck fuck," and felt the shame of tears rolling from his eyes.

27. Frederick Breathwaite

Now the autumn really sinks down around us, Breathwaite thought, standing on Queen Louise's Bridge, gazing out over the gunmetal gray water of Peblinge Lake. Already heavy dusk at five thirty P.M. The damp autumn smell off the mossy water filled his nose and touched his heart with chill fingers. Leaves of yellow, red, and brown lay scattered across wet green grass on the bank. He shuffled through big soggy yellow leaves heaped on the bridge walk, in the gutter, like scuffling through soggy cornflakes. He remembered that this Sunday, daylight savings time would end. *What is it now, do we win an hour or lose one?* Spring ahead, fall back. Curiously he observed his own melancholy; it had been so many years since he'd felt himself this alone. Facing disaster. Too strong a word? What else to call it?

He began walking again, north, paused just before the embankment to look at a stone sculpture of a young man and woman who sat facing each other, leaning forward to peer into each other's faces. The young man had his elbows on his knees, palms on his cheeks; the girl had elbows on knees and palms joined, wringing her hands, which were extended toward the boy. Their gaze was fixed on each other—or rather, she gazed at him, while his glance was slightly downcast. The lake water glistened between them, and Breathwaite could see the Lake Pavilion on the far bank, Codan building rising behind it like a sore thumb. He considered the girl and boy gazing at each other. A pair of opposites. *We have all come from lovers. For what purpose? To become lovers. Mate. Like mayflies. Ephemerals. Infinite motion. What's it called? Chain of . . . No, chain reaction. Cause and effect and cause. What came first, the penis or the egg? Of what fucking use are we?*

Some sensation at his back turned him. On the other side of the bridge, several people were standing in a loose row, leaning back against the railing, the dusky lake behind them, but they were facing in his direction. A chill crawled over his flesh, a distinct chill, infusing the moment with a distressing sense that he had been caught in some subliminal ghostly confusion. The hair on his body lifted. Were they looking at him?

His eyes flicked from face to face—man, woman; man, woman; man, woman. Six of them. Three couples, they seemed to be. As if moved by his thought, their bodies regrouped, man to woman, as if to demonstrate that they were indeed three couples.

Was he going mad? It almost looked like some scene from a Hollywood musical. He almost expected them to begin to dance, sing, tango—an older couple, sixties, perhaps, the man with a battered leather satchel beneath his arm, woman in a blue wool coat; a couple in their forties, man in a leather jacket, cap backward on his head; another couple somewhere between, dark-haired man wearing a gray beret with a woman whose blue eyes were so light that Breathwaite could see them shining across in the dark all the way from where he stood.

Breathwaite's confusion focused. He smiled. *Dance*, he thought. *Turn into Gene Kelly and Debbie Reynolds and Fred fucking Astaire and whoever else.* Then, as though they had never been looking at him at all, the three couples turned and moved away along the bridge, two of them in one direction, one in the other, melding into the after-work pedestrian traffic.

They were gone.

Am I going nuts?

He glanced back at the sculpture: stone girl and stone boy peering at each other. Lovers on the bridge. *We have all come from lovers. For what purpose?* He thought of Kis. Sweet Kis. Sweet angel. *Please God don't let her love me so much that I hurt her.* Then he noticed the date at the base of the sculpture: 1942. During the German occupation. *So that's the story. The impotence of their love against a mad world.*

Off Queen Louise's Bridge to North Bridge Street and left on Blågårds Street to the square to visit Jes. He thought of phoning first, but that would only give the boy a chance to beg off. *On my way out, Dad. Can't wait. Another time. Sorry.* Catch him by surprise. Take the chance and hope he's home, hope for the best, hope.

Listen, son, you've got to listen to me. And use your head. I've got an opportunity for you that you can parlay into a berth for life. Funny expression, *berth.* Don't use it. He'll say, *I don't want a berth, Dad. I don't want to spend my life sleeping. I want to wake up.*

Sure, sure. Truist bullshit. *This is real life we're talking about here. Not airy fairy floss. You've got a head on your shoulders. This job is a real shot at life. You'll travel. You'll earn good money. Don't throw everything away because you don't like the way the world is screwed together.*

I want to make a difference.

This will make a difference for you.

He stopped outside the building. Sooty gray stone that needed sand-blasting. Badly. *They'll gentrify this square in no time. Triple in value. He'll be okay. If he takes the job and gets his butt back in school.*

Breathwaite stared at the bell register for a moment. Instead of Jes's name, alongside the bell it said, "HVT6."

Breathwaite smirked—*High Value Target 6*—decided he needed fortification, and stepped into the Café Flora a couple of doors down, ordered a quadruple Tullamore at the bar.

The very young barmaid looked startled. *Thinks I'm some rich fuck. Or dangerous, maybe.* "On the rocks, please."

"The *what*?"

"The rocks. On ice cubes."

"Just ice cubes? Nothing else? No lemon?"

"Oh, Jesus, no. Just ice cubes." *This is not fortifying me.* "Just ice." *Justice.* "Please."

She took some time studying the bottles on the shelf behind her.

"Second shelf, fourth from the right," he said. "No, not that, that's bourbon, the next one . . . Right." He watched her carefully pour four two-centiliter measures into the glass, then dip her fingers into an ice bucket and scoop out a single cube. Breathwaite laid a hundred on the bar and laughed at himself for perceiving this as another example of his luck gone sour. *The center cannot hold.* He tipped her five crowns for the finger sweat bonus and swished the whiskey in the glass to let the rapidly melting little cube chill it, then threw it back in two snaps and returned to the door of Jes's building.

Instead of ringing Jes's bell, he rang another at random, on the third floor, not to alert Jes yet. *No warning. Just Dad there at the door, in your face.* Whoever it was mercifully buzzed him in, and he began the long, slow climb to his son's sixth-floor walk-up.

On three, he paused to catch his wind. A door opened, and a young man's shaven head ducked out.

"Sorry," Breathwaite wheezed. "I must have rung you by mistake." He pointed upward. Without a word, the young man's bald head disappeared behind his shabby door again. On the fourth, Breathwaite began to hear noise, music from above. He was feeling the climb. Too many cigars, even if he didn't inhale. Much. Well, that was another cozy comfort that would regulate itself with the economy. Start smoking El Cheapos. Or quit altogether. Sit around and chew your fingernails instead. Free habit. Bite yourself.

On five, the noise grew louder, and louder still as he ascended the sixth flight. He stood on the landing outside Jes's door, waiting for his lungs and heart to quiet down. Stenciled in white paint along one edge of the door were the words *SUCCES SUCKS*.

Learn how to fucking spell! Or was that some kind of intentional irony?

He could not avoid hearing the voices from within, punctuated by short bursts of jazz.

"Listen to this, listen to this!" Jes's voice, and then the sound of a record, discordant horns and a dramatic voice, recorded apparently, speaking in English, with urgency, shouting that he wanted to slit the bellies of frigid women, to pour gasoline down chimneys, to poison dogs; shouting accusations that a drunken cherub had been murdered, that the murderer was a son of a bitch in a Brooks Brothers suit . . .

Breathwaite was surprised then to hear laughter from several mouths, male and female, it sounded like. What the hell was funny about that? Breathwaite opened the lapel of his Burberry and looked at the jacket of his suit. It was not Brooks Brothers, but they would hardly know the difference.

He sighed. Then he turned back and descended the stairs. The descent was easier.

Another quadruple Tullamore in Flora. The girl remembered this time and gave him two ice cubes dug out with a tablespoon. He sat by the window and smoked, nursing the whiskey. *Try again tomorrow. Or the next day. Don't take no for an answer.* There was a copy of the *BT* tabloid folded on the vacant table beside him. He leafed through it as he sipped the whiskey and enjoyed his Wintermans. That was maybe cheap enough, Wintermans. He could ration himself.

The news in *BT* was bad enough to match the autumn gray evening. War, torture, murder, rape, street violence, hospital waiting lists, racism, a shooting in Ålborg—gang execution—and suicide bombers in Palestine and Baghdad. A small item in the lower corner of one page caught his eye: "Police: Mysterious Death Explained. Cancer Diagnosis." It told the story that the mystery surrounding a man who had been found dead under suspicious circumstances had been solved when his doctor stepped forward to explain the man had recently been diagnosed with cancer of the spleen. The breach of confidentiality was condoned by the police and medical profession. Apparent suicide. The man's wife was quoted as expressing understanding that he had wished to spare himself from a long and painful death.

Interesting.

A thought fleeted across his consciousness: those couples on the bridge. Musical comedy. But they hadn't been smiling.

Then it was gone.

28. Adam Kampman

Adam squatted before the shelves of Jes's brick-and-plank bookcases, examining the titles and the bindings. They stirred a hunger in him. Not many of the author's names were familiar, but there were a few he recognized from school: Kerouac, Baudelaire, Neruda, Rimbaud. The ones he didn't recognize at all intrigued him even more. Still others he knew well—Michael Strunge, Dan Turèll—but could remember little he had actually read of theirs. But Jes knew them. He quoted them left and right, along with his sayings of Jalâl and another Eastern poet he called Rumi:

> *We have many barrels of wine.*
> *People say we have no future.*
> *That is fine with us.*

The three of them were warming up here in Jes's apartment before going on to the North Bodega on Solitude Way, which Adam had promised to show to Jytte. She had never been into a serving house in Copenhagen and had seemed fascinated when he'd told her about it the night before. They met today at Pussy Galore to wait for Jes to get out of work in the key-and-heel bar. Adam ordered beer for the two of them and paid with money he had taken from his savings account. It seemed so simple. It was *his* account, *his* money that his father had forced him to save up ever since he could remember.

Fifteen percent of everything you get—birthday money, Christmas money, Easter money, anything you earn—goes into the account, and you don't touch it. You let it grow. That's how you build a fortune. Let your money earn money and don't let yourself be distracted by the expensive gadgets kids your age waste their time and money on.

When he was still very young, it had occurred to him to ask, "If you never use it, what is it for?"

"For the future."

"When is the future?"

"You will know it when you get there. And this way you'll be ready for it."

Now that he had started his future, it seemed appropriate to make a withdrawal. There were 177,000 crowns in the account, but most of it was in long-term bonds that Adam could not touch until he was eighteen, in three months. But seventeen thousand had been available. His father had had him sign papers to invest in long-term bonds every time there was an accumulation of twenty thousand. This morning, Adam had filled out a withdrawal slip for two thousand, then torn it up and filled one out for seven thousand. Then he'd added a one in front of the seven, shoved the slip across to the teller, and held his breath.

"You want this in cash?"

"Yeah."

"How?"

"In cash. In money."

"Yes, Mr. Kampman, but large notes or small?"

Mister! "Some of each."

He had also taken his passport with him just in case. He figured he could go just about anywhere he wanted with that much money, and Jytte didn't have to be at work again before Monday. If he wanted to, he could just invite her to come away somewhere with him. He could hide away until he was eighteen—that was only three months away—and cash in all the bonds. He could live for a long time on 160,000 crowns. He could maybe go to Jes's friend's farmhouse in Jutland and hide away there until he was eighteen. Maybe Jytte would come with him. Suddenly everything seemed possible. He would never have to see his father again. He could maybe start some kind of business. Maybe he could buy a sausage wagon. He could have a lot of books in the wagon and sit there and read all day in between customers, read things like the poems Jes had recited and the ones he played on his CD player with the strange jazz music behind the voices. Someone named Ferlinghetti. And Kenneth Rexroth.

Jes came out of the kitchen with three more green bottles of beer, which he opened by pressing his cigarette lighter against the cap, and the three of them raised the bottles, clanked them together. Another record was playing now, some kind of blues, where a man sang, *Going to Chicago, baby / Sorry I can't take you. / Ain't no room in Chicago / Fo a monkey-face woman like you . . .*

Jytte laughed so she had to spit her beer back into the bottle. The candlelight gleamed in the green glass and in the wet on her lips, and Adam watched sidewise from the bookcase. She was so beautiful.

Jes put on another record and started dancing with her. It was a slow song by Bob Marley, and Jytte pulled away from him with a skeptical smile. "No woman, no cry? Is that how you think?"

"People don't understand that song," Jes said. "It's a tender song of admiration for a woman, telling her not to cry."

Adam sat in a broken cane-seated chair and flipped through a book of photographs by someone named Man Ray. Strange pictures, some of naked women. Now Jes and Jytte danced faster to "I Shot the Sheriff," and Jytte asked, "What is that supposed to mean, anyway? That he didn't shoot the deputy? Why?"

"You know why?" Jes said. "You want to know why? Why do you think?"

"How do I know? Maybe the deputy is cute."

Jes laughed. "*You're* the cute one. I'll tell you why I think. 'Cause the deputy is a subaltern."

"A what?"

"The deputy is subordinate to the sheriff. The sheriff is the guy who's responsible. He's the repressive authority. The colonialist. The way I see it, the narrator in the song is out to cut off the head of the oppressor."

"Well, doesn't the sheriff work for somebody, too?"

"It's a metaphor, Jytte," Jes said, pushing his face close to hers, and Adam could see they were going to kiss. He buried his own face in a thin little black-and-white paperback titled *Howl*. On the first page it said, "Unscrew the locks from their doors! Unscrew the doors themselves from their jambs!"

He flipped further forward, read a long kind of chant which repeated the word "holy" about twenty times and then went on to name a bunch of body parts that were holy—the skin, nose, tongue, cock, hand, asshole, and then that everyone is an angel.

But even as his eyes took in the words with amazement and excitement and wonder, he could not ignore his awareness that Jes and Jytte were moving into the next room. He heard Jes whisper something to her, and then he could no longer concentrate on the page as his ears tried to filter through Bob Marley's song to what was happening in the next room. He heard a distant, audible gasp and knew instinctively it was Jytte and what it meant.

He put his hand over his eyes, but he could not stop listening. He rose and stood in the middle of the bare wood floor. There were empty beer bottles and heaped ashtrays and stacks of CDs and CD cases, empty pizza boxes and books and magazines and newspapers everywhere. The record ended. He heard Jytte gasp again, more clearly, then whimper. He looked at his beer bottle where he had placed it on the floor alongside three tall, thick candles, their flames guttering. He leaned down and, one by one, blew out the candles, then quietly let himself out the door.

29. Birgitte Sommer

Hunched forward on the leather sofa, Lars sat watching the TV news. The musty training suit from ALDI hung around him like a sour robe, and his little finger dug up into one nostril. Birgitte watched from the shadow of the living room doorway. He took the pinky out of his nose and studied it for a moment, then put it between his lips. She turned away, swallowing so that she would not gag, before stepping out into the half-light from the flickering TV screen.

"I'll be late," she said.

He removed his finger and held it down by his side. Was he wiping something on the leather of the sofa? He said nothing. She watched his face in profile, slack and self-absorbed, aimed at the screen.

"There are some meatballs defrosting in the fridge," she said. "And a fresh pack of dark rye," she added, annoyed with herself for bothering. Let him feed himself. Still he said nothing. Her impulse was to just walk out, but she hadn't told her lie yet. Then it occurred to her that he was intentionally denying her an opportunity to tell the lie, that he was out-maneuvering her. The thought startled her, that a thinking being might be home after all behind that oblivious facade. Now the finger was up in the nostril again.

"Do you think you could stop picking your nose long enough to say good night?" she said, more harshly than she intended.

The hand came down again as he turned to face her. "What?"

"I said I'll be late."

His gaze moved down her body, her leather jacket and tight gray pencil skirt, dark stockings. "Lot of sudden meetings, aren't there?"

"It's a dinner. I told you about it months ago. You should write things in your calendar." It was so easy to lie to a man who never listened to her. To her surprise, the lie was pleasant in her mouth. Like a numbing poison to spit into his despicably self-absorbed face. How had she managed not to consider this for so long? How strange the way things happened. Slow, invisible changes, a crack spreading infinitesimally until suddenly the wall breaks down and you see the man you live with is a stranger. Worse than a stranger.

"I thought the dinner was yesterday."

"No. I told you. That was a strategy meeting."

He looked at her again. A fragment of a smile touched his lips. "Strategy?" Then he looked back at the screen. She opened her mouth to speak, but his face turned abruptly to her again. "Tell me," he said, "is somebody fucking you?" His face showed no emotion.

She smiled, could feel the meanness of it. "No," she said. "Unfortunately nobody is fucking me, and that's a big problem."

"So you're going out to solve it."

"No. As I told you months ago, I'm going out to a dinner."

"Where?"

"North Port, if you'd like to know."

"Where?"

"You're suddenly so interested. At the Barcelona."

"Who is it for?"

"It's a colleague's fortieth birthday."

"Who?"

"Harald Jaeger."

"Didn't he just get divorced?"

She could think of nothing to say, so she said, "What is this about, Lars? You've been ignoring me for months and suddenly you're suspicious. Well, are *you* fucking somebody? Since that's the way you think and the word you use. Are you?"

"I'll drive you to the Barcelona. I'll come in and say happy birthday to Harald."

"No, you won't."

Now he was on his feet, moving toward her, and her head tipped back to look up into his face, the sudden contortion of his mouth. "You're fucking somebody, you bitch, and you're not getting away with it!" He grabbed her arm.

She stumbled back, jerking her arm from his grasp. "You bastard! Get away from me!" But he had both her arms now, and he dragged her forward off balance toward the sofa. She flailed her arms, unable to break from his grip. "You bastard, get your filthy snot fingers off me, you *smell*, you *stink*!" He was pushing her down on the sofa and let go with one hand, which he shoved up inside her skirt, freeing her one hand, which she balled into a fist and hammered down on the side of his head.

He yelled, and both palms flew to his face. "My ear! You punched me right in the ear! I'm deaf! You made me deaf!"

She was on her feet now, but the certainty of her disdain had abandoned her. She stood over him, reaching, but stopped short of touching him. "Are you all right?" she asked stiffly.

"No!" He sat hunched, palm cupped on his left ear, lifting it away to move his head, then covering the ear again, moving the palm away. Then he leapt to his feet and glared at her, his face trembling with indignation. He looked like a little boy on the verge of furious tears. She almost smiled, he looked so silly.

"Are you crying?" she asked.

"No!" he bawled, and spun away, hurried toward the stairway, took the steps two at a time, and she heard the bedroom door slam shut.

In their six years together, she had never seen Lars like this before. She thought of that expression on his face, the squinted eyes, the lips spread flat across his face, head twitching, the tremor of his voice shouting, *"No!"* and the sight of him, hunched forward, knees, long legs pumping as he ran up the stairway.

Her thigh hurt where it had struck the side of the coffee table. The TV was still running, a smiling man pointing at a weather chart. She retrieved the remote from the carpet and clicked it off, looked for her bag, which she'd lost in the scuffle, stood at the foot of the stairs, irresolute. Slowly, she climbed the steps and stood before the bedroom door. She heard a strange noise coming from behind it, a rhythmic, high-pitched yelp.

My God, was he crying?

Her cell phone rang in her bag. She put her hand in and silenced it. Then she opened the bedroom door.

30. Harald Jaeger

Jaeger sat in the dark, staring at the illuminated face of his cell phone. She was not answering. Long overdue and not answering. Every time he used his thumb to jab the key for the repeat call, his little finger, swathed in bandages to a bulbous girth, throbbed with pain. He had gone directly from Vita's to the emergency room at Gentofte, where he was received by a slender nurse, bare-legged in her hospital whites, and a young doctor, who shared his every thought with her as though to secure her agreement.

Jaeger was directed to lay his hand on the table while the two of them touched and poked at it.

"That's a nasty finger," the young doctor said to the bare-legged nurse. Jaeger could see her underpants through the thin white material of her uniform.

"Not pretty," she said.

The doctor jabbed it directly with his plastic-gloved index finger, and Jaeger yelled. The doctor apologized, smiling as he did so.

"Very nasty gash beneath the nail," he said. "But probably doesn't need a suture."

"Probably doesn't," the nurse said.

"Probably just bandage it," he said.

"Probably just disinfect and clamp it, then bandage it," she said.

"Of course," said the doctor. "Disinfect and clamp, goes without saying."

Jaeger could not take his eyes off the translucent material of the nurse's white uniform as she went to the cabinet for a bandage kit. Curious, he thought, that he couldn't see her bra strap. Then it occurred to him she was not wearing a bra, was wearing nothing at all beneath the flimsy uniform but a pair of panties. He could see the fuzzy yellow hair on her bare slender legs. Now he focused discreetly on her chest as she rolled back the cuff of his shirt and lifted his hand gently into a stainless-steel kidney bowl.

"This might sting a little," she said. "I'm just going to wash and disinfect the cut before we bandage it."

"Then we'll clamp," the doctor said. "And you'll be all set."

Her hands were gentle with him. Jaeger felt water of gratitude come to his eyes at the lightness of her touch, the tenderness, sponging his palm and between his fingers. She lifted out the hand and laid it on a clean white towel on the table and gently daubed it dry. The doctor placed three deep, narrow metal canisters on the table beside the towel and a glass jar prickling with long sticks whose ends were wrapped in cotton.

The trouble was that her uniform blouse had buttons and pockets where her nipples would be. He could see the swell of the breasts, which were cute, about as large as good-sized halved grapefruits, but the nipples were concealed behind those damn pockets and buttons. You couldn't even see an outline of them. He wondered how broad the areolae might be and whether they were pink or brown, smooth or nubbly, how thick the nipples themselves might be.

"Now we'll have to disinfect the part of the cut which runs beneath the nail," she said. "If the pain is too great, tell me and we'll take a break and do it more slowly."

"Can't it be anesthetized?" Jaeger asked, looking away from her to the doctor and back to her. He didn't really mind her hurting him, but he didn't like the doctor witnessing it.

"We only anesthetize if absolutely necessary," said the doctor. "You wouldn't want to risk immunity."

"The anesthetic can be even more painful than the treatment itself," the nurse explained.

"Can be more painful," the doctor added quickly. "And costs taxpayer money."

"Mainly it's the discomfort," she said.

"And the risk of immunity?" Jaeger asked.

"That too."

"Well, I'm sure you don't want us squandering your tax money," the doctor said briskly into Jaeger's face as the nurse dipped one of the swabs into each of the three canisters and placed it beneath the edge of his split, swollen, blackened nail. Then she shoved.

Jaeger yelled. With her free hand she patted his knee. Then she twisted the stick. He yelled again.

"I know," she said. "I'm sorry. We're almost done."

"Almost all done," said the doctor.

"Except for the clamp and the bandage."

"That's a nasty finger all right," the doctor said as the nurse applied the clamp and padded the cut with gauze, wrapping it several times around the finger, securing it with bits of white tape she had cut in advance and stuck along the edge of the metal table. Then she began to pack the whole thing in some kind of perforated condom-looking thing of black latex.

"How'd it happen?" the doctor asked.

"Ex-wife."

The doctor looked startled. "Did she *bite* you?"

"No, actually, it was her father."

"Her *father* bit you?"

"No no no, he slammed the door on my finger. *Twice.*"

"Did he do it on purpose?" the nurse asked, and there was such a willing eagerness to condemn such barbarism evident in her pale blue eyes that Jaeger nearly lied to her. Instead, he said, "On purpose or not, he *did* it. Twice." He thought they might suggest a police report, but they were finished with him.

In the hall outside the treatment room, he heard the nurse laugh at something the doctor said to her, and indignation flared in his heart. He fished out his cell phone with his unbandaged hand and awkwardly dialed 112 with his left thumb.

"I'm calling from the emergency room at Gentofte," he said. "I'd like to report an act of violence."

"Is someone in danger now?" asked the policeman or whatever he was.

"No, but someone, my father-in-law, slammed the door on my finger. Twice."

"Has it been treated?"

"Yes."

"Are you ambulatory?"

"Yes."

"Then I suggest you come into the station if you think you want to report that, sir. This is the alarm central. It's for emergencies."

The line went dead.

Jaeger didn't know if he was more ashamed or furious. He recognized, though, that the pain in his finger was buoying him. As long as his finger hurt, he was angry, and as long as he was angry, he could keep afloat. He didn't dare begin to speculate about what might be waiting for him when the anger abandoned him to his feeble intellectual devices. *I'm not stupid! Why am I so stupid?* And he could not bear to think about what Vita had implied—no, accused him of!

Being in Gentofte, he suddenly remembered a man he knew named Elsnab who had a legal practice on Gentofte Street. He got the number from information and called. Elsnab agreed to see him if he could be there by four thirty.

The offices were on the second floor of a low, broad building complex, a minimall that included two small supermarkets, a uniplex cinema, two toy stores, a candy shop, and a butcher. Elsnab's office was above the candy shop and butcher. The reception desk was not manned, or womanned, and Elsnab sat in the empty waiting area with him. Elsnab had a whiskered, receding chin, bulbous nose, and protruding eyes.

"Ever been to the movies in that cinema down there?" he asked. "Ingenious. They weren't doing so well, so they tore out every other row—you know, to give everyone lots of legroom. Doubled their business. By halving their seats. Ingenious. Very pleasant. What the hell'd you do to your finger?" he asked.

Jaeger told him the story.

"So you want to sue your ex's old man?"

"I want to assert my right to see my little girls."

Elsnab touched the sparse salt-and-pepper whiskers on his inward-slanting chin. "How old're they?"

"Four and six."

"You love 'em, huh?"

"Love 'em to death."

"How's that?"

"It's an expression. It means I love them a lot."

"I'd drop that expression if I was you. You love them enough to leave them in peace?"

"What! You mean just give them up?"

"They're young enough to forget you."

"I could never do that, *never*. My father left me and my mother alone when I was thirteen, and I swore I'd never do that to my children."

"But that's it. You were thirteen, so you remember him still. If you were four or six, you'd have forgotten him. His face would just disappear from your memory. There've been studies. You'd have forgotten him and he'd have forgotten you. And probably when you were four or six, he wanted to leave anyway, but he couldn't get himself to do it, thought he could make it work, tried but just kept sinking deeper in hell until finally it was so hot he had to escape clean. He should've done it earlier. You could learn from your father's mistakes. Let everyone forget everyone. Let the mother get on with a new life, let the kids have a new father. Let the father start again."

"I could never do that."

"Because you think you're afraid of hurting them, but what you're really afraid of is hurting yourself. Look, you feel terrible right now, right? And you're afraid that it's always gonna be this way, that it'll get even worse. But it will only get worse if you keep tramping around in it. You got the door slammed on your finger. What do you think that did to your little girls? They're not getting better off by you staying around to get doors slammed on your fingers. They'll get worse, and the ones who suffer most are the little girls. In ten years' time you'll be dealing with drug problems, alcohol problems, pregnancies, abortions, piercings. Who knows? Even sex films—who knows? Prostitution! You want to see your little girls in sex films? I mean, when they're older. Leave them in peace now, and you avoid all that. They forget you, you forget them, their mom meets a new guy, and inside of two years they'll be calling him Daddy, and you're free to make a new life for yourself. Kindest thing all around. Believe me. I been there."

"Never could," Jaeger said.

"Think about it, Harald. Give yourself a break."

"You left *your* kids?"

"Hard choices. Man's got to rise to them. Think about it."

Now, in the dark of his apartment, what Jaeger thought about were the little faces of his little girls lying in their beds with the blankets up to their chins, smiling up at him as he sang them to sleep at night.

"Sing the onliest girls one, Daddy!"

"Yeah, sing the onliest girls one!"

And Jaeger sang the makeshift song he had stitched together for them over the years, sung more or less to the tune of "If You Were the Only Girl in the World":

> You are the onliest girls in my world.
> And I am your only dad.
> We'll swim in an ocean of glittering pearls,
> Where nothing that happens is bad.
> And there while the sun shines with gentlest rays,
> I will care for you all of my days.

He could not stand it. He tried the phone again but only got the message service. If she looked at her call register, she would see that he'd called ten, fifteen times. Why didn't she at least phone back? It was nine P.M. She should have been here three hours ago. He'd called her after he'd seen Elsnab. She'd promised.

Abruptly he rose and flicked on the light, paced the wood floor. Seven steps from end to end. Five steps from wall to wall. He put his good hand over his eyes and turned his head from side to side, leaned on the window ledge, and gazed down at the windows of the building across the narrow street. There were three stories of windows down beneath him, studded with light. He could see a man and woman seated at a table by one window. The woman raised a coffee cup to her lips. The man was smoking a cigarette. He could not see the man's face, but the woman was smiling, and an agony of loss opened and grew within him. That no woman was here to smile at him, to want him to want her.

"Oh, Birgitte," he whispered, "Birgitte, Birgitte, Birgitte," and spun from the window. Their cups and snifters still littered the coffee table from the evening before. Abandoned debris of a lost evening, a lost night of passion, of now lost happiness and joy.

One of the snifters had a lipstick smudge on the rim. He poured the rest of the cognac from the split into the glass and sipped from it, placing his lips over the lipstick smudge, closing them on it as the cognac burned his throat.

Then, on the floor beneath the coffee table, he saw her scarf, gray and white and red. He seized it, silk, buried his nose and mouth into it, and inhaled. He could smell her perfume, the flesh of her slender neck, the tang of her hair spray. He managed to tie it around his nose and mouth like the bandanna of a bandito and, closing his eyes, breathed in its perfumed scent; and imagining her gaze, her eyes, beneath him, above him, imagining her cuntful smile, he did the only thing that remained for him to do now.

With his left hand.

31. Adam Kampman; Harald Jaeger

The North Bodega seemed different to Adam at night when sunlight didn't slant in the window from Solitude Way. It seemed more closed off. And none of Jes's friends were here now, either. At least the bartender was the same, a tall, sorrowful-looking man with skinny legs and a big belly. His name was Erik. Jes had made a point of introducing Adam to him, and Erik had shaken hands with sorrowful formality, blue eyes peering out over the elaboration of pouches beneath his eyes.

Adam ordered a bottle of Carlsberg Hof and sat at the corner table with it. From there he could observe the entire barroom. He took a newspaper from one of the empty tables and pretended to read it while he watched the room surreptitiously. It seemed to him he had made great progress in the past few days. Here he was—a boy who had hardly ever even drunk a beer before—in a serving house, on his own, on a first-name basis with the bartender, pockets full of money. He had quit school, thrown away his schoolbooks to seal the bargain, made some new friends, even invited a girl out.

That, however, had not been much of a triumph. In some way, it seemed his new friend and the romantic interest canceled each other out, considering that Jytte was in bed with Jes at this very moment and they were no doubt fucking. Adam felt the heat of a blush crawl up the back of his neck. Did Jes think of him as some kind of dupe, that he could just snatch his girlfriend away from him like that? On the other hand, he couldn't very well claim she *was* his girlfriend. He had never even kissed her. He had no claim on her at all. Still, he felt miserable about it, even if that misery was not as bad as his previous misery of nothingness. At least now he could sit here over a beer and nurse a broken heart. At least he wasn't hiding under the covers of his bed, sinking into the annihilation of sleep, being taunted by his father. Here he was out in the middle of life itself.

The door jingled open and a short, stocky man came in, smoking a cigarette. He glanced around the room, and Adam had a sense that the man's eyes rested on him for a moment too long before he took a place at the corner of the bar. Adam looked up, and their eyes met before he turned quickly back to his newspaper. Still, he watched the man secretly, saw him twist out his cigarette in the ashtray and immediately light another as Erik the bartender served him.

"Triple house vodka," the man said. His voice sounded at once husky and effeminate.

The only other customers in the room were an older woman with painted red lips sitting alone in a window niche and two men with tattooed arms drinking strong gold beer from the bottle at a table by the wall. They seemed to be friends but were muttering angrily to each other, cursing, as if sharing anger at a common outrage. The woman chatted with the bartender from time to time in a mix of heavily accented Danish and heavily accented English. She was tall and very thin and moved her hands when she spoke, in a slow, dreamy manner. Adam thought she looked old and used and sad, but when she smiled, her face brightened attractively. Her blouse was open three buttons so Adam could see the fleshy curve of her small breasts.

There was some mystery here, it seemed to him. He was being admitted to the mystery of a hidden part of life away in the north of the city. He felt more alive than he could remember feeling for a long time.

He glanced again toward the man seated at the bar with his triple vodka and cigarette. His clothes were messy, lumpy, pale blue jeans and a cheap, dark rain jacket. The man glanced over at Adam and seemed to stare for a moment before looking away. Adam felt as though he were remembering an old and faded nightmare. Was he going nuts?

Again the door jingled—there was some kind of metal wind chimes it struck when it opened—and a man leaned in, glancing quickly around the room, holding the door from closing as though deciding whether or not to enter. A neatly trimmed red beard and mustache circled his mouth, and he wore a rumpled gray suit and red tie. Adam noticed the man's eyes were chafed and the little finger of his right hand was wrapped in a thick dark bandage.

The woman in the window niche gestured dreamily with her long fingers. "Here is Danish chantleman," she said.

One of the angry men at the table across from Adam shot a quick look at the man in the doorway and grumbled, "You plan to close that door or what?" He wore a sleeveless shirt that showed his thick, tattooed arms and shoulders.

"Excuse me," the man said, shutting the door carefully. "Excuse me." He sat just beside the window niche and ordered a draft. "And please give the lady what she might like."

"I know you was chantleman," she said, and lifted an empty stem glass to the bartender. "I am Tatyana," she said, and extended a long hand in a slow, dreamy reach.

"Harald."

Their fingers touched, and she said, "You have cigarette for me?"

Jaeger asked the bartender for a pack of ten.

"With the filter," said Tatyana.

The one angry man—the one with the thick bald head—muttered to the other, "Tatyana's found a purse for herself," and the two chuckled and coughed. The bartender delivered the cigarette pack and tore it open for her, then poured peppermint schnapps into Tatyana's glass.

"To chantleman," she said, raising the stem glass.

Jaeger was fascinated by the movement of her hands. She looked like some kind of fallen Eastern European nobility. He willed his gaze away from her slender cleavage, up to her thin poppy red lips.

"But you are vounded," she said, and touched his hand lightly with the tips of her long fingers.

"It's nothing," he said.

"Hero," muttered the bare-armed angry man.

"Are you Russian?" Jaeger asked the woman.

"Never Russian," she said. "I am on way to Stockholm but am stopped here by love. Since three years I am stopped here. He was wery kind to me."

"Was? Did you leave him?"

"I could never to leave his kindness. He is dead since eight months. Now I wait to come me over him until I continue my journeys. He leave to me his domicile. Little apartments beneath the level of the sidewalks. I sell this and move on when I am strong again."

Jaeger nodded, looked into his beer. Sorrow everywhere he turned.

She touched his hand again. "You wanted I should be Russian?" she asked. "Then you do not spit upon me, perhaps?"

"Why in the world would I spit on you?"

"The Danish peoples they spit upon me two times. They spit upon me because I am Polack. And they spit upon me because I am Jew."

"I'm a Jew myself," said Jaeger.

"No surprise there," muttered the angry man.

She stared at Jaeger. Then she reached up to the green-glass shade of the lamp hanging over his table and tilted it back so it shone into his face. "Let me to see your eyes," she said, and studied him. Then, "You are *not* Jew."

The angry tattooed man muttered, "Can see clear down to his foreskin."

She made a little sign to Jaeger to disregard them, shaking her head. Jaeger looked at her cleavage, her thin red lips, her tea brown eyes. Her smile registered and approved his inspection of her.

"Jewish women are best," he said.

"Perhaps you wife is Jew."

"I have no wife."

"You have been with Jewish woman?"

"No."

She laughed huskily and only now reached for a cigarette from the open pack he had bought her. Jaeger fished a lighter from his pocket, thumbed it clumsily in his left hand, and she drew the hand to her with a gentle touch.

"You do not take cigarette, too?"

"Don't smoke."

"Do not smoke but carry lighter to light cigarettes of women. I am right. You *are* chantleman."

Adam carried his empty bottle to the bar and ordered another Hof, turning his back to the man who had been watching him. Or had he? He wanted to take a good look at the man's face, to remember it if he showed up again, but he was afraid to provoke him. What did he want? Was he the same man from before, following him? Or was he just going nuts?

As he sat again with a fresh Hof, he glanced up. The man was trimming his cigarette along the edge of a large black plastic ashtray, and it seemed to Adam he was watching him sidewise. He wanted to get away now. Something bad seemed about to happen. But he thought if he left his beer unfinished, it would look queer. And what if someone came after him? All that money in his pocket. But where could he go? Not back to

Jes, not with Jytte still there. Picture walking in on them fucking. The thought both excited and depressed him. He could rent a hotel room, but where? And how much would it cost? How old did you have to be? What if he left and the man at the bar followed him? He would run. He was younger, surely he could run faster.

With a jangle of the metal chimes, the door popped open again and Jes leaned in, spotted Adam, and headed straight for him. "Hey, man, what'd you leave for? I been looking all over for you."

Without knowing he would do so, Adam snapped, "Fuck you, Jes."

Jes raised his palms in front of his chest. "Whoa!" Then he straightened his posture to imitate Jalâl and proclaimed formally, "When one is greeted with salutation, offer a greeting nicer still. So, my friend: Fuck you twice, please." Jes got a beer from Erik and straddled the chair across from Adam. "Hey, man," he said, "I'm sorry if it hurt your feelings that I, you know, fucked your friend."

Adam sneered. He felt this unexpected mood taking hold of him and followed it unwillingly as it dictated his responses. He wondered how to stop it.

"Hey, I didn't know you had the hots for her. I thought you were just, like, acquaintances. And she was so cute and so . . . *ready*."

"Just fuck you, Jes."

"You ever been laid?"

Adam's sneer intensified, and he said nothing.

"Hey, it'll happen, Adam. You're young."

"Oh, and you're so old, right? The sayings of the wise man Jes. *Ha*."

Jes rose and made an Arabic fanfare with his right hand. "If any do a bad thing in ignorance but then repents and make amends, assuredly mercifulness and forgiving will forthcome."

Adam chuckled. He felt the evil mood begin to lift from him, and he began to feel that maybe the man at the bar was just a stranger after all.

The angry man reached one thick, tattooed arm over the back of his chair toward Jes. "You the kid who works for that key-and-heel place, right? That spic perker?"

"At least he's not a prick jerker," Jes said with a smile that put Adam's nerves on edge. He didn't want any trouble.

"Let's go," he muttered. "Let's go back to your place."

The tattooed man stared blankly at Jes while Erik rang open the register, shuffled to the jukebox, and dropped in some coins, punched buttons. Daimi came on singing, about her need to find a man who would treat her like a goddess on Solitude Way.

Jaeger and Tatyana started dancing. The tattooed man lifted his beer bottle to his lips without taking his eyes from Jes.

"Something wrong?" Jes asked with a smile.

"You'll know when it is, mac."

"Well, good. For it is said that God has sealed the lips and covered the eyes of the ungrateful who have forgotten how to speak nicely to people."

The tattooed man turned his eyes back to his friend. "You know what the fuck he's talking about?"

"Not a trace."

Adam was on his feet, and Jes let himself be edged to the door, still peering back at the man, who muttered, "*Tarzan*, huh?" with sneering lips, tilting back his beer.

The door jangled shut behind them, and Adam hurried toward North Port Street. Jes sauntered behind him. "Come on," Adam whimpered. "They may come after us."

"They won't come after us. They're losers, man. Losers. Racist assholes."

As they turned the corner, Adam glanced back and saw the bodega door swing open. "Shit, they're coming! Come on, let's get the fuck out of here!" He began to run just as Tatyana appeared around the corner of Solitude Way, snuggled up against the arm of the man with the bandaged little finger.

32. Adam Kampman

A rattling plastic bag cradled in each arm, Adam and Jes climbed the six flights to Jes's apartment.

"We should've bought plastic Tuborgs," Adam said.

"No, my boys," said Jes. "We are talking about delayed gratification here. We suffer the extra weight now in order not to have to suffer the taste of beer out of plastic later. Plus, this labor increases our thirst, so our enjoyment of beer from glass bottles is even greater. Plastic is multinational shit. Glass is good. Millions of peaches, peaches for me. And you!"

Adam was winded. "What do peaches have to do with anything?"

"You don't know The Presidents of the United States of America? You're in for a treat, my boys."

"Hey, thanks for letting me stay, Jes."

"Hey, you pay your rent, you're welcome. The rent is beer. We have thirty-two bottles of beer. Think of it. People might say we have no future, that's fine with us. Hey, did you see the guy with the finger? At the bodega? That guy works with my father. He works *for* your father. He lives around here. I see him once in a while. What a mess, huh? You see that woman?"

"Looked pretty good to me."

"Man, you *are* fucking horny."

The apartment had been littered with empty bottles, heaped ashtrays, and pizza boxes when Adam left. Now he was startled to find the living room all tidied up, glass ashtrays emptied and polished, drinking glasses and plates and utensils washed and stacked in the little kitchen. Even the floor had been swept and the pillows on the ragged sofa plumped.

Adam squatted before the refrigerator and started stacking beer bottles on the shelves.

"I smell a Jutland girl," Jes said, and slipped down the two-step hallway to the bedroom, tiptoed back, whispering, "There's a Jutland girl in my bed."

"In your bed?"

"Yeah, and I think she's naked. Have you ever seen a Jutland girl naked? Dear God, man, you're trembling, you are literally trembling. Listen, listen, here is what you got to do. You go in there quietly and you sit on the edge of the bed and you just watch her. Just watch her face. And when she opens her eyes, you smile at her. Don't blush or fumble or get scared. Just smile right into her eyes. She smiles back, which she surely will, then you lean down and kiss her on the mouth. Not hard or fast—just slow and light. And let what happens next happen."

"I can't do that."

"You got to. Come on. *In.* In in in."

Adam stood in the bedroom doorway. An oblong of coppery light from somewhere outside fell obliquely across the bed, touching Jytte's face and her chest beneath the pale bedspread. Beside the bed was a chair, and Adam could see her clothing folded neatly there. A bra, too, hung over the back of the chair. His heart lurched. Jes shoved him lightly and whispered, "Get in there."

On watery knees, Adam crossed the bare gray planks of the floor and stood beside the bed. It sat very low off the floor, and he felt he towered over the sleeping girl. This wasn't right. He looked back over his shoulder. Jes jabbed his index finger downward. *"Sit!"* he whispered.

It wasn't right. She would be so disappointed in him. But he sank to the edge of the bed, not sitting, but on his knees, hypnotized by her pretty, calm face. Her cheekbones were high and luminescent in the coppery light, her jaw strong, her nose, and her skin so clear, so silken, to his eyes. He wanted to reach out and slide his finger down the soft beak of her nose. *Bone in the nose,* he thought, and remembered the time when Jytte threatened to tickle him. The memory brought a smile to his mouth just as she opened her eyes and looked into his face. Her eyes got big and round and so blue, he was afraid she might scream, but then they settled in recognition, and she returned his smile. There was an understanding in it, an acceptance, and she lifted up a little on her elbow to meet his slowly lowering mouth.

33. Harald Jaeger

Jaeger held his breath and slipped his arm from beneath Tatyana's neck, slid quietly out of her bed. A car passed outside on Griffenfelds Street, its headlights sweeping through the shallow basement windows, across the bed. She looked so very thin and fragile there in the fleeting light.

His jacket was slung over the back of one of the two chairs in the dining alcove, and he lifted the cell phone from his inner pocket with his left hand. His bandaged finger was throbbing. He looked around for a place where he might call in privacy, without waking her, but there was only this one room, a complex of asbestos-covered whitewashed pipes across the low ceiling, an armchair leaking its stuffing, and a battered drum table in one corner, the dining alcove, a bureau, a scrap of kilim in the center of the gray, stained wall-to-wall. There must be a bathroom.

He found it behind a curtain, a very narrow, very deep room at the end of which was a white toilet bowl. The room was so narrow, his shoulders barely cleared the walls. Fear clutched at him as he moved deeper into the length of the room, a sense of being trapped here, no way out but back, and if someone suddenly appeared, charged him . . . He could not run, could barely turn, his naked back a square target. He dialed Birgitte's number with the thumb of his left hand while he peed, and it occurred to him he had not used a condom.

Sweat broke out on his brow. *Don't worry,* he thought. *She's okay. She's clean. She's not sick.* But the image of her naked on the bed reentered his mind, so thin and fragile, her sharp, exposed hip bones. *Jesus,* he thought with horror, *I went down on her! What the fuck is wrong with me!*

Birgitte did not answer. Impulsively, he left a message. "This is Harald. You've *got* to call me," he rasped into the phone. Then he added, "Did you tell Lars about us yet?" Immediately distressed by his impulsiveness, he clicked off. He had to do something, get dressed, get away.

As he turned, he glimpsed someone moving up behind him and gasped. Arms circled him, Tatyana's, long and thin, floating around him. She nestled her cheek against the back of his neck. She was as tall as he, a little taller.

"You gave me a shock," he said, trying to turn, to slip past her. But she pressed close to him within the narrow walls, pressed her belly to his. He could feel the blades of her hip bones digging into his own, feel her damp cunt against him, and despite himself, he got stiff. She kissed him with her tongue, then drew back and looked into his eyes.

"You were calling to your wife, perhaps?" she said.

"I have no wife."

"I am thinking you have someone."

"I have no one."

A smile turned in the line of her thin lips, in the strange oval of her amber eyes. "You vant perhaps to have me?"

"I—" His telephone rang. He lifted it to his ear. "This is Harald," he said.

A man's voice replied, "Yeah, this is Lars."

Jaeger froze.

"I called to tell you the answer is yes. Birgitte told me about you. She asked me to tell you to stop calling her, okay? She's not interested. So go bother your own wife and leave mine alone, okay?"

Jaeger clicked off. He wondered if Tatyana had heard.

"I am thinking you have someone," she said.

"No. Yes. I did have. It's over."

"I am thinking you should need glass of tea."

34. Adam Kampman

Adam felt taller, stronger. Even lying down. He felt muscles in his arms and legs and back he had never considered before. He lay beside her on Jes's bed, and she was curled around him, her fingers on his chest, her face close beside his ear, and the world seemed to him new and full of wondrous surprises.

From the next room, he heard the sound of bottlecaps popping, and Jes appeared, barefoot, carrying three Tuborgs in one hand, their necks laced between his fingers. He wore a white T-shirt emblazoned with black block letters that said, SAME SHIT DIFFERENT DAY.

"Have a *pivo*," he said. "You'll feel like a new man. Trouble is that new man may want a *pivo*, too." He distributed the bottles and sat on the side of the bed where Jytte lay, tapped her hip. "Shove over, make room."

"Jes! I'm not dressed."

"What else is new?"

He slipped under the covers and tipped back his bottle for a long pull, eyes looking upward as he drank.

"What the hell are you doing?" Adam demanded.

"Aren't we friends?" Jes smiled into Jytte's face. "Aren't we all friends?" He kissed her lips lightly.

"Girls from Jutland don't do this," she said. She was smiling, too.

"I think girls from Jutland don't have rules. I think girls from Jutland make rules." He flipped back the top of the covers and looked at her breasts. She lifted her chin, met his gaze, her smile proud. Jes's fingers rose to one nipple and circled it reverently. "So beautiful. Adam, have you ever seen anything so beautiful?" Without waiting for an answer, he lowered his face to the nipple. Jytte sighed—that same sigh Adam had heard earlier, so long ago, from the other room. But now he was here. Her eyes found his, smiling, inviting, enjoying revealing to him the pleasure she was experiencing, and he leaned down to the other breast.

She crooked one arm around each of their necks as they curled around her.

"Hey, man," said Jes, "it's like Romulus and Remus and the she-wolf who suckled them. No, you're Beatrice. You're our *bel viso*. Beautiful vision."

Adam raised his face. His eyes were wild, his chest heaving.

"You're all fucked up," Jes said, and Jytte giggled.

"God," he whispered, "God, I'm so hot!" and his face moved down her belly over the little paunch, toward the golden fleece, and her thighs clamped lightly around his ears as he heard Jes's words, muffled from above: "Welcome to the *vita nuova*, pardners."

SATURDAY

Fuck You, Dad

35. Adam Kampman

Adam's father and mother played golf on Saturday mornings. They took the BMW and drove the twins to his mother's parents on their way to the course. Jytte had the weekend off. They were always out of the house by eight A.M.

Despite the fact that Adam had not been home all night, he had little doubt that they would follow their routine. As they always did, no matter what. *The end is here, but golf goes on!* The only thing that kept them from their golf Saturdays was heavy rain, ice, or snow, and today the sun was blinding white, low on the horizon, pools of light in every hollow of the roads and sidewalks, tree branches with their sparse, wizened leaves limned silver.

Adam approached the house with caution, stood behind the trunk of an oak on the other side of the street. One half of the garage door was up, the side his father always used to park the Beamer. Still, he watched the house. There was no movement through the long row of leaded-glass front windows, no sound from the back garden. All was as usual. Routine.

He stepped up the walk between the poplars, slid his key into the front door, and opened it a crack, waited, listening. There was no sound. He let himself in and shut the door carefully behind him, stood still in the foyer for a moment, head cocked. Nothing.

In his room, he took the blue canvas suitcase from the top of the armoire, zipped it open, and laid it out on the bed. He packed his favorite jackets and slacks directly on their hangers, emptied drawers of folded underwear and rolled socks, folded shirts, an extra pair of leather shoes, runners, two sweaters, his alarm clock. He decided to leave his CDs. They all seemed dated.

As he stood considering whether to take a couple of neckties, he heard a sound behind him and spun to see his father there.

"I thought you were playing golf!" Adam yelped.

His father smiled. "Obviously." The smile was the kind he wore if he beat you at ping-pong or Monopoly. He nodded toward the suitcase. "What's this?"

"It's a suitcase, Dad."

"Ah-ha. And I notice it's packed. You plan on going somewhere, do you?"

"That's right."

"Where?"

"I'll send you a postcard."

"I think I'd like to know now, son."

"Fuck you, Dad." Adam hadn't known he would say that. But now it was said. He zipped the suitcase shut and looped the strap over his shoulder. "Please get out of the doorway, Dad."

"When I get a reasonable explanation. You're off the track, son."

"Fuck the track."

"Put the suitcase down. Sit down. And we'll talk. Then we'll see."

"Fuck you, Dad!"

"That the best you can do to explain yourself? Your vocabulary used to be much better than that."

"I don't have to explain myself."

"Oh yes, you do. We all have to explain ourselves sometime or another, and this is your time. You have to explain yourself to me. Now. So just put the suitcase down. And sit."

Adam glowered at his father. The calm of his voice, of his face, was more infuriating than if he had shouted, scolded. Adam wondered if he was strong enough to shove the man aside, to force his way past him. He couldn't allow himself to do as he had been told. He could not. If he just headed straight for the door, his father would have to step aside, and once he was past, he could run for it, get out. His father wouldn't follow him out to the street. He wouldn't make a scene where the neighbors could see.

His father lifted his brow. "Put the bag down now, Adam."

Adam moved straight toward him, fast. His father sidestepped but caught his wrist and twisted the arm up behind Adam's back.

Adam cried out, *"Ow!"* and he could hear the sob in his own voice. "Dad! What are you doing? Ow!"

His father shoved the arm up another notch, then suddenly let go. "Now," he said, and Adam looked into his face. He could see the doubt there, saw that his father doubted what he had done and didn't know what to do next. For the first time in his life, he saw doubt in his father's face. He saw it. And he was past him.

"I fucking hate you," he whispered, and was in the hall, down the stairs, his father moving fast behind him.

"If you leave now, Adam, don't think you can just come back."

"Fine!"

"Get back here!"

"Fuck you!" He had the front door open now and was out in the air, hurrying down Tonysvej. He could feel the small hard malevolent smile tightened upon his own mouth, but he didn't dare look back for fear his father might see the tears rolling down his cheeks.

MONDAY, MONDAY

A Boy Named Isaak

36. Martin Kampman

At his desk, Kampman gazed out the window over the botanical garden, sipped a Danish water, and contemplated strategy. Rain streaked the tall narrow windows that lined the outer wall of his office. It had been raining all day, and the sky hung like a marbleized gray ceiling, low over the city. Autumn, and his boy was playing the fool. This was *not* the season for nonsense. This was the season for completing a shelter and ensuring the larder was full.

Worse still, his idiocy was being backed up by the system. Kampman had been on the phone with Viggo Sand, the filial director at his bank, only to learn that Adam's access to his account was not only legal but also confidential. Kampman got the information, but only obliquely; it seemed Adam had withdrawn the not yet invested capital—"a certain amount, but only a smaller portion of the account"—and there was no way to keep him from taking the bonds in three months when he turned eighteen. His only recourse was to freeze further deposits, but what was in was in. "Those eggs are scrambled, Kampman, but I wouldn't panic."

"I'm not," said Kampman. "I'm examining the situation. Can I change the access date to when he's thirty?"

"Sorry. You can only freeze further payments."

"Well, you do that for me, then."

The conversation with Adam's high school principal yielded even less. They could and would release no information on Adam's status or grades without the boy's permission.

"But I can tell you that for his first two years your son has the third highest average in his class."

Kampman wanted to know about the *third* year, about *now*. "Is he attending?"

"Why don't you ask him?"

"I'm asking you."

"It would not be correct for me to tell you."

Kampman was surprised to see his hand trembling when he laid down the telephone receiver again. It offered little consolation, though a certain grim satisfaction, imagining the expression on the face of the alumni fund treasurer when he saw the much reduced figure on his next check to them. And when the treasurer phoned him for an explanation, he would be pleased to give it to him.

He had no idea where to turn now. The boy's mother hadn't a clue, either. As far as they knew, Adam had not made a single close friend in his two years at the high school. And no girlfriend.

The face of the au pair surfaced in his thoughts. Jytte. Of course.

It seemed to Kampman that this was something of an exercise in perception management. He was convinced that the girl knew where Adam was. Something about the way they'd been chatting over tea the other night. She was out to get her nails into him, thought she could make her fortune here. But getting the information would be tricky. She was a self-important little tart; he'd get nowhere trying to intimidate her. It would be all about how she perceived his approach. He would be the concerned father appealing to a young woman he had come to respect; then when he had the information, he would offer her a lift home. In the car, she would have her notice. The employment agreement the girl had signed with his wife required them to give her thirty days, which she would receive as a check and no need to meet up again. She would no doubt tell him that she had been hired by his wife and would prefer to hear *this* from her, too.

Feel free to give her a call. She'll tell you the same thing, though no doubt less directly.

He left the office at six—and still he was the last to leave, he noticed with scowling pleasure, glancing into each office along the hall to the elevator. No, Claus Clausen was just stepping out of the men's room, buttoning his coat. Kampman's nod was gauged not to invite chitchat, and they stood silently, side by side, in the elevator car as it descended.

"Good night, Mr. Director."

Mr. Director. What are you kissing my butt for? "Night."

As the Mercedes glided north on Bernstorffs Way, Kampman chatted with the chauffeur.

"Do you have children, Karl?"

"Two sons, Mr. Director."

Kampman thought he should have known that. And their ages. "How old are they?"

"Twenty-two and twenty-eight. The young one's in business school, the older one's a plumber with his own business and two kids of his own."

"That must be a pleasure."

"Nothing like it, sir. Those little ones are the jewels of my eyes."

"Well, sure, but I meant it must be nice that the two boys are all settled in their work."

Karl glanced back in the rearview mirror. "As they say, Mr. Kampman: Little children, little problems; big children, big ones."

Kampman chuckled. He watched the back of the man's neck, ruddy skin crosshatched with wrinkles, his black gray hair curling up in back. *Time for a haircut*, Kampman almost said, annoyed at himself for soliciting succor from his driver.

Karen was in the living room with her feet up on the red ottoman, a stem glass of wine balanced on the arm of the easy chair.

Kampman registered the wine with a silent glance. "I'd like a word with the au pair," he said.

"I let her go early." Light glinted in her stockings as she turned her feet toward each other on the ottoman.

"Oh?"

"I didn't want you interrogating her."

He said nothing for a moment. She sipped her wine. It occurred to him that Karen knew something. It also occurred to him that her tone was out of character.

"I can understand you're upset," he said. "I am, too."

She glanced at him. "*You're* upset?"

"Naturally."

"How can you be so, so, so *cool* if you're upset?"

"Let's not paint Satan on the wall, okay?"

"Martin," she said, "our son is missing."

He stopped himself from saying, *Red wine won't bring him back.* Instead he said, "Now why don't you tell me where he is." A calculated gambit he immediately saw would work. He saw it in the shifting of her eyes, in the careful, labored manner with which she put the wineglass on the end table and licked her lips, already wanting to pick up the glass again. If he bent to kiss her, he was certain he would smell tobacco on her breath.

"What are you talking about, Martin?" Shrill edge to her voice.

"Karen." Quiet but firm.

She lifted her feet from the ottoman. "I have to look in on the twins," she said, and rose, slender and graceful in her bare feet but no match for him. With a single step he moved to block her path to the staircase. Then, remembering the scene with Adam last Saturday, which he had kept to himself, he decided to limit the movement, keep it to a gesture. He wondered whether she had been in contact with Adam, whether Adam had phoned her, told about what had happened between them. *Well, yes. Sure I grabbed his arm. The boy was totally out of control.*

"Karen, I know that Jytte and Adam are involved. I'm certain she knows where he is and that she told you. This rubbish has to be stopped immediately."

He could see she hesitated to pass him, even though the path from her chair to the stairway was only halfway blocked. There would be no more violence here. He had decided that. The boy had caught him by surprise. It would not happen again.

"I think he needs time."

"You might be right," Kampman said. Her eyes scanned his face with rapid surprise. "But I need to know where my son is. I won't have this information kept from me. I certainly wouldn't keep it from you."

She stared at her feet, toes pointed in.

"He's staying in North Bridge," she said. Then she reached for the wineglass, and he knew he had won.

"I'll need the address."

37. Frederick Breathwaite

From where he stood on St. Hans Square, near a sculpture that resembled some kind of elaborate swastika, Breathwaite could see into the window of the Dome of the Rock Key & Heel Bar. What he saw through the window was his youngest son wearing a blue workman's smock and grinding a key on some kind of lathe. It stung him to see his youngest, most intelligent boy dressed as a worker, performing the labor of an unskilled workman. Kirsten would call him a snob if she could hear his thoughts, but it was not snobbishness; it was respect for the boy's intelligence and fear of how he was branding himself in this country, where a person who played at being an unskilled laborer ran a very real risk of ending with that as his only option. In the United States, you could reinvent yourself repeatedly. You could probably do it here, too, but only with great effort. Here you were expected to have your papers in order. It was a small country. Every failure was noticed, registered. There were people everywhere who remembered you, and opinions were seldom revised for the better.

Breathwaite still had hopes for Jes. Jes was capable of doing what he himself had almost done. Jes was capable of more, much more.

Outside the shop was a little wooden pony ride. Breathwaite could remember slotting coins into one like that on one of the Greek islands when he and Kis vacationed there with the kids many years before. He remembered Jes, the baby, delighted as Breathwaite fed drachmas into the slot for him while his older brothers smashed each other with some kind of volleyball in the pool. Where had it been? Crete? And later, Lesbos, still later Cephallonia and Lefkada and Ithaca.

Breathwaite had told Jes the stories of Sappho and Alcaeus, stories his brothers wouldn't sit still for but which lit the fire of imagination in Jes's eyes. He told the boy about Oedipus and Sisyphus and Homer. They traced together on a map the journeys of Odysseus around Cephallonia back to Ithaca, and Breathwaite told him about the modern Ulysses, the pacifist, who would not harm his wife's suitors as Odysseus had butchered his, who longed for his son as surely as Telemachus longed for the return of his father. He read him the modern Greek poets, too—he could remember reading George Seferis to him, about the soul's need to look into itself for self-knowledge.

Jes had not been more than eight or nine, but his eyes glittered with comprehension of the journeys, the Homerian monsters and the Joycean parallels, and Breathwaite knew that this was the one to put his money on. This was the boy who had it. He could have been whatever he wanted. If only he stayed with it, he could be a university professor, more. He could be a learned man, an authority, a person the world came to for wise counsel. Or a CEO with fat perks. A leader of industry, of professionals. He just needed a fix of the sweet life to keep him pushing the wheel.

This kid had so much going for him. Breathwaite would not abandon him to a career in IT, and he certainly would not sacrifice him to a key-and-heel bar. All he needed was a little taste of success, of the possibilities, a little bit of money—he would finish his university and go on.

Breathwaite opened the door of the shop and stepped in. Jes glanced up. "Hey, Dad," he said curtly, and the little man with gray hair curling up from beneath the rim of his black cap raised his face from the shoe last.

"Is your father, Jes?" he asked, sliding off his stool, wiping his palms on his smock. "I see you boy's face in you, Mr. Breathwaite," he said. "I am Jalâl al-Din. We have speak in telephone. Welcome. You will have tea?"

"Thank you, Mr. Din, I only need a word with my boy."

"Is clever boy! Very clever!"

"Thank you."

"I'm working, Dad," Jes said, and Breathwaite tried not to hear ironic echoes from the boy's childhood. Was that the kind of father he had been? *I'm busy, son.*

"I saw a nice place over on Ahorn Street. You know the Ahorn Room? Meet me there for a beer when you get off. I've got something to tell you."

"I don't have much time, Dad."

"You go with father," said Jalâl. "You go now. I finish here."

"No, no," said Breathwaite. "I can wait. Meet me for a beer, Jes."

"Just *one*, Dad."

Breathwaite killed time strolling down Guldbergs Street, past Café Rust. He stopped to read a graffito painted on the outer ocher wall: "Meat Is

Murder." The papers had recently carried a story about a shooting in the road here. Two men wearing ski masks in an idling car had fired a dozen or more bullets that riddled the wall and cobblestones, caught a young man, a karate trainer, in the leg and the buttock. Another bullet pierced the hand of a girl who happened to be standing there. A miracle no one was killed. The journalist interviewed a witness, a young man with dazed eyes. "Apparently anything can happen here now," he said, and would not give his name.

Breathwaite wanted Jes out of here. He could sell his apartment for a handsome profit, let some other young idiot earn his street creds here while Jes moved up and on.

Right on Ahorn and into the Ahorn Room, a new yuppie bar he had read about in the entertainment supplement of *Politiken*, all chrome and prime colors in a modernized semibasement. It looked like a bad imitation of something out of Kubrick's *A Clockwork Orange*. Breathwaite ordered a vodka martini straight up, and the barmaid mixed it by twirling a long chrome stirrer between her palms. A bearded man, the owner apparently, ambled over and said softly in New York–accented English, though loud enough for Breathwaite to hear, "Sweetheart, you're bruising the gin."

"That's how I was taught to do it," the girl said, smiling.

"Well, better unlearn it. Observe and be enlightened." And he danced the stirrer up and down in the mixing glass while Breathwaite looked away and lit a cigar, suppressing the urge to tell the man that she had not been bruising gin, but he *was* bruising vodka.

The vodka eased his annoyance, and he considered the fact that the American could not be any older than he himself had been when Jes was born—thirty-seven. It seemed absurdly young to be a father, even as he recognized the absurdity of the thought. In fact, thirty-seven was not at all young to become a father; he was nearly old enough to be his youngest son's grandfather, and maybe that was the problem. But it was said that being born to older parents enhanced the child's intelligence.

That's probably a crock of crap, too, he thought, gazing through the low window beside his chrome chair out to a fenced side yard patched with withered weeds. The chain-link fence reminded him of his boyhood in Queens, as did the arrogance of the bar owner. *There is no provincial like a native New Yorker. When you come from the biggest city in the world, nothing is good enough to satisfy your ignorance.*

It occurred to Breathwaite that he was developing an animosity toward his fellow American expatriates, and he wondered why that should be. Although his children all had dual citizenships, he himself was still technically an alien here; the Danish authorities required that he surrender his blue American passport before being issued a red Danish one—something he could not bring himself to do. The kids had both passports as their birthright. He suspected the two older boys were closet Republicans, Bush and Fogh supporters. Bush-men, lost in the Fogh. Jes, he was certain, leaned lefter than left, but that would correct itself in time. Everyone moved right with age, but what the hell happened to someone who was already right of center in his youth?

Morose thoughts. But the vodka helped as the level of clear fluid in the cone of the cocktail glass receded. It occurred to him that the greatest share of the drink was in the mouth of this glass. What remained at the pointed cone bottom wouldn't fill a thimble.

He called to the barmaid, "Would you please bruise me another vodka."

She chuckled, began spooning ice into the shaker just as Jes appeared down the little front flight of stone steps.

"Make that two, please. Doubles." Good chill dry martini might be just the seduction needed.

Jes rendered a perfunctory hug, taller by an inch or two, though half the girth of his father, before he sat and said, "So what's up, Dad?"

It stung Breathwaite that his son felt free to be so curt. He wondered if his own impatience with his own father had ever been so naked, supposed that it had been, supposed that he had never succeeded in concealing his disappointment that his father had never visibly addressed his wife's (*my mother's!*) roll in the hay with the fucking laundryman, that his father's kindness might have been mere weakness. He recognized and appreciated the irony that he could admire the pacificism of Joyce's fictional cuckold, Leopold Bloom, but never quite forgive his own father for the same behavior in reality. *Maybe the problem here*, he thought, *is an excessive appreciation of irony; insufficient recognition of the slaughtered emotions that lie beneath it.* Even now, forty-something years later, Breathwaite could reach in and pick at the scabs and feel the blood of anger ooze from the wound.

He wished to hell that he had been kinder to his dad, hoped he had been kinder than it felt just now that he had been.

"What's up?" he said now to his son. "A vodka. Straight up, in fact," he said just as the waitress came around from behind the bar with a little tray bearing two classic cocktail glasses of pure clear chill liquid. Breathwaite did not fail to notice the barmaid's appreciative glance at his good-looking son. And he was pleased to see that Jes's time could thus be purchased; the boy's eyes gleamed at the sight of the glass. Father and son lifted them by the stem and toasted with a glance.

"Your boss seems a nice enough fellow," Breathwaite said.

"Well, you know how it is, Dad: You can't teach a monkey to speak and you can't teach Danish values to a sand nigger."

"A *sand nigger?*"

"Maybe you prefer 'camel jockey.'"

"What in the hell are you talking about, son?" Breathwaite was almost losing it, his son's cracks had so unnerved him. "Are you implying that I use language like that?"

"Easy, Dad, it was meant as irony."

"Irony?" There it was again. "Toward *me?*"

"If the shoe fits, repair it."

Indignation swelled within him, and Breathwaite felt the moment spiraling away before it had even begun. He wanted desperately to drop this, but how? He calmed his voice. "Do you think I'm a racist?"

The boy shrugged. "Maybe not."

"You *know* I'm not. So what are you talking about?"

"*I was being ironic, Dad.*"

"Irony is pretense. Be careful who you pretend to be, Jes."

"Amen, Dad."

Breathwaite wondered if he had really been so quickly, so easily, outmaneuvered. He let the moment steep for a bit as he took out his cigars, offered the opened metal box, and was heartened that his son accepted. Breathwaite lit them both up, puffed, sipped his vod martin. Then he said, "Listen, Jes. Don't quote me on this, please, I wouldn't want to hurt your brothers' feelings, but I've always considered you the sharpest of the three . . ."

"I know that, Dad, and I never much cared for having that laid on me."

"What? The fact of your potential?"

"My potential is *mine*."

"To use for what?"

"For what *I* deem worthwhile. For what *I* deem worthwhile."

"And what is that, pray tell?"

"*My* business."

"I can't believe we're talking this way, son."

"I wish we weren't."

Breathwaite sipped his drink, thinking about what he had to offer the boy, recognizing he would never get there from where they were now, recognizing that retreat was the only way to keep the option open now, and trying to envisage a way forward to retreat to. Then he thought he glimpsed a way. Lightly he said, "You remind me of Gilgamesh, son."

"And how is that?" Jes asked with a cutting smile that Breathwaite rebutted with a smile of his own, one of rue and affection. "'Gilgamesh,'" he recited, "'Gilgamesh. Whither rovest thou? The life you seek you shall not find.'"

"Did *you*, Dad? Were you even seeking?"

"Jes, I am not your enemy. I'm your father."

The boy made a flourish with his hand and affected a foreign accent, speaking with a formality apparently designed to convey more irony: "And when someone asked of the great prophet Muhammad, 'Who is most deserving of my kindness?' the Prophet replied, 'Your mother.' And the questioner asked, 'Then who?' And the Prophet answered, 'Your mother.' And he asked again, 'And then who?' And the Prophet replied, 'Your mother.' The questioner asked again, 'Then who?' The Prophet replied, 'Your mother.' And once again he asked, 'Then who?' And the Prophet answered, 'Your father.'" Jes lifted his glass. "*Skål*, Dad."

Breathwaite crossed back over Queen Louise's Bridge through the chilly evening drizzle, thinking, *Mission aborted*. But he took comfort in the fact of the boy's openness. At least he had not hidden behind false smiles and superficial politeness. That anyhow was something. In the anger and impatience he expressed, there could be some key to understanding, and that key might open a door to a place where he could see the value of what Breathwaite was about to offer him.

"Tell me," he had asked the boy, "have you become a Muslim?"

"No, Dad, I just want to understand. That's the problem today. Nobody wants to understand. We bomb them. They bomb us. We bomb them better, they bomb us sneakier. Who's asking why? Who's asking what's happening? The other day I was talking to this guy in a bar, and he was spouting all sorts of ignorance about the Koran, and I asked him if he'd ever read it. 'Why the hell would I?' he says to me, and I ask him, 'Can you even try to imagine yourself as a Muslim?' He says, 'Can you imagine a Muslim trying to imagine himself as a Dane?' It's so fucking hopeless."

"It's not really hopeless, son. It's a matter of setting your hopes in line with your options."

Again the smile that was not a smile opened on his teeth, and he lifted the martini glass. "Like you did, eh, Dad? *Skål.*"

One thing cheered him, though—that the boy was not angry at his mother. They would need each other when he was gone.

38. Martin Kampman

The light turned green, and Kampman gunned the BMW up onto the bridge ramp to cut around a slow-moving Volkswagen he didn't want to be stuck behind. Through the drizzling window, he glimpsed Fred Breathwaite lumbering along the pedestrian pavement in the opposite direction. He wondered if Breathwaite was holding out on the Irish contact, angling for something he could hold for himself, possibly set up his own little consultancy firm and siphon off those contracts. Might try to keep his whole European Union network intact, invest that last piece of money into his own operation, run it from home. Then, as the BMW rolled past Sacrament Church on North Bridge Street, a thought surfaced, and he fished the cell phone from his shirt pocket.

He had overshot his corner, so he cut a quick right onto Chapel Way and pulled up to the curb alongside the yellow wall of Assistens Churchyard, beneath the dark trees jutting up from within. He found the number in Dublin and hit call, sat behind the wheel listening to the series of double rings on the other end. Then the ringing stopped, and it sounded as though the phone on the receiving end were being dropped down a chute. Just as he was about to ring off, a blurry, suspicious voice said, "Yes?"

English was not Kampman's forte, but he plunged in, explaining who he was, whom he was trying to reach in connection with their Copenhagen visit.

Suddenly the blurry, suspicious voice rang clear. "Martin! Is that you, Martin Kampman?" As though the blurriness had been from Kampman's end.

"Yess, Sean. It iss good to be hearing you. Vi look from to you wisiting with us." Pleasantries taken care of, Kampman went for the point. "Sean, you know your old friend Fred Breathwaite—yess, Fred!—he is decided upon to be leaving us . . . Yess, ha ha, ha ha, you are right, he hass had enok of the Tank. I will tell you this for we are planning a little farvel cermony to him at the dinner this week. I am thinking you will wish to know this as old friend to Fred . . . Yess. We wish to say good-bye in the good way to our Fred . . . Yess, Freddy, ha ha."

Kampman noticed in the rearview mirror that a strained smile was still plastered across his face even after the silent phone had been returned to the dark of his shirt pocket. He studied the smile, trying to determine whether he would look as idiotic to others as he appeared to himself—lips spread wide, teeth parted, cool eyes nestled in twin beds of incipient wrinkles. He let the smile drop, saw the normal control return to his features, and sat staring into the cool blue of his own eyes for several moments, thinking.

That should close that door for Fred. The question now was to be certain Jaeger was securely in place as a buffer between himself and the Irish. He did not really trust the Irish. They seemed a very foreign race to him, a people with little respect for the clean line, without Northern European values. They were as foreign, to his mind, as the Japanese, although the Japanese at least understood hierarchy. The Irish respect for hierarchy, he thought, was mere form without content, as opposed to the Danish, in which it was content without visible form; in principle, everyone here was on a first-name basis and you gave your hand to everyone in the room, but in descending order of importance.

The Irish were too sentimental, but he didn't trust their sentiment. Their famous hospitality was dazzling but insincere, rooted in drink and late night contests over who could stay clear longer, although there seemed no important consequences for those who eventually succumbed, even for those who—as they said—became "drunk as a lord."

When Kampman accompanied Breathwaite to Ireland the summer before, he was received with what seemed to be great warmth, but he was aware of the fact—had overheard it at breakfast one morning—that behind his back they referred to him as "Martin the Mortician." As he was entering the buffet room in Killarney, he distinctly heard Sean ask Breathwaite, "And how is Martin the Mortician today, Freddy?"

Breathwaite snorted. "Not accustomed to late nights, Sean. He'll be fine."

Sean put the edges of his little teeth together and, hand on heart, pronounced in stentorian tones, "The Morte d'Arthur! Long live the Mortician."

Breathwaite chuckled again, while Kampman—who had not yet been seen—backed out of the room and retreated to the lobby window, gazing over the sweep of lake and mountain behind the hotel, owned and administered, he knew, by Germans. That was the kind of people he was dealing with—Irish name-callers who left the administration of their properties to Germans.

He squared his shoulders and marched back into the buffet room, went directly to Sean's table, beaming. "Morning, Sean, morning! How are you today?" Then he waved his hand in front of his own nose. "Big cigar smoke last night," he said, referring to the fact that Sean and Breathwaite had still been slouched back in their lounge armchairs over long cigars and deep whiskeys when Kampman, unable to contain another fizzy water, had capitulated and gone to bed.

Sean set the edges of his little white teeth together and giggled while Kampman sent a message to Breathwaite—whose breakfast plate, he noted, was a mess of egg and sausage, tripe and blood pudding, and baked beans in red water—by turning his back without a greeting. *We will see who is used to what, Freddy boy.*

On the Aer Lingus flight home, while Breathwaite drank complimentary champagne and Kampman sipped juice, he smiled at his subordinate and asked, "By the way, what is the word in English, you know, what is it for *bedemand*? You know, the ones who bury the dead people?"

Clearly caught by surprise, Breathwaite hesitated. "Ah . . . uhm . . . ah . . . mor . . . morticians?"

Kampman snapped his fingers. "Right! That's it. Morticians. They're the ones who bury dead people, right?" And he smiled into Breathwaite's red eyes.

Now Kampman keyed the ignition and pulled away from the churchyard, continued down Chapel Way to Åboulevard, and cut left to come in from the other end of Blågårds Street. He parked on Kors, outside a greengrocer's, and walked through the drizzly evening up to the square, looking for the address the au pair had given Karen and Karen had given him.

A tall, skinny man with dirty hands hobbled over to him with a strange, listing gait. "Excuse me. Can you spare three crowns?"

"No," Kampman said, and looked away, heard the man immediately repeating his request to someone behind. Beggars were a thorn in his eye, an insult to the social welfare system, which itself had become an insult to the individual citizen.

The buildings on the square were an unattractive mix of workers' quarters from various periods with a grubby little park in the middle. Kampman was only too aware of the sad history of this area with its activist squatters and autonomes covering their faces with ski masks and hurling unearthed cobblestones at the police. He knew a movement was under way to gentrify it, but it was far from gentrified yet, and it was no place for his son.

The address was in a six-story building between a café with unwashed windows and a secondhand bookshop that was still open, judging from the baskets of cut-rate paperbacks flanking the door.

From close beside him a woman's voice said, "Hey?" and he turned to see the au pair, her face full of confused question. Good. Karen apparently had promised her that she wouldn't repeat where Adam was staying. This little tart would quickly understand how he got the address and why he was here, and that would be the end of confidences between them. He recognized at once, too, that her being here was no coincidence. As he suspected, she and Adam were shacking up. Now that he had all his information, he could go right for the kill.

Kampman smiled. "Ah! Good. I have something for you." From his inner pocket he removed a business envelope with the flap tucked in and Jytte's name printed on the front. She took it from him automatically, which didn't really surprise him.

"What is it?"

"Your contract calls for a month's notice. That's a check for a full month, to the end of November. And you won't have to come in anymore—so really it's almost six weeks' severance. My wife is making other arrangements."

Now *she* was holding the envelope out to *him*, but he didn't accept it. "I was hired by Karen," she said. "If she isn't satisfied with me, I would prefer that she tell me so directly."

Kampman's smile broadened. He loved this. He loved this girl. "You may phone Mrs. Kampman if you wish. She and I agree that it was inappropriate for you to get involved with our son."

Her eyes blazed. "What do you mean, *involved*!"

Kampman was still smiling. "You're blushing, my girl."

"I'm not your girl!" She shoved the envelope at him, but his hands were in his pockets. "It's up to you, of course, my girl, but don't you think you'll have use for it?"

39. Adam Kampman

Their first Hof of the day dangling between their knees, Adam and Jes sat with their feet up at either end of Jes's battered sofa. Jes wore a T-shirt with FUCK IT printed in block letters across the chest. Adam leaned over the stuffed sofa arm and picked through the teetering, tall stack of books atop a standing cinder block. He lifted as many as he could manage into his lap and ran his fingers over the covers, reading titles: Homer's *Odyssey*, *Bullfinch's Mythology*, James Joyce's *Ulysses*, Søren Kierkegaard's *On the Concept of Irony* and *Fear and Trembling*, the Koran, the Old Testament of the Holy Bible, the New Testament, Baudelaire, Rimbaud, Ibsen, Dostoyevsky, Joyce's *A Portrait of the Artist as a Young Man* . . .

"Man, you read a *lot*, Jes!"

"Read little, understand less."

"But all these books!"

"I don't read them, I rape them. I read ten books at a time."

"Do you really read Kierkegaard?"

"Of course I read him! I'm a master of the rotation method and a knight of infinite resignation, too. KIR, as opposed to KMRDA—kiss my royal Danish arse. You mean *you don't* read Kierkegaard?"

"We were supposed to read *Either/Or* last year, but I couldn't, I just faked my way through it. I tried, though."

"What kind of Christian are you if you don't read Kierkegaard?"

"I'm Lutheran."

"Ah! So you believe in Christmas pork and Easter beer."

"What are you?"

"Me? I'm an agnostic-polytheistic Muslim and apostate-Catholic Commie-Jew champagne-socialist pseudo-sand-nigger mountain Turk."

Adam was grinning. "What do *they* believe in?"

"Irony."

"What are your parents?"

"My father was raised cuckold, but he's lost his father faith and converted to materialism. My mother has a personal relationship with Jesus

Christ, whom she identifies with me. When I was a kid and found out my father was Catholic, I asked if I could be a Catholic, too, like him, and he said, 'If you want to be a Catholic like me, you don't have to do a god-damned thing.' That's when I figured out his real religion, a contemporary variation of the ancient sect of Epicurus. Same as all the other sixty-eighters, rich now all of them and sitting on the power they seized in the name of something else but then found out they had in fact gained entrée to the wine cellars and larders and gold vaults. And they like it there. They like their pleasure and comfort. Tickles the palate. Last judgment be damned. Tell me, do you believe in the resurrection of the body and the soul and the last judgment?"

Adam swigged his beer. It was almost empty, and the little bit remaining made him feel sad. "I don't know," he said. "I guess not."

Fetching two more bottles from the case on the floor, Jes asked, "So you don't believe in accountability?" He opened the bottles by hooking the cap edges against each other and yanking. He passed one to Adam, dripping foam.

"Well, I don't know about that," Adam said.

"Well, you ought to find out. Otherwise your life will have no foundation. And you know what happens when you have a life without a foundation? It runs along okay for a while until one day you look down and see there's nothing beneath you and you fall. Like in the cartoons. Straight down into the sands of doom."

"So do you believe in accountability?"

"I believe in inquiry. I believe in magic in a young girl's pussy. I believe in beer. And I'm in the process of finding out about accountability."

"How do you do that?"

"You crawl down your well, all the way to the bottom, and the descent is difficult. Maybe in the end I'll join the Theosophists or the Rosicrucians. Or learn to sing the Ragnarokian rag. Tell me, Adam, do you believe in anything at all? Aside from pussy. I *know* you believe in pussy. And you're taking instruction in beer." Having said which, he tipped back the bottle and drained it.

"Yeah, gimme another lesson, willya?" Adam said, and followed suit, standing the second empty bottle beside the first. Jes passed him a new one, and he took a long swallow and sighed. Then for some reason he thought about his little sisters' sweet twin faces and wished he were kinder to them, and he said, "I guess, well, I guess I do believe in kindness."

"Are you kind?"

"Not kind enough."

"You do have a kind face. The kind I'd like to push in."

"Ha ha."

"Do you read at all, or do you just fake it all the way?"

"I do read," Adam said. "But I don't know, I guess I have been faking it. I don't really . . ." Suddenly a truth seemed to hit him full in the face, and he felt terror. "Jesus Christ," he said. "I don't think I ever really understood anything I read. Not anything at all!"

Jes leaned across to him and squeezed his biceps. "Hey. Hey hey hey, take it easy on yourself, boy. Recognizing you don't understand a fucking thing is a great step forward, believe me. There's a Greek word for that moment."

"Really? What is it?"

"Can't remember." He squeezed the biceps again and said, "Flex the muscle. Come on, show me what you got there."

Adam flexed and Jes stretched his fingers around the bulge. In a fake foreign accent, his Jalâl voice, he said, "You are strong boy. Big. Strong!" Then, "We need some music."

"And another *pivo*."

"*Mais oui, mon ami!*" Jes shuffled through his CDs, popped one on, and scaled the jewel case over to Adam. "Know that one?" he asked while he popped two more bottles from the case.

"*Highway 61 Revisited*. Dylan. Man, that guy's got a weird voice."

"Oh, *man*," Jes said in a weepy tone. "*Listen*. To the man's *words*."

They leaned back against their respective sofa arms while Dylan blew his kazoo siren to an electric background and launched into his version of the story of God and Abraham and Isaac and Abraham's capitulation to God's demand that he cut the throat of his only son out on Highway 61 in the midst of American commerce and war, threatening violence if he did not.

"Now *that*," said Jes, "is faith. Now that is faith. Right?"

"I guess."

"*Wrong*. It's fuckin' fear, man. Kierkegaard in *Fear and Trembling*, he says, well, he writes it in the name of Johannes de Silentio—Johannes the

Silent—he says that he cannot understand the Abraham story, and his conclusion—ironic, natch—is that he is stupid because everyone else understands it, but he can't. What he's saying, to my mind, is that the story is not based on faith but on good-old, bad-old, old-fashioned fucking shit-in-the-pants fear, and that's what Dylan says, too. The world is corrupt. The Judeo-Christian God is corrupt. God is in cahoots with the world, which is a great highway of fucking commerce where you can sell anything—telephones that do not ring and forty red-white-and-blue shoestrings—and you can sacrifice your beloved fucking son rather than buck the system. Man, what father doesn't sacrifice his fucking son, *son*? They're scared shitless themselves, and they're even more scared for their sons not being scared, because if their sons aren't scared, then they have to admit that they themselves are scared. And scared of what? Scared of a God who demands that you sacrifice your fucking son? *No*, man! I don't buy it. It's a vicious fucking cycle and a sham, and you need a good lawyer. Now Muhammad, he says that Abraham is one of the great prophets, and he says that we *do* not and we *can*not understand the greatness of God, we can only submit. *Allah Akhbar!* Allah is great, man is little. But what do we submit to? 'Cause God never speaks to us! God never tells anybody anything. God is the silent fucking sky, man. It is only the father of the son on earth who puts the knife to your neck. Look at the New Testament, too. God sacrifices His only son for the sins of man? He's just like Abraham, man. He wants Abraham to kill his son. He lets His own son get tortured to death in agony by puny little ants He could snuff out with His little finger. I tell you, Adam, this is a problem that we got to deal with, this killing of sons."

"But isn't it, like, a symbol? Or a metaphor?"

"Am *I* a symbol? Are *you* a fucking metaphor? Men don't even believe any of this stuff, but they're conducting the pattern. Kill a son today. Feed him to the fuckin' machine. 'Cause if we *don't* do that, then the son is going to survive and look at us and say, 'Uh, like, Dad, you're a corpse, man. I think your dad cut your throat about two thousand years ago, so don't shake your head or nothin'.'"

The case was empty, so Jes fetched cold bottles out of the fridge and popped them open. The green-glass bottle was cold against Adam's palm, and the first swig burned coolly in his throat. He drank as he had seen Jes do, tipping the bottle back at his mouth so the beer made a swirling, sucking sound out the glass neck. He liked the sound and the feel of it in his mouth and the way it made him feel. The CD had ended, and they sat in silence.

Then Adam noticed that he had taken down a third of the bottle in one pull, and it occurred to him that this was already his fourth bottle—the empties stood in a row on the stained, chipped surface of the coffee table—and a sense of sadness invaded him.

"Damn," he said. "These go so fast. Look, three pulls and the bottle's empty."

"That bottle's not empty," Jes said. "It's more than half-full." He flourished his hand before him. "In the sayings of Jalâl, fear of the thirst when well is full is the thirst you never quench."

"You're gonna end up a Muslim, Jes."

"Worse things to be."

Adam chuckled. "Jes the perker."

"I hate that fuckin' word, man. Don't use it in my home, okay?"

"You use it yourself."

"Only ironically."

"Ironsick Jes," Adam said, and started snuffling laughter.

"Man, you're fucking wasted on four beers-sick." He fished an Advokat out of the pack in the pocket of his flannel shirt and lit it with a stick match.

"You smoke fucking cigars-sick?" Adam liked this word game. He felt very clever for having invented it and flattered that Jes was playing along.

"My old man-sick got me hooked on the fuckers." He held up one finger. "*One* fucking cigar-sick and I'm hooked-sick. Hey, man, we need some more mu-sick." He hopped up and shuffled through the CD stack.

"I got to pissick," Adam said.

"Well, don't forget to flush-sick after you. And don't pissick on the seat-sick, you prick-sick."

"We're fucking sick-sick, man!"

Giggling, Jes picked out a CD and slid it into the player. "Hey, man, more old-gold-sick."

Bob Dylan came on singing "Black Diamond Bay." Jes sang along, about going to "grabanotherbeer." Adam stepped back out, trying to zip up. "Shit, my zip-sick is stuck."

"Well, don't get your prick-sick caught in it."

The door opened, and Jytte stood there, panting. "Lock the door! Adam's father's on his way up!"

"Fuck him anyway," Jes said, and glanced at Adam. "Fuck-sick him, right?"

Jytte's face was flushed. "I *hate* him!"

"Don't do him that honor," said Jes, but Adam saw then she was crying. "What did he do to you!"

She wiped her eyes with the back of her wrist. "He *fired* me!"

"I'm gonna fight him!" Adam said. "The *fuck*! The bully *fuck*!"

"Whoa whoa whoa whoa whoa," Jes said, maneuvering Adam to the sofa. "You can't fight your own father with your fly open."

Jytte giggled, sniffling.

"Sit down here now—"

The bell rang and knuckles rapped the door at the same time.

"He can't see you from the door. Let me do this," Jes said, and opened the door a slit, stood with one shoulder to the jamb, the other behind the edge of the door. Adam watched his back. *If he lays a hand on Jes!* He heard his father's voice.

"I'd like to talk to Adam."

"*Who?* You mean like the father of sin?"

The voice was cool, almost friendly, but Adam knew the tone only too well as he heard his father say briskly, "That's okay. I need to have a word with my son. *Now.* His mother is sick."

"She is *not*!" Jytte shouted from inside.

"Mmmm. May I . . . come in?" Adam's father said.

"No, you may not," said Jes. "So I'll just say good night, good luck, and good-bye. Hurry up, please, it's time." And he shut the door, spinning the dead bolt. "Now I know why there was a lock on that door all this time," he said, facing the others.

The doorbell rang immediately and knuckles rapped the door. There was an authority to the knock that twisted in Adam's stomach.

Three knocks, a pause, three knocks again, a pause.

Adam whispered, "Did he recognize you?"

"Don't think so."

"But he'd see your name on the bell."

"You haven't noticed the name on the bell? How unobservant of you." He flourished his hand. "Permit me to antrodoos mysalf. HVT6. Fifth look-alike to President Saddam Hussein. High value target 6 only. Relative safe-ety. Now, let us cerebrate cereblate and dance to mu-sick!"

40. Martin Kampman

Incredulous, Kampman glared at the battered slab of wood not three inches from his face. He balled his fist, about to hammer it again. Then he noticed the words printed aslant across it: SUCCES SUCKS. Clever Dick hanging his pictures where his nails were. Slowly he relaxed his hand. He glanced at the doorbell for a name and smirked: "HVT6." Snot puppy with that T-shirt, FUCK IT. He had almost smacked the boy's face, he almost regretted *not* having done so, but he was also painfully aware of his strategic miscalculation the weekend before when he had used force on Adam. The art was to win without employing force, to will things into place. Somehow he had to get Adam out of that apartment without force. He was aware that it had also been a miscalculation to say that Adam's mother was sick. That could be checked by a simple phone call, exposing his own desperation.

Well, he wasn't desperate, but he *was* determined, and he *would* have Adam home again and back in school before any real damage had been done, and he would see to it that the boy's bank account was tied up out of his reach for a long time to come. Adam would *not* be allowed to ruin his life or to spend more money on that little tart, and this foolishness would be toppled by the weight of its own stupidity.

He swung the BMW out of its place on Kors Street and edged it up onto Blågårds Place, pulled in alongside the low wall at one end of the little park. From there, he could see the door of the apartment building while he let his mind work, considering his next step.

The girl was the key to it. When she was out of the way and Adam's funds were blocked, the boy would return. He would have no other option. Time to get the Tank lawyers moving to lock up those bonds before the boy's birthday. No, get someone else. Keep this private. He had three months in which to get that done, a little less than three, but even that was too long. He wanted the boy back on track within three days.

His cell phone vibrated in his shirt pocket. Karen. "Have you found him, Martin?"

"I know where he is, but he doesn't want to come out. Exactly as I suspected, he's with that girl."

There was a silence. "Does he have money?"

"Unfortunately, he emptied his savings account. Seventeen thousand crowns. The girl is out after the gold," he said, and held his breath, then added, "She is definitely a gold digger."

There was another silence. Then: "Something is missing," Karen said. "You don't suppose Adam—"

"Missing? What?"

"My gold bracelet. You don't—"

Kampman watched his face in the rearview mirror. He was smiling. "Your gold . . . Do you know what that cost?"

"—suppose Adam would take—"

"Adam? I just told you he has seventeen thousand crowns in his pocket. No, why would he take a bracelet? Are you *sure* it's missing?" In the mirror he watched the performance of his face as he spoke, remembered a transactional dynamics course he had taken years ago, "Do You Know What Your Face Is Doing While the Rest of You Is Negotiating?"

"I *always* put it in the box in the back of the top bureau drawer."

"We *have* a safe."

"I know, but I wear the bracelet almost every day, and it's such a bother pulling away the chest of drawers to get to the safe."

"Mmm."

"If Adam didn't, then do you . . . No, I really do *not* believe that Jytte—"

"My God, she knew," he said. "I knew she was involved with Adam and she *knew* she was getting the sack . . ."

"The sack? You fired her? Without—"

Calm voice. "I only suggested to her the other night, when I drove her home, that Adam needed to have peace for his studies and that I trusted I could count on her, otherwise—"

"You might have told me."

"I had every intention of telling you. But it all went much faster than I would have guessed. She's a nasty piece of work."

Silence. Then: "What now?"

"Call the police. I'll be home right away."

"Do we really have to involve the police?"

"No police, no insurance. Do you know what I paid for that bracelet?"

Kampman detoured to Strandboulevarden on his way home. He parked the BMW in the shadows beneath a cluster of linden trees on the parking island across from her window. It was dark in her room. The little vent window on top of the tall casement was open, perhaps ten feet up from the sidewalk. And there was that sturdy red mailbox fixed to the wall beside the window ledge.

There was no way she could be home yet.

Karen sat in the living room with a glass of wine, her bare feet propped on the ottoman, when Kampman let himself in.

"That took a while," she said.

"Traffic. Did you speak to the police?"

"They'll send someone out tomorrow afternoon. They wanted one of us to come in to them, but when I told them who you are, they gave in. They'll come sometime tomorrow afternoon." She sipped the wine.

"Did she have a key?"

"Yes. I asked Adam to have one made, and he knew it was for her, so I presume he gave it to her. It would make sense. Nothing unusual about that."

"Then we'll need the locksmith, too. To change the lock cylinders."

Karen began to cry. "I just can't believe that girl would do this. She seemed so sweet."

"Appearances deceive, honey."

41. Jes Breathwaite

Depression had descended upon the room like a Copenhagen autumn twilight and long since had begun to bore Jes. He was tired of participating in the group consolation over Adam's father's bullshit treachery. Even the huggy consolation had given way to solipsistic gloom. He didn't want to trample on their wounded young hearts, but he sat on the floor, back to the wall, holding a beer bottle between his knees, trying to think up a gentle way to get them to see the comic elements at work here: Adam hunched forlornly on the sofa, his fly straining to burst on the two safety pins he'd clasped it shut with; Jytte biting her fingernails meditatively over the prospect of no longer having to work for a bastard of a ligustrum privet fascist. I mean, get a life. And at the slow rate they drank their beer, how did they ever expect to break the morbid spell?

He considered fishing his *Sayings of Jalâl* notebook from his knapsack to clown them out of it: "People of the book, do not go to excess in your religion of gloom. Do not grieve for an ungrateful people, be they Muslim, Jew, Christian, or bloody bastards."

"Woba golves," he said experimentally.

No reaction. It was so silent in the room, he could hear the water bubbling in the radiator pipes. Another of gloom's details. But then it gave him an idea. "Time for a bit of music-sick," he said.

"Do you have any Thomas Helmig?" Jytte asked.

"Certainly not. You'll hear this." He slid on Dylan's *Blonde on Blonde*, clicked forward to "Visions of Johanna." "Behold the glories of the English language at its best in the mouth of a world-class poet. Not to mention depression-ripping ironics, Adam-sick. As we sit here stranded, doing our best to deny it—"

"What's wrong with Thomas Helmig?" Jytte asked, drawing her feet up cozily beneath her.

"You are comparing Grand Prix melodies with art."

"Thomas Helmig has beautiful language."

"Anything to compare to these visions of Johanna? You can't hardly *do* that in Danish. I mean, listen to Mark Knopfler's words, listen to Counting Crows, listen to—"

"There are lots of fine songs in Danish! C. V. Jørgensen!"

"He's good."

"Good? He's a genius! He's a poet!"

"He serves a purpose."

Jytte sneered. "What do you mean, *purpose*?"

Jes could see he was getting her piss to cook, and that was much better than depression. "To show us that Danish can handle rock. To an extent."

"Why, he's *just* as good as this! Better!"

"Can't you hear he's an attempt to transpose Dylan to Danish? To co-opt him to a Danish setting? Even his voice, for chrissake. His crowded lines, even his nasality."

"And Kim Larsen!"

"He's good."

"And Lis Sørensen!"

"Now *she* is *good*. Oh, Lis, Lis, Lis," Jes chanted ecstatically. "I want you *sooo bad*!"

"This is boring," Jytte said.

"Boring!"

"Yeah, I think it's boring. You can't even understand what he's mumbling. We don't have to listen to American music all the time."

"Why not? Music is the best thing that's come out of America. Or you can listen to Danish copies of it instead. Or British copies. If you want some original Danish music, listen to Poul Dissing and Benny Andersen. 'Nina comes naked from the bath / while I eat a cheese sandwich . . .'"

"What's wrong with that!"

"Nothing. I *love* it! I'm just saying we're not going to get any further in Danish by imitating. The language is too small. Help me out here, Adam."

"Hov!" Jytte was now sitting straight up, her blue eyes blazing. "Danish is *our* language."

"Right, like crowns are *our* money. Why live in a big world when you can stay closed up in a tiny one?"

"Don't tell me you *like* the EU!"

"Not particularly, but I like isolation less. Someday the Danish Language Council is going to wake up and see that they can't decide what's

Danish and what's not. Language doesn't come from the tower to the streets. Language comes from the streets up. Case in point: Until like last month, you couldn't find the word *fuck* in Gyldendal's *New Danish Word Book*, but show me one Danish kid who hasn't been using the word since like they could speak! I mean, just *look* at English. Look at how many more words it has!"

Jytte was on her feet now, shouting, and Jes *loved* it. "That's just because for every word in English they have the same word in Latin or French, too!"

"It's because English isn't afraid to *grow!*"

"You're only half Danish anyway. You grew up speaking English to your father, right? Or not even English—*American*."

"Poor me. The new Danish pariah. People with two languages. The poor two-languaged children. *Quel problème!*"

"Two-tongued, maybe," Adam said suddenly, glaring at him.

Jes was startled, but then he perceived the lad was defending the damsel against his attempt to get her blood circulating again. He rolled with the punch, laughing self-deprecatingly as though found out. "The sleeper awakes. Speak again, O toothless wonder-sick."

"Fuck you-sick!"

"Fuck-sick you too-sick!" Finally it was getting fun again. Dylan was singing "Leopard-Skin Pill-Box Hat," but Jytte was not ready to take it for fun yet.

"French is a more beautiful language than English," she said. "And Italian is, too."

"Italian is good for operas, and French is dead for all practical purposes. Committed suicide trying to construct long French substitutes for IT and TV terminology. But French literature, of course, is quite another matter."

"Spanish is a more important language," Jytte said officiously, and Jes looked at her with a smile. He had gotten more out of her than he would have dreamed. She'd already dropped at least two masks, but the real Jytte, he was convinced, was still concealed somewhere under this jingoistic one. He could have gobbled her up. Maybe he would. Such transparent defense could only be a vestibule leading to very, very hot pants.

"And where did you come from, little goose, little goose?" he said.

"Don't you call me 'little goose'!" she snapped, chin raised, eyes clear and cold, and he saw suddenly that he had gone too far for her. But he couldn't resist another little dig.

"I'm sorry," he said. "I meant little goose-sick." He kissed his lips at her.

Still glaring at him, she said, "I think I'll go now."

"I'll walk you," Adam said.

"No." She was slipping on her shoes.

"Let her go," Jes said. "She's homesick-sick."

"Let me walk you, Jytte."

"No. No, thanks, Adam." She kissed his cheek.

"Why go, anyhow?" Jes said. "Can't you take a joke? I was just fucking with you. Don't be so self-serious. It's a mortal Danish sin. Stay and we'll have a party, celebrate that you don't have to work for that asshole tomorrow."

She was looking at his T-shirt, a small, bemused smile on her mouth. "Fuck it," she read out. And, "I think I want to sleep in my own bed tonight."

Jes watched Adam follow her to the door. He sure did like her butt in those dirty beige jeans she was wearing, but he was beginning to wonder where she was coming from. He was about to call after her, *Who sent you?* thinking of William Burroughs going mad in Paris and Tangier, but realized it would be lost on her. Dylan was now singing "Just Like a Woman," and Jes snorted. *Breaks just like a lit-tle girl . . .* But she hadn't broken. He couldn't figure out what had happened. Who can read the heart of a Jutland girl? What was she so fucking uptight about?

"Night, Jytte," he called as she hugged Adam and closed the door behind her without a word.

Fuck it, he thought, and glanced at his shirt in the mirror over the CD player. TI KCUF. He liked that. TIKCUF.

Now Adam was depressed again. Fuck depression, anyway. The lad was sitting on the floor in a corner, head bowed, elbows on his knees.

"What the fuck is wrong with you, man? Come on, forget your troubles, come on, get happy, for chrissake. Tikcuf. Tikcuf it all."

Adam looked up. His eyes were wet. "I was just remembering something," he said, thick-mouthed. "When I was, like, ten years old once. There was a picture of my father in the newspaper because he had got some big promotion. Director of something or other. I was so proud of him, and I told him that. 'God, Dad, I am *so* proud of you.' And he looked at me, really cold, really, and he said, 'What are you kissing my ass for?'"

And the kid started weeping. Literally weeping snot. Jesus.

"Hey, Adam, listen to me. Do yourself a favor. Don't waste your tears on the man. Fuck him. He's not worth it. Don't be sad, be *mad*. Don't let the bastards getcha. Come on, have a beer. Fuck *him*, anyway!"

42. Frederick Breathwaite

Trying not to consider the distance from his earflap chair to where Kirsten slept, across the archipelago of carpets, down the hall, in their antique four-poster, Breathwaite sat up in his library, reading. Sweet woman who still desired him, and what could he give her now? How discreetly but indefatigably she tried. Until his pale response, his limp hugs, his chaste caresses, finally succeeded in fatiguing her. It seemed to him now only a matter of time before she gave up, too. *How long can a woman of passion do without? Please realize, sweet Kis, that it is not by choice that I have chilled. I am not able.*

And it seemed she was ready for a surrogate. Came home from work today excited about the puppies her boss's golden retriever had had. "Freddy, they are just *so* cute! If you just *saw* one, you would melt."

"Mmm."

She caught the drift, read the tone, and he saw she was getting sad again. The swangler. He modified, in hopes of dispersing the clouds of sadness. "Of course if we ever did get a dog, it would definitely have to be a golden. They're more like another species of human than a dog. Lovely creatures."

"They are *so* beautiful, Freddy. It's almost like holding a *baby*!"

"Let's think it over, shall we?" he said, and saw she *knew* what that meant. And went to bed. And he sat there wondering why he was such a fuckless fuck.

But the muscle of his heart was too soft at present to bear such thoughts. He discharged the matter by reassuring himself that Kirsten had to be protected against herself, against her sentimental enthusiasms. All she saw was a cute puppy; she failed to perceive all the trouble involved, the housebreaking, the vet expenses—and not to mention what she was not yet even aware of: that they would have to be looking for a new apartment, and not every apartment allowed dogs. Or that *she*, rather, would have to be looking for a new apartment. Another thought he did not wish to follow just now.

No.

Staring into the air, redolent with Cohiba smoke, he thought again of those people on the bridge. Had he been hallucinating? Or just suggestive in his weakened state? Already he could feel his memory evolving the moment from a glimpse to a scene. He pictured them going into a dance on the dusky sidewalk, lake gleaming behind them, singing some Tin Pan Alley love song. Life as a musical comedy. Or Dennis Potter weird. Lars von Trier's dancers on the lumber train of falling darkness. Like the "Lonesome Polecat" dance in *Seven Brides for Seven Brothers*, which Breathwaite remembered from when he was about eight. Was he going nuts?

He turned his attention instead to the new issue of the *New Yorker* that had arrived that day. He read a short story by V. S. Naipaul about a doomed affair between a man and woman of two different classes in England, attracted to each other because of the distance between them, which, once breached, destroyed the illusion of the otherness that had drawn them in the first place. There were some other levels in it that he could not quite grasp, could not quite follow to a satisfactory conclusion.

Pondering it, he poured another dram of an inexpensive blend, lit a cigar, then paged forward to an article about Isaac Bashevis Singer that surprised him. He had read and enjoyed a couple of collections of Singer's stories but had never realized or considered how complex the man's life had been. One sentence toward the end disturbed him, stating how much a refugee flees from, not least himself. In other words, you can leave your shore but not your soul behind.

Breathwaite looked at his watch: one A.M. It seemed a bad time of night to encounter such a sentiment. He flipped back to check the name of the man who had written the article, Jonathan Rosen, paged further back to his bio note, which offered no enlightenment about the man other than that he was about to publish a novel entitled *Joy Comes in the Morning*.

He wondered whether that was a double entendre about a woman named Joy, realized it could only be, considered how Kis loved French breakfasts, how he wished he could deliver that joy to her tomorrow. He thought about what his own morning might bring, then about the fact that it was already morning, that a mere six or seven hours separated him from the new day.

More musical comedy: Kelly, O'Connor, and Reynolds, dancing and singing, "Good Morning."

Those people on the bridge. He shivered.

It hardly mattered. He could sleep until nine or ten if he wanted. No, he would have to get up, not to arouse Kis's suspicions. Then he could slip back into bed if he wanted. It didn't matter anymore. The only thing that mattered was how he handled the Irish visit at the end of the week.

And he still had not spoken to Jes about the opportunity he had engineered for him. It was all he had to leave the boy. He had to make him understand the value of this little inheritance. The phrase *résidence secondaire*, which he had read in one of the *New Yorker* articles, popped into his mind, and it seemed such a grand and eloquent term compared with his own secondary residence, the little beach cottage in Gilleleje. Kis could sell it and buy herself a small apartment in the city. Or go up and live there. That would keep it in the family, at least. If she could get permission from the authorities to turn it into a year-round residence. She could have a puppy there if she wanted. To fill his empty shoes. Jes had always loved the cottage. Breathwaite remembered him there the summer he had graduated from high school, wearing the white student cap. Such a hopeful time. He remembered the graduation day. Jes had been at the top of his class, one of the highest averages the school had ever seen. And valedictorian. Shook them all up talking about 9/11 as an effect rather than a cause. Might have seen the seeds of this nonsense there. Not that he was wrong, but a man had to learn to be strategic about the good.

Breathwaite remembered the boy's joyful face as he climbed into the open-backed truck with the rest of his class, decorated with pine branches, stocked with cases of beer, the truck pulling away, honking, all the boys and girls in their white caps, up on their feet, hoisting beers, cheering, Jes's head tall above them all, his face glowing as they drove through town to stop at the homes of each student for a drink and snacks. Fine tradition.

Breathwaite and Kis had hurried back to the Tank, where they would receive Jes's class, when it was their turn, in the main hall at a long table draped with starched white linen, decked with bowls of strawberries and tiger prawns, chips and dip, a glittering row of green bottles of beer for those who preferred it to the Crémant magnums in their gleaming ice buckets. Cheers and honking and toasts in the summer afternoon. Just four years ago, when everybody was still happy. The boy could have done anything he wanted, anything. But he flitted from one thing to the other and landed in a fucking Pakistani key-and-heel bar.

Breathwaite's stomach growled. In the kitchen, he poked around inside the refrigerator, found a container of vanilla ice cream that was nearly half-full. He ate it straight from the container with a soup spoon. The ice cream was too hard, too cold. He had to melt the first few spoonfuls against his palate, and his teeth began to ache, his temples. Then the sugar carried its optimisms to his brain, and he thought, *Complex organisms take longer to gestate.* Jes would find his way, and he would do well, with that quick intelligence he had. His son would prevail. His son. His youngest son.

He finished the ice cream and stuffed the empty container down deep into the garbage bag where Kis would not see it and then wondered why he did that. She never complained about his appetites. It was his lack of one particular appetite that was the problem.

Back through the library he fetched his cigar, still smoldering in the ashtray, sipped his whiskey, and let himself out onto the balcony. The street below was empty and still. A bicycle rattled past on the bike path, and he watched its red taillight drift off out of sight.

Something happened in his gut as the cold ice cream made its way lower, and he heard the mournful sound of a long fart moaning into the night. Another. Another.

He snorted. Ice-cream farts. Threw back the rest of his whiskey and swallowed without tasting it, then looked ruefully into his empty rock glass. Irish crystal. Gift from his colleagues there. He had an urge to fling it down at the roadway. Instead he took a last pull at the cigar and flipped it over the railing. He watched its red glow spiral downward for a good few seconds before it exploded silently on the road into a scatter of sparks that quickly died out.

Quite a drop, he thought. *From here to there.*

Then he went inside to refill his glass.

43. Jes Breathwaite

"I think . . . I think I love her," Adam said.

Jes said, "Nah."

The two of them were back at their opposite ends of the sofa again, legs stretched out onto the coffee table between the long, glistening flanks of empty green bottles. From the CD player, Bob Marley sang a question about how long they would kill our prophets.

"I *do*," Adam insisted.

"You may think you do, but you don't."

Jes glanced at Adam, who sat with his head back, eyes closed, mouth open and wet.

"You know, Jes, you're kind of cyncical."

"*Cyncical*, am I?"

"Cynlical."

"Right."

"I *mean* it."

"Right."

"If you keep on saying that, I'm gonna get very angwy."

"*Angwy?*"

"Fuck you, Jes."

"No, fuck Jytte. You'll feel better."

"I'm telling you, Jes, I'm not kidding."

"Right."

"You don't know how I feel."

"Do. Been there."

The Marley record ended.

"Hear that?" Jes said.

"What?"

"Water. In the pipes."

"So?"

"They turned the heat on. Summer's really dead."

"So?"

239

"It's autumn. Anyone who hasn't found a home by now won't find one. Whoever is alone will stay alone, will sit and read, write letters all evening, and wander along the boulevards, back and forth restlessly while the dead leaves carry on the wind."

Adam squinted disbelievingly at him from his end of the sofa. "What the fuck are you talking about? I thought you were my friend! Are you mocking me?"

"*Relax*, man." Jes rose and stooped before a bookshelf, searching. "I was not mocking. I was *sharing*. Where the fuck is it? . . ." He rummaged through the shelves. "Where the fuck is it? Oh, fuck it! It's Rilke. He says that you have to love your solitude and hear the sweetness in the lamentation of the suffering that comes with it. Because you can't take anyone there with you. By its nature, solitude is experienced alone. And to be kind to those you have to leave behind. And not to expect anything from your parents—just accept the warmth of the love they offer even if it does not understand you."

"*Warmth?*"

Jes looked at the boy and thought of his own father and felt pity. His own father was so full of delusion, but he was not a bastard, he was not like Adam's. "You know, people are so afraid of being alone, so afraid of *failing*—of failing to do what everybody else tries to do. It's all a failure. A failure to realize the failure that we're being expected to live up to. Listen to this."

Jes remembered something more. "You know what else Rilke said. He said that solitude is great and difficult to carry sometimes. So difficult that we try to exchange it for *any* intercourse, anything at all, no matter how cheap it might be. But then he says that it's necessary to be alone, the way a child is alone among grown-ups with all their 'important business.' But you find out that all those 'important' things are useless. All the 'important things' that the grown-ups try to do. It's hard to be alone and it's hard to love; to really love is the hardest thing we have to do, and the most important thing. Young people don't know about love—they have to learn about it, but we're impatient and we throw ourselves at each other and we *fail* in our love. We have to learn how to love but first we have to learn how to let our solitude develop."

Jes was surprised to see Adam watching him intently. "I don't understand," he said. "It, that doesn't sound like you, I—"

"It's *not* me. It's Rilke. But it's also me. All I'm telling you is not to be afraid. You're like a little tree that's full of fear, that hasn't been watered. It's afraid it won't grow, but you'll grow to be just what you're destined to be. Rilke says that, too. Don't fear the rain. Don't fear the seasons and don't fear the rain. Rain is sacred. Water is from God. What do you say?"

Adam looked into Jes's eyes, standing above him. "You believe in God?" he asked incredulously.

"What do you think, I'm an asshole? Of course I believe in God. I just haven't figured out who or what He or She or It *is* yet. Maybe I never will. But I'll keep on trying. Now let's have more mu-sick and beer-sick!"

IRISH NIGHT

WINE COMES IN AT THE MOUTH

44. Karen Kampman

With mascara and pencil and eye shadow, Karen Kampman did her eyes at the vanity table, glancing from time to time at the reflection of her husband, who stood behind her, before the full-length mirror, fitting the gold-and-pearl studs into his tuxedo shirt. She studied his face as he watched himself in the mirror, meticulously fastening the antique studs into each buttonhole. She wondered if he could see that she was looking. Nothing on his face seemed to suggest that he could, but neither did anything on his face seem to suggest anything at all of their exchange earlier in the week about the bracelet.

She remembered then the expression on his face once when she overheard him in response to an admiring comment from someone at a dinner, responding that the shirt studs and cuff links had belonged to his great-grandfather. Which was not true. She had been with him when he bought them, from an antique dealer on Bredgade. They were eighteen karat, red gold with natural pearl inlays. They had cost a fortune. Martin knew nothing about his great-grandfather or his grandfather, either; Martin's father had been raised by a single mother who had never told him who his own father was. The secret died with her.

But looking at his face—its expression of warm modesty—as he told that lie, she almost came to doubt the fact. She asked him about it afterward, and he said, "No, no, I told her it was from the *time* of my great-grandfather," so convincingly that she concluded she must have heard incorrectly. She thought about that from time to time, wondering whether she *had* heard right or not. If he really had lied about that, though, she felt the lie was an endearing one; Martin was ordinarily so devoid of sentiment that it touched her to think of him lying about this, saw the lie as a glimpse of emotional pain otherwise scrupulously hidden from view. She had almost begun to think of him as unfeeling, so that little glimpse of pain, of a fear of inadequacy, enlarged rather than diminished him in her view. *If* indeed she had not misheard what he said. The question now seemed important. Extremely so.

Four mornings before, the au pair girl had visited her to return the house key and to deliver her bracelet in an envelope.

"How in the world do *you* happen to have this?" Karen asked her.

"I wish I knew," the girl said, but her face suggested she had a good idea of how. "I found it in my room, in that envelope. My room is on street level and the top part of the window is always open. It's too small for anyone to get in through it. But it would have been easy for someone—especially for a reasonably athletic person—to climb up on the window ledge and drop that through. I found it on the floor beneath the window."

Their eyes locked. The girl did not blink.

"What are you suggesting, Jytte?"

"I won't suggest anything. But I can see no other way it could have got into my room."

"And how did you happen to know it was mine?"

"Why, I've seen you wearing it. All the time."

"You would have had many opportunities to take it from my drawer."

The girl's eyes narrowed, but her voice was calm enough under the circumstances. "I am *not* a thief. I did *not* take it."

"I didn't say you were a thief, Jytte. I only said you had the opportunity. You might have just wanted to borrow it."

"Is that how you think? With all your, your *wealth*. That everyone wants to 'borrow' from you? I wasn't raised that way, Mrs. Kampman."

The formality was cold; they had been on a first-name basis from the start. "I'm not saying you were, Miss Andersen. It is just all very curious. And you *did* try to steal our boy."

"Steal your . . ." The girl laughed flatly. "Adam is older than *me*. *He* invited *me* out. And we were hardly together at all. I can't understand why that should be grounds for firing."

"Mr. Kampman was very unhappy about it."

The girl glanced at the bracelet. "Yes, he was, I can see that."

"What are you suggesting?"

"I won't suggest a thing. I'm only here to return my key." She clicked it down on the kitchen tabletop. "After all this, I'm happy not to be working here anymore. Your husband was not very polite when he drove me home the other evening."

"Are you suggesting that he—"

"Mrs. Kampman, I am not suggesting anything at all. I am saying directly that he was not polite. He drove me to my door and he sat in his car for some time afterwards looking at my open window."

Again their eyes locked, and the implication was clear. Martin could have seen the open window. He was certainly fit enough to climb onto a ground-floor window ledge. Karen could not help being impressed by the girl's dignity, by her refusal to accuse directly, by her not lying about Adam. Yet this could also all very easily be calculated. The girl might be a schemer, an *intrigante*.

For reasons she did not fully understand, she had not told Martin. When he came home from the office and asked whether the police had been by, she smiled and told him it hadn't been necessary after all. "I found it."

"Found what?"

"My bracelet. Here in the kitchen. I must have taken it off to do something and forgot about it."

"Doesn't sound like you."

"Well. What else could it be?" She watched his face but saw nothing in it. She halfway expected him to suggest that Jytte had taken it but then lost her nerve and returned it. Somehow she hoped he would. It would be at least some kind of evidence or indication against him. But he said nothing.

"By the way," she said, "Jytte came by to return her key. On her own accord. I thought that was admirable. Under the circumstances. So we won't need the locksmith, either."

"Let's hope she didn't have a copy made."

Karen could see nothing in his face. She chuckled. "Every thief thinks everyone steals."

"*What?*" Now his eyes were cold, fixed on her.

"It's just an expression, Martin. At least the bracelet is back and no one tried to steal it after all, so everything is fine."

"Everything is fine? Is my son back?"

Now he fixed the stud to the collar button and stood back from the mirror to examine the effect. He lifted his white braces up onto his shoulders and adjusted them, fiddled with the cuff links on the starched French cuffs.

Is he watching me in the mirror? she wondered. What was going on inside his mind? The placid, cool expression on his face seemed suddenly like some stranger's, like a mask. Who *was* he? The envelope that the bracelet had been in was an ordinary one you could buy in the post office or a supermarket stationery section. Plain white, self-adhesive flap. The kind most everybody used. The kind *they* used. There was a bundle of them in the drawer of the telephone table downstairs. The cellophane had been torn open. One was missing. But she could not remember whether she had taken it. It was really too absurd to be thinking such things about him. Yet she remembered something else.

One evening after dinner, they sat with their coffee in front of the TV, watching the late news as was their custom. But this time Martin had taken three glasses of wine with dinner, very unusual for him, and he was talking more than usual. Entertaining her. He had her laughing and seemed to enjoy that. It was cozy. Then the commentator started interviewing a high executive from McKinney, and Martin said, "Ah! It's Anders Madsen. I worked under him years ago. He taught me one of the most important lessons of my career."

"What? What did he teach you?"

Martin glanced at her, a meditative smile on his lips, as though he were considering whether to say what he would say. "He taught me that if someone makes something difficult for you, you take the first opportunity to make it twice as difficult for him. It doesn't matter what. And it isn't important whether they know right off that it was you who did it. It will be known. The effect is cumulative. People know who they're up against. They think twice." He looked so pleased as he told her, his smile so expectant of her admiration and complicity in the revelation, that she mirrored his smile, not to hurt his feelings, not to deride the gift of his confidence. She chuckled. "You're a tough guy all right." And was touched by the rare openness of pleasure her admiration clearly mirrored in his own face—even if it was false admiration. But there were so many other things she had always admired about him.

Now he turned from the mirror, black butterfly in place at the throat of his pleated shirt, jacket roll-buttoned, immaculate white rectangle in his breast pocket, shiny stripe down the outer seams of his black tuxedo trousers, draped just so on glistening black shoes, gold wristwatch with crocodile

band, ruffled shirt flat on his flat belly, his close-cropped hair immacu-
lately brushed, faint scent of cologne from his lean jaw.

"The car will be here in ten minutes."

She rose to display her long black Jaeger dress, piped with black spangles,
black net gloves to the wrist, filmy dark shawl over her bare arms and
shoulders.

"Elegant," he said.

She could see nothing on his face.

45. In the Hotel Bar

In the D'Angleterre bar, half a dozen Tank personnel milled about inside the King's New Square entrance, sipping Crémant, waiting for the others. Neither the guests of honor nor Jaeger had arrived yet, and Breathwaite kept an eye on both entries because the Irish delegation might very well appear from the sneaky little back door above the three-step stairway from the hotel lobby. Probably would, in fact. They were Kerrymen. Kerrymen were said to prefer to come up from behind so they could get ahead of you. Breathwaite had armed himself with a few such sayings in case they came in handy for the evening.

A Kerryman is the only person who can enter a swing door after you and come out first.

He had an idea, though he was never certain, that they enjoyed these things, unlike Århusians, who, it seemed to him, did not appreciate Copenhagen jokes about people from the Jutland capital.

How long does it take an Århusian to clean the basement windows? Three hours: one hour to dig the hole, one to find the ladder, and another to wash the windows.

Breathwaite considered springing that one on their jittery spin doctor, Ib Andersen, who hailed from Århus and was currently hopping around from couple to couple, dealing out witty comments no one could understand, while his wife trailed close behind, holding his arm like the string of a balloon that might float up and lodge itself against the ceiling.

Breathwaite mentally rehearsed another: *A Kerryman is standing on a country road, leaning against a fence, and a Rolls-Royce pulls up. The window lowers and a Brit in the backseat says, "My good man, can you tell me how to get to the Dingle Road?" The man scratches his head and says, "The Dingle Road. Well, let's see now, you continue straight up this road, across the little bridge to the crossing where the great oak used to be, and . . . No, no, wait. You've got to back up here and turn around, drive about five miles toward the . . . No, no, no, that's not it, either. You've got . . ." Whereupon the Brit says to his chauffeur, "Driver, move on, this man is obviously an idiot," and the Kerryman says, "Well, sir, I may be an idiot, but you're the one who's lost!"*

The PA system was playing Bob Marley's "Three Little Birds." Breathwaite was worried. He had been on the phone with Kampman, and if Jaeger didn't show, Kampman had threatened to let the spin doctor make the welcome speech, which would leave Breathwaite twice removed from the action. Kis was at his side, looking gorgeous in a narrow charcoal gray Jackie Kennedy–type cocktail dress. Breathwaite was trying to remember to keep his gut sucked in so as not to spread the lapels of his ruffled shirt across his belly, thinking that maybe he could make love to Kis later. He could try. She looked so good. She was holding her champagne glass by the edges of its base and snipped her fingernail against the bell. The ring was flat. She smiled at him, and he saw the smile was saying, *Cheap glass.* She had a valuable collection of antique glass herself.

"The glass expert," he said to her. "You can see right through me."

"And I like what I see. All the way through."

"Think so?"

"Know so."

Now Kampman stepped in with Karen on his arm, wearing his inscrutable smile. His wife looked elegant in a simple black dress, her tight blond curls, a simple gold necklace and bracelet. Breathwaite had always admired her. Kampman nodded, greeted the spin doctor, Birgitte Sommer, and her husband. Breathwaite recognized that the message was for him to go to the CEO if he wanted his existence to be acknowledged. He was not much for it, but thoughts of the job for Jes spurred him. He stepped across and smiled and had to put out his own hand and wait a moment before Kampman accepted it.

The edges of the CEO's mouth spread into a narrow smile. "Do the Irish appreciate your hotel choice? An English hotel?"

"The Irish are pragmatic," Breathwaite said. "They like it here."

Kampman lifted one eyelid over his smile and chuckled, lifting and dropping his shoulders a couple of times. Breathwaite had never disliked the man but felt he was learning to. Then, from the corner of his eye, he saw the three Irish delegates appear at the top of the little stairway from the back door: Sean Cronin, Gussy Dunbar, and Anroi Dignam.

Breathwaite stepped quickly toward them and said loudly, "Three Kerrymen walk in the back door of a bar. The bartender says, 'What's this? A joke?'"

Cronin smiled with the edges of his little white teeth joined and giggled quietly. Gussy Dunbar gazed at him with a practiced look of bewilderment, while the twitch of Dignam's lip was his smile. They shook hands all around as Sean Cronin told a story, smiling merrily:

"I had a lovely encounter with a beautiful young Danish woman today at an automobile rental office. It pleased me very much. As I was applying for the automobile, she inquired after my year of birth, and when I said 1943, she looked most skeptical and said gravely, 'Oh, Mr. Cronin, I am thinking nineteen *fifty*-three.'" And he giggled merrily.

Gussy Dunbar continued to look bewildered, and Dignam leaned toward Breathwaite's ear and muttered, "You will notice for the moment I am saying nothing."

Cronin seized Kampman's hand and exclaimed, "Ah, Morten, Morten, how good to see you again. Are you well?"

Kampman smiled his narrow smile. "Wery vell, sanks. And actually my name is Martin, not Morten."

"Whatever made me say Morten? Well, it is good to be vell. Vell vell vell."

Breathwaite was fearing the worst. No sign of Jaeger and Sean Cronin full of mischief. This whole thing could blow up in his face. Then he noticed that Sean was carrying what appeared to be a bottle wrapped in colorful paper, and the three Irishmen surrounded him while the company looked on.

Kampman, to Breathwaite's surprise, struck the bell of his glass with the tines of a cocktail fork to call for silence.

"Now, Freddy," Sean said, "we have heard the sad news that you have decided to withdraw from the Tank, and it has made us very sorrowful indeed. So sorrowful that we bought this bottle of spirits to cheer ourselves up. But then we got to thinking that, well, perhaps you will be sad at not seeing us anymore, either, so we decided to give the bottle to you instead."

Breathwaite glanced at Kampman, who was smiling happily, then at Kis, whose mask, he could see, was close to slipping. The intensity of the hatred he felt for Kampman at that moment, for the pain and embarrassment he had caused Kis, was almost enough to make him throw it all over. But what could he do? He squeezed Kis's hand. She returned the squeeze, but her blue eyes were hurt. He bent, smiling, to kiss her cheek and whispered, "It's nothing. Don't worry. I'll explain," cursing himself for not having done so earlier. He remembered then Kampman on the plane back from Dublin: *That's it. Morticians. They're the ones who bury dead people, right?* And felt the fury running down his arm toward his fist. He wanted to hammer it into that smug fucking face. But there was still Jes. That was a done deal. This was just an extra surcharge on the package.

At that moment, he glimpsed Jaeger drifting through the King's New Square entry. He looked like hell. He was wearing not a tuxedo but a rumpled beige suit. His eyes were red, with gray puckered pouches sagging beneath them. There was a big, filthy bandage on one finger and something that looked like a glob of mayonnaise at the corner of his mouth, smeared into his obscene little red beard.

Breathwaite squeezed Kis's hand again and reluctantly let it go as he moved over toward Jaeger. A strange-looking woman was trailing a few paces behind him and to one side, long and very thin, moving with slow, dreamy steps, her eyes fixed with dreamy tenderness on Jaeger's profile. Breathwaite, smiling, said softly, "Got a handkerchief? Wipe the right corner of your mouth . . . Again! . . . More." Then, "Do you remember the speech? Yeats. Not *Yeets* but *Yates*. William Butler. 'Wine comes in at the mouth / And love comes in at the eye . . .'"

"I remember, I got it down," Jaeger said, and his breath reeked of beer and mustard.

Breathwaite glanced at the strange woman, not certain whether to greet her, but she crossed to the bar and took a glass of Crémant from the tray held by a black-liveried waitress. She perched on a stool at the bar, crossing her thin legs so you could see clear up to Christmas. Breathwaite had Jaeger by the elbow, steering him toward the Irishmen. "Give it five minutes before you speak," he whispered. "I'll give the signal."

They moved past Birgitte Sommer, whose arms were twined around her husband's one arm, while he—Lars was his name, Breathwaite remembered—glared with narrow eyes at Jaeger.

Jaeger pumped Irish hands as Breathwaite washed down his bitterness with Crémant and introduced Jaeger as his successor, his left arm around Kis, massaging the nub of her shoulder. Bewildered Gussy Dunbar seemed to see Kis for the first time; he seized her hand and kissed it, gazing intensely into her eyes. "You are a magnificent figure of a woman," he murmured, while Dignam muttered to Breathwaite, "Nothing spoken, no regret."

To kill time, Breathwaite tore the wrapping paper off the bottle Sean Cronin had given him. "Ah!" he exclaimed, gladdened and moved to discover a limited-edition fifteen-year-old Jameson.

"You'll like the nose on that," Dignam muttered. "Now don't quote me."

Glancing at Kampman, Breathwaite said, "I'll *bury* my nose in it," then regretted the dig. There was still Jes.

"Freddy," said Gussy. "Breathwaite: Now you'd be a Lambeg man, would you not?"

Breathwaite thought of his ancestor, the informer, and said, "No. My people are from Tipperary."

Gussy's bewildered eyes ruminated. "Never heard of a Breathwaite from Tipperary."

"At least that's what my father told me. Maybe he lied."

"And haven't our fathers all lied to us!"

Breathwaite's secretary was beside him, whispering, "It's time for the seating." A table for thirty had been set sidewise along the King's New Square window in the restaurant alongside. Breathwaite slipped his Montblanc from his inside pocket and struck it against the whiskey bottle until the conversation in the room hushed. Kampman now had his inscrutable smile on again and was watching him.

"Now it is my pleasure," he said, "to give the floor to my young colleague Harald Jaeger, who"—he glanced at Kampman—"will be succeeding me as international liaison."

Jaeger fumbled in his pocket for some crumpled sheets, and with his first word, Breathwaite remembered that Jaeger's spoken English was not particularly good.

"When this is my first time to be doing this," Harald said, a flush creeping slowly up from his collar into his cheeks, "I am remembering that the first time is always special."

There was a mutter of laughter through the room, and Sean Cronin threw back his head, smiling with the edges of his front teeth, and said, "I hope it as good for you, then, as it is for us!"

More laughter broke out, louder, and Jaeger's cheeks flamed. His eyes jumped back and forth as a smile slithered desperately over his mouth and a giddy laughter chuckled from his throat. Breathwaite slapped him on the back. "Good one, Harald!" Hoping it might pass as intentional.

"So it is a pleasure—"

"I *am* pleased," said Sean. "And please do remember that those who share the same bed do not necessarily share the same dream."

Now everyone was laughing, even Breathwaite. It was impossible not to succumb. The large strange eyes of the long thin woman at the bar were gazing with iconic compassion upon Jaeger, whose own eyes jumped about the room, from face to face, clearly seeing no one. He lifted the champagne glass in his right hand, his bandaged pinky jutting out at a vaguely obscene angle. Apparently, he had abandoned his printed text. "To velcome our guests from Ireland I vould read a digt, a poem by a poet from the wery special Wiking city of Dublin. The poet is Vilhelm Botler Yeets . . ."

Cronin clapped his hands once, grinning. "Oh, I love it!" And Jaeger lifted the glass formally in front of his nose. With profound seriousness and sincerity now, he began to recite:

"'Love comes in your mouth . . .'"

There was a moment of tense silence through the room. Then Jaeger started giggling.

Please please please please please, Breathwaite chanted silently in the dark realm behind his eyelids. *Please get a fucking hold of yourself!*

"I start again," Jaeger said.

"But the first start was so perfect!" exclaimed Sean Cronin.

Now Jaeger had it. Or so, apparently, he thought. He cleared his throat. The room fell to a desperately respectful silence, and Jaeger recited:

> Love comes in at your mouth.
> Vine comes in at your eye.
> This is all vi shall know of love
> Until vi grow old or die.
> I raise my glass to look at you
> And cry, *Skål*!

Clearly everyone had in silent complicity decided to hear wrong, or not to hear, even the Irish, even Sean Cronin. All toasted solemnly, all applauded, and Breathwaite's blushing secretary passed around the seating plan.

Kampman stepped up to Breathwaite. "Excellent poem," he said. "Your choice, I presume." He was smiling.

AFTERMATH

While There Is Still Time

46. Frederick Breathwaite

Warm and dry in Martinus's restaurant, Breathwaite equipped himself with a cigar and a large draft, served by the dark, eponymous Martin with his welcoming smile. Breathwaite sat at a table behind the plate window and puffed meditatively at his apostolado, gazing into the dim November light on Victor Borge Place and North Free Harbor Street. Outside, it was drizzling. A woman bicycled across the square, holding an opened black umbrella over her head. Two tables down from where Breathwaite sat, a young, angular fellow wearing a straw Borsalino and narrow, black-framed spectacles sat hunched over a latte, reading Sun Tzu's *The Art of War*, jiggling a pen over a pad, clearly prepared to take notes.

Breathwaite's cigar was slightly stale. He studied the cracked wrapper and reminded himself that he had no income now and was diminishing his capital by the day. Start smoking cheaper. Better sooner than later. This was a twenty-crown cigar. In ALDI supermarket, he could get a wooden box of five panatelas for fifty crowns—never mind that engraved on the wooden cover were the words *Original Colombo Cigars* or that they were manufactured in Germany, not the world's foremost cigar producer. They were cheap and they were smokable. He could allow himself two to three a day, and in time he would forget the taste of Cohiba.

He wet his mouth with the beer. In the future, when the weather was good, he might consider taking his beer from the bottle on a bench; you could get a perfectly drinkable bottle of pilsner from ALDI or Fakta or Netto for a crown and a half. He pictured himself swathed in his Burberry, Stetson tilted over his eyes. On a park bench. Daintily tipping back his pilsner. Colombo panatela clamped between his teeth. (*'Scuse me, sir, I forgot, just one more question, please . . .*)

He would miss his cafés and serving houses. The little pleasures. A sardine on dark rye at the White Lamb, served by an amiable one-armed waiter. Rough-cut Irish bacon and egg on toast at Dubliners, where the waiter says, "Get it down your neck now, it'll do you good," and it does;

the continuing saga of bacon propels you through the day as it negotiates the course of your alimentary canal, sliding through on its own delicate grease. And the draft so nicely tapped in Rosengårds Bodega; decorous matchboxes of the Eiffel Bar, where a double goes for a modest tune; the friendly dour face of Hans at Café Under the Clock; the friendly fellows of Femmeren—the Fiver—on Classensgade; or a selection of bracing cheeses at Krut's, where the former proprietor, Peter Kjaer, was in the process of distilling his own single-malt in the Scottish highlands, Bruichladdich vintage 2003 single-cask, an ex-bourbon cask treated with oloroso sherry.

Of course, there was an alternative, a very real alternative. He could do it the way his father had. Use it all up fast and shuffle off the coil. What did it matter now?

The irony had come afterward, as a kicker. After all the bitter kissing of Kampman's butt, fighting to salvage the unsalvageable, he won the confirmation, a concession.

"Martin, about that job for my boy . . ."

Martin stared at him with that deceptively mild expression. Then, "Send him in. We'll take a look at him."

As if he were an object, a piece of meat, a donkey. Even *that* Breathwaite swallowed. But then Jes, finally cornered at a table in Pussy Galore, listened politely to Breathwaite's offer and said, "Thanks, Dad. Really, thanks. But I don't want a job like that."

"Jes: It's part-time. You'll make a hundred grand a year for a few hours a week, have time to finish your degree, and have a foot in the door for a spot that most kids your age would give their left nut for. Even just the experience would—"

"I don't want a *spot*, Dad. I want a life."

"Here we go with the rhetoric. How much are you earning at that key-and-heel bar? A hundred crowns an hour?"

"Eighty."

"Eighty! And you're telling me no? Wake up, son!"

The boy leaned across the table. With his long body and long limbs, he made Breathwaite think of a praying mantis. "Dad, maybe *you* should wake up. Or maybe not. Maybe not. You know what happens when the dead awaken. They find that they have never lived."

It was an interesting moment for Breathwaite. He seemed to watch it from three different viewpoints. The surface view was that his son was sufficiently culturally fluent to so easily call up an appropriate quote from an Ibsen play that was more than one hundred years old; beneath that, he admired that the boy could use the quote in a debate over serious matters, like a skilled chess player selecting an old but excellent gambit; beneath that was the fact that his own son was telling him he was a dead man who had never lived. Two points of admiration, one of pain. And even if he could discount it as the observation of a callow youth, nevertheless the pain struck deep. Yet he noted with interest that it seemed to draw neither blood nor tears. So maybe the boy was right. Maybe he was already dead. Maybe he was a dead man who had forgotten to jump down into his grave. Or maybe there was another interpretation—that death *is* an awakening, life a mere illusory slumber. And what did it really matter, anyway? He was no longer even certain that he regretted any of it.

You were given a life. You used it. Or it used you. It got used up. You got used up. The only regret he felt keenly now was the hurt he had caused Kis. He should have told her what was happening right from the start. But how could he have known that Kampman would use that maneuver with the Irish? *Bastard!* He'd already had him down, but he'd had to deliver the last lethal kick in the head. Coup de grâce.

"Did you have to do that, Martin?" Breathwaite had asked him in the office the day after. "To Kis."

Kampman had shrugged elaborately. "Things should be up front. I naturally assumed she would have been the first you'd tell. And I wanted to give your friends an opportunity to say a proper good-bye. They thanked me for it, in fact."

People think they are excused from their treachery because they report it to your face. Get him back. Engage the enemy. Never was good at it. But it was Kis whom Kampman had hurt. And now that there was nothing left to lose, Breathwaite investigated his heart for the desire to take revenge, to hurt the man back for what he had done to Kis. Or was it he himself who had hurt her?

Whatever, now Kis was pissed, and he was swangled again. The sweet angel was not pleased with him. Perhaps she would never be pleased with him again. The permanent displeasure of a sweet angel was like a world of enduring sunlessness. Swangled again. Swangled forever, dick-less wonder.

Let your fountain be blessed, take delight in the wife of your youth, let her breasts fill you with pleasure, be entranced always with her.

Proverbs, he thought, *5:18–19*.

And, *What good has my capacity to spout quotations ever done me?*

Those three couples on the bridge revisited his thoughts. He had been working the memory, constructing it, so that by now it really was a scene from a musical of his own composition, and the three couples danced mournfully in the misty evening, lake glistening behind them beneath the smoky sky. The dance they did was full of sorrow, and the lyrics to the musical were by Chaucer. Mournfully they kicked and pivoted, dipped and sang:

> What is this life?
> What asketh man to have?
> Now with his love,
> Now in his cold grave,
> Alone, without company.

For a moment, a split of a moment, Breathwaite thought he was going to weep. But nothing happened. Instead he lifted the wet butt of the aposto-lado to his lips and drew.

It was half smoked, the pint of pilsner half drunk. He already knew, despite his Babbitt calculations, that he would be ordering a fresh pint, that he would be removing from his breast pocket another apostolado tube in order to enjoy the ritual: Screw the cap off the tube, tip out the cigar, grasp the end lug of the red cellophane zip strip with his fingernails and tear it around the circumference of the cigar, remove the cellophane from the cigar itself, carefully undo the band, not to destroy the wrapper (remember how his father used to say, *You like music, son; here's a whole band for you*), nose the cigar, tongue it, tear off a strip from the cedar coil inside the tube, light the cedar with which to roast the tip of the cigar, then place the cigar between your lips and draw, fill your mouth with good smoke.

This was life. This was a reason to live. This was an excuse for living. He puffed the half-smoked apostolado and gazed out Martin's window across Victor Borge Place, scattered with big soggy yellow leaves. He thought of his mother and father, years ago, attending a one-man Victor Borge show on Broadway. When? It was the mid-fifties, late fifties, maybe. When he was a child. He remembered them coming home afterward in a taxi, Dad wearing his blue suit, Mom in fashionable black, a white fur pillbox hat on her pretty head, flushed with happiness, so amused by the Dane's monologue. *Is that what brought me here? That Victor Borge had made my parents happy?*

Strange it seemed to him that that had been back in the United States, land of weak coffee, thin beer, and surly cabdrivers, in New York City, in Sunnyside, Queens, some five decades before, when he was a boy, and now he sat on Victor Borge Place in Copenhagen, fifty years and eight thousand miles away. His beautiful, unfaithful mother was dead, his idealistic, compassionate father, the amusing, sardonic Victor Borge . . . all dead.

There was a little blue sign with white letters—VICTOR BORGE PLADS/J E OLESENS GADE—fixed to the brick above the gaudy blue-and-white sign spanning the whole girth of the wall diagonally across from Martin's window. In enormous letters, it said, STØVSUGER BANDEN. It had always amused Breathwaite that the word for vacuum cleaner in Danish was *støvsuger*, literally "dust sucker." A functional language. *Støvsuger Banden* meant "the Dust Sucker Gang." A cut-rate vacuum cleaner shop. Electrolux. Eurocleaner. Universal World Cleaners. What is a universe without a Universal World Cleaners dust sucker?

Directly out in front of the window where he sat were benches and dead bare bushes, a glass bus shelter, a Plumrose sausage wagon giving off orange light in the dull, dim afternoon, its rear glass window reflecting the broad sign of the Vasketeria—"Machines and Dryers"—and the cozy front of Erland's serving house.

And on the opposite corner, a 7-Eleven occupying the ground floor of an elegant fin de siècle building. End of what century? The nineteenth. *Twentieth also finished now, by God.* Across from 7-Eleven in the other direction, moving counterclockwise around the square, a Wonderwear lingerie shop with a picture in the window of a woman in panties and bra so erotic that it would have been illegal when he was a boy. Used to study the ads in the *New York Times Sunday Magazine*, gaze rapturously at a black-and-white woman in her underwear rowing a boat in the Central Park Lake: *I dreamed I rowed a boat in Central Park wearing my Maidenform bra.* Word for bra in Danish is *brysteholder*, literally "breast holder." Picture a woman in a breast holder running a dust sucker. *I dreamed I sucked dust in my Maidenform.* Maidenform. Maiden. Old-fashioned word for virgin. Maidenhead. Hymen. *Jomfruehinde* in Danish—"virgin membrane," "virgin film." More poetic in English.

What is to be learned of all this I see and think and remember? he wondered.

Half a dozen dark autumn trees are scattered about the square, a yellow-and-orange ambulance screams past on North Free Harbor Street. Above the dust sucker shop sign rises a wall of bay windows, cozy lamps, and curtains. An Ethiopian-looking woman crosses the square pushing a baby carriage. Tall and slender and so magnificently black, a long, olive-colored veil billowing around her in the air. So beautiful. Why do some Danes object? Try to make policies against head coverings. No veils, no head scarves in school or on supermarket checkout cashiers. Why? Shall we also ban all nostalgic 1950s photographs of lovely Danish girls in head scarves? See the Muslim women sometimes so covered that all you can see are a pair of eyes peering out a slit at you. Mysterious. Who are you in there? What are you thinking? Might just as well be wearing veils ourselves, all of us, for all the secrets in our skulls. We peer out the slit of our eyes from amid them.

Now a chubby young man in punk attire, unnaturally red hair stritting up like the comb of a giant rooster. (*Wonder is* strit *an English word or only Danish? No longer know. Who I was is fading into who I am.*) What sadness behind that boy's young posturing as he bops his head to the music from his earphones. Wrapped in private music. Just as that woman was wrapped in her veil.

Just as I am wrapped in private thought. No, my thought is fed by the world I see around me. That boy is wrapped in private music that blocks out the sounds of the world around him.

Another orange-and-red ambulance screams past. Two emergencies. Double suicide? *My father and my great-granduncle, the informer from Lambeg.*

Some ancient uncle in the Sunnyside branch of the family had known him. Said he had been an intelligent and kind man. That was what nobody could understand. Why did he turn informer? Remember Dad saying, "What in the world made him do it, then?"

"Pretty simple, really. He did it for money and privilege and position. What else? Didn't expect it would blow up in his face. Fooled himself. Wound up putting a bullet in his own forehead."

Dad, too. Not a bullet, but the pills. Washed down with gin—Cork blue hundred proof. No note. *Why, Dad?*

It was after Mom died. Must've loved her, despite what she'd done. And maybe done again, who knows? How old was he then . . . let's see, she died in 1992, would've been seventy-three, he was four years older. Seventy-seven. Not young, but these days you expect more. Was it the loneliness? Or something else? *Did you finally decide your pacifism was just cowardice? Or worse? Indifference? Vomit yourself out your own mouth?*

How was it, Dad? Breathwaite wondered now, and realized he was talking to his father inside his skull. *How was it in the end when the pills and gin mixed in your blood? Did your body fight to survive, to undo what you were doing to it? Did you feel a dread sickness of approaching death washing up through your arteries beneath the blank ceiling of your numbed consciousness, patched over perhaps with fleeting bits of thought like a fevered dream? Was it too late then to stop, or did you think with the last sparks,* Yeah, yeah, get it over, get it done. Out, out.

Then Breathwaite half remembered a dream he'd had last night about his father. What? His dreams had been taking him to strange places he had never been before but that he could remember, and there was discourse of some kind, and it was not pleasant.

The discourse with Kis:

"How could you have kept that from me, Fred?"

"I thought you said the job and position and all of it didn't matter to you."

"That is not the subject. I am talking about your keeping such a thing from me. Letting me find out like that. What else is hidden away?"

"Can't you forgive me?"

"It's not a matter of forgiving or not. It makes me sad."

Swangled. *Kis is pissed. Has a right to be. I should learn to understand that, learn to suffer with grace. Learn to take it. Try to learn to be a human being for a change. Maybe I could. Consider Kis. Looks so sad about this. As my mother was. Have I made Kis unhappy? Consider your wife.*

Then he remembered something else, a dream fragment, the word *wifle*. Your little wife. Your rifle.

Ah!

The rifle over the fireplace in act one. In the trunk. The antique chest. *Frederick Breathwaite, for the crime of having not made sufficient use of your life or setting an example worthy of the three sons you created or being worthy of the beautiful wife who loved you, you are hereby sentenced to recapitulate the act of your father and his great-granduncle before him.*

Ah!

Breathwaite raised his hand toward the bar. "Martin!" And lifted his empty pint glass. "Another, please."

Then he lifted the last apostolado from his breast pocket and began to screw the cap from the end of the aluminum tube.

47. Harald Jaeger

Jaeger looked up from his desk—formerly Claus Clausen's desk—in the tiny cramped office that had been Clausen's and saw his colleague moving past, leather meeting planner beneath his arm, on his way to the Mumble Club. Clausen saw Jaeger looking and leaned in around the jamb, his tall, rangy body draped up against it.

"How goes?" Clausen asked.

"It goes."

"Y'okay?"

"All in all," said Jaeger. "I miss my windows . . ."

"Great windows."

". . . but it is almost worth it that I don't have to attend those meetings anymore."

Clausen's smile dripped with pity, which Jaeger did not wish to have and which he feared might have been intentionally taunting. In a bid to appear lighthearted, he said, "Listen, now that you sit in on those meetings, why don't you propose another office for me? One with windows."

"Of all people, you should know, Harald. That's not how we play the piano here."

Jaeger felt the naked droop of his own lips. *Big boys don't cry.* But clearly Clausen saw it, too.

"Guess it's been pretty tough for you, Harald," he said. "Did they stiff you bad on the money? What are they paying you now?"

You insolent prick! Eat this: "Well, Claus, it's like this. Being asked that is like being asked how big your dick is. If it's big, discretion dictates humility. And if it's little, well, you just don't much want that information getting around, you know?"

Clausen looked hard at him. Jaeger's instant of satisfaction led immediately to regret. This man could hurt him even more than he was hurt. But before he could try to make amends, Clausen was gone. And now he had said it. Clausen knew he had seen behind the towel that day in the showers. *You idiot.*

He and Clausen had not been out for a drink or a meal together since what Jaeger referred to, in the privacy of his thoughts, as his "reversal of fortune." The phrase was consoling, seemed to lend a dignified formality to the mess of his life. It seemed to him that in the snap of two fingers he had lost virtually everything of the little that had remained after the divorce: title, corner office, windows, secretary, a third of his salary, the apartment he could no longer afford to meet the mortgage payments on, and, worst of all, his two angels. And now, apparently, his friendship with Clausen.

He was struggling to maintain some semblance of pride, and he would not suggest to Clausen that they meet for a drink. Clausen would have to take that lead. If he suggested it to Clausen and was turned down, the refusal would be one more blow of the hammer driving him deeper into the pit of loss. So he had to wait and swallow the indignity of waiting, counting the pennies of the aftermath of his disgrace. At least, he thought, he no longer had to worry about calamity descending upon his life. It had descended.

And at least he still had a job. If only he had not made that crack to Clausen.

Kampman had called him in and with seeming profound regret informed him that he had reviewed the personnel budget with the board and that he had been instructed to make some rotations. "And"—he firmed his lips as if with brave sorrow—"to let some people go. Even my own secretary. We'll be moving Clausen around. And we cannot afford to maintain the current department head structure."

Jaeger felt sweat soak the back of his shirt, beneath his arms. Jaeger, who was two years older than the CEO, felt as though he were being lectured by his father. In a way, he realized, he thought of the CEO as his father. *Please understand me; I hate you.*

"I will certainly understand," Kampman said, "if you feel unable to accept what I can offer."

Only after he had left the CEO's office did Jaeger hear echoed in his own ears the sound of his own voice thanking the man profusely for the demotion and decrease in salary, see in his mind's eye the picture of himself clutching and shaking the CEO's hand, which declined to respond to the clinging pressure of Jaeger's.

Now, at his new desk in his miserable little windowless alcove, he looked at the hand that had so instinctively and ignominiously betrayed his own dignity, or the scrap of it that remained. He stared at the five-fingered traitor, the pulpy tip of the pinky with the pink crescent edge of nail that had begun to reappear.

Someone passed in the hall, and he glimpsed Birgitte Sommer on her way to the Mumble Club. Had that been the edge of a smile of malicious triumph on her lips? As he sat there gazing out, the new woman from accounting passed and glanced in, smiling. Jaeger had met her only once, and they had hardly spoken. When he'd introduced himself, she had offered her hand, and as he moved to take it, she stepped closer and he accidentally cupped her breast in his palm, jerked his hand away as if stung, face full of apology, but she'd only smiled. With plump lips that were made to be kissed. And her butt so gorgeous that it was almost painful for him to behold. Now, as if his mental response to its power had radiated out into the hallway and nudged her, she dropped the pencil she was carrying and bent to retrieve it, drawing blue green denim tight around those globes of marvel. Jaeger felt himself stiffen as his heart lurched, pumping blood toward his center, rallying for action. She straightened again and smiled once more, the tip of her tongue, its underside, slipping out to wet her upper lip.

Oh God, Jaeger thought. *Oh God, oh God, oh God, you are so fucking beautiful!*

At the nadir of the long deep tiled toilet, Jaeger sat with his pants around his ankles, elbows on his knees, *trying*. Another of his losses. He had never had this problem before. *Never.* On the contrary.

The curtain slid aside on its rod, and Tatyana appeared. Jaeger coughed to alert her to the fact that he was present.

"I vill not look," she said. She was naked. "Haf you had success?" she asked, looking away from him, in sympathy with his leaden bowels.

"Nul and nix," he said. "Can't even take a successful crap anymore."

She lifted the telephone shower from its hook on the wall and began to wash herself in its feeble spray, five meters from him, turning her long thin body in the narrow space between the walls. She hummed in a minor key as she washed, eyelids lowered, a smile on her lips. The melody was deeply sorrowful, but through her smiling lips and with its resonance in the high narrow space, there seemed some reverse power at the core of its sorrow, some reverent beauty.

He studied her, the lines of her, the childlike buttocks and the mysterious cleft between, the fork of her limbs with its vertical lips—an enigmatic tilted smile, her tiny breasts, china-delicate hands, fingers, wrists, feet—the feet on which she stood, toes lightly spread to negotiate her balance. The electric light from behind the curtain limned the lines of her in the steam of the water, and it seemed to him then that her body was a screen both shielding and revealing the light that blazed within her being.

He stepped out of his pants and shoes, stripped off his shirt, and stepped forward to kneel before her. She opened her eyes and beamed her smiling mouth down at him.

"Vhat kind of bird are you?" she asked, and touched his face.

He pressed his cheek against her cunt, arms doubled around her narrow hips, and began to murmur a silent prayer of thanksgiving.

48. Martin Kampman

Kampman pulled the Toyota into the garage and entered the house through the boot closet, limping slightly, his eyelids half-lowered with memory of sounds and words and sensations that would nourish him for three weeks to come. It was late. He would sleep in the basement guest room. But first he would allow himself a cognac from the XO he kept under lock in the living room. He would sit in the dark with it and contemplate the details of his evening. This was *his* time. No thought of Adam, no thought of *any*thing.

In the hallway, he thought he smelled cigarette smoke. Karen again, no doubt. But in the house? That would have to be mentioned in the morning. He knew she smoked, but she usually at least tried to hide it.

He crossed the living room in the dark, slipped out his key pouch to fit the key into the cabinet lock, lifted out the XO and a snifter. The smell of smoke was heavy here. Then a light clicked on behind him, and he spun toward it. Karen sat in her chair with a glass of wine, the floor lamp lit beside her, a cigarette smoldering between her lips.

"Who *are* you?" she asked.

He felt his head twitch. "I beg your pardon?"

"Who *are* you?"

"How much have you had to drink?"

"Who *are* you?"

For a moment he could think of no further response, fixed as he was in the sharpness of her gaze. Then his mouth opened and he said, "Are you out of your fucking mind?"

Her face showed no sign of having heard. "Who *are* you?" she said again.

"Who am I? I'll tell you who I am. I am the man who takes care of things. I am the man who gets up first in the morning and who is first into the office and last out in the evening and who takes care of things. There and here, too. That's who I fucking well am."

She twisted out her cigarette and rose, looked him up and down, laughed a single, mirthless note, and left him there.

49. Birgitte Sommer

It was not the fish. The fish had been three days ago, and she was still getting sick. Sporadically. In the bathroom, she dipped the stick of the litmus paper into the vial of urine. It turned green.

Lars was sitting at the kitchen table over a cup of coffee, picking his nose and leafing through the real estate pages of *Berlingske*. She watched him from the shadows of the shallow hall. Then he glanced up and his hand slipped beneath the edge of the table.

"Hey, honey, listen to this," he said. "'Istedgade. Handyman's special. Two hundred square meters. One point five mil.'"

"*Istedgade!* Isn't that all prostitutes and drug addicts?"

"Was. They're on the way out. It's getting to be prime real estate. Now is the time to buy. We could fix it up and sell it for at least twice that, maybe three times, in just a couple of years. Meanwhile we could rent it out."

"Where would we get the money?"

"Borrow it. You know very well the interest rate is down practically under the inflation level. With the money we made off that, we could pay off the place in Gilleleje just like *that*." He snapped his fingers. "And still have half a mil surplus." She looked at his fingers. He looked into her eyes, and his own took on a deep, intense shade of blue, almost violet. His voice was hushed. "We could be rich, honey."

Birgitte stepped through the doorway and sat across from him. "Lars," she said, "I'm pregnant."

She could see the smile begin to lighten his eyes before his face went still. She could see what he was thinking. She had already sorted this out. There was only one way to do this, only one thing to say. Everything now depended on it.

She smiled and shook her head. "He and I never got that far."

Lars was still watching her.

Only one thing to do. Her smile broadened. She shook her head again. "Never. He and I never did it, Lars. It's yours, honey."

50. Adam Kampman

There was music at the North Bodega tonight. Three men wearing black peaked caps trimmed with shiny metal piping, the word *jazz* spelled out in metal on the crown, a trumpet player, guitarist, and bass man. The bass, a short, dark-haired man with a strong jaw, also sang. He was singing "Dream a Little Dream of Me."

Adam sat by himself at the corner table, sipping a Hof, surprised that he was enjoying the music, the man's moody, sad voice. He knew this song from somewhere and had never liked it, but he liked the way this man sang it.

Across the room, the man Adam had seen before with the bandage on his finger sat at the alcove table with that strange-looking long thin woman. The bandage was gone, and he was holding her hand and peering deeply, almost reverently, into her eyes. She returned his gaze. They were very still, almost like a painting.

The singer in the black peaked cap was making faces as he plucked the bass, now doing "Oh, Lady Be Good."

I'm just a poor boy
Lost in the wood.
Lady be good
To me.

Jes and Jytte had not shown up. Adam wondered whether they were together, wondered whether he cared. Jytte's feelings for Jes seemed to fluctuate constantly between admiration and annoyance, while her feelings for him seemed more like she considered him a little brother, even if he was older than her. He realized the other evening, listening to her argue with Jes, that he didn't love her anyway. He realized he didn't know what love was. He didn't know what anything was or meant, and somehow that realization was bracing to him. He felt as though he had walked into a brick wall of ignorance, slammed his face flat up against it, wiping out any thought he had ever had, or thought he had had, and now it would be necessary to rethink everything. Everything. He knew nothing, nothing at all, and the sudden awareness of that had the power of revelation. He was free.

Life now was like a blank picture, an empty box, and what he had to do now was slowly, carefully, to fill that emptiness. He would take on nothing without carefully examining it first. And the first thing he wanted to do was read a book. He had been forced to read so many books in school and had answered questions about them in class and on examinations and had received very high grades for his answers, but it was all fake. He understood nothing of it. Now he would take one book, *one*, and he would read it, scrutinize it, and he would not put it aside until he understood it. He would take nothing for granted, nothing at face value. All he had to do was select the book, and he had all the time in the world to do that, and he would take his time. It was exciting to think about. Out of all the books that had ever been written, he would now select one, and he would read it. He would look at every word from every angle he could imagine, and he would find understanding.

Or else he would create it.

The singer ended his song and said with his gravelly voice, "You have been listening to the Asger Rosenberg Trio, and now we will take a short and very intense pause before we come back singing again. And remember, as a very wise man once said, 'A little beer is good for you.' So by extrapolation, a lot of beer is a lot of good for you."

The men laid aside their instruments and went to the bar, and Adam noticed then, around the turn of the wood, half-hidden against the wall, that man again. It was definitely the same man. He thought so. It could be. The man slid off his stool and began to gather his coins and cigarette pack and matches from the bar.

Adam decided. He swallowed the rest of his Hof, slipped on his jacket, and went to the door. The man zipped his jacket. Blood was pulsing in Adam's ears. He took his time opening the door and paused outside, pretending to look at something he took out of his pocket, watching from the corner of his eye as the man approached the door. Then he started walking.

He turned right from Solitude Way onto North Bridge Street and heard footsteps continue behind him. A quick glance over his shoulder and Adam saw it was the man from the bar. He decided to keep going to the next corner and to cross, and if the man was still there, he would act. He slowed his pace to time his approach to the corner with the green light, crossed slowly. The man was close behind him now. On the opposite pavement, Adam spun toward him.

"Are you following me?"

The man jerked back and glared at him. Then he said, "What are you, fucking nuts?"

"You mean you're *not* following me?"

"Get lost, you little asshole. What are you, a faggot?" He stepped around Adam and moved quickly away, and Adam started laughing.

The man spun back, muttered, "Idiot," and crossed to the other side of the street fast.

Adam couldn't wipe the smile off his face. He kept chuckling as he continued down North Bridge Street, turned right on Blågårds. He hoped Jes was home. He wanted badly to talk to him, to try to explain what was happening, how the one thing seemed to lead to the other.

Words appeared in his mind. *What you don't know you only have to ask. Ask who? Someone, yourself.* So simple, yet it seemed to have the force of revelation.

On Blågårds Place, he spotted Jytte sitting on the low park wall, talking to someone—Jes. They were both drinking from bottles of Tuborg. There were others around them, too—the guys Jes had introduced him to at the North Bodega. Jes spotted Adam, too, and bowed to a plastic bag at his feet, lifted out a bottle, and chucked it to Adam, who barely caught it. Beer geysered out as he popped the cap, and Jes flourished his hand before him and said, "My friend: Allow me, plice, to offer you the woba golves of Jalâl. There is pain and there is suffering in the world, but we are all in the hands of God, who wears the woba golves of the eternity. All else is sport and play."

Jytte was sniggering. Adam laughed a little, too, but there was something here he didn't like. Jes kept going on and on.

Then, over Jes's shoulder, Adam saw a man approaching from behind. He thought he recognized him. He thought it was Jalâl.

51. Jalâl al-Din

In the back of the shop, Jalâl washed his hands carefully, working the rough grains of scouring powder along the edges of his fingernails, into the creases of his knuckles and palms. Then, holding up his hands like a surgeon's, he turned to Khadiya, who draped a clean white linen towel over them and rubbed them dry. It was their daily ritual, the way she helped Jalâl out of the world of commerce and back into the life of family and spirit. When she had dried his hands, she rolled down the long sleeves of his gray dishdasha for him and patted his cheek. He kissed her forehead.

"You have some old bread for me?" he asked, pulling on a sky blue padded ski jacket over his dishdasha and switching a wool pakol for his lightweight kufi cap. She handed him a plastic bag stuffed with leftover bread and pita of the past days.

"We eat at nine," she said.

"My boy Zaid is coming today?"

"Tonight we dine alone again," she said, and touched his cheek to comfort him. "He will be all right," she said. "He needs only some more time."

Jalâl smiled ruefully, nodded. He let himself out the front of the shop, stepping around the little wooden horse ride, which he dragged in each night and out again each morning when he opened at nine, even if no one ever rode it. Someday perhaps it would give pleasure to some small ones, his own grandchildren, perhaps.

He locked the front door with a key and, from the street, surveyed the front of the shop quickly. Time to wash the window. Dome of the Rock. It pleased him. It was a good enough business. It fed and sheltered them all. He knew he would never be a wealthy man, but he would never be a poor man, either. He earned enough for his family and a little extra for charity, too. And it pleased him to employ the son of an important man. A good boy, who listened to the things Jalâl had to say to him.

It could have been Zaid working for him, but that had been the source of their angry words, Jalâl's assumption that the boy would help him in the shop. It was necessary for Jalâl to learn to understand that this would not be so, to listen to Khadiya's counsel about this, unreasonable as it seemed to him.

He crossed Fælled Way, heading toward North Bridge Street, plastic bag tucked beneath his arm, greeting the fellow merchants he passed on his way in the common Arabic they used on the street.

"Salaam aleikem."

"Aleikem salaam."

Jalâl belonged to no mosque. There must be no compulsion in religion, Muhammad had said, and no exaggeration. Jalâl constructed his own manner of observance. He read his Koran with care. He meditated the words, and he also read the thoughts of learned imams and considered them. It was a way to live in peace with other men. It was good.

On the corner of North Bridge, a young man sat cross-legged on the cold sidewalk with a small cardboard box in front of him. Printed on a paper propped against his knees were the words *Homeless & hungry.* The young man's head was bowed.

Jalâl dropped two crowns into the box.

"Have a good day," the young man said without looking up.

"God's blessing," said Jalâl. So many orphans now in Denmark. How did this happen in a land that had always made provision for the poor? But even the poor here were hardly poor in the material things. They were a well-fed people for whom hardship meant no playing toys for the children or no vacations on a sunny beach. He thought of his days in Kabul, after the Russians had come in and killed his father. Then there had been days of very little food, when a full loaf of bread was a luxury, a single egg a precious thing. These people had not known such hunger. Perhaps far in the past, but not this generation and not the one before that, either. Of course, they had the Germans here under the last great war. He understood that, as they would understand him. But the hunger here now was different. Jes, who worked for him, was skinny as a beggar, haunchless, but he did not want for food or any other thing he chose—education especially. Things were changing.

He turned toward the lakes, passed the halal butcher on his way out of his shop.

"Salaam aleikem."

"Aleikem salaam."

He passed an electronics shop, a clothing store, a café where young people sat entertaining themselves. He scanned their faces, expecting, hoping always, to see the face of his own youngest, Zaid. Jalâl had not seen the boy for eight, nine weeks now. Longer, perhaps. Last time they had expressed anger toward each other. Jalâl had expressed anger while the boy sat silently, sullenness lowering over his face like a curtain. It made Jalâl angry. It made him want to strike the boy's face. Angry words filled his mouth and spilled out, and then the boy raised his voice, too, rose from his chair, crying, and fled from their home. Eight weeks ago. Longer. Anger was not of use. Jalâl's anger was at himself. The boy's absence was constant pain in Jalâl's heart. He accepted the pain as his due. They had argued over money, the money Jalâl would save if the boy would work for him. A father and son should not argue over money. He knew the boy was in contact with Khadiya, and he trusted that Khadiya would inform him if Zaid was in a dangerous situation. He had no choice but to trust Khadiya's reassurances.

Yet tonight again, the two of them would dine alone. *Oh, my Zaid! Forgive me and come home so that I may forgive you and bless you and have the blessing of your presence again.* If any do something bad in ignorance, but then repent and make amends, assuredly God is forgiving and merciful. With God are the keys of the unseen.

On the bank of Black Dam Lake, he opened the mouth of the plastic bag and began to break off pieces of the old bread and cast it out onto the surface of the water. Swans and ducks and the other funny little squeaking birds, like ducks with pointed bills, began to paddle toward him. There was a lot of bread today, and many birds came. Pigeons materialized around his feet, pecking at the crumbs, and seagulls hovered in the air above his head, swooping to get the larger pieces before they struck the water. One of the gulls was especially aggressive and successful at seizing far more than his fair share of the bread. He would catch a lump in his beak and swoop up again, swallow it, and be back in a moment for more.

Jalâl smiled. Greedy bird. He paused in his distribution of the bread and looked up at the gull hovering above him.

"What sort of bird are you?" he said. "Not the falcon of a king. Not a peacock to delight the eyes. Not a parrot asking for a sugar lump, or a nightingale singing like a man whose heart is in love. What exactly do you do? You swoop and seize. You want more than you need. You have forgotten that God feeds but is not fed—God, who owns everything and gives it to us to share and who knows nothing of taking profit from every exchange."

His prayer did nothing to deter the bird, but it brought comfort to his own heart. It was a prayer written by the poet Rumi, from whom Jalâl had his name. When the bread had been distributed, he stuffed the bag into his jacket pocket and dusted the crumbs from his palms. Then he decided to take a long circle home to exercise his legs. His body grew stiff from sitting too long at his workbench in the shop.

Back across Queen Louise's Bridge, he stopped to glance at the statue of a boy and girl sitting and gazing at each other. He smiled, thought of Zaid, who would surely soon be thinking to choose a young woman. He must choose wisely to have good fortune. Jalâl walked the whole length of Peblinge Lake, turned up Åboulevard, then right on Blågårds Street.

Perhaps somewhere he would see Zaid. Perhaps if they just saw each other on the street, in a neutral place, their eyes would meet and the memory of their angry words would fall away like scales from their eyes. They would approach each other and embrace and would be wiser in the future. Jalâl would be wiser. He had learned something about his anger and his will. When we choose incorrectly, God offers pain to help us choose the way back to the correct path. It is for us to choose. We must be attentive to the lessons that are available to us. We must remember that God forgives and that there is not anything green or withered but is an open book to God.

As he entered Blågårds Place he noticed, at the center of the small group of young people standing, talking, by the wall, a figure that was familiar to him. He saw only his back, and for a moment he grew confused with hope that it might be his youngest, Zaid. But this figure was much taller than Zaid. Then he saw it was his other "son," young Jes, whose name sounded like "Yes" and who helped him in the shop.

He started across to greet him, for it was important to render greetings—to treat all as good neighbors in order to help them to be good neighbors.

52. Jes Breathwaite

The beer was good in him. Jes felt its radiance glowing around him. He felt as though he had become his own father, had given birth to himself. He felt like a messenger of the gods, a prophet of mirth, a preacher of laughter. He perceived wonder in the eyes of his flock, Adam and Jytte and a couple of others from the North Bodega who stood off to the sides, slouched against the wall, grinning.

Jes rotated his hand before him as a flourishing fanfare.

"Consider," he said, "the fig. God has more than one child. There is the fig, the apple, the cherry, the olive, the onion. I say unto you, marry the women who please you. Two, three, four, but if you cannot treat them equitably, then stick to one."

His public sniggered.

"Do not take my words for mockery or sport, you apes and swine and slaves of seducers that do not understand. For yours is an evil state, you shaytaans of dhulma! You in the dark who cannot emerge from it. The intercourse between the man and the woman is of the sacredness." He made a ring of his left thumb and forefinger and, tongue lolling, drove the right index finger through it.

His public laughed.

"But do not marry the orphan girl for her wealth, and always provide to the nakedness of the ignorant the clothing of wisdom."

Out of the corner of his eye, he saw that Adam and Jytte were not laughing. They were not even smiling. What was this, the turn of the worms?

"Take on your woba golves, O you of little mirth," he pronounced, popping his eyes. "Take not the dark without the light or without the daily clove of garlic for the sick, little organ in your neck, and remember that with God are the keys and the heels of the unseen, and do not take into your hand the boot of the man who has slain your daddyo . . ."

Something in their faces stopped him. They seemed to be looking behind him, and their faces were troubled. Jes turned and saw Jalâl there, in his gray dishdasha and kufi and padded sky blue ski jacket.

The little man's face was impassive, and he said quietly, "You thought perhaps I was doing you a joke when I told to you these things I told?"

Jes's lips parted, but no words came to his mouth.

"This I did not expect from you," Jalâl said quietly, and Jes glimpsed hurt in the luster of his protruding eyes as he turned and hurried away across the square.

The man's short legs moved swiftly, and Jes followed, trying to keep up, calling, "Jalâl!" and then again, more loudly, "Jalâl! Jalâl! Jalâl!" trying desperately to catch up with the man.

53. Frederick Breathwaite

The view from Breathwaite's south windows was dim, smudgy. The dome of the Marble Church up past Grønningen looked dirty through it, the green copper towers of the city tarnished.

He considered washing the windows to improve the view. Surprise Kis when she got home from her job. Win a smile. But Kis was not smiling these days. She was sad. She had never been sad for this long before.

"Because I lost my job?" he had asked her.

"Because you lied, Fred. You didn't tell me. For how long?"

"It wasn't a lie, exactly."

"You can lie by not telling something, too."

"I wanted to spare you."

"You wanted to spare yourself."

Take more than clean windows to make her smile. She needs a man.

So instead of going to the slop closet for a bucket and sponges and Windex, he went out into the hall, removed an ornamental bowl from the top of the antique trunk, flipped open the locks, and lifted the lid. Beneath folded blankets and tablecloths, surplus towels and old photo albums—which he stacked on the polished hardwood floor—was a false bottom. He wedged it up and removed a half-meter-long, clanking felt bag, closed by a knotted drawstring. Then he repositioned the false bottom, returned blankets, tablecloths, towels, and photo albums, closed the lid, and re-placed the ornamental bowl.

In the library, on top of his antique mahogany desk, he unknotted the drawstring and took out and assembled the parts of his thirty-caliber Winchester underlever rifle and screwed on the telescopic scope. The rifle was not really built for a scope. It was meant to fire heavy bullets at short range and was not particularly accurate. So the telescopic sight was not of much benefit. But he used the sight only to play with. His objective today was short range. Very.

He checked the chamber. Empty.

He got the tall aluminum ladder from behind the utility closet door and climbed it to the top shelf there, felt around for a box of thirty-caliber cartridges, climbed down again, and pressed the bullets into the loading mechanism, one after another, each falling into position with a pleasing mechanical click. This was the rifle he had always wanted as a boy, ever since he had seen James Stewart in *Winchester '73*.

Years before, when Jes was ten or eleven, Breathwaite had had an opportunity to buy it from a colleague who hunted. He'd had dreams of taking up hunting, bringing Jes along, having something physical to share with the boy, but also to lift himself up a notch in Danish society. Hunting was an aristocratic sport. He and Kis had been invited to a party at the home of a baroness, and there had been talk of the hunt. The baroness herself had trophies mounted on the walls of her library—a deer's head, the skin of a two-meter alligator she'd shot years before on the Bernard Baruch estate in South Carolina. An invitation to the hunt seemed imminent.

But he never got far. He never even really started. Hiking in the deer park with Jes one autumn Sunday, they observed the deer and stags in rut, and Jes asked, "Will you be shooting *them*, Dad?" And he saw in the mirror of the boy's gentle eyes the reflection of his own once cherished innocence, and he knew he would not be getting up some dawn to go out in expensive hunting boots to stalk and kill an animal. Even if that innocence was dead in his own heart, he would not trample on its corpse for his boy to see. He would not enlist in a society of animal killers to fabricate an identity. Not even that he *would* not, he *could* not. Because it was not for the meat or the hunt or the sport, it was for the identity: Frederick Breathwaite, hunter. Deerslayer. Strictly uppa crust.

Who are you, Fred? Who are you?

Now, however, with the rifle across his knees and his death a mere arm's length from him, he was free of that. He carried the rifle in the crook of his arm out onto the south balcony, let himself out into the nippy late afternoon. He sighted through the telescopic mount, set the crosshairs on the head of a man climbing onto the East Port trestle, followed him up and across to the street. Could pick him right off if he wanted. *Bing!* Maybe miss. See dirt fly up where the bullet hit beside him. See the man look around, wonder. Or he could put this in the sports bag he never used and carry it across the city, station himself in the bushes of the botanical garden and watch Kampman's window, lever a cartridge into the chamber, wait for his face to appear, sight, squeeze, watch him drop.

Or he could take off his shoe, put his big toe on the trigger and the muzzle in his mouth, and . . . Leave that terrible mess for Kis? No.

He pumped the cartridges out of the rifle, broke it, checked the chamber to be certain it was empty, and stuffed it back into the felt bag, which he knotted and returned to the false bottom of the antique chest.

With a Tullamore rocks and his last Cohiba, he sat on the balcony on the two-man outdoor sofa. The concrete wall was a little more than a meter high, topped by a brass rail that needed polish. He could step up onto the wall, step off, leap, dive, fall. Let the city clean the bloody pavement. He'd already paid for more than that in taxes.

Leave a note: "Dearest Kis, I am so sorry, but I could not face and did not want you to have to face the pain of a long dying with this cancer . . ."

Not a lie, really. Just a metaphor.

Or I could just climb up and fall. An accident. Lost my footing. Take the camera up with me, make it look as if I'd been going for a telescopic picture of the Marble Church, say, and lost my footing. Took a wrong step. Drank a few whiskeys. Misjudged my balance under the influence. Drunk is something I love getting but hate being. To the edge. Faced away from the plunge to snap a picture of the roof, faulty gutter up there, insurance purposes. Staggered sideways. Stepped away from an approaching figure. Optical illusion. Startled me. Blank air sucked me down into its boundless well.

Bang!

The impact of a body on the pavement from this height makes a terrible loud noise and actually rattles the walls and floors above. Infinity of pain in an instant as life is driven from the body in one shot, all those friendly cells that gathered together to become you—under the direction of what or who?—dispersed on impact.

The undoing of me. Skull cracked like a hollow rock. Spillage of gray brain. Drops of it sprayed about, skull fragments flying all over the place, teeth! Free of them at last. All systems stop. You are dead. You are a dead man.

An ether rises from the mess. The essence of you, but not the *you* you know as you. That *you* was a mere shell and a surface. Disposable wrapper. You knew nothing of the infinity you bore in the capsule of your body, for you wasted your life on superficial trivialities. Gone gone gone the chance you had. Game too complex and scary. You stayed on the sidelines. You were scared. Pleasured yourself, turned your back on the masses. Be gone, faint heart. Pale fire. Lukewarm you. Spewed from your own mouth. Judge, jury, defendant, and executioner in a single step over the edge of the wall and down. *Whoosh!* Be vomited out the mouth and washed away by sacred rain and wind, return to the cosmic weird economy, foreign particle in the WC bowl.

And that's it.

But no, before the little will-o'-the-wisp of spirit disperses forever in the autumn breezes, a current from the sky snakes down, as such Copenhagen streams of air will do, and lifts it for one last tour of the city. One last peep. Lifted from the fallen broken bones and splattered fluids that were Breathwaite on East Railway Street and rising to let the last breath of B take in one last time the assortment of embassy mansions and the apartments of nobodies alike, anybodies, rather, everybodies, elegant buildings along the eastern streets—sandblasted, clean, and well tended from the foot of the furrowed stone walls past sturdy heavy carved wood doors and tall slender segmented white window frames to the red-clay roof tiles, formed of a worker's thigh.

Breathwaite's last eternal instant of fading light sees all this and more, and his heart brims with a love for the place that he understands suddenly is profoundly felt. This is a city where a human being could live a human life, even as his guttering remnant was swept farther, across the tracks, past the Grønningen windmill, past a wall of old luxury apartments, the faces of no longer quite wealthy Danish barons and baronesses, counts and countesses, cheeks bulging with their dinners, pressed against the well-appointed windows to witness as Breathwaite is carried on the air past the relicts of their lives, the treasured objects they preserved of gone times, over the ocher naval barracks of Nyboder, toward the harbor, over the green cupola of the Marble Church in all its portly grace, flanked around by famous potbellied theologians looking upward, pointing, *Look! There's a flying Breathwaite up above! The knight of infinite resignation who lost it!*

And look down, quick, now, there's Amalienborg—an open-courted royal castle, wondrous! he thought, drifting back across the fortress of Kastellet and Langelinie, where he saw the tiny mermaid on her rock, watching the sea. And he thought this would surely be the end of his little closing tour, but a fluke of the wind decided to show him more. Rapidly through the Centrum first, whipping back and forth, light as a feather, over the copper towers of Christiansborg and the twisted dragon tails of the stock exchange, lifting up again, high, high, higher up, so he could see it all in one clean sweep! Look! Back over there the tower of the Savior's Church, and there's Rosenborg Castle! And there's the Round Tower and Nikolaj Church, and look there, look there, Mercury on a Butcher Street roof, balanced on the toe tips of one foot like a beautiful green acrobat, a dancer defying gravity with a helmet of wings, and look there! The lakes! You see them all from up here—Black Dam and Peblinge and St. George's, so like a river, so like the boxcars of a train, a water train on its way to circle and celebrate our great city!

See the gardens! The parks! All the statues given us by brewer Jacobsen of Carlsberg and the thirsty love of beer! All out to the west side and Frederiksberg and the canals, too, and over to the north and south toward the bridge and Amager—you never really saw, so little of it, so much more to see and see again, you never understood. Only too late now you see how beautiful this city is, what a privilege to be here, a human city where a human being might choose a human life.

Too late, too late, for Breathwaite is no more.

The night tinkles like ice in glasses. Brown leaves blow and are glued to pavements with frost, and a roaring, restless air rattles shop windows, tries doors, and slides past, raw with frosty cold.

And that's it.

Breathwaite opened his eyes. He could not see her face for the light from the room behind her. Then she stepped closer. She was smiling. Sad Kis was smiling.

Am I dead? Am I dreaming?

Why is Kis smiling? he thought. And, *Who knows the heart of a woman?* He looked at the Chinese archer kneeling alongside the concrete half wall. The sculpture looked clumsy, stupid. All this stuff they would have to get rid of. The air was nippy and smelled agreeably of death.

"Hello, love," Kis said, and sat beside him on the two-man, her warm thigh flush against his. She had the look of a woman who had made a decision. She leaned into him, her body so incredibly light. He could smell her scent, the aroma of all the secret potions she used, creams and oils and vapors and colognes, all the things she had used all these years to conjure the power of her femininity, her power as a woman. Which she was. Though he, he thought, was hardly a man. But she leaned into him as though he still were, as though he still could be, as though she loved him, as though he could make love to her, tireless in her attempts, and he felt a stirring. But a stirring was not enough. He was dead. He had fallen and risen and floated all across the city, and he was of no use to her. Why did she persist? Why did she place her delicate fingers on his thigh, on the inside of his thigh, moving upward?

"You know I can't," he said.

She smiled up into his face, that taunting, salacious smile. "Why not let me worry about that?" she said, and the clear, deep-throated timbre of her voice vibrated deep inside him, stirring him more. She touched him and murmured, "Mmm . . . That feels like the Fred I used to know."

He said nothing as she lowered her head and placed her open mouth against him, exhaling, her breath seeping hotly through the material of his slacks as her blue eyes peered up and found the complicity in his gaze.

"Oh, Kis," he whispered, his palms lifting to her perfumed hair, and the thought of all the things they would have to get rid of dissolved under the starry autumn sky, in the tender hot insistence of her breath.

A NOTE ON THE AUTHOR

Born and raised in New York, Thomas E. Kennedy has lived in Copenhagen for over two decades. His books include novels, story and essay collections, literary criticism, translation, and anthologies. *Falling Sideways* is the second book in his acclaimed Copenhagen Quartet to be published in the United States, following *In the Company of Angels*. His Web site is www.thomasekennedy.com.

SACRAMENTO PUBLIC LIBRARY
828 "I" Street
Sacramento, CA 95814
07/18

D1020089

For Sara,
who always makes me smile.
—C.B.C.

To Liam and Aya,
who, along with me, turn being SILLY into an art form.
—H.K.

An imprint of Rodale Books
733 Third Avenue, New York, NY 10017
Visit us online at RodaleKids.com.

Text © 2018 by Courtney Carbone
Illustrations © 2018 by Hilli Kushnir
All rights reserved. No part of this publication may be reproduced or transmitted
in any form or by any means, electronic or mechanical, including photocopying, recording, or any other
information storage and retrieval system,
without the written permission of the publisher.

Rodale Kids books may be purchased for business or promotional use
or for special sales. For information, please e-mail: RodaleKids@Rodale.com.

Printed in China
Manufactured by RRD Asia 201805

Design by Jeff Shake
Text set in Report School
The artwork for this book was created with pencil and paper,
then painted digitally in Adobe Photoshop.

Library of Congress Cataloging-in-Publication Data is on file with the publisher.

ISBN 978-1-63565-074-7 paperback
ISBN 978-1-63565-075-4 hardcover

Distributed to the trade by Macmillan
10 9 8 7 6 5 4 3 2 1 paperback
10 9 8 7 6 5 4 3 2 1 hardcover

Today I am going
to the zoo
with my family.

I cannot wait
to see the animals!

A tour guide
shows us around.
She pretends to talk
to some ducklings.

4

It makes me laugh.
My heart feels
warm and fuzzy
like their feathers.

We see elephants
playing in the water.
They have long trunks.

My brother and I act like elephants, too. My insides feel wiggly like their trunks!

Next we see lions.
Our guide asks
if we know how to roar.

The answer is yes!
We all roar
as loud as we can.

Then we see the monkeys.
They make funny faces.
We make funny faces, too.

The monkeys get angry!
The tour guide tells us
not to tease them.

Soon it is time
for lunch.

We have
a family picnic!
I feel as light
as a bird.

My brother eats
his banana
like a monkey.

I laugh so hard
that water goes
out my nose!

15

Dad helps us
to calm down.

We breathe slowly.
We count to ten.
The giggles go away.

After lunch,
we see a polar bear.
He is sleeping.

I put my hands
in the air like claws.
I feel big and strong
like a bear.

I pound on the glass
with my pretend paws.
The tour guide points
to a sign.

She tells me
loud noises can scare
some animals.

I stop to think.
Our guide is right.

It <u>is</u> scary to wake up
to loud noises.
I will be more careful.

The last stop of the day
is to see the penguins.
They are my favorite!

I waddle around
with our tour guide.
I thank her for
such a great day.

We pass a park
on the way out.
We stop to play.

I make lots
of funny faces.
My family does, too!

I feel like I am full of tiny bubbles about to burst!

My giggles are back.
But now I know
how to calm down
if I need to.

I close my eyes.
It is so much fun
to laugh, play, and
pretend.

What am I feeling?
I am feeling SILLY.

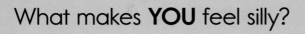

What makes **YOU** feel silly?

Also available:

Look for these other titles in the
DEALING WITH FEELINGS series:

- **This Makes Me Sad**
- **This Makes Me Angry**
- **This Makes Me Happy**
- **This Makes Me Scared**
- **This Makes Me Jealous**

To learn more about Rodale Kids Curious Readers,
please visit RodaleKids.com.